DARK TALES

OF LOST

CIVILIZATIONS

"As a boy, some of my favorite stories were those of lost lands and civilizations, made popular by such writers as H. Rider Haggard, A. Merritt, and Talbot Mundy. I daydreamed of falling through some hidden cave entrance into a lost and forgotten world (sans injury of course) and if asked about my career ambitions I would have answered that I wanted to be one of those specially lucky explorers. As I gradually became aware that such civilizations weren't terribly likely in our closely-examined world, that fantasy became a bit bruised. But now Eric J. Guignard brings back a bit of that magic with Dark Tales of Lost Civilizations, an anthology mixing the values of pulp fiction (returning us to a milieu where such stories seem more possible) with contemporary standards of fresh description. Here we have lost islands, civilizations on the brink, and uncharted lands imaginatively described with new mythologies. David Tallerman, Mark Lee Pearson, Jamie Lackey, Folly Blaine, Jonathan Vos Post, and JC Hemphill—to mention just a few—all shine, and the new Joe Lansdale piece with a unique slant on a western railroad story is a special treat."

—**Steve Rasnic Tem**, *Bram Stoker and World Fantasy Award-winning author of several novels (including his latest,* Deadfall Hotel*) and numerous collections of short fiction.*

"Bright new voices offer chilling glimpses of the darkness beyond mere night."

—**David Brin**, *author of* Earth, The Postman, *and* Otherness.

Dark Tales
of Lost
Civilizations

EDITED BY ERIC J. GUIGNARD

dark moon

LARGO, FLORIDA

DARK MOON BOOKS
an imprint of Stony Meadow Publishing
Largo, Florida

www.StonyMeadowPublishing.com
www.DarkMoonBooks.com

Dark Tales of Lost Civilizations

www.ericjguignard.com
E-mail: eric.guignard@gmail.com

Interior Illustration by Ron Perovich

First edition published in March, 2012
Library of Congress Control Number: 2012931548
ISBN-13: 978-0-9834335-9-0

Made in the United States of America

dark moon

This is for all of you who helped make
my first anthologist venture a success.

And this is for my wife, Jeannette,
and son, Julian,
who helped make my life a success.

CONTENTS

Introduction

Eric J. Guignard

=[]=

It begins with discovery.

A shard of pottery lying on the bottom of the ocean. A block of stone unearthed from the sands of a distant desert. A hastily-scrawled message, slowly fading from the parchment it was inked upon.

From these innocuous relics, great mysteries and legends arise. Who left such remnants behind? Where in history did they exist and how does it relate to us? What were their glories? What were their failings? Why did their society ultimately collapse? What does it all mean?

We wonder questions like these, at one time or another. It is human nature to seek knowledge, to understand the world around us. And with these questions we step back in time for a moment to reflect on those who came before us; the countless races and cultures that have fallen to dust, many of whom are now completely forgotten.

You see, mankind has thrived on earth in a number of mysterious and wonderful civilizations, not the least of which is our own. However, the world as we know it also amounts to only an infinitesimal speck of sand within the great rolling dunes of time. Life existed long before us and will continue to do so, in some form or another, on this world, or perhaps one of the countless others struggling in the universe. Organisms tend to band together, sharing needs—shelter, food, language, and soon a culture begins. A civilization is born. Some flourish while others die quickly. All eventually collapse.

The fascination of history, of knowing the experiences of people that lived before us, has endured as long as humans have been self-aware. Close your eyes and imagine the earliest accomplishments of Homo sapiens—do you see them as I do, etching hieroglyphics on the cave wall, inventing stories of their forefathers to explain phenomena around them? Since then, think of the great splendors and mysteries that have existed on our planet, those which thrived in eras past and even those which are still yet to be. How many peoples considered themselves to be the most advanced, yet now are barely remembered through crumbling relic and lore?

Cambodia's Angkor Wat was the largest preindustrial city in the world, "grander even than Greece or Rome," as described by French explorer, Henri Mouhot. Built in the twelfth century, its architecture, waterways, and intricate carvings were never before seen and still today are considered as brilliant marvels. Drought and invading armies brought ruin to the great temple after only a few centuries of use.

The pyramids of Egypt are chronicled in every history textbook as a harkening to the ancient wonders of the world. Technologically advanced, the splendor of Egypt was evinced in science, architecture, culture, and military power. But how could such a powerful nation at the height of prosperity collapse? The country suffered from a long and slow period of disintegrating finance, ultimately leading to bankruptcy. Class warfare and civil strife erupted, fragmenting the nation into numerous warring families. Sound familiar?

Consider also Mayan civilization, stretching across all of Mesoamerica between the eighth and ninth centuries. Peasant revolt and agricultural abuse led to their decline. There is Pompeii, destroyed in a day by volcano. Rich Babylon, conquered in war and left to decay in the desert. Biblical Gomorrah, burned for its sins.

And those are just a few exceptional peoples we are aware of. But what of the civilizations we are not intimately familiar with, the perplexing mysteries which are footnoted in the great book of the unknown? How many of humanity's secrets are waiting still to be rediscovered, hidden under jungle vines or even beneath the asphalt streets we walk upon?

What became of the Indus Valley people, a culturally-advanced society which is considered India's oldest known civilization? With a population numbering over five million during the Bronze Age, they were contemporaries to Mesopotamia and ancient Egypt, yet suddenly vanished at the height of their power.

What occurred to the "Lost Roman Legion"? Over four thousand of Caesar's most feared soldiers vanished . . . only to appear inexplicably in the Gobi Desert, seventeen years after going missing?

What is the large city that lies over two thousand feet underwater, off the coast of Cuba? What is the reason for the Nazca Lines in Peru, images which stretch over thirty-seven miles in length? What is the origin of the mystical healing practices at Anuradhapura? What happened to the colony at Roanoke, Virginia?

I foster the fascination of these questions and have assembled this book as a collection of *explanations* to such curiosities. Hypotheses, if you will, to suggest answers to baffling enigmas or perhaps even "alternative" interpretations to what you *think* you may know. What we have learned over our lives, after all, is not infallible.

Within *Dark Tales of Lost Civilizations*, each author offers a unique perspective to unexplained mysteries or to a society of beings, whether they are historically known or only rumored to exist, in great and fearful whispers.

Has there ever really existed the great continent of Mu? What is it that lures explorers to distant lands where none have returned? Who, not *what*, are responsible for causing our nightmares? Where is Genghis Kahn buried? What happened to Atlantis? Who will displace mankind on Earth?

Included are accounts of archaeologists and scientists, treasure hunters, tragic royalty, spirits, and even the Witches of Oz. Each story illuminates a particular race of life and explores the genesis of their origin, or the cause of their destruction, or perhaps just contributes a chapter to their legacy.

Ask each author as to what inspired them, and the answers invariably would revolve around a sense of wonder, sparked by those relics of life and their unsolved mysteries.

For out of ruins, come questions.

Some day, peoples of the future—whether our own descendants or perhaps explorers from a strange, alien world—will look upon our crumbling remains and wonder, *what happened?*

—Eric J. Guignard
Chino Hills, California
December 7, 2011

ANGEL OF DESTRUCTION

Cynthia D. Witherspoon

=[]=

Angel of Destruction was my first acceptance into the Dark Tales anthology and it set the bar for future submissions. Thus it seems only fitting to begin this book following that same rationale. Cynthia D. Witherspoon has crafted a short story which is simply one conversation that takes place in a single scene, but it is so succinct and powerful that it remained with me long after I read it—the true mark of a great story. As one civilization is collapsing, a darker truth emerges, one that could affect so many more . . .

=[]=

My world was ending. No, that wasn't right. My world *had* ended. Not in the glorious battle foretold by the priests of Nimrud, but with sickness and silence. My father was dead. My brothers. My young husband. All were considered great men. The heroes of our empire who kept it alive after a traitor claimed the throne of our ancestors. But even great men are deceived by the gods. And even heroes rot in false palaces outside the grave.

We were under siege. Visions of the final victory had led us to the city of Harran in this, the year of 609. Yet those visions failed to describe how our enemies would cage us here until the disease of fire and famine would kill us faster than their spears. My dear husband had laughed when the townspeople began to succumb to the illness. He considered it a punishment for the lower classes who were caught climbing the city walls daily. I had laughed with him, silently rejoicing in our superior status. Yet we were no better than the traitors. I had spent hours wailing and ripping at my veil as proof of that. Now, I was edgy. I knew what was coming next and I was simply working up the courage to act upon my duty.

"Calm yourself, Eilina." My servant since childhood slipped into my foreign chambers with a smile that was uncalled for in this time of sorrow. "It will do you no good to panic in the coming days."

"What is left for me to do, Arbella?" I snorted as I resumed the pacing which kept me from acting out in anger for my plight. "I have the blood of warriors coursing through my veins. Woman though I am, I wish to avenge my people. My father's throne!"

"Warrior?" The old woman nodded as she placed a covered basket by the door. "Aye, you are that, though you've had no training. Your desire to survive is evident of that."

Her words stopped me as none other could have done. I whirled around with every intention of putting the maid in her rightful place when something held me back. Perhaps it was the gods clamoring to bring peace to this stricken house. Or perhaps, it was my own sense of kindness which kept me from striking the old woman. Either way, I dropped the hand I had raised and collapsed on the pallet which served as my bed.

"I know what I must do." I reached for the jeweled blade meant to take my life and lifted it from its place by my bedside. "And I will. Long before the barbarians come to take me away. Just . . . not now. Not when there is a chance for us to escape this wretched city."

"There is no escape, princess." Arbella stroked the side of the basket with one long, crooked finger. "At least, not for the others."

"What do you mean, the others?" I frowned as I replaced the blade. "There are no others."

"No?" She raised her eyebrows in mockery. "What of the others in my status? The servants? The women of the harem? Surely you realize that their fates were sealed the moment your father drew his last breath. Just as yours was."

"My fate." I spat out the word as if it were a curse. "My fate was to bear my husband's children. Continue the line of Assyria's great rulers. My fate was stolen from me. And nothing you can do will ever bring that back."

"Ah, but that was not to be, princess." Arbella nodded as she approached my bed and knelt before me. "Otherwise your men wouldn't have died nor would you have been betrayed by your priests. No, your destiny is for far greater things."

"What do you know of my destiny? My fate?" I shoved her away from me in order to stand. "You are no prophetess, servant. You have no right to speak such words to me."

Arbella nodded. "Then perhaps it is time for you to do your duty, princess. Allow me to retrieve the blade you are so quick to sit aside."

When she stood, the servant extended her hands to offer me the blade. I wanted to take it from her. I wanted to prove to this impertinent woman that I wasn't the coward she saw me as. Instead, I shook my head and nodded toward the basket.

"What is it that you brought for me, Arbella? The method of escape you spoke of?"

"It is." The woman grew serious as she searched my eyes. "Your gods have failed you, princess. But mine has not. Promise your allegiance and you will be saved."

"Your gods?" I laughed despite myself. "Arbella, are you confused? Mad? You are just as Assyrian as I, after all. My gods *are* your gods."

The servant shook her head, waiting for my laughter to cease before she spoke. "No, princess. It is you who are confused. I was stolen from my home by your father's men long before you were born. Brought first to the harem, then to your chambers. I am no more Assyrian than the Medes attempting to break down the palace gates."

"Not Assyrian?" I frowned as I distanced myself away from her. "How can that be? No slave so close to royal blood would be of conquered stock."

"I am much more than a slave, Eilina. And it wasn't difficult to convince your father to place me in your rooms."

I watched in fascination as the woman I'd known since I was a child began to shift into someone else. The lines carved by age fell away from her face. The silver in her hair darkened to a hue of red that could only be described as unnatural. Indeed, even her bones straightened so that she no longer struggled to stand, but faced me as an equal. No, it was more than that. She faced me as a superior. A goddess among men. I would have fallen to my knees before her had it not been for her eyes. They mesmerized me. Kept me still.

They glowed a shade of green I'd only seen in the jewels brought back by our soldiers from the East. Arbella spoke and her voice broke through the spell cast by her unusual eyes.

"I am the first to have been cast aside by a man, but it was a god who saved me." The magnificent creature moved to the door and I watched as she lifted the lid of the basket. "You will be *my* first, and we will wreak havoc on those who wish to control us."

"Who are you?" I found my voice at long last, and I was surprised at how steady it sounded given what I'd just seen. "Are you a goddess? A witch?"

"Promise your allegiance, child, and I shall tell you all that I know. Otherwise, I will leave you here to do what is expected."

I didn't hesitate as I nodded my acceptance of her offer. Perhaps she was right. I was a coward. But there was something about this mysterious woman that I wanted to mimic. She had a gift more powerful than any noble I'd ever known. And I will admit, I wanted a taste of such power when I had so little remaining as my father's kingdom collapsed around me.

"You must say the words, princess." Arbella stood, cradling something close to her chest. "I cannot accept such a commitment on silence alone."

"I pledge my allegiance to your mysterious god, Arbella. Please. Let me be as powerful as you are at this moment. I ask for nothing more."

The woman turned with a chuckle. "Of course you would ask for power instead of your life. You are truly your father's daughter, Eilina."

For the first time, I laid eyes upon the creature she cradled so lovingly in her hands. It was a snake, its black skin as shiny and polished as stone. My first instinct was to flee the room. Take my chances with the enemy soldiers outside our gates. Yet as before, I found myself frozen in place by the voice suddenly whispering in my mind.

I want this. I need this. I want to become one of them.

I reached for the desert cobra with none of the hesitation I'd held for the dagger. Suddenly, I knew what I wanted. What I needed. Without my father telling me what to do. Without my brothers guiding me. Without my husband commanding me. I would be more powerful than they had ever been in life. And I knew just how to make it so.

I wrapped the snake around my throat with a tenderness I rarely possessed, stroking its flat head as its forked tongue caressed the side of my throat. It wasn't until I felt the pinch of the snake's bite that I realized what I'd done. I'd betrayed my ancestors. My people. I'd failed in my duty to die as an honorable member of the royal family. But as I began to chant alongside Arbella in a bastard form of Aramaic, I found that I didn't care. It didn't matter. I wasn't Assyria's princess anymore. I was my own person. My own woman.

And I would survive this.

I barely felt Arbella as she removed the serpent from around my throat. I was too lost in the images rushing into my mind and within moments, I knew the creature's story. I knew of Arbella's power.

She was telling the truth when she said she had been the first true immortal. The first woman, cast out of a beautiful garden because she dared to question her husband. My childhood servant had once been known as Lilith and, in her desperation, she found power through the serpent. I knew this was the fate she had spoken of before. The destiny which was born out of the destruction of my ancient empire. I was to be immortal, the first of many who would serve a fallen angel by stealing the souls of men away from the god who had wronged her. I had become the second next to Lilith. A creature they would call many names, but always be drawn to.

Succubus.

Demon.

Vampire.

And so, I embraced the poison which changed us into something so much more than mortal. I became a goddess. A beauty who would bow to no man.

One who would rise forever as an angel of man's destruction.

=[]=

Cynthia D. Witherspoon has had numerous short stories published in anthologies and has been the recipient of several writing awards. Her collaboration with K.G. McAbee, The Brass Chronicles, *is her latest project; with the first book scheduled for release in October 2011 by Carina Press. She currently lives in South Carolina with her husband and Jack Russell terrier,*

THE DOOR BEYOND THE WATER

David Tallerman

=[]=

I have been a fan of David Tallerman's work long before I started this anthology and it pleased me to no end that he was interested in participating in this collection. Not only was he quite enthusiastic about this project, but he also provided wonderful advice as I set up the foundation of the book and met with publishers and agents. A nice bloke to work with and a smashing writer—made my job as an editor almost an easy one! The Door Beyond the Water really encompasses the heart of what this anthology is all about; the resolute explorer who searches uncharted land in the name of science, only to uncover a dark horror that was never meant to be found.

=[]=

The message came to him in dreams, before the second moon of the season: *A man comes to free the imprisoned one.* Nothing more than that.

But for Cha Né—who was shaman, who saw beneath the mystery of things—that sentence was enough to darken his heart with fear such as he'd never known.

The next night he confronted his spirit-guide with the inevitable questions. "Who is this man who comes? Is he of the mountain people? Is he from the hollow tribe?" It hardly seemed possible, unless the ancient truces had been somehow corrupted. "I must know, Shanoctoc."

The feathered guide had hesitated long before answering. "He is Montague Evans. He is not of the three tribes, nor of the lands between the water and the mountains. He is a white man, of the tribe of Henry Johnson. He will arrive before the third moon."

Then Cha Né's guide, his one companion in the Otherworld, sank into the waters of the lake—was swallowed amidst shivering liquid tendrils.

Cha Né knew, without knowing how, that it was the last time they would ever meet.

Day 24

This morning finds us high upon the first incline to the plateau, and so perhaps a day's hike from its summit, certainly no more than two. It's hard to say more certainly, for Johnson's account becomes increasingly erratic around this point, and his comments upon matters of time unreliable. However, we have the map appended to his diaries and the corroboration of the guides. They tell me we draw near to the lands of the Lam, whose territory comprises the whole of the summit region.

Will the Lam prove peaceable? The guides claim so, but they are less than trustworthy themselves of late. They appear nervous, more so the further we ascend. I worry that soon I may no longer be able to rely on their advice.

That concern might be easier to bear if I weren't already ill at ease myself. Undoubtedly, the blame lies in my reading and rereading of Johnson's account. It's a task I'd eagerly give up, were it not for the fact that in his lucid moments he made insights that I'd hate to be without. Unfortunately, those moments of clarity grow scarcer the further I read. More and more, the valuable detail of the day's journey is outweighed by description of his nights, and of his dreams—and the narration of those dreams becomes more outlandish with each page. I have no doubt that by this stage in his expedition he was almost lost to the dementia that would soon ravage his mind entirely.

I often think back to that time when I first became properly aware of Johnson. For months, I'd been hunting a means to corroborate my theories regarding the diffusion of myth in regions cut off from outside influence. I'd heard the rumors that still occasionally circulated, the wild-seeming tales of the ethnographer's last, disastrous excursion. I knew of his earlier notoriety, his controversial and often bizarre essays. But he had been forgotten for the most part, or was remembered only in hushed tones.

That only added to my growing curiosity. The freakish legends surrounding Johnson began to fascinate me, as much if not more than the remarkable similarities between our ideas. However, it was chance rather than diligence that brought me to the accounts of his last expedition, for I hadn't so much as guessed at their existence before I found them moldering in the depths of the library. It didn't take me long to realize that the lands he'd investigated would be perfect for my own fieldwork, or—despite the protestations of certain faculty members—to organize a trip upon his established route.

Often, too, I find myself remembering my visit to him, after a long day's journey by train. Even in the asylum, Johnson was kept apart. His mania, they said, disturbed the other patients. I recall the expression on his face, how despite the excruciating brightness of the electric light, he seemed lost in darkness. More, I remember his screams. "Astasoth! Astasoth!" He repeated the meaningless word endlessly.

With memories such as those, accompanied by Johnson's alarming journals, what wonder is it that my thoughts are unsettled? Is it so strange that I should be troubled by nightmares myself?

=[]=

Cha Né never questioned his responsibility. He was shaman of the Shanopei. Thus, he was guardian of the gate. Neither the mountain people nor the hollow tribe had a shaman, for there could only be one guardian, and always he came of the Shanopei.

Within the lake tribe, the only other was his novice, Cha Poc. Cha Poc was barely more than a child. The boy would not be ready for many years, for—by nature weak of body like all prospective shamans—he was still ravaged by sickness after each journey through dreams. At present, he lay in the adjoining hut, which Cha Né had built upon his arrival. The boy burned with fever, drifting between this world and the other.

Under any other circumstances, Cha Né would have said that if Cha Poc should die then that was as it must be. Another would be found to take the boy's place, for the tribe had never been without a shaman. In the meantime, he would stand alone until another took his own place.

Yet now, Cha Né found himself wishing the boy was older, that he was stronger—that he could be relied upon.

It was a weak and unworthy thought. It was the surest measure of his fear.

Day 26

We achieved the rim of the plateau late this morning, after hours of exhausting climb. However, this small victory has presented fresh difficulties, for our guides have left us, as they threatened they would. They've started back toward their village on the western shore, where Harley and our base-camp await. God only knows what Harley will imagine when they return without us.

Their last comment still rings in my ears: *Death dwells beyond the lake,* or something to that effect. I choose not to guess at their meaning.

There's no doubt we grow close to where the Johnson expedition was routed. Halfway toward the further edge of the plateau, Middleton was forced to take over after Johnson's undeniable breakdown. There followed a further eight days of hasty retreat back to the sea. Through it all, Johnson raved of some being seen only by himself that dogged their steps. Under that intensely morbid influence, Middleton too began to lose his grasp on sanity. When the expedition finally reached their shore encampment, to be reunited with the two members of their party who'd stayed to maintain it, they were all six in a state of uncontrollable mania.

Not one of them ever elaborated on what had happened, and Johnson and Middleton were quite incapable. What details I now know are the composite of three sources: Johnson's original journals; hurried accounts penned by Middleton before his own breakdown; and some barely meaningful notes scrawled by the last of the party to succumb. All of these texts I have with me now.

I wouldn't wish to exaggerate the similarity of my nightmares to those detailed so intensely by Johnson. I've read his descriptions countless times and been undeniably affected by them. It's unsurprising that they should haunt my rest as they do my waking hours. This is the only reasonable explanation.

I do find it curious, however, that it isn't the more outlandish details that disturb me, from the period when Johnson was unquestionably deranged, but those earlier incidents he narrated with some measure of sanity. Yet perhaps even this isn't really so strange. Henry Johnson was a dreamer, with an appetite for the most bizarre aspects of the cultures he studied. In this, he was very much an anthropologist of the old school.

I believe myself a more rational man than Johnson, and of stronger mind. Thus, I can sympathize with his writings where they remain within the boundaries of the sane. Beyond that point, they can only appall me.

=[]=

Henry Johnson had been a dreamer. Not by nature an evil man, he had nevertheless fallen easily into the service of the being beyond the gate.

Cha Né had no choice but to battle with Johnson in the Blind Lands. Afterwards, he had defiled Johnson's mind to its very core, and then—for long days and longer nights—had pursued him through nightmares, hunting and destroying any last snatches of reason.

Cha Né had taken no pleasure in this profanation of his role as shaman. Yet nor could he deny its necessity. He had intended Henry Johnson's madness to serve as warning so that others would not follow. He had done the unthinkable to protect the tribes under his care from an indescribable fate. He would do the same again.

For all that, Cha Né knew now that he had failed.

He had observed the progress of this new intruder from his perch upon the Sun-drenched Cliffs. Montague Evans had reached the Plains of Frozen Light, guided by cloying words of promise from behind the Endless Gate. In this world, the invented world, he could be no more than two days from the worldly shadow of the Gate. Then, in dreams, he would also reach its true form.

Already there were signs that he was succumbing to the ruinous thing waiting for him. Already the battle seemed half lost.

For it was something more and less than a man he'd seen there, staring back from the far cliffs. Montague Evans's dream-self was changing.

Day 27

Last night, in my dreams, I looked out over a vast plain. Great, mottled cysts rose from its surface, which otherwise was glassy and radiant.

Amongst these curious mounds, crystalline towers reached into colorless skies. Those edifices were carved in perfect yet nonsensical angles, as if manufactured according to some altogether inhuman geometry. Their upper levels were pitted by what I told myself must have been windows, though I could see no other means of ingress.

In my reverie, I imagined a voice. I knew it was in my mind—but that it wasn't *only* in my mind. Nor were there really words as such, rather a current of sound that somehow held meaning. I can't even truly say that I heard it. For I had no sense of either mind or body, and such terms do little justice to what I felt myself to be. In waking, I find it all but impossible to explain. Our language is hopelessly ill-suited for such things.

I spent an indeterminate time crossing that plain, just as, in reality, we'd traversed the plateau of the Lam through the previous day. Other than the voice, there was no sound, no sign of any presence. The surface beneath me was adamantine. There was no sun in the sky, no stars. I progressed at a steady pace, moving as if through the exercise of will.

Eventually, with no clear sense of time having passed, I came to the edge of the mesa. So far, my experience had been not wholly unpleasant, at worst like the queasiness that accompanies the first decline into real drunkenness. Now, abruptly, it veered toward the nightmarish.

Before me, a great sinkhole interrupted the landmass on which I stood. Upon its far side, a sequence of steps joined the higher and lower levels— or what appeared to be steps, for their excruciating size meant that no man could have used them so. At the crater's base swam a fluid of rainbow color, which swirled with unreasonable currents and eddies. All around the basin, cliffs of an opalescent substance ran, shining brilliantly.

None of those details were frightful. Indeed, the liquid and the cliffs surrounding it were startling and splendid. No, the object that filled me with fear—and much worse, with recognition—stood at the base of that distant, gigantic stairway. At the point where it met the luminous waters of the lake, two columns reared. They were of black rock, polished yet unreflective, seeming almost to absorb the light. Hieroglyphs engraved the twin obelisks from base to tip. I couldn't read them, nor even identify them, yet they filled me with dread.

Even the columns, however, awful in their way, weren't the true source of my terror. Rather, it was what lay within them. Another kind of blackness was spread between the pillars of black rock. It wasn't simply an absence of light, or that there was nothing there. Instead, there stretched an endless void—not the lack of space but its absolute reflection.

And there was worse, even than that. The voice in my head, the not-sound I'd unquestioningly followed—it issued from that impossible dimension. It's meaning, now, was almost clear. I knew it had led me here, and for a reason.

I was helpless. Whatever purpose I'd been summoned for, I would certainly have played my part—had I been alone.

The realization crept upon me slowly. I was being watched. The figure was hard to distinguish, for it perched upon the precipice to my left and shone in similar manner. At that distance, it was as if someone held a mirror up to the sun. However, somehow I felt sure that this image of light was another presence.

Just then, a whim made me think to look down at myself. Or was it more than that? It was as though a message had reached me from that strange being upon the far cliff. Suddenly I was overwhelmed by the thought that I should examine my own form, which before had been so shadowy and ethereal.

No longer. Now it was quite as solid as the ground beneath me. In color, or absence of color rather, it was like the twin pillars. My torso was reminiscent of a shell, armored with great, interlocking plates. I raised my hand. It was a hand no longer. Like my body, it was encrusted, and my fingers were gone—fused into a great pincer.

Strange to tell, in my dream none of this dismayed me. I must have been monstrous, and the memory chills me now. But there was something in the tone of that ever-present voice from beyond the gate that lulled my doubts. More than that—it flattered me.

I can't say for certain what roused me then. Amidst so much awfulness, what detail stirred enough revulsion to jolt me into wakefulness? I wish I knew.

For sooner or later, I'll have to sleep again. If I understood what might wake me from such half-known terrors, perhaps the prospect would appall me less.

=[]=

Cha Né had spent the afternoon in preparation.

In shallow dreams, he had hunted upon the shadow-lake for Shanoctoc, hoping against hope that his only agent in the Otherworld hadn't truly abandoned him. When Henry Johnson had encroached upon the Endless Gate, the shaman and his spirit guide had consulted for two days, planning for every eventuality. Could the approaching threat really be so much worse? Could it intimidate even such a thing as Shanoctoc?

Cha Né woke with no answers to his questions. Angry and dispirited, he'd begun to make arrangements of his own. He had already gathered the ingredients he'd need. The base constituent was water from the lake, for it belonged almost as much to the Otherworld as to his own. The most powerful was the root of the Malaka, which grew in a single patch upon the far shore. But there were many other components, most virulent if used in the wrong proportions, and so the process of preparation was a slow one.

Finally, Cha Né removed his loincloth and his ceremonial garments, retaining only the charms he wore around his neck. Naked and squatting before the blazing hearth, he proceeded to rub the ointment into his body and face. Only when he was sure that he was entirely coated did he allow himself to relax, to meditate.

He felt the salve begin to dry, to work itself subtly within him. The pain rose slowly—until the heat beneath his flesh exceeded the blast of the fire without.

Cha Né held himself still. He remained calm. And eventually, the pain subsided. The heat inside him faded; so did the warmth from outside. All sensation died, by slow degrees. At first, it was like falling out of the world, like sinking into numbing water. But even those comparisons required feelings that, moment by moment, were lost to him.

Then unexpectedly, abruptly, it was over. The descent into deepest trance, the near-death of mind and body, was complete.

When Cha Né opened his eyes again, it was within the Otherworld.

Day 28

Eventful as they've been, only now do I find a moment to write of these last two days.

Yesterday we passed through the lands of the Lam. The tribe did nothing to hinder us, and we saw little sign of their presence. We camped without disturbance, and early this morning came upon the edge of the plateau.

I confess that I'd been expecting further bad dreams during the night, and their absence had left me in good cheer, perhaps even a little giddy. Yet as I looked out from those jungle-trimmed heights, the excitement turned to ashes in my mouth.

The view was unmistakably that of my nightmares from the night before. Across from us, where the cyclopean steps had descended, a river tumbled through the brush. The waters of the lake, whilst not so variedly colored, were of equally vivid blues and greens. The cliffs were of similar proportions, though of unspectacular grey stone. As for the two black pillars, I saw two great rocks, one to either side of the distant river at the point where it met the lake.

Once the first flush of alarm had passed, I forced myself to consider how my imagination had so accurately anticipated geography I'd never seen. Surely, my subconscious mind must have pieced together details from Johnson's journal and the crude maps drawn by Middleton. It was hard to believe, but I could think of no other rational explanation.

Just as I'd managed to calm myself, the Lam descended upon us.

In my state of agitation, I almost fired on them with my revolver. I might really have done so if Harris hadn't caught my arm. As soon as he did, I realized what the others had seen already; we were not being threatened. No man in the delegation was less than ancient. They were the tribal elders, and they wanted only to talk.

Without our guides, however, even that was no easy task. I managed as well as I could with my smattering of the language. As far as I could tell, they were trying to warn me. I say that without egotism, for they spoke to no one else, though I'd done nothing to identify myself as expedition leader. They talked of a door, or so I thought, and they pointed often toward the twin rocks at the river outlet. But beyond that, I could make no sense of it.

When they realized their appeal was beyond my understanding, their manner grew more excitable. Finally, tired of their ranting, I insisted to the others that we continue onward, before the day was altogether wasted.

We left the elderly tribesman shouting and pleading at our backs and began our descent. Whenever I glanced behind, I could see them watching from on high, and the sight unsettled me more than I could explain. I was glad when our progress cut them off from view.

The plateau proved lower on this side. By noon, we'd reached the heavily jungled rim of the basin. We could clearly see our objective, the lakeside village of the Shanopei, as a clutter of shelters upon the far shore. However, it was evident that there was no direct route between us and it. The only way down was to circumnavigate the basin and descend alongside the distant river, passing the mysterious twin obelisks. After the tirade I'd endured from the tribal elders, that prospect unsettled me more than it should have. But on another, perhaps more academic level, it intrigued me. I couldn't help wondering what secrets those barely-visible hieroglyphs might hold.

Intellectual curiosity, of course, won over. Against the protests of my companions, I insisted we make haste, so as to camp upon the lower level.

While we marched, I chided myself for being so easily unsettled by the recollections of a lunatic and the prattling of natives. They are wild people here, with wild ideas. My role as a rational man is to suck the poison from those concepts, so that more restrained minds can inspect them without threat of harm or infection. Re-reading my previous entries, I see to what extent I've failed in that regard—how I've allowed myself to fall under the sway of phantasms.

Well, no more. I am a man of science again. The travails of our day's journey have worn me out, but in that weariness I discover an unexpected depth of peace. As we make camp beneath a purple sky, and before those great carven rocks, I find myself calm for the first time in longer than I can remember.

In the fading light, those vast columns have a surprising, uncanny beauty. From my position by the campfire, I can just discern the rows of pictograms that reach from base to tip. Perhaps they offer one more version of the fantasies that so dominate the lives of these people.

Whatever the case, they're a mystery for tomorrow. I feel serene, and very drowsy. Twice I've lain down to sleep. But there's a noise here, a curious, incessant murmuring. The others tell me I'm hearing the river. I'm certain, though, that it was more audible when we examined those twin rocks this afternoon.

The sound, however, is more soothing than distracting. I'll try to ignore it—or stop struggling with it, rather. Tomorrow will be the crucial day of our expedition. Tomorrow is what I came so very far for.

I must try to rest.

I must sleep.

=[]=

Cha Né perched upon the Sun-drenched Cliffs.

He was deep within dream, so submerged that his body was only a fragile memory. He had torn through membranes of space and time, through many shades of consciousness. The way back was tortuous, hard to recollect.

The sky above was blank and cold. The luminous waters below curved and swelled against brilliant rocks.

Cha Né waited. Finally, in a distant flickering of darkness, the avatar of the thing behind the Gate entered the Otherworld. It sparked into being upon the kaleidoscope of the lake and began immediately toward the Gate, regardless of the shifting surface beneath its hooves. It moved with an awkward creeping motion, bowed beneath its carapace, claw-arms clacking rhythmically. The Gate surged and writhed in anticipation.

Cha Né allowed it to approach. When it was close, he rose and moved cautiously nearer, casting vast shadows. The avatar didn't notice him at first; but when he leapt again, this time landing clenched in its path, it raised its snout and gave a scratching cry.

Cha Né squatted between the avatar and the infinite darkness of the Gate. It tried to maneuver around him, claws outstretched, head held low to protect its one cloudy eye from his brilliance. Cha Né shifted, keeping between it and its object. His thoughts, as he reached toward it, were a tangible thread of light that quivered in the ether.

Cha Né could feel the mind of the man, Montague Evans—like a dream or the memory of a dream. It no longer controlled the form encasing it. Cha Né felt the man's fear and recognized it as his own. He knew as well the price, if the thing behind the Endless Gate should be unleashed. He had no choice. Burn out the mind of the man and the cancerous presence anchored to it would be vanquished too.

Cha Né faltered.

He could still taste the acid tang of what he'd done to Henry Johnson, of intelligence ground down to violent madness. What if this one were different? What if he could be reasoned with? Turned back? Could be saved?

Even as Cha Né thought it, the avatar scented his reluctance—the instance of weakness it had anticipated. In that moment, it lunged. The viscous web of its consciousness clutched at Cha Né, a cloud that howled around, within him. He felt his form fracture. He felt the drag of his body, the empty shell still squatting in the invented world.

He'd come too far, too deep. He couldn't remember the path back.

Broken, leaking light, Cha Né lay buoyed upon the liquid ground. The avatar didn't concern itself with him. It continued its creep to the Endless Gate, its milky eye still diverted, but its claws now clicking steadily again.

Cha Né's senses were failing. He saw the world as through a crust of ice. Yet he could still feel the umbilical cord of consciousness between himself and Montague Evans. He concentrated, focusing upon a last, hopeless transmission. He pressed through insect-thoughts, through drone-thoughts, into the screaming red of human mind below.

Even then, they had no language in common. They were so different. Could emotion bridge that gap? Could despair? "Free it in this world and you free it in our world. Montague Evans, listen to me . . . it will devour *everything* . . . "

Then the link was broken, melting into translucent dusts. If the avatar, or the mind of the man encased in it, had understood, it showed no sign. The thing continued its warped motion, until it stood before the undulating black of the gate. The surface bent in dreadful curves as the avatar reached for the hieroglyphs of the pillar. The darkness throbbed, rolled out like storm clouds. Soon the creeping thing could no longer be seen amidst the pulsing ebon swell. But where it had been, something else was emerging—condensing.

Cha Né couldn't move. He couldn't look away. He could only lie still, watching.

It had been imprisoned for countless moons—for time beyond time.

It must be ravenous.

Day 29

My dreams last night were awful beyond imagination.

I'm sure of this. Yet, I can't remember—or only the most indistinct details. A black and vacuous gateway. A strange, bright being, which spoke to me perhaps. Terror. Joy.

My memory is like a tattered cloth. Better to remember nothing than these half-grasped horrors, these flash-bulb grotesques that seem to be the shattered memories of a stranger.

Of the many things that petrify me this morning, this is the worst—this terrible sense of dislocation. I feel I've witnessed something dreadful. Maybe I even played a part in it. But that part is a void inside me. It belongs to someone—to something—else.

We've arrived at the village of the Shanopei. They would be unknown to the world were it not for Henry Johnson. Their evil superstitions would never have left this sheltered cove. Yet Johnson came, as I have come. Those superstitions have spread, as typhoid spreads.

This is what I sought. Now that I'm here, I can't but question my motives, and their repercussions. I told myself it was the correlations between my work and Johnson's that drew me. These are the reasons I offered my companions. Half-truths at best. It wasn't Johnson's theories that brought me but his madness. No, not even that. Those revolting horrors, the cancer in his mind, the darkness that finally devoured his sanity . . . that was my lure. I opened my mind to the blackest dreams. Now I think those things may consume me.

The village of the Shanopei is gone. Only gutted remains survive, scorched in impossibly arbitrary fashion. There are no bodies, though the paraphernalia of life suggests the recent presence of people. There is nothing alive here. We can't even hear the singing of birds.

This was not the work of men. There are no tracks. It's as if some force fell on the village, and desolated it, and was gone.

I fear it hasn't gone far.

The sky is crimson and purple and black, as though blood were bruising behind it. It's cold, so cold that the ground is hard, though yesterday we sweltered beneath tropical sun. The waters of the lake are viscous, swirling outward from the center. They give the impression of appalling depths. Tendrils of fog rise from the water to gather about our feet. There's a carrion scent in the air, a murmuring that is something like music. The sky is without color. The cliffs, through the mist, are crystalline.

I'm hallucinating. But the others claim they see the same. I can make out the bay, the canoes tethered there, the ravaged village, the river tumbling through mud flats into translucent water. Another scene lies on . . . over . . . *through* that one. At first, I could distinguish them. Now they seem to coexist.

The others want to retreat back toward the plateau. They insist I stop writing and go with them. I wish I could. I'm frozen, by awe and fear, and by the need to leave some record in the face of what I fear.

I remember Henry Johnson, tethered deep in the bowels of the asylum. The word he'd been calling incessantly since his arrival—and they told me his throat was cracked and torn by then, that it was a miracle he could make any noise at all—I believe that word was a name. *Astasoth.* I've known its meaning, I think, all along. I could have understood. I chose not to. *The imprisoned one.*

I'll leave this journal here. If I don't survive, perhaps it will. I hope it's never discovered. I hope it's lost forever. I can't tell anymore what's real, what's delirium. The lake is obsidian, bubbling and frothing, flailing the shore with fluid tendrils. Beyond the beach, a well leads further down than I can see.

Something is rising.

I can't see. The fog devours everything. I hope it isn't real, that I'm insane. I'll follow my companions, to the path that leads up the cliff side. What else can I do? This wasn't my fault. A record—a record, at least. In the face of it. What else?

I hope this journal won't be found. I hope I'm mad. Let me die in the jungle, and rot, and never be remembered. Let me die mad and forgotten!

I fear I'm sane. I fear . . .

I know. Astasoth is free.

And it has other plans for me than death.

=[]=

***David Tallerman**'s horror, fantasy, and science fiction short stories have appeared in around forty markets, including* Lightspeed, Bull Spec, Redstone Science Fiction, *and John Joseph Adams's zombie best-of* The Living Dead. *Amongst other projects, David has published poetry in* Chiaroscuro *and comic scripts through the award-winning British* Futurequake Press, *while a short he co-wrote won numerous awards in the 2011* Two Days Later *horror film contest. David's first novel, comic fantasy adventure* Giant Thief, *came out in February 2012 from UK publisher* Angry Robot; *its first sequel,* Crown Thief, *is due toward the end of the year. David can be found online at* http://davidtallerman.net *and* http://davidtallerman.blogspot.com.

TO RUN A STICK THROUGH A FISH

Mark Lee Pearson

=[]=

Writing from Japan, Mark Lee Pearson brings an intriguing contribution to this collection. He explores the lore of an islander people through the eyes of a girl, Izanami, as she ages and the world changes around her. To Run a Stick Through a Fish *is one of the shortest stories in this anthology, yet the author is able to fill it with an immense diversity of life and emotion. For the noble Ainu race, heritage is to be cherished, whether through family, magic, or by "knowing a dog."*

=[]=

Izanami was named after the divine mother of the Ainu race, and she kept her naval string in a small cedar box, which she concealed in a raccoon skin cloak.

Her Grandmother, Huchi, who had the gift of tongues and tattooed lips, told Izanami that the divine mother had been born of a goddess and a dog. The goddess came sailing north on a celestial ship from the lands of the gods, and when the vessel hit rocks she was marooned on the island of Shizunai. There she was stranded and alone with only her gold, silver, brocade, and jewels for company until a dog befriended her. The dog led her to a cave and ravished her and ten months later the goddess gave birth to the divine mother, Izanami. Thus began the Ainu race.

"Hapi, was my father a dog?" Izanami asked her mother one evening as they harvested elderberries from the mountainside. She was twelve and curious to hear about her own origins.

"Yes, he was a dog," said Hapi. "But nothing like the dog in Grandmother Huchi's tale. That dog didn't disappear. He didn't leave his mistress's side. He remained faithful, continued to provide her with food and love, and they had many children together."

Izunami had more questions. She wanted to know if her father was still alive and, if he was, where was he, but Hapi cut her off, denying any claim to divinity. She told Izunami to forget her father since he was a disgrace to the Ainu people and to the name of dogs. Then she plucked a succulent elderberry from a bush and popped it into Izanami's mouth.

Izanami's Grandfather, Ekashi, was the greatest fisherman in Ezo and a speaker of rains. He maintained that the Wajin in the south, who sought to erase the Ainu race from existence, had fabricated the origin story to that end. For what woman in her right mind would admit to being known by a dog?

Huchi insisted that every Ainu woman admitted at one time or another of being known by a dog; it was an affirmation of the female's role in her society.

On the night of Izanami's thirteenth birthday, Hapi disappeared. The local fishermen combed the coast; the hunters searched the forest and mountainside, but to no avail. They called upon a Saaghalian magician to divine her whereabouts. The magician was short and hairy and wore straw sandals and a robe, which reeked of wet bark. He sat alone for a long while in her mother's darkened room. When he emerged he said she had died and her body would never be found. Izanami beat him out of the house with her fists, and Grandmother Huchi cursed the cannibalistic dog under her breath, but nothing could foil the truth of the magician's prediction. Hapi's body was never found and the smell of wet bark never faded from the house.

Izanami went to live with her grandparents, Huchi and Ekashi, in a hole in the ground. Huchi continued to relate to her the suspect stories of her ancestors. She told tales of the famine and how the Ainu people had once feasted upon their brothers' flesh to stay alive. Izanami balked at the thought. She wondered if Huchi had ever ingested the flesh of her brothers and sisters, but she dared not to ask.

Ekashi taught Izanami vigilance, invisibility, and how to produce fish from a handful of sand. He also showed her how to summon the rains. She ran a stick through the fish her grandfather caught and pushed it in the ground with its mouth facing the sky. They prayed to the skulls of a pair of raccoons, and he presented her with the raccoon skin cloak her mother had worn. He threw seawater over her and they danced upon the beach until the sun rose and when they caught sight of the cumulus clouds that had appeared on the horizon they shrieked and wept tears of elation.

The following year was dry too, so they traveled to Peneshiri to cut the birch tree with a knife. On the way home a pair of hungry bandits brandishing fishhooks and spears ambushed them. Izanami watched Ekashi slay the two men with his fish knife.

One night when Izanami was fourteen, a local boy followed her home. He was the son of a hunter and his body was covered in downy hair and he moved with the stealth of a pine marten. That night on the edge of the forest, Izanami discovered what it meant for a man to be a dog. It was not as she had imagined.

In Huchi's tale, the male deity, Izanazi, inquired of the female deity, Izanami, whether anything had formed within her body before making an advance. The female deity, Izanami, had coyly replied, *yes my body has a place completely formed, and it is called the source of femineity*. The pine marten had made no such inquiry of her. He threw down his jeweled spear and ripped the crystal mountain from the muddy quagmire of her youth by instinct alone.

Two days later the pine marten disappeared while on a hunting trip in the mountains and she persuaded the Saaghalian magician to divine his whereabouts. The short, hairy magician arrived, still carrying the reek of wet bark, which brought back memories of her mother. She left him alone in the place where she had known the dog the night previous and when he emerged from the undergrowth he said the boy had been chased down and eaten by a bear and his body would never be found.

Izanami resolved to kill the bear in revenge. She set out that night and tracked it across the lowlands and through the mountainous terrain for eight months, until she became exhausted and was forced to give up, crawl into a cave, and lie down on a bed of rushes.

That night a dog came to her in a dream. He claimed he was her father and told her she must speak to the gods, take dirt from the footprints of the bear, and turn it upside down. He explained that this would cause the bear to be turned upside down and rendered unable to move. She would then be able to catch it and exact her revenge. The fiery spite in the dog's eyes reminded Izanami of what her mother had said about her father being not the kind of dog from Grandmother Huchi's tales.

Izanami woke in a panic and debilitating pain, to find her raccoon coat soaked with blood and what appeared to be her entrails splayed across the floor of the cave. For a wild moment she believed the bear she sought had mauled her in her sleep. She lay there for six days and nights, enduring the sleepless agony and the persistent spite of her father, waiting for death to cover her with a shroud. But her spirit refused to let go and on the seventh day she crawled out of the cave and buried the body of her stillborn child in the raccoon skin coat.

Izanami returned to the village and her grandparents' hole in the ground. She forgot about the bear and the hunter boy, but the mangled face of her stillborn child never left her. While she was away, Grandmother Huchi had weakened in body and spirit. She remained holed up while Ekashi continued to produce fish from handfuls of sand and Izanami gathered berries and fruits from the lowland hedgerows, and mushrooms and mountain vegetables from the highlands. When the seasons were dry they sacrificed raccoons and prayed for the rain. But the gods did not always listen and the people of Ezo suffered a season of spoiled crops.

They buried Grandmother Huchi the following fall. Ekashi withdrew from society, leaving his work to Izanami. He refused to eat and pray. His body withered, and before spring could make its round again, Ekashi passed away.

Izanami sacrificed an entire forest of raccoons for her grandfather. That was the year of the torrential rains; the year the earth bore an abundance of fruit for the people of Ezo. From time to time she would run her hand over the little cedar box that she kept hidden in her cloak.

The people of the village avoided her. They said she would summon a tsunami to your door if you gave her so much as a passing glance. They said she was the one who breathed the fog that concealed the beautiful autumn moon. They said she was the one who threatened the turtle with death if the rains didn't come. But it was clear that she had grown to possess an undeniable beauty, like her mother Hapi, and when the ships from the south finally arrived, bringing Wajin in search of land and settlement, a sailor took her for his lover, but she could not trust him.

She became skillful in the art of invisibility. One night she became invisible and followed the sailor back to his ship. There she overheard him telling his comrades how he had known the dog's daughter. She heard how her father the dog had hunted down, savaged, and cannibalized his people. He laughed as he referred to her as a bitch, a beast, a barbarian. She looked on in fury as he lay down beside a goddess of the crystal mountain. Spurned, she built an effigy of straw and nailed it to a pine tree, prepared fetishes of the guilder-rose, and buried them upside-down. She chanted, "O demon, I offer this image of the man I despise to thee. Take his soul and carry it together with his body to the fiery depths of Hell. Turn thou my enemy into one of thy kind; make him a demon."

The sailor disappeared, but Izunami didn't need the Saaghalian magician to divine his whereabouts. Besides, it was a vanishing custom.

The Wajin settlers built houses of wood above the ground and erected magnificent shrines to the gods of the south. The season was dry when the officials came to count her head. They dragged her from her hole in the ground and told her she lived in a different country now. They changed her name and wrote the new name on a register in a language and script she could not read. When the official spoke, she didn't listen. Her hand was in her robe, her fingers running over the grooves of the tiny cedar box in which she kept her two tiny navel strings.

The stories of her ancestors that Huchi had told her and the customs Ekashi had taught her roared inside her head. She resolved to never again run a stick through a fish and face its mouth to the sky.

=[]=

Mark Lee Pearson is from the United Kingdom. Aircraft toolmaker, translator, and father of two little monsters, he has a degree in Philosophy and English Literature, and a Masters in Japanese. When he was nineteen years old, Mark founded the legendary indiepop label, Ambition Records, *in his Southampton bedroom. He now divides his time between teaching junior high school students in Japan how to communicate in English, and trying to communicate his own ideas about the nature of the universe to the world. His stories have appeared in various magazines and anthologies including* Apex, Andromeda Spaceways Inflight Magazine, *and* Space and Time. *For more information check out* markleepearson.blogspot.com.

QUIVIRA

Jackson Kuhl

=[]=

Out of the submissions I received, few struck me as unique and colorful as this next selection. Connecticut author, Jackson Kuhl, infuses humor and mystery with an exceptional ability for story telling. Quivira *is a legendary city of gold and has come to symbolize the misfortune that befalls those who search for it. Where* Quivira *actually was ever located has long been a mystery associated with the ruse of misdirection, purposely guiding those that get close to travel the wrong way. If it exists however, it just goes to reason that someday, someone will find it . . . or is even the legend itself a ruse for something else?*

=[]=

The Sioux tell a story about four brothers who went hunting and came across a buffalo. The buffalo said to them, *Sure, you can eat me—I taste real good—but when you're done, lay my bones together so my hoodoo will make me whole and alive again.* The brothers promised to do this and killed the buffalo. But after they finished supper and the youngest brother gathered up the bones, the others mocked him. Buffalo can't talk, they said—they must have been hearing things. Besides, what good would putting the bones back together do? And so the older brothers, bellies full, went to sleep.

The youngest brother left them and walked up a hill to lay out the bones. Leg bone connected to the shoulder bone and so on. He finished and watched as the moonlight fell upon the skeleton. Before his eyes the bones knitted together, flesh grew, hair sprouted. The buffalo rose and walked away.

When the hunter went down the hill, he discovered his three brothers had transformed into enormous rattlesnakes: this was their punishment for ignoring the buffalo. They slithered into a hole to live beneath the hill. The youngest brother put his head in the hole and told them, *Even though you're now serpents, and jackasses as well, you're still my family.* So from that time onward the Sioux would bring offerings to the entrance of their hill, whereupon the snakes would give the tribe powerful medicine to use in battle against their enemies.

This story came suddenly to the head of Tobias Clayton Lyddy as he picked himself up from the scree he had just rolled down like a wheel of cheese. Having walked three steps off the trail to piss, his fingers undoing his fly as he trod, he became aware of a cunning illusion in the landscape: a crevasse in the ground that, through perspective and an arrangement of brush, was indistinguishable from solid earth until Lyddy's boot heel met nothing but wind and curses. He tumbled into darkness. Lay there some moments at the bottom, wondering if he was broken completely or if just parts were.

Staring upwards, wiggling fingers and toes to confirm their assemblage, Lyddy saw a cavernous dome far overhead, the underside of the mesa he had been circumnavigating. Sunlight sliced down through pierced rents. Lyddy had tripped into one of these. But rather than plummeting straight to the rocky floor, his fall had been interrupted by a landslide of bruising stone.

After he realized his legs would hold him, Lyddy stood. Faced the clusters of buildings cut into the walls of the enormous cavern, many of their facades etched with winding serpents. That's when the story of the four brothers jumped into his brain.

He had heard the story years ago around a campfire, one of those impromptu nights when the paths intersect of a half-dozen Conestogas and a couple of prospectors and maybe a few rowdies on the run from a warrant, a night where bottles of whiskey are passed around. Stories told about Indians and ghosts and the Devil swapping fiddles for souls. The teller had said the tale of the four brothers was from Sioux lands—up north, in the Dakota Territory. But seeing the snakes under the mountain made Lyddy think he had found where the three siblings had sidewinded off to.

Lyddy was fresh to New Mexico. Had held over a dozen claims, each of them squeaking out just enough to keep him in shovels and cornmeal before he would shake his fists at Jesus sitting at the Right Hand and light out to buy another patch someplace else. Nebraska, Colorado, now the Territory. He had heard descriptions of pueblo cities, square stone houses and courtyards built into the sides of canyons, and he imagined these were them: wedges of sandstone fitted together to make walls, black gaps for windows and doorways. Empty places, their architects disappeared. Some Indians, like the Hopi, knew about the cliff villages. Shunned them. Refused to even discuss them. Or so Lyddy had been told.

These buildings weren't square. They were cylindrical, without corners, with painted snakes wrapped around them. Lyddy was ringed by shelves upon shelves of giant hat boxes, rising up toward the fractured ceiling of the mesa.

He crossed the cavern floor, climbed a ladder to the lowest tier. He was surprised the wood and fiber twine held his weight.

"Hello there, hello?" he called.

No answer except his echo. He approached the buildings, the wet armpits and back of his shirt turned icy, once away from the smolder of the desert. Up close he saw the snakes weren't painted. Instead formed by thousands, millions of deep hash marks incised into the adobe plaster, cut so their shadows formed scales and rattles—murals, appreciable only from a distance.

Lyddy wandered among the hat boxes. Encountered not so much as a mouse. The darkness was too thick to see within the buildings.

He left, slipped and scrambled back up the slope, clambered through the hole. The horse and pack mule were nowhere to be seen. Lyddy swore and slapped his hat against his knee until he found them a hundred yards down the trail. He led them back. Both shied away from the crevice, his chestnut with the crooked blaze whinnying and pulling sharply on the reins. The animal instinctually feared the pit and the broken limbs it threatened, Lyddy reasoned. He hobbled them a safe distance away under a pinyon.

He slid to the cavern floor again with an oil lantern and a pick taken from the mule's load of supplies. Lit the lantern. Restarted his exploration. Now he could see inside the silo structures. Dwellings, he guessed, bowls and blankets and metates arranged on low benches. As if the owners had straightened up before leaving on a trip. No, Lyddy thought, that was wrong—it was too neat and tidy, as if nobody had ever lived here at all. More like a storefront window, items arranged for display. Corncobs lay shriveled in dishes. Whatever liquids had been in the gourds had long since evaporated.

Other chambers were mysterious to Lyddy, oubliettes dug into the rock, their only entrance or egress a ladder descending into shadows his lantern couldn't resolve. His heart beat too hard to go down into them.

The Cliff Dwellers, they called them. The makers of these places. Built them and then vanished.

Lyddy searched and searched, amazed, dumbstruck, down alleys and across courtyards. He stopped peeking into the houses, their furnishings redundant. Truth was, they unnerved him. Some of the interior walls were painted. Handprints, bighorns, snakes. Ordinary animals. But there were also lizards walking on two legs. And strange figures with square heads and geometric features, feathers sprouting in place of hair. Kachinas, Lyddy knew. Spirits. The Hopi and Zuni carved fetishes of them. Their weird faces, their staring eyes. Lyddy didn't like them.

He passed a black window. The swinging light of the lantern caught something. A glint, a glimmer. Lyddy thrust his lantern through the opening.

A golden statue.

Less than a foot tall. Standing on a bench beside the usual bowls and dishes. Blocky head, ears like pie slices. A kachina fashioned from gold.

Lyddy stood slack-jawed, asking himself if he was seeing what he was seeing. He waved the lantern, the light catching and reflecting the surfaces of the figure.

He forgot his dislike, went inside. Picked it up. Heavy in his hand, heavier than it looked. Heavy because it was made of gold. He pushed his thumbnail into it, marked the surface.

Solid gold.

More metal than he had panned or picked in a decade of prospecting. Just lying there, in a hat-box house under the earth, down a hole Lyddy had accidentally tumbled into.

"Hello there, hello?" A voice said.

Lyddy yelped, turned.

A man walked into the house, calling again, "Hello there, hello?"

Lyddy dropped the figure, almost the light too. His knife leapt into his palm and he thrust in the same instant. The man grunted, collapsed.

Hands shook so bad he couldn't stab the blade again if he wanted. He went over. Held up the lantern, looked down. Gazed at his own face, his own clothes—*him*, lying open-eyed and dead on the stone.

Lyddy sprinted from the house, through the alleys, sprang down the ladder, up the slope. His chest constricted and his guts cramped. Didn't stop until open sky was overhead.

"Hello there, hello?"

Nearly jumped out of his skin. A mirror image of himself shuffled erratically by the horses.

Lyddy lunged for his Winchester in the saddle scabbard. Pumped the lever.

"You'll stop in your tracks or I'll blast you," said Lyddy.

The other man halted. "Easy," he said, holding up his hands. "I don't mean nothing."

Identical, clothes and all. Only minus the mustache and beard, as if fresh from the barber. Just like the last one.

"Who are you?" Lyddy said fierce. "Where did you come from?"

"Just now?" He rubbed his neck. "From one of the cellars. You know, those rooms where the only way out is a ladder."

Lyddy shook the carbine. "I'm not crazy. *You're real.* Now tell me where you come from."

The other man shook his head, baffled. "Same place as anybody, I suppose—from my mother." He looked sideways, overhead, all around. "It's like I was asleep and just woke up."

There was a bottle of rye in the saddlebag. Lyddy fished it out single-handed. Poured half down his throat.

Wherever the stranger came from, he wasn't lying. Lyddy felt that. And he *did* act groggy, as if he rolled off a cot moments before.

Certainly didn't seem dangerous. More dazed than anything.

Several items occurred to Lyddy in quick succession. Lyddy was the only one of the pair who possessed a firearm. If there was one statuette down there, there were bound to be more. Gold is heavy. They were miles away from anybody else.

Lyddy lowered the muzzle.

"There's gold down below," said Lyddy. "You help me carry it up to the surface, we can split it fifty-fifty."

The man scratched his cheeks where a beard should have been. Wobbled on his feet. "That sounds fair," he said.

Lyddy nodded, slung the Winchester over his shoulder. "Good. Now what should I call you?"

"My name is Tobias Clayton Lyddy."

"That's *my* name," said Lyddy.

"It's the only name I know. Don't I have just as much right to it?"

Lyddy considered. "I'll call you Clayton."

This cheered the other man. "And I'll call you Toby."

"No," said Lyddy, "You'll call me Mister Lyddy."

Come sunset, Lyddy and Clayton chewed their beans and bacon, facing each other across the campfire. Lyddy sat with his back to a scarp of red sandstone, the carbine across his lap. Clayton chattered away, talking fluff, telling stories Lyddy already knew. Lyddy grunted at intervals.

Flakes of ash and sparks rose into the night sky and Lyddy wondered, *Had there even been another man besides this one?* Yes, he decided, there had been—and moreover, Lyddy had cut him dead. But the features couldn't have been his. He had gone a little crazy, his eyes playing tricks on him. In the bouncing firelight, he wasn't even sure Clayton was the same as him.

"I wonder what would've happened if I had married Jenny Allen," said Clayton. "She sure had peepers for me."

The statement arrived out of nowhere. "She wanted to marry *me*," said Lyddy. "You weren't there."

"Sure, sure." Clayton stared at the stars, smiling. Remembering? "How many kids you think you'd have by now if you had married her?"

Lyddy said, "I haven't thought two seconds about Jenny Allen in years." Which was a fib.

If he had been deceived by the man's face then he could have been deceived by the gold too. Maybe it wasn't a golden kachina he had found— maybe it was made of pyrite. Or maybe he had never seen anything at all. What was real and what were tricks?

No. Lyddy didn't like that. The gold was real so the faces of Clayton and the other man were real too. Whatever Lyddy saw was part and parcel with the place. Some strange Indian medicine. If he wanted the one thing, he had to accept the other.

If he wanted the gold.

Lyddy slept rough that night, dozing every few minutes before jarring awake, but by the time the eastern sky was smeared pink and purple, he had a notion. He and Clayton would return to the chamber, grab the statue, and search for others. There had to be others. When they had loaded as much as Lyddy's two animals could carry—Lyddy would walk, leading them both—he would make a careful map of the crevice and the surrounding countryside. Head back to civilization. Live like a king. Tell no one. If he ever needed more, he had the map. Only Lyddy would know.

Because killing a man who resembles your twin and popped out of nowhere can't be a crime. If no one else knows about a man living, then no one else should care if he stops.

The dead body was right where he had left it. Both Clayton and Lyddy studied it for a long while.

"If that isn't the damnedest," said Clayton.

The same frayed threads were on the jacket cuffs. The same scar on the temple from when Lyddy fell down the kitchen stairs at six years old. The only difference was the body had no lip or chin whiskers. Like Clayton.

Lyddy pulled off the hat. The dead man's scalp was smooth and hairless.

"Perfect match except he's bald," said Lyddy.

Clayton shrugged. "Any morning every man in creation decides whether to shave his face or not. This guy just kept going."

It bothered Lyddy. He and Clayton grabbed the corpse's collar and dragged it inside a building, not the one with the statue but another empty hat box. His hand brushed its cheek and he shuddered—the skin was cool and dry and raspy, like very fine sandpaper.

They began the extraction. Lyddy had a sack with a drawstring. In went the golden kachina. Then they searched the other buildings, scoring the adobe beside the doorway when a chamber was clear. There were other items too, buffalo hides and eagle feathers and woven blankets, junk things. They ignored those. Only gold interested them. They found other kachinas all right. Some bigger, some smaller. Not in every house. But in enough.

Lyddy and Clayton filled the sack with as much as it could carry without the seams tearing, their coat pockets too, then trudged all the way out and up to dump it. Lyddy thought maybe the figures would vanish in the sunlight, but no—they were real. The gold blazed in the light, dancing like reflected water on the surrounding rock.

"It sparkles, all right." Clayton winked. "But not like Jenny Allen's eyes."

Lyddy turned on him, hands balled. "Why you gotta bring her up again?"

Clayton patted the mule's muzzle. "Little point throwing punches. I was there too."

"No. You weren't," said Lyddy. Then: "What kind of life could I have given her? Coaxing weeds from the dirt. She deserved better."

"You don't know it would've always stayed that way. She would have married you poor or sick."

Lyddy said, "Money is the only thing that matters in this lifetime. Women, marriage—they all follow after."

The two left the gold with the nervous old stallion and mule and went down to liberate more.

"You know where I reckon we are?" said Clayton, as they returned along their circuit.

Lyddy said nothing. He was still hot from before. But he had been puzzling the same question in his head. *Quivira.*

Clayton laughed and clapped his hands. "In the Year of Our Lord 1539, Coronado traveled north from Mexico into the Territories. Searching for the Seven Cities of Gold."

"He found the pueblos of the desert but no gold," said Lyddy.

"The Indians he talked to pleaded ignorance. Eventually he met an Indian guide who promised to take him to Quivira, one of the seven. He led Coronado's expedition into Kansas."

There they found a place the guide called Quivira, Lyddy thought. *But it was only more mud huts and naked savages.*

"Right. It struck Coronado during the long weeks of plodding over hill and canyon that if *he* had a city of gold, a good way to protect said city would be to lead plunderers *away* from it with promises of taking them *to* it."

"Which, Coronado surmised, had happened to him."

"Exhausted, depleted—hornswoggled—Coronado gave up the hunt."

"Returned to Mexico."

"But first he ordered his men to strangle the guide."

And here Lyddy was. Not the Quivira Coronado found but the Quivira he wanted to find. All because Lyddy had glimpsed an old Indian footpath from the main road and estimated it shortcutted across the desert to his claim and then after stepped off it to piss. There may not have been seven cities but there was one of them, in the Territory, right where Coronado had suspected it lay. But underground, hidden from the Spaniard's greed—and maybe even from most of the Indians he talked to.

"Hello there, hello?"

Lyddy jumped even though he should've been used to it by now. But that morning his carbine was slung across his back instead of above-ground with the horse.

The figure tottered into view around the curve of a house. Lyddy shrank back, Winchester aimed. This one was just as hairless as the last—more so, even lacking eyebrows. And shaped different. The legs and arms were truncated, like those of a dwarf.

"Don't shoot," the little man said, holding up his stubby fingers.

Lyddy took a few breaths, licked his lips, adjusting to the newcomer's presence. *Another porter,* he told himself.

"I won't if you help us move the gold," said Lyddy.

Clayton leaned in and whispered, "I thought you said we was gonna split it halfsies."

"Sure," Lyddy hissed back, "But he don't know that."

"Ah," said Clayton. "The old double-cross." He squinted at the newcomer.

"I'll help," said the stranger.

"Good." Lyddy put the gun up. "We'll call you Shorty. Now let's go."

They freighted another load. But on the return, Lyddy couldn't find a chamber without a score mark beside the doorway. They had cleaned out the kachinas from this level.

So Lyddy commanded they set off to explore the city to find other treasure rooms. They climbed ladders to higher terraces, shone the lantern into countless doorways, breathed the cool niter-tanged air. Only empty chambers awaited them.

Lyddy and Clayton led the way. Shorty stumbled after them. He had some kind of bad itch—he unbuttoned his shirt to scratch his chest and shoulders better.

"You know," said Clayton, "For a town like this with so many people, there don't seem to be any water."

Lyddy had been thinking the exact same thing at that exact same moment. He recognized that he needed to quit this place by morning; he had only two skins left and his animals hadn't drunk since yesterday. By his reckoning, the nearest watering hole was some ten, twelve miles off. Whatever they grabbed today was what Lyddy walked away with.

"Maybe it all dried up," said Lyddy.

"No, Mister Lyddy. I don't believe anybody ever lived here," said Clayton. "It's like it was built by one set of folks for another set who never bothered with it."

They searched for hours, climbing higher and higher, lunching on some cornbread Lyddy had brought along. Shorty pecked at his.

"What's wrong?" Lyddy asked, annoyed. "You too picky to eat?"

"Not to my taste," said Shorty and he tossed the bread away. Coat and shirt discarded completely, he toddled over to scratch his spine on the jamb of a doorway.

There was nowhere else to go but the top shelf. In a courtyard they found a ladder leading through a tunnel-like square.

Lyddy pulled himself up and out of the hole. The other two muttered and fussed below him. "Both of you shut your yaps and come on," he called down.

Clayton and Shorty huffed up the ladder after him. Lyddy sniffed. Musty. Bad. He held the lantern overhead.

Bones.

The cavern's attic was like the other levels—the round rooms, the snake etchings—but polluted. Littered with femurs and humeri and skulls. They spilled from chamber entrances, packed too tight to contain them all, like waterfalls of white calcium. Not just human bones, but buffalo bones, horse and cattle and deer bones, too. Tiny ribs of mice or rats cracked under Lyddy's feet.

Clayton stooped, picked up a leg bone. "Smashed," he said, studying it. "Like to get the marrow out."

"So?" Lyddy's head raced, not knowing what to think or do. "Beef marrow makes for a good soup."

"This is human," said Clayton.

"Man corn!" said Shorty.

Lyddy spun on him, waved a fist. "Shut the hell up, Shorty."

Shorty cowered. Eyes slit.

"He's right," said Clayton. "I've read stories. About bad times what done in the Cliff Dwellers. Civil war. Murder. No food. Hungry stomachs."

"What stories?" said Lyddy. "I never heard those stories. How can you know that?"

Clayton shrugged. "The paintings inside the houses. It's like they're words to me."

The lantern light bobbed, tremors reverberating through Lyddy's grip on the handle. "We should go," he said. "Take what we got and go."

Shorty screamed, charged Lyddy. He dropped the lantern, whipped the carbine from his shoulder. No time to aim—he swung the stock like a club, batting Shorty's shoulder. The arm sheared off, dropped to the ground. It was empty and desiccate like the hive of a paper wasp.

Clayton smacked Lyddy on the neck with the leg bone. Lyddy fell.

Clayton threw away the club. He stooped to retrieve the lantern, still lit.

The old double-cross, Lyddy tried to say. It came out as a sigh. He lay stunned and immobile.

"I imagine the story of this place was scrambled as it moved north, all the way from here to Dakota," said Clayton.

The Indians brought gold and skins and what-not to the hole in the hill, thought Lyddy. *In exchange, the serpent brothers gave medicine to their kinsmen to help in their battles.*

"Yessir. And the snake medicine was making extra warriors. The Cliff Dwellers must have built this place for the new people to live in. Though they weren't people exactly." Clayton walked over to the ladder well. "But that's a lot of mouths to feed—especially if the new ones don't like corn pone. So it went to pieces."

The Indians built high to get away from the ground. Snakes live on the ground. Or under it.

"So many people you could have been," Clayton said. "Instead you got stuck on gold."

Maybe there never were four brothers in the story. Maybe there was just the one to start.

"I presume you're correct," said Clayton. His voice echoed in the vertical tunnel, the pool of light diminishing as he descended. "Now I'm gonna go see how old Jenny Allen's getting along."

If she would've married me poor, she'll sure marry you rich.

"Ha!" Clayton whooped. "So many decisions to make, so many opportunities." He sounded far away. "So many different people I could be. Have fun, Shorty!"

"Mmhphgr," said Shorty. Somehow he had disarticulated his jaw and swallowed Lyddy up to the waist.

=[]=

Jackson Kuhl *is the author of* Samuel Smedley, Connecticut Privateer *(The History Press, 2011). His website is* www.jacksonkuhl.com.

DIRECTIONS

Michael G. Cornelius

=[]=

The following story is another that, the moment I read it, I knew right away I had to have it. It really pushes the boundaries of what I was visualizing to be included in this anthology, and it just fits so perfectly. The lost civilization in this next tale is one that is long beloved in our imaginations and has been popularized in modern culture the world over. In this account, Michael G. Cornelius explores the lives of four sisters, each a unique voice, as they lament their mortality in the lost and wonderful land of . . . Oz.

=[]=

West

It wasn't a schoolgirl.

That's not how I pictured my death.

My delicious evil deserved far better than to perish at the hands of a raw-boned, wastrel youth from Kansas. Kansas! How ignoble that I, terror of the Winkie clan, scourge of all western Oz, should be reduced to oblivion by the cursory actions of a mere child, a slip of a girl in blue calico and pig tails. Pig tails! My murky beauty outshone everything about that girl, and still I fell before her.

No, that wasn't supposed to be my end! I was destined for greater infamy. In my mind's eye, my end came only at his hands; only the Wizard was wild enough to destroy me. But only at the end of a terrible battle, and only at some great, Pyrrhic cost. I may finally be defeated, but I would make sure all of Oz would live to regret it.

I saw that final battle every night in my dreams; every night when I lay down on my straw-filled mat, my soul swam with images of the carnage and destruction I would wrought. My flying monkeys and Winkie army would descend upon the Emerald City like a horde of black locusts, destroying and devouring everything in their path. They had been trained for this moment, to think of nothing save devastation, to care not for their own lives but only for the glorious rancor of annihilation. And there, in the midst of broken wings and oozing pustules of green, rent flesh being torn and tasted by crows, stood he, the Wizard, half-walking, half-floating through the carnage, calling me out by name. Finally I would have broken through that placid demeanor, pierced the mask of civility, to the true man underneath! His anguish fed the recess of my soul which, until that very moment, had always hungered, always pained for such rich nourishment. How I loved the clarity of his rage, the sweet tenderness of his fury! Crying, he would call me forth, summon me from my lurking shadow, and I would appear, all in black save the few drips of spent blood that splattered my misshapen face. I would smile, and bow, not forgetting the old courtesies before a wizard's duel. And our match—legends would be writ of it for centuries to come! Songs would be sung, stories told, a stone monument built to the devastation we would cause! I would face him, and in the pit of my stomach, I would feel a new sensation, something I had never known before. A quivering in the pit of my belly, a quavering, a new sensation, something entirely foreign to me—

Fear.

For the first time, for the only time, fear. I would tremble, shake, and relish the moment, this moment, my last moment on this earth. Then the duel would begin. My greatest magics I would call upon—dark spells that I had preserved for this very instance. Each of us would rise to new heights of power, our conflict a lover's dance, intimate, he and I, side by side, face to face, as we parried and thrust, as we wounded and bled. I know I would ultimately lose—I must, he is the Wizard of Oz—but my story would be ended that day, ended as it should be, as all evil must be ended. In glorious, savage defeat. He would emerge bloodied, hardened, victorious, but lamenting his costly victory. He would curse my name, scorch the very earth where I now lay crumpled with his vast powers. He would be exalted for all time; and I, reviled. But we would be remembered, the two us, forever locked in combat, forever locked in a bloody, awful embrace.

In the moment I awoke every night from this dream, this beautiful dream, I would gasp, then catch my breath with surprise that I was indeed still alive, still whole. Then I would remember that it was, still, just a dream—that it had not yet come to pass. I slept well on those dreams, relishing my continuing nightmare. In those minutes after I woke, as I lay in my bed feeling the coolness of the rock beneath the straw that supported my body, I wondered what he would do with my broken, bent corpse. Would he avenge himself further? Use his powers to blast me from all recognition? Or would he prefer a more visceral revenge? Would he take a woodsman's axe and tear my arms and legs from me, scattering bone and flesh and sinew, ordering that each vile limb be taken to some remote corner of Oz, the locations never to be revealed, lest some dark magic revive my bones and return me to this plane of existence? Or would he, in his infinite power and sagacity, mourn me, bow his head over my body in sympathy for what might have been, for what might have become of me— of us—had I chosen to use my powers more wisely, more judiciously, more as he has? Oh yes, I could see that, see the great and powerful Oz shed a tear over my passage, even as he stood amongst the hundreds and hundreds of dead bodies my rancor had created. And I hated him for it, hated the very thought of it. I prefer to picture him as I like him best, his visage crossed with such deep anger, splattered with the green blood of my fallen body, grabbing at my haunch to tear my leg from my torso. His hair is matted with my gore, but his fury is such that he barely notices; one last indignity, and he spits at me, spits into the crushed canyon of my face, and watches as his spittle mingles with my blood and creeps slowly down my countenance, following the trail my tears would go if I were capable of expressing such thoughts or feelings. Oh yes, the irony of that ending, of my blood tears as my dead form cried over what I myself had wrought with girlish, impish glee. That pleased me. That gave me hope. That was how I was to die.

Not like this. Not through *her*. Where is he? In my last moments as I leave this world, as my hopes and ambitions and beautiful evil melt away, where is he, where is my Wizard, come for his revenge at last? Only he can kill me; only he can be the cause of my destruction. This is not my story; this is not my end. The cruelty of this moment, the reckless loss of life she has spared through her actions . . . what a world.

What a world.

North

It wasn't sweetness.

That's not how I pictured my death.

Truth be told, I never had a stock answer for my end. I pictured it, yes, but in a hundred different ways, in a hundred different times. I was old, that I knew, old but not enfeebled. I was still radiant, still beautiful, my hair still shone, my breasts still heaved, my smile still expressed the benevolent power of my heart. There was still time for accolades; still time for parades; time for mercies and gratitude and time for me. Time to sleep, time to rest, time to be alone with this world. But that time has slipped on by, so fast, so fast, and now I find myself here at the end, and I wonder where it has all gone, where it all went.

It all started off with such promise. I was beloved, a vision in white and gold, luminescent even against the sunniest of skies. I was the breath of stale air everyone needed, the voice who always said what everyone wanted to hear, no surprises, no missed expectations, just the same, stale, saccharine goodness everyone wanted from me. I wasn't mercurial, aloof, tempestuous like my sisters; I wasn't—well—a *witch*. I was me, or better yet, me to the tenth power, smiling, always smiling, always happy, always pleasing everyone, always sensible. The Good One. That's what they called me. The Good Witch of the North. As if to be Good was simple, was natural, as if to be always Good, always mild and always pleasant, always just too-darn-nice, was easy. And the sad truth is, it is. It is easy, it is simple, if you don't mind being phony, being plastic, being a cookie-cutter vision in white crinoline and chiffon frosting swirls. It is easy to be perfect, as long as you don't mind not being yourself anymore.

And I didn't mind. Really. I was loved. Beloved. What need had I for freedom? I had bliss. Bliss, I thought, is better. And so I came when they called. I kissed foreheads, I smiled benevolently, I bestowed luck and good tidings. I came to bless the births of every child in Oz; came to toast the retirement of grand ladies and gentlemen; came to celebrate the opening of a new Munchkin bakery or shoe repair shop. I came to their parties, I came to their parades, I came to their celebrations, always smiling, always waving. They expected me to come; they depended upon it. And so I came.

And sometimes, sometimes, in the lull of a celebration, in a quiet moment between an Ozian minuet, or before the main course was served, someone, some small person, would turn to me, and in a quiet and always respectful voice, ask me, "Dear Good Witch of the North," (for, indeed, they always referred to me as a Good Witch,) "dear Good Witch of the North, could you please, pretty please, rid us of our evil tormentor, the Wicked Witch of the East?" And then, batting at me with coy and hopeful eyes, the same small person always added one last "Please?," more a hope than a request, as if that was the reason I had done so little to help them before, as if the reason I had done nothing to alleviate their suffering and their torment was that this one, small person had not said "please" to me already a dozen hundred times before.

And what do I do, when some small person asks me this? I smile. I smile as benevolently and sweetly and kindly as I can, because I know that that smile is the only help I can give. I cannot explain to them the diminutive power of sweetness, the relative feebleness of kindness; nor could I tell them the formidable power of my evil sisters, who reign over me with appalling ease. I could not tell them that kindness only has power in the hearts of good men and women, and every child in Oz; kindness was light and truth and honesty and honor and square dealings with kith and kin and stranger alike. Kindness was all I had to give; and they took it, took it wrapped up in a pretty pink bow and a sugary smile, a helpful spoonful of sucrose to ease the passage of the vile cod liver that was always sure to follow. But my kindness was nothing compared to the power each of my sisters wielded. They who knew no kindness and possessed strength far greater than I; they who depended on no one, who cared not to be loved, who had no need to be so needed, they had true strength. I could not explain to these small people that I was powerless against them; that my ministrations did no real good. Oh, I had my tricks; I offered my protection, and my sisters, perhaps out of some sympathy deep in their black hearts, they let that pass. But my starlit wand knew no true magic; it knew nothing of transfiguration or transubstantiation. Why else must I be kind? I want to explain it to them; I want to grab their small necks and shake and squeeze so hard they gasp for air, they choke, feel as constricted as I feel day in and day out, constricted with kindness and goodness and sweetness and caring and understanding. I wanted to wring their small necks and explain to them the true power of the witches of Oz. But I couldn't do that; I needed them as much as they needed me. And so I only smiled. Pat their little small heads and tell them I shall do the best I can. Let them think the fault lies within them, that they did not ask kindly enough, or sweetly enough. Let them blame themselves. For they cannot blame me. Then no power would I have at all.

And so I sit and wait. I smile, and wave, and smile, and wave. This is what I have become. A symbol of light, rather than the light itself. A symbol of kindness, but impotent to act. Soon I shall fade away, become the statue in the square I so longed that they would build for me. And I will forever look kindly on them, their benevolent goddess, smiling and helpless, and useless, as useless as I am now. I was their perfection, their sweet confection of sugar and light and pink chiffon and white riffles and blond curls and starlit wand all balled up into one fading figure, slowly getting smaller, softer, kinder in this light, only now waving, and smiling, and smiling, and waving.

It was they who killed me; their love, their need.

They killed me with kindness.

East

It wasn't a house.

That's not how I pictured my death.

I mean, seriously. A house, falling from the heavens, dropped by a torrent of magic wind right onto my head. Who in their right mind ever believes that they will die by having a house dropped on them? Surely there is no imagination fertile or twisted enough to conceive such a possibility. And yet, here I lie, part of the foundation, proof that truth is, indeed, stranger than fiction.

This is not how I was supposed to die, not me, not a good, strong woman doing the best she can to set the world right. And it was not my time! I was not ready; I was not done. No, I died before my time. It's not fair. But then again, what in all the land of Oz ever truly is fair?

I pictured my death much differently. I was old—truly old, ancient—enfeebled. I am in my bed. A wizened doctor, nearly as old as I, is nearby, but there is little he can do. Time, that great enemy and friend, has finally caught up to me. It is no matter. I am surrounded by the ones I love. Oh yes, I can love. My heart is not so hard as to excuse the possibility of love. I knew there would be a man someday. A man whose values agreed with mine, who saw the world as I see it. Flawed. Fractured. In need of structure, in need of discipline. He would help me to implement order, to bring stability to chaos. We would wed, and have children—two, both sons—and by the time of my death there would be great-great grandchildren, and me, the old matriarch of the clan, respected, revered and feared, as truly old women often are. But there would be love, the proper kind demonstrated in the proper manner, and they would sit by my side, my sons closest, then their wives, and children, and so on in this manner. There would be no disappointments, at least none allowed in my presence; a proper family, educated, brought up in the right manner. Something to be proud of. A legacy. Someone would hold my hand. I would go quietly, though not peacefully. Still, I would not prolong the event. It would not be proper to rage against time and nature in such a manner. All things must end, but only in their time.

Oh, I know what you say. What man would love me, me, a witch, ugly and bent as I am, black in my heart and soul? You believe the lies they tell in the Munchkin villages. You believe I am what they say I am. It puzzles me why their word is always believed over mine. My word is as inviolate as anyone else's; my family is storied and has long, noble roots in this land. They are nothing more than mere peasants, plain folk villagers. They have no education, no culture. They need us to help them, to civilize them. That is all I have done. Yes, I have imposed rules. The rule of law, the rule of order. What government does not? Show me a government that allows chaos and I will show you a government that will soon fall. It is the very job and duty of government to impose order. And I am that government here.

My rules are not so strange, so different. They are—quite reasonable, if you look at them from the proper perspective. These folks, these munchkins—why, left to their own devices, they drink, they carouse, they row in the streets. What's that you say? Let them rule themselves? They are not fit for such duty. They are not fit for much of anything, to be honest, not even good manual labor, small as they are, though dozens do work in my castle. They can clean, see to animals, lift small loads. They are like donkeys, and make good pack animals, given the proper training and incentive. On their own, they are wild. They lack breeding. They lack manners. They indulge in the most terrible of behaviors. Why, did you know they actually have guilds dedicated to sweets? Sugar will rot their teeth, and hardly represents a nutritious diet. Restrictions must be put in place, for the benefit of the people themselves. I have only their interests at heart.

Oh, do not be put off by their childlike appearances. They would drink (something fierce!) had I not prohibited liquor. They would fornicate in the streets like dogs if they had their druthers. Laws must be passed and so they were. And who could argue that things are not better? There is order now, there is discipline. They work and do as they are told. How is that not better for everyone?

What's that? Yes, I closed the newspaper office. Yes, the libraries too. Why? Well, that must be obvious. Too many contradictory ideas—it's not good for them. They confuse easily, you see. One idea. One course. One way, the right way. That's the proper method to civilize a populace. The school? No, no, there is still a school—a school *I* opened, a school *I* organized for them. Now they all learn to read and write and to count to one hundred and learn all about their duties as citizens of the state. I tell you, I had to completely restructure the educational systems around here. Their previous standard of learning was appallingly low and the subject matters were ridiculous. Music? Art? Have these ever benefited anyone? Sure, they make for fine leisure pastimes, but leisure is the only area where the Munchkins excelled. Kindness lessons? Such drivel! Why not deportment, that's what I said. Proper etiquette and deportment will help you get on in the world. And do I receive thanks or praise? Of course not. But in government, no one can truly expect such commendation. No one ever thinks to thank their betters. Such is the way of the world.

What? No, no, that simply is not true. Just another lie they tell in the square. Of course they still have their festival days, still gather together in great numbers in celebration. It is only the scope, the—what is the word—the *focus* of these festivals, well, of course that has changed. It's all part of their re-education. Part of their learning. But I have not forbid them from gathering, from coming together in celebration. I only impose that they do it at certain times, under certain conditions, to celebrate the glory that is today, to toast the success of the state. And why not? Why should the people not be allowed to celebrate their own successes—oh yes, theirs as much as mine, for I do it all for them, every law, every commandment, every cleansing, every raid, every mass arrest, every new law, it is all for them, for the betterment of their lives. Why is that so hard to understand?

Well of course there has been punishment. There must be punishment! If someone breaks the law, they must be punished. Is that not the way in the Winkie land? Is that not also true in Sapphire City? You find my punishments cruel and unusual? You simply do not understand the depraved nature of the little beasts. Nor the simple effectiveness of such measured and tested policy. And these punishments are not cruel. The method of execution is swift and sure. No one suffers here. There is no need to suffer. Everyone gets what they deserve, whatever that may be.

Regrets? Oh, I've many, but most are for my people, the poor Munchkins. I fear my work is only begun. I fear what will happen to them without my strong, reasoned hand. Will they slip into anarchy, back into the revelry of yore? They need me, you see. They need me to fear because that is the only way they will ever change. Well, perhaps my lessons have sunk in. Perhaps these short years have been enough. I can only hope. They are my legacy, after all. Not the family I always planned on, or the happy life I envisioned. Not my simple, plaintive death. No, a house has put an end to all that. It is up to them, now. To carry on as I led them. To follow my example. To stay the course. It would be better for them. I know that. I absolutely do. And perhaps, in time, they will see that for themselves.

And perhaps, now that I am gone, they will finally learn to appreciate me.

<u>South</u>

I wasn't supposed to die.

Not I, the most powerful being in all of Oz. More powerful than my good sister, more powerful than all the evil in Oz put together, more powerful than the charlatan Wizard and his foolish band. I, and I alone, am power incarnate.

And they took it all away.

I, and I alone, was destined to forestall death. That was my power, my right. And I had earned it. I was good . . . mostly. More truly I was power and, wielded for the right or the might, it did not matter. What I did was good because I did it. No one could say otherwise. But I did do good, I did. I was judicious and wise, more sorceress than witch, more goddess than sorcerer. I was Diana in her orb; Athena of the gray eyes; Venus in the heat of a luxurious bed. I was woman; one woman, every woman. I was birth mother, wet nurse, and shriveled, aged widow to all of Oz. I outlasted, I outperformed. I was never to die.

I remember the moment I first felt my powers. I was thirteen, and my womanhood had yet to come upon me. There were four of us total, all girls; but I was the eldest, and it fell to me to lead. I was a natural at it. Mama was busy; Papa had abandoned us years ago, and Mama raised us all herself. She wasn't perfect; she did the best she could to give us food, clothing, a roof. What if the small thatch hut leaked? What if it was damp in autumn and cold in winter? What if we huddled together near a small fire for warmth, our shivering bodies covered only by a tattered woolen blanket and a thin layer of lard and dry leaves Mama would smear on us? We were dry, we were fed (though not often well), we had a roof. What right did we have to complain?

So Mama drank; it helped. And Mama could rage; oh how Mama could rage! Sometimes, at night, she would come into the room we all slept in, drunk on rye whiskey and full of wrath. I shared a straw bed with my youngest sister, Locasta, and I protected her as best I could. Mama favored us anyway, perhaps because we resembled her more, with our golden hair and pink skin; who can say. On the other bed of straw were my two middle sisters, Momba and Sally, as dark as we were fair, and somehow their raven hair and black coal eyes enraged Mama all the more. She used a broom on them, too often. It stung; I saw it in their eyes each night. But soon, perhaps too soon for those so young, they learned not to cry. It did them no good anyway, and such weakness—well, Mama abhorred such weakness.

During the day, when Mama had gentleman callers come 'round, we would escape, deep into the woods. There was a special place we all went to, a virid, still pool surrounded by a tall grove of sycamore and elm. The three oldest of us would rush out of our shifts and wade into the cool waters; this was our joyful time. Locasta would always hesitate, timid and afraid of the sea monsters our other sisters teased her lurked under the water's edge. I would patiently grab her hand, walk her in. I would smile, to reassure her. And she would smile back, a timorous, wan little smile; but she would never relax.

Those happy moments were truly few; life was hard. But we were daughters of the North, the cold wastelands of Oz; we were used to hardship. And Mama could be sweet sometimes. On our birthdays she would give us walnuts and sing to us, pet us and hold us in her lap. I loved Mama in those moments, loved her with a ferocity I had never felt before or since. But those moments were fleeting; the drink, the men, they all came soon again, and life continued as it did before.

Then, one day, in the woods, wading pell-mell in the water, I felt funny, felt strange, as if a warm shock passed right through me. There was a cramp, and a grimace of mild pain. And there, in the water, I saw something red, ruby red, thicker than water and lazily drifting toward the murky bottom of the pool. Blood. I gasped; my courses had come, but I did not know that then. I only knew fear, terror, but I could not show this to my sisters. And the other two, they did not know; they only grumbled as I rushed them out of the water and bundled them home. Locasta, I think she suspected, but she said nothing as we trod home as fast as we could. She only smiled, a paean to me, that same forced smile I still see every night in my dreams before I go to sleep.

I told Mama about what had happened, and she was excited, powerful excited. She told me I was a woman now; that I was to stay home and help her in her work. I didn't know what that meant, and I was sad to see my childhood slip away without any warning at all. But Mama said we needed the money, and so reluctantly, I did as she bade me do.

She sent the others off to play and took me to her room. She pulled out an old white, muslin dress; her wedding dress, she told me with a low mirthless laugh. Am I to be married, Mama? I asked with a fearful voice. Mama laughed again, but said nothing. The dress was long on me, reaching past my feet, but Mama told me to pay it no mind. She told me to lie down on the bed and wait until she came for me. I did as I was told, my mind a sea of possibilities as I waited for Mama to come.

But she didn't come. Instead, a man came, a deserter from the Winkie army. He was dressed like a soldier and smelled of the same whiskey Mama favored. He leered at me. Such a pretty little thing, he said. I said nothing. I didn't know what to say. I don't think he minded none. He came over to the bed. He sat down next to me. He touched my hair. His calloused hand caressed my face. He was old, and stank of grime and frailty. I didn't like him. His hand began to move lower, past my chin, my tight bosom, down the length of my leg. It moved as if on its own volition; his eyes never left my face. But mine were fused to his hand, to his lecherous advancing hand, wondering what he was going to do with it, what he was going to do to me.

He started to lift up my dress, slowly, past my ankle, my calf, my knee. I knew then in an instant what he was going to do to me. I didn't know what to call it, or what Mama would call it, but I knew what he wanted. I just knew that when I touched myself in certain parts down there I felt a pleasure, real vague and hazy-like, and I knew that he wanted that pleasure, wanted to steal it from me and take it all for himself. My breath caught. He was strong; he was man. I knew I was powerless to stop him. But then, in an instant, in the sudden flash of inspiration, I knew I was wrong. I felt it, coming from somewhere deep inside, deeper than my gullet, deeper than any depth I conceived lay inside me. Power. Anger. Control. I knew then I was stronger than him, stronger than any man in Oz.

I knew it.

I immolated him, right there in Mama's room, watched with a stony face as he burned to a crisp in front of me. Mama heard his cries, not the kind she was expecting, and she rushed in. When she saw him aflame, Mama screamed; she howled at me; Glinda! she said. What did you do? I felt my hand move through the air as if it was the paw of some great forest beast. I grabbed Mama by the neck, and then there was blood, lots of blood, spurting over the tiny cabin's walls. Mama sank without another word. I moved through the fire and the ruby red liquid as if nothing could touch me; and it couldn't. I was indomitable, impregnable, unassailable now. As my entire life burned down around me, I found myself glad to leave it behind.

I went deep into the woods, found my sisters by the still, virid pool. Momba and Sally, my two dark-haired beauties, were laughing and splashing as usual, their play as rough as always. My sweet pale Locasta, the image of my eye, sat on the bank, looking forlornly at the blue water she dared not enter alone. She saw see me come; and the way I moved, the way in which the forest parted as I advanced, terrified her. But I took her hand; I cooed and calmed her fears.

We never went back home. I built a house for them by the pool, and a few years passed peaceably enough. Then they left, one by one, and quickly, too. They left to make their way. They left to know the world. Momba first, to the wide-open spaces of the western wild; she always chafed under anyone's thumb, Mama's or mine. She was most like Mama of all of us, though I never told her so. Then Sally left too, my rigid marionette, who in many ways had become the Mama, keeping our tiny home tidy and clean, cooking meals of sallow root vegetables every night. Sally left for the wider world, for the cities of the East. Even Locasta, shy Locasta, left me all alone. For her there was a man, one who lived nearby, a temporary and futile gesture; he was the first of many men who would be there for her. And that was fine with me. They each had their own paths and I was happy to forever leave this place.

I went south, to the warm, temperate climes of Oz. There I stayed, powerful and resplendent. And my sisters you know, too. You know them, in fact, better than I. You know of Momba and Sally and even of Locasta, though you call her for me. You gave her my name. But I am the Glinda. I have the power. And of them all—of everyone in Oz—I am the power. I am the potential, I am the kinesis, I am the future. Or so I thought.

Perhaps in absolute power I became complacent. I rested too much, on my many laurels. For now I am oblivion, doomed to be forgot. West, North, East—you remember them, each and everyone. You remember them, their deeds and their infamies, their smiles and their silver slippers. But do you remember me? The good witch, the sorceress of the South? The goddess of all Oz? No. They have their legacies; and perhaps they alone are mine. For I see now that power is nothing. Even when it is absolute. It is still intangible. Memory is all. To be forgot, like me, to be disregarded and left out, left behind, that is the fate of so many of us. To be forgot, to never be thought upon. No one will lament my passing; no one will even know I am gone. I simply will go. Too late I have learned that to have power is not to have time immemorial; it is not to have legacy. Such things are made of sterner stuff than power, and for all my might—for all my deeds, both good and ill—I leave nothing behind to mark me, nothing behind to show I was here. All I was, all I am, will simply, quickly, be forgot. Too late I have learned.

To be remembered . . . that is true power.

=[]=

Michael G. Cornelius *is the author/editor of eleven books, several plays that have been produced on stage, and numerous stories, poems, and essays. His books have been sold to* Chelsea House, McFarland*, the* Vineyard Press, Variance Publishing, SynSine Press*, and shorter works have been sold to or appeared in works from* University of South Carolina Press, Lethe Press, Alyson Press, Dark Scribe Press, Jan van Eyck Press*, and others, and has appeared in such journals and magazines as* Americana, Futures Mystery Anthology Magazine, The Spillway Review, Velvet Mafia, Lachryma: Modern Songs of Lament, Clever Magazine, CreamDrops, From the Asylum, Scroll in Space, The Piker Press, The White Crane Journal*, and more. His work has received dozens of favorable reviews in national magazines, journals, and newspapers. He was a finalist for the* Lambda Literary Award *in 2002, and has also been nominated for an* American Library Association *prize, an* Independent Press *Award, and others.*

QUETZALCOATL'S CONQUISTADOR

Jamie Lackey

=[]=

I had only recently become acquainted with Jamie Lackey's short fiction, but what I've read, I've loved. Needless to say, I was thrilled to unexpectedly find her submission to this anthology sitting in my in-box one morning. Unfortunately, that first story did not fit the theme of this collection quite right, so Jamie went back and wrote up this next little masterpiece in just a few days. Rewriting the exploits of the Spanish explorer, Hernán Cortés, Quetzalcoatl's Conquistador is wicked and brilliant. Beware the ones you trust—Quetzalcoatl may be coming.

=[]=

Hernán Cortés took a long drink of the fermented cactus juice the natives called octli. It was a far cry from the fine Spanish wine that he deserved, but there was none at hand and he needed a drink. His relationship with the governor of Cuba had soured, his men only served him because he'd scuttled all their ships, and now Marina, his native concubine who'd been serving as translator and advisor, was dying.

He was feeling a bit odd, himself. He could only trust that God would protect him from whatever afflicted the woman.

He stormed through the camp, looking for someone to punish for his foul mood. The night air was heavy and cool, a welcome relief from the heat of the day. The coughing bark of a jaguar echoed through the dark trees, and the men around him flinched.

The sound of distant drums caught his ear, and he froze. The wind shifted, and the sound faded. No one reacted. "What are you waiting for?" he snapped at his attending officer, Bernal Diaz. "Send out a scouting party! Find the source of those drums!"

Diaz blinked. "What drums, sir?"

"There were drums. Before the wind changed."

Diaz's eyes flicked to the flask in Hernán's hand. "I didn't hear them, sir. But I did hear a jaguar."

"If you slay it while looking for the natives, you can keep its skin."

"I don't think that's a good idea, sir."

"Take some men into the jungle. Lead them yourself."

Diaz glanced at the flask again. For a moment, Hernán thought he would disobey. He was delighted—that would give him reason to have the man whipped.

Then Diaz sighed and looked away. "Of course, sir."

Hernán longed to strike the man across the face for his insubordination. But his command was already brittle—he didn't have the power to punish glances. And he didn't have the energy to think of another way to put the man in his place.

Hernán hoped Diaz was one of the ones who spooked at every sound in the jungle night. Maybe the drumming natives would manage to put him down before they were eradicated. Or maybe the jaguar would rip his throat out.

The thought cheered him, and he continued to walk aimlessly through camp, pretending to check on his men, until he found himself outside of Marina's tent.

He went in.

It stank of strange, resinous native incense and blood. The doctors must have been at work. Marina lay on top of a cot, clad in a simple white robe. Bandages adorned her wrists and ankles, and a low fire flickered in the middle of the tent. The stifling heat was almost unbearable. Sweat coated Hernán's face and soaked through his light clothing.

Hernán took another drink. The cactus wine burned down his throat. He passed his flask to Marina. Her fingers, when they brushed against his, were hot and dry.

Hernán watched her drink. She was so beautiful. Worthy of him. Worthy of the Spanish wine that would never grace her tongue. He brushed stray strands of her dark hair away from her face. "The priest says that you won't last the night."

She laughed. It was a wild, dark sound, and her eyes were black in the flickering firelight. Shivers coursed along Hernán's spine. "Your priest, for once, might know what he's talking about."

Hernán frowned, pushing away his sudden unease. "Don't blaspheme, Marina."

"Malinalli," she said. "My name is Malinalli."

"You were baptized as Marina before Jesus, our Lord and Savior. You mustn't fall back into your heathen ways, especially not now. The gates of heaven will open or close to you by morning."

Malinalli said something in her torturous native tongue.

For a moment, Hernán almost understood her. He fought off a wave of dizziness. "What are you burning?"

"Copal. It is sacred to my people."

The drums returned, louder this time. Hernán shook his head, and they faded.

Malinalli held out her arms. "Come, my lord. Lie with me, one last time."

He hesitated. She was ill and her return to her native ways was troublesome.

"Please," she said. Her desire-roughened voice stirred him. Who was he to deny her final request?

Heat came off her body in waves. She smelled like her copal incense and orchid blossoms. The drums came again, pounding in his ears. She pulled him onto her cot, and he took her, rough and fast.

The warmth from her body flowed into him as they became one. When he pulled away, her body was as cool as the night air, and his skin glowed brighter than the fire.

"What is happening to me?" he asked.

"Quetzalcoatl is coming."

She spoke again in her native tongue, but this time he understood her perfectly. Her native words felt right in his ears.

He fell to his knees and clutched at the solid gold crucifix around his neck. He prayed. "Holy Father, who art in heaven—"

Malinalli laughed again, and he realized that he'd been speaking Nahuatl. The words died on his lips. He reached for Latin, but it was gone. He tried to cry out in Spanish, but his voice failed him. He could not even shape the Lord's name.

Malinalli pulled the crucifix from him and tossed it away. "Your god has no power here."

"How have you done this?" he asked.

Malinalli shook her head. "My god chose you long ago. Before you were even born."

"Chose me for what?"

"You will be his Tēixiptla—his vessel. He will take your flesh as his own and walk in glory." She pulled a knife from beneath her thin mattress. The obsidian blade glistened black, and blood-red gems gleamed from its golden hilt. Malinalli held it out, and Hernán's hand reached forward of its own accord.

"I offer my life to you, Quetzalcoatl." She stood, naked and glorious before him, her arms spread, palms up.

"Why?" Hernán asked.

"He will remember my sacrifice and be kind to my people. Kinder than Moctezuma, kinder than you. This is the only way I can help them."

A weight settled over him, moving his body like a marionette. Hernán stepped forward, crushed his lips to hers, and thrust the knife between her breasts.

Her blood was cool on his bare skin, refreshing as a mountain lake. A shimmering, green-blue bird, its tail two long, trailing feathers—a quetzal, he knew now—burst out of Malinalli's chest and plunged into his own.

Pain raked his body as it entered his heart.

Hernán struggled against the heathen god. He tried to dive for his crucifix, but his body refused to obey. He felt the Lord's light ripped from him. His thoughts grew fuzzy, hard to control. His skin shone like the sun.

=[]=

The Aztec Emperor, Moctezuma, gave him a worthy welcome. He and a legion of his finest warriors met Quetzalcoatl and his host's men on the wide road into Tenochtitlan. The heat was punishing for his mortal shell, especially clad in metal armor. But his deception had to remain complete, for just a little longer.

Moctezuma presented him with flowers from the emperor's own garden, as well as feathers from Quetzalcoatl's sacred bird. Quetzalcoatl was moved by the gesture. He abandoned his caution for a moment and laid his hand upon Moctezuma's brow. He whispered a blessing in Nahuatl. Moctezuma's eyes widened and he fell to his knees. His warriors did the same.

His host's companions gaped. "My lord, what did you say?" one of the two priests asked.

Quetzalcoatl sighed. The invaders' language was unworthy of his voice and he loathed having to speak to them. He was growing tired of these priests. They asked too many questions, and their weak offerings to their own god offended him.

"These people are simple and easy to impress," he said. The invaders' sense of superiority was their greatest weakness. But they were still a threat, here on the open road, with their guns and hot metal armor. They would not be a threat tonight, after the feast he knew the emperor will have prepared.

"They will make us welcome in their halls, and feast us like gods," he said, forcing a companionable grin.

The priests, gluttons both, were much pleased by the idea. "It's good you managed to learn some of their heathen tongue before that woman died," one said.

Quetzalcoatl looked forward to killing them.

=[]=

They feasted. Quetzalcoatl and Moctezuma sat together and talked, far from the invader's prying ears. "There is a sickness spreading among my warriors," Moctezuma said. "I feared that we had displeased you."

Quetzalcoatl shook his head. "The sickness comes from the invaders. I will use their blood to burn it away."

"When? My men are dying."

"We will move on them tonight."

Moctezuma bowed his head. "Thank you, Lord. It shall be as you wish."

"We will sacrifice the priests upon my altar. I want to taste their hearts. The others, we will allow a choice."

"That is most generous."

"Generosity is important in a good ruler."

Moctezuma had the grace to blush. "As you say. I will strive to be more . . . generous."

=[]=

The battle was easily won. The invaders were drunk and overconfident, and they trusted him. Quetzalcoatl seized the two priests and dragged them to his altar by their hair. He bent one backwards over the stone and cut his heart out with a single slash of his obsidian knife. The other chanted slurred Latin that broke into sobs as Quetzalcoatl brought the heart to his mouth and consumed it. Flesh-warm blood ran down his face. The other priest followed the fate of the first, his broken Latin no defense against sharp glass.

Quetzalcoatl turned to the rest of his host's men. "I am Quetzalcoatl. Will you follow them," he waved a hand to the mutilated priests, "or will you follow me?"

Bernal Diaz stepped forward and spat on his cheek. Quetzalcoatl admired Diaz's spirit . . . and his heart was delicious.

The remaining Spaniards converted, cowering at his feet and offering prayers for mercy.

Quetzalcoatl placed a hand against the stone altar and felt the power of the sacrificed blood pulse inside him. He closed his eyes and willed a change in the world. He could feel plagues that the invaders had carried to his land spreading among the warriors around him and beyond. He destroyed the threat with a thought. He turned to the men surrounding him. Already, some were standing taller.

"I will lead you to glory greater than you ever imagined," he said.

It only took a few months for Quetzalcoatl to teach his people everything his vessel had known about the invaders and the way they fought.

He led them to Cuba. They stained the sands red with their enemy's blood, and even more invaders knelt and prayed at his feet.

Then Quetzalcoatl strode onto the deck of one of their beautiful sailing ships and looked east. The sunrise painted the ocean the same blood-red as the sand. The invaders had gold that would make fine tribute . . . and he longed for a taste of fine Spanish wine.

=[]=

Jamie Lackey attended *James Gunn's Science Fiction Writer's Workshop* at the *Center for the Study of Science Fiction in 2010.* Her work has appeared in *The Living Dead 2, Bards and Sages Quarterly*, and *Stories from the Heart: Heartwarming Tales of Appalachia.* She works as an assistant editor on *The Triangulation Annual Anthology Series* and she reads slush for *Clarkesworld Magazine.*

Königreich der Sorge
(Kingdom of Sorrow)

C. Deskin Rink

=[]=

This next selection really encompasses two lost civilizations: The brutal and short-lived Nazi war machine, and also what they discover deep under the arctic earth. It is a chilling tale of uncovering slumbering evil and the consequences for such ill-considered desecration. C. Deskin Rink takes you into the world of the ancients; the not-unfamiliar realm of green soapstone and eldritch metal. Madness and death await in the Königreich der Sorge.

=[]=

April 17, 1939

Herr Generalfeldmarschall Wilhelm Keitel:

Please convey my sincerest apologies to the Führer for tardiness of this message. Industry has been our sole determination for these last six days to the near exclusion of all else—including at times food and drink. I have so much wondrous news to impart that I scarcely know where to begin!

Major Holtz and I waited five days for the rest of our men to finally arrive in Nazyvaevsk—a truly squalid little town if ever there was one. Why the Soviets extended their railway network to that filthy little nook of the world is quite beyond me, I assure you. No more than two score of the most toothless, boil-encrusted wretches to ever walk the earth make up its entire citizenry.

Thereafter, we requisitioned sufficient yaks to convey ourselves, our possessions, and our equipment, then set off overland for the village of Marblehead.

We made good progress during this leg of our trip. The spring thaw ensured that snow never truly hindered our passage except in the few instances where slushy ground forced us into lengthy circumnavigation. On midday, April 3, we arrived at the tiny village of Marblehead—quite ahead of schedule, I might add. I found the villagers to be, on the whole, amicable—if somewhat given to the usual stoicism and taciturn demeanor common to non-Aryan peoples living so far north. However, to be utterly honest, they do not seem entirely wholesome to me. True, they are dour, but that is not the reason they bother me so. When I chanced to observe the interiors of several of their households, I saw little shrines arrayed with blasphemous figurines and grotesquely carven idols. I must confess that, despite my disquiet, I felt a certain thrill upon recognizing a few members of that loathsome pantheon: Hastur the Inscrutable; lifeless yet ever-living Xan; hermaphroditic and ophidian Xethogga; Ihmapheses or The-One-Who-Waits. I recognized them from the cache of occult books confiscated from that gypsy-wizard the Einsatzgruppen rounded up back in 1935—particularly the images betwixt the rotten pages of the largest tome, the *Torzul Balceor.*

I checked my map and instruments before we set out the following day to discover that we had passed beyond the sixty-sixth parallel and were now within the Arctic Circle. From the rough maps the gypsy-wizard had drawn, I could tell we were getting close.

After two more days of travel, we discovered a collection of unusual stones protruding betwixt the patches of brittle grass that dotted the hard earth. These stones were of an unusual, soapy texture and green complexion. They were each approximately four meters x three meters x six meters and arranged in such a manner that I could scarcely doubt they had ever been anything but masonry blocks.

Digging in the area revealed nothing, but as we traveled further north we encountered yet more of the curious stones. They were badly worn by innumerable years, but on the surface of some I could make out the barest hints of nigh-effaced sigils or runes. I need not explain the thrill I felt when, upon closer examination, it became clear that they bore striking similarities to certain scrawled hieroglyphs within the pages of that accursed *Torzul Balceor.*

We tarried only long enough to make accurate sketches before pressing onward—since by now, I knew that something must lie just beyond the horizon. Three days later I was proven correct. Right where the old wizard's map indicated—right where it was supposed to be—a ruined city built in some long forgotten age! I could not help but wonder: Is this the place? The fabled place which the ancients whispered about betwixt hours of night and nether night? The place which the mad author of the *Torzul Balceor* mentions only obliquely—the place which he calls "The Kingdom of Sorrow"?

Unfortunately, what remained of that place was precious little indeed. It was quite clear that all the edifices had long since tumbled down, long since been reduced to their foundations. Only half-buried chunks of the strange masonry remained: arranged in accordance with floor plans that completely defy my ability to comprehend.

Immediately it was also clear that someone else had been here before us. We found hastily abandoned digging apparatuses, tools, the remains of tents, and partially collapsed pits that could hardly be anything else except the sites of excavation. Though we inferred the truth long before we saw any evidence of it, examination of the materiel showed it to be of Soviet origin.

That the Soviet camp was hastily abandoned for an unknown reason is readily apparent but, given the state of disrepair that we found it in, I can only conclude that it was abandoned at least two years ago. This is, of course, in accordance with what the SS decoded from certain intercepted pieces of Stalin's personal correspondence.

The remains of the Soviet camp proved quite a boon since we found several wooden structures they had erected to be still standing. Repairing them took only half a day and saved us the trouble of logging enough trees to build new shelters—a process which could have taken over a week.

After setting up our own camp, we spent the next few days digging amongst the ruins. Although much of the Soviet equipment has been rendered useless, that which is still in working order has proven invaluable: particularly the hoists and counter-weighted troughs. Pity that the petrol-powered shovel is badly damaged as it would be of great help. It may be possible to repair the shovel, but not without the correct replacement parts.

Most of the stones are nondescript, either because they are smooth by design or have been rendered that way by the ceaseless grind of wind and snow. We uncovered a few pieces which evince worn sigils, but such is their sorry state that attempting to read them is a fool's errand. However, we did uncover a couple smaller pieces which appear to be the remains of some sort of bas-reliefs. Although worn nearly to the point of unintelligibility, it is still obvious that they depict horrific creatures which I am at a loss to categorize amongst all the known types of fauna—or flora! Exactly what these creatures look like—or what ghastly pursuits they are engaged in—is best not described. Indeed, my eyes hurt when I look upon the plaques, and the men refuse to look upon them at all.

As I conclude this letter, I must confess that I am in a state of considerable excitement. Just this morning some of the men, whilst rooting about some of the more complete foundations, discovered a large area of loose dirt covered by a pile of flagstones and other debris. Curiously it seems that the flagstones had been laid there somewhat recently and in a manner that seemed to suggest an attempt at concealing or covering up something beneath. We spent the better part of the day removing the flagstones until we revealed a mighty trapdoor composed of the same soapy green stone and bearing a metal ring so large that only Major Holtz possessed strength enough to lift it even the tiniest bit. Tomorrow we plan on constructing a large lever or other sort of apparatus in order to lift the door.

Before I go on, I must state that I am not a man given over to superstition or childish belief in spirits, specters, or ghouls. There is nothing I have ever encountered throughout my many wondrous travels that cannot be explained through, rational, scientific means—no matter how supernatural and terrible it may appear at first. That being said, there is something about this door that fills me with a nameless dread which I have hitherto never known. Perhaps it has something to do with the large, metal brackets that seal it shut. These brackets can be nothing other than arcane locks—although they bear no place for the insertion of a key. Perhaps it has to do with the monstrous images carven on the door, leering faces and writhing figures which I am glad that time and erosion have worn away to near the point of complete obliteration. Perhaps—perhaps it is the fact that I am doubtless the flagstones had been laid in haste by none other than the Soviet expedition two years ago. Did they see something down there that made them abandon their anthropological efforts?

Yet despite my trepidation, despite my dread, despite it all, I cannot help but feel a certain thrill at considering what lies beneath that hideous trap-door. Wondrous treasures of long-lost civilization! Atlantis! Lemuria! Catrazzarr! Mu! Their secrets lie so close! What antediluvian cycle birthed this nameless city? If I listen close enough, I can hear the cold winds whistling over that nighted trapdoor—I can hear the cold winds whispering of the secrets lying just below our feet. Tomorrow we construct a mighty lever to pry the trapdoor open. I doubt that this night will find me asleep for even an instant, such is my state of anticipation.

Your Ob'd Servant
Dr. Werner von Eichmann PhD. M.D.

April 26, 1939

Herr Generalfeldmarschall Wilhelm Keitel:

As I stated in my last letter, we had been preparing to breach the stone trapdoor which so hindered our progress. On the morning of April 18, I instructed the men to attack the hinges and locking mechanisms of the door with pickaxes, but to no avail. Even Major Holtz's great strength could not so much as dent the dark metal; he managed to break two pickaxes before I bade him cease. I spent the remainder of the day testing out various types of acid on the metal of the locks and the stone of the door itself. Both seemed curiously impervious to my chemicals and I was about to abandon hope when one of my last tests revealed the metal at least slightly vulnerable to strong hydrochloric acid.

It took nearly another day for me to bring a batch to the desired concentration of thirteen moles. We had to wear gas-masks and rubber gloves while handling the compound so toxic were its fumes. Although it was highly concentrated and even though I employed my entire supply, the locks refused to dissolve completely. After an entire day of effort we succeeded only in making the locks pock-marked and corroded like old iron—weakened, but not destroyed. Again we went at them with pickaxes, but still with no visible results. Whatever kind of eldritch metal was used in their construction, by God is it strong! Finally as the sun began to dip below the horizon, Major Holtz set upon the locks with a masonry block. This block must have weighed upwards of 250 kilograms. I have no idea how Major Holtz managed to lift it even one time, never mind the score or so times it actually took to finally shatter the stubborn locks.

Even though the hour had grown quite advanced, we unanimously decided that our enterprise could not wait until the light of dawn. Once again Major Holtz's strength proved invaluable—I thank you for allowing him to accompany us. The mighty ring that allowed for the door to be opened could only be enticed to lift from the ground the barest fraction of an inch through the total application of his physical might. Once he had lifted it, we managed to jam a metal rod underneath it and prop it up.

Through the night we worked to construct a series of pulleys that would draw the trapdoor up with steel cables. We worked in shifts for two days until it was finally complete, and when it was, we required no less than the strength of all the men and two yaks to force the door to budge. We made several attempts with no visible success and I began to worry that something held the door shut from within. But then, on the eve of April 21, with a mighty groan and a crack like thunder, the door lifted from its jambs. Frantically, we tugged at the hoist until we had pulled it open and dropped it with an almighty bang onto its other side.

The lateness of the hour brought about a particularly black, moonless night—but the square of darkness gaping from the open trapdoor was blacker still. A smell like the grave issued forth from that nighted mouth, a putrid stench from the unknowable recesses of inner earth. It was tinged with an awful, clinging dampness that, I think, was even more horrible than the stench itself. Major Holtz later said that the stench reminded him of death; not the death of aeon-old mausoleums, but the fresh death of charnel killing fields. Yet he also said that he could detect nothing that resembled blood, but could pick up bare hints of odors which he could put no name to. He described these hints of other scents as akin to rot, but not rot in the common sense. It was almost as if, he said, the very stone and dirt beneath was not wholesome stone and dirt, but carrion flesh. I think that was when I first noticed that Saturn hung exactly over the trapdoor, shining balefully down upon us with a malice whose source I could not describe—but could not fail to notice.

No matter what rewards I promised, none of the men could be enticed to be the first to set foot into that hideous abyss. I suppose my ravenous curiosity got the best of me, for I seized an electrical torch and declared the men spineless and frightened women—I would make the plunge alone.

Thank God for Major Holtz, for he immediately offered to accompany me and, appealing to the honor of the men, he enticed four to accompany us. Truly the pure blood of our Aryan forefathers sings in his veins.

Before descending, we decided to tie a rope to a nearby masonry block and uncoiled it behind us so that we could beat a hasty retreat if need be. We set up a radio—but this later proved in vain, for nothing but static was ever received on either end.

Crossing the mouth of the trapdoor, we descended a sort of irregular staircase that plunged drunkenly into the stygian depths. The walls were made of the same cyclopean blocks of soapy, greenish stone as the rest of the city. For the most part they were devoid of any markings whatsoever, but once or twice I thought the beam of my torch landed upon a bas relief of a cruel face or twisted figure—only to have it prove blank stone upon closer inspection. Above us the ceiling rose to such heights that, when I cast my beam upward, it vanished into the gloom long before reaching the top. Once or twice when looking upward I fancied that the cone of light from my torch illuminated things resembling leering, carven faces or inhuman statues protruding from the ceiling or walls, but whenever I took a second glance I was always proven false.

After what seemed an eternity we finally reached a level surface. We found ourselves in a network of chambers, each so vast that even if they were fully lit, men standing on both sides would not be visible to each other. Lengthy exploration proved that these chambers were hexagonal in configuration and each one abutted another so that they formed a perfect honeycomb. I found this geometric arrangement to be, if you can believe it—reassuring. I must confess that I had half expected some unimaginable perversion of geometry wholly beyond the ability of the human mind to grasp.

Grand arches rose to adjoin each chamber with the other, arches so high that they made the Arch de Triumph seem positively dwarfish in comparison! Sometimes, when the darkness did not press in quite so close, I could illuminate impossibly high-groined ceilings with the feeble beam of my electric torch. The walls, ceilings, and arches were all composed of that same soapy, green stone and utterly devoid of markings or ornamentation. In later rooms I was thrilled to discover the mangled, twisted remains of machinery. Imagine! In a place whose age counted in the thousands—machinery!

We found apparatuses which must have been stoves, waste disposal units, filtration systems, automated elevators, and lighting fixtures. But we also found networks of crystal tubes and bulbs which may have been used for some unimaginable alchemical purpose—or something else entirely. We found arcane cylinders which stretched beyond our view, metal globes that hung in a lattice of magnetized filaments, interlocked rings that seemed to describe the orbit of planets—or at least I fancied they did. What ancient civilization was this that could manufacture such marvels? If we could but decipher it, unravel its secrets—how the world would tremble before Germany's might!

Of all that remained, however, none was small enough to be easily transported without pack animals or mechanical aid; in short, the entire underground demesnes was, except for rubble, entirely devoid of portable contents. It was almost as if whatever men—if they had been men—who once lived there, departed with the entirety of their belongings. But most disturbing of all is what I have yet to tell you: I have previously mentioned that each device we encountered was in a state of utter disrepair—but I did not mention that this was due in no part to the passage of aeons and the natural decay wrought by time. Each item, each gleaming edifice, each irreplaceable wonder of lost centuries, had been destroyed with what was undoubtedly deliberate violence. I cannot even begin to speculate upon what sort of doom fell upon this nameless place.

As we progressed deeper into the chambers, we discovered scorch marks on the walls, cracked stone, and clustered arrangements of small pits which could have only been bullet-holes. Curious it was that we even found bullets in some places, deformed, but obviously of contemporary design. I admit to feeling a great sense of unease when I realized that these bullets must have been fired by members of the Soviet expedition. Eventually we stretched what rope we had to its utmost. Unwilling to allow this minor inconvenience to halt our dizzying plunge into that dark chest of wonders, I asked for two volunteers to return to the surface for more rope. Grenadier van Austen and Grenadier Isaacson raised their hands. Instructing them to return quickly, I sent them on their way.

In order to save batteries, I ordered the electric torches to be switched off periodically. In that absolute midnight, the ticking of my pocket-watch was like the clamor of a locomotive. After waiting for nearly an hour, we began to grow agitated. The men we'd sent to get more rope should have returned by then. Although I wished fervently to continue our delving, I knew that without more rope, we would be liable to get lost. Becoming entombed forever within that pitchy crypt was hardly a prospect I relished.

Angry that van Austen and Isaacson had been too afraid to return, I reluctantly ordered the group to begin following the rope back out to the surface. We activated our torches and made quick progress through the tangled heaps of machinery and interlocking chambers. Soon we reached the staircase and regained the surface. The seven men we had left behind waited for us there. I demanded to know what happened to the two cowards we'd sent up earlier, but my questions elicited only blank stares. The men guarding the entrance professed that we were the first and only to emerge from the abyss. Of van Austen and Isaacson, there had been no sign.

I became quite unnerved by this, but Major Holtz quickly enlisted two of the bravest men and made a return descent through the trapdoor. He was gone nigh two hours and we had quite begun to fear the worst when, just as Saturn ascended to its highest point within the ebon firmament, he stumbled back out with his companions. Despite his best efforts, he had not been able to detect the barest hint of the two vanished men.

On only a few occasions have I ever seen Major Holtz visibly display fear or unease, such is his degree of emotional mastery and exposure to horrors of war. This was one of those occasions. He professed to have heard a distant pounding from somewhere in the deep, somewhere far beyond where we had thus far dared to travel. A pounding not unlike some huge, slippery bulk against a stone barrier.   Since then, I have made sure that all teams sent to explore the chambers below stay together at all times and are well armed. This may seem a foolish precaution, but it makes the men feel slightly less apprehensive when they can touch the cold steel of a revolver on their belt. So far we have had no further disappearances. Nor has anyone reported hearing anything else unusual during his time underground. I can only deduce that van Austen and Isaacson became lost and are still down there, wandering alone in the darkness. Hourly, we hope to see them reemerge alive and well from the depths, but the trapdoor only yawns wide in a mocking imitation of a laughing mouth; in my heart, I know that they will never be seen again on this earth. Please send my regards to their families. Van Austen was a bachelor, but Isaacson had a wife and family, I think.

At nights, I stay up late and gaze at the stars because my sleep is brief and shallow when it comes—if it comes at all. No one else reports hearing that hideous pounding, but I swear, it keeps me nightly from my slumber. On the rare occasion that I manage to close my eyes long enough to dream, I find them filled with imagery of the most dreadful nature. Twisted, rubbery, slimy, grasping appendages that constrict me unmercifully. Boiling glacial skies and the hint of a distant black tower or castle flung up against even blacker mountains. Some of this imagery is not new to me, I feel as if it has lurked in the corners of my eyes ever since I beheld that accursed tome, the *Torzul Balceor*.

Your Ob'd Servant
Dr. Werner von Eichmann PhD. M.D.

October 1, 1939

Herr Generalfeldmarschall Wilhelm Keitel:

Major Josef Müller reporting:

I write concerning the disappearance of your comrade Dr. Werner von Eichmann.

As per your orders and those of the Führer, my platoon traveled along the route indicated, following in the steps of Dr. von Eichmann's expedition after he departed from Nazyvaevsk, five months prior. We found Dr. von

Eichmann a few miles outside of Marblehead, half-dead from frostbite and suffering dreadfully from exposure. He was alone.

At the sight of fellow Germans, Dr. von Eichmann erupted into relieved hysterics. He refused all food and took only a hurried swallow of water before bursting into a torrent of half-formed words and syllables that tumbled over each other in their haste. He described an impossible tale of an ancient, chthonic city filled with fantastic technology. He described how he and his men explored the haunted cockles of that place for twenty-six days, hauling up wondrous device after wondrous device. I will relate his tale to you, Herr Generalfeldmarschall, but it certainly must be a work of fiction invented by his starved and dehydrated brain.

On the twenty-sixth day of exploration, von Eichmann and his men discovered a gleaming artifact of oblong configuration and roughly the size of a man. Just as he began directing its removal, a hideous pounding thundered through the catacombs. It echoed from the walls so that it came from all directions at once. One of the men, Grenadier Jack Neihoff, grew so terrified that he fled screaming into that labyrinth of nighted corridors. The men tried to go after him, but von Eichmann stopped them since such pursuit would in all likelihood be foolhardy and futile at best. At worst . . . at worst was something they dared not imagine.

After nearly a minute, the pounding tapered off to a series of regular, dull thumps. The lowered volume reduced the noise's proclivity to echo and allowed the men to infer its source to be the room immediately adjacent to them. Of course, given the way Dr. von Eichmann describes the size of the nameless city's rooms, it must have taken them considerable time to cross into the next chamber. What caused them to investigate the source of that dreadful pounding rather than flee outright, I will never know. Dr. von Eichmann could only guess that, perhaps, some sort of madness had come over them in that hellish abyss.

The next chamber proved identical to all the rest—limitless, composed of green soapy rock and filled with naught but darkness and wreckage—save one aspect: In its center were four stone trapdoors, sealed with bands and locks of singular, dark metal and nearly identical to the mighty door they'd pried open on the surface.

It was from one of these doors that the terrible pounding issued. The stone slab shook as though subjected to hammer blows imparted by some unseen agency beneath the door. But the most terrifying, soul-shirking characteristic of that dismal room was realized only when Dr. von Eichmann allowed his gaze to drift from the shaking door to a door farther back.

Here, Dr. von Eichmann required several more draughts of water, guzzling them down as though they were nepenthe. Finally, with a strained voice and wild eyes, he continued. It had taken him some time to finally regain control of himself since what he revealed next—although it lacked any visceral horror—it carried implications of a most unspeakable magnitude. In the back beyond the shaking, rattling door, beyond the other two doors which lay still there was the fourth and final door yawning wide and completely thrown open!

This proved too much for the party and they fled in abject terror. Von Eichmann was nearly abandoned when he tarried alongside the oblong artifact to scribble its location, but he came to and tore recklessly for the surface with the others. The pounding began anew to beat out an abhorrent, mocking tattoo that chased their every footstep but—when they finally, gratefully, blessedly regained the snow-dusted surface—it ceased.

Grey clouds gathered overhead and soon a wet snow began to fall, which did little to lighten their already damp spirits. Another party, led by Major Holtz, yet remained underground. Reluctantly, they decided to wait to see if their companions would emerge.

After an hour, with undeniable clarity, the terrible pounding echoed up once more from the depths. It started and stopped at random intervals, but one fact was undeniable—it grew stronger with each passing minute. The men began to talk of working the pulleys and levers attached to the trapdoor in order to close it. Dr. von Eichmann argued against them—he could not even imagine even an ounce of the despair he would visit upon the men remaining in the catacombs should they rush to the exit and find it horribly sealed and find themselves entombed for all time. But just as Dr. von Eichmann began to lose the argument, the pounding abruptly stopped.

In tense silence, the men waited. Quite suddenly, they beheld the drunken swaying of two points of light at the bottom of the utterly black staircase. From the way the two electric torches swung around, Dr. von Eichmann could tell that their bearers were in distress. He called down to them repeatedly and received terrified screams in reply.

Immediately, the men heaved on the cables that held the trapdoor open in an attempt to slam it shut. The two specks of light grew nigh and Dr. von Eichmann knew that they were running at full tilt for the surface. He shouted down encouragement, begging, pleading, praying that they would reach the surface before the stone barrier entombed them forever. As the straining pulleys and winches hauled the trapdoor closer to vertical, Dr. von Eichmann made out a third, more distant, point of light whipping to and fro further down the stairs. The faint crack of far-off gunshots echoed up the staircase with the emergence of this third point.

By then, the first two points drew so close that they had expanded into blazing halos of light. Von Eichmann could make out quite clearly the forms of Major Holtz and another man scrambling desperately up the ominously large stairs. Dr. von Eichmann shouted at them to hurry. He tried to get the men to pause in their attempt to close the door, but to no avail. By now the door was vertical so that it teetered precariously close to tipping over and slamming shut.

More gunshots rang out from the shadowed passage. Major Holtz had drawn close enough that flashes of his blonde hair were occasionally visible in the crazed pitching of his electric torch light. A terrible smell that von Eichmann described to me as a combination of spoiled milk and the stench of low tide issued forth. It was clear that, as he ran, Major Holtz was firing backwards into the shadows at something unseen. A moment later Dr. von Eichmann could make out Major Holtz's screams; he was screaming with all his might for the door to be slammed shut.

The men heaved against the cables holding the door up. The door pitched and wobbled. No matter how they strained, its weight denied them utterly so that it remained stubbornly vertical. Less than an inch of lateral movement would incline it sufficiently as to cause it to topple shut, but try as they might their strength proved wholly insufficient. Just as Dr. von Eichmann felt his hammering heart must explode from fear and exertion, Major Holtz leapt from the opening to tumble out into the snow. He wasted not a moment for words, but instead heaved with all his considerable power against the opposite side of the trapdoor. This final shove proved just barely enough and the door swung down to close with an almighty bang. Although it obviously pained him to do so, here, Dr. von Eichmann paused in the telling of his tale to whisper quietly that—amidst the crash of the door slamming blessedly shut—he heard faint cries for help echoing up from those he'd just entombed.

But tragedy of the man's premature burial went unrecognized, for more pressing matters were yet to be attended to. Major Holtz had already heaved one of the heavy green blocks that lay scattered near the door back atop it. The men aided him as swiftly as they were able and, working in teams of two, they had soon dragged four blocks atop the door. Just as the fifth block was dragged into place, the door shook with that all-too-familiar pounding. The blocks atop it rattled and danced, but after two horrific minutes, the barrier had moved not at all. Then, as sudden as its onset, the pounding ceased.

That horrible, fishy, rotten stench lingered around the door for nearly an hour longer then it too disappeared. Most of the men were too stunned to react to what they had felt and heard and simply sat shivering in silence with their stuttering breaths misting in the air. Hidden behind a white shroud of clouds, the sun now sank slowly below the horizon to cast the sky in haunting blacks and deep blues.

I asked him then what happened to Major Holtz and the others. He paused for a long time before trying frantically to convince me that they were dragged, screaming, back into the abyss. He claims that several days after they departed that hellish place, the pounding came anew—and in the darkest hour of night, each of his companions vanished one by one beneath the cold light of Saturn's gaze. He claims they left naught behind but their agonized cries. He claimed that he would be next. He claimed that we would all be next.

I, for one, believe not a word of his tale. Our scouts have scoured the areas he described and detected nothing resembling even slightly the nameless city or the horrid trapdoor. It is possible that Major Holtz and his party have made their way back to safety, or that they were killed by the Red Army somewhere on the tundra—but I am convinced that, in his madness, Dr. von Eichmann's murdered them whilst they slept.

After von Eichmann told me his tale, there came a low thudding or pounding. I knew it to likely be distant artillery fire, but von Eichmann would not be convinced and stood to his feet and let out a soul-shirking laugh. His white beard bristled and his eyes blazed with the light of madness. From his pockets, he dug out a collection of hand-written notes and cast them at me, cackling, wailing and shrieking.

"Don't you understand, Herr Lieutenant? Don't you understand?! After we shut the door, it rattled and shook. We thought that we'd trapped the thing—but it was not pounding on the door from beneath. *It had already escaped and was pounding on it from the outside in victory*! What fools we were to think we'd won—what fools we were to think that such an entity was necessarily visible to the human eye! We let it go free!

Burn the documents, Herr Lieutenant! I beg you! Burn them and disavow any knowledge of finding me or of the expedition. Please Herr Lieutenant, I implore you! Burn them. Burn them all! Burn yourself and burn me! The vaults are not for our eyes! Burn! Burn it all! *Uuah! Uuah!* The Kingdom of Sorrow spreads over the Earth! All bow before the unspeakable High Priest! Before His grace and His might! The worm rises to his invisible throne in the sky! *Uuah! Uuah-Xethogga!*"

Dr. von Eichmann broke into a series of wordless shrieks and then, casting his canteen to the floor, he rose with arms outstretched to throttle me. My guards tried to restrain him, but he broke free. He tore through our camp and eventually managed to lock himself in the cab of one of our trucks. There, whilst heroic attempts were made to force the door, Dr. von Eichmann retrieved a spare Luger from the driver's compartment and shot himself in the head.

Very Respectfully,
Major Josef Müller

=[]=

C. Deskin Rink *is a human organism. His writings include* The High Priest *available at* CastMacabre.org *and* Ankor Sabat *available at* Pseudopod.org. *Visit his website at* ankorsabat.blogspot.com.

GESTURES OF FAITH

Fadzlishah Johanabas

=[]=

Dr. Fadzlishah Johanabas is an interesting guy. He's a young neurosurgeon in Malaysia and one may not immediately equate an individual who is anchored in the scientific world of medicine as someone who would be passionate about writing speculative fiction. However, after reading Gestures of Faith, *you'll quickly find that he has honed his craft of writing with as much precision as . . . well, a surgeon's knife. This story follows Thoth, an idealistic youth who may not have the powers of his peers, but could be the final hope for the once-mighty people of a declining Island nation.*

=[]=

The great Poseidon sat alone facing the rising sun. The rest of the temple, from the sea-blue marble floor and colonnades, to the double rows of pristine white columns supporting the elaborate triangular pediment and slanted roof, were well maintained. The gigantic orichalc statue within the naos, the heart of the temple, however, was fading. The gold leaf that layered his entire form had peeled off in places, and the trident he held upright was dull when the pointed tips should have captured the first rays of sunlight and lit the open-aired temple like a beacon, welcoming all to the island kingdom.

Pastel hues of blue, pink and orange filled the heavens as the sun blinked awake from beyond the eastern horizon of the ocean. In the soft light, the floor of the temple reflected Thoth's solitary form. He alone knelt and kissed his forehead on the cold marble before the statue. He remembered a time when he was little and his mother still alive; there would be at least fifty worshippers to greet the rising of the sun.

"If only there were more like you, child."

Thoth sat up and smiled at the Oracle as she walked into the temple from the side. The colorful beads at the tips of her fine braids tinkled with each movement. Her hair was white, her face etched deep with creases, but her slender body was still graceful, her steps sure and fluid. She smiled back at him before kneeling beside him to pray.

He waited for the Oracle to finish her ritual before speaking. "Has

Poseidon spoken to you, Oracle? Everyone is worried about the war going on against the Greeks."

Her half-smile was a sad one. "The Lord of the ocean deep has remained silent."

"I pray that everything goes well. Master Leus says control over the elements is erratic at best."

"The sages too? I thought only the magic of my order is failing."

Thoth looked at the statue's stern, bearded face and shuddered. "I should go back to the Hall of Ages. The test is today, and Master Leus will require my assistance."

"Your lovely friend is taking the test too, isn't she?"

"Yes, Oracle."

She nodded, sending the beads in her hair jostling against one another. "I shall pray for her success. Give my regards to Leus as well."

"I will. Thank you, Oracle." Thoth bowed at her and padded out of the temple.

Beyond the temple grounds, the city was rousing. Boats and ships with masts slanted to either side had their white sails unfurled as they made their way in and out of the capital and its surrounding islands via canals that cut through the islands like spokes on a wheel. In the early sunlight, the metal-coated walls that circled the concentric ring islands gleamed like the haloes of a full moon; the yellow brass of the outermost island wall, the white tin of the middle island wall, and the red orichalc wall of the circular island that was the heart of the greatest civilization on Gaea. The buildings, great and small, were primarily white, and stripes of red and black decorated most of them. Tropical trees and ferns co-existed with buildings, roads and walls in glorious harmony. At the exact center of the inner island, the high emperor's palace stood proud with its graceful spires and columns, gold and orichalc arches, and fountains sprouting from life-like statues, tumbling down in gentle cascades into pools of water-lilies. The palace proper was large enough to house all ten rulers of the island including their retainers, whenever they convened at the capital.

The circular Hall of Ages stood just beyond the gold-plated gates of the palace. Great columns lined the outer wall, each thicker than two great elephants that populated the eastern plains of the land. The pristine white building in itself was simple compared to the palace, but the real wonder floated above the domed roof made of crystal. A model of Helios, a silent globe of yellow-orange flame, burned at the center, with ten other globes of varying sizes orbiting the miniature sun. Great sages, generations ago, had constructed the floating model of the Helios system using their accumulated knowledge of astronomy and magic. Even midway down the hill from the temple, Thoth could make out the green and blue of Gaea, and the smaller Luna orbiting it.

Thoth's sandaled feet clattered against the pavement, arranged into repeating motifs of blue-and-white. It was a good thing the path toward the Hall of Ages lay empty. He prayed to Poseidon to guide his feet so that he would not be late. Thoth had seen Master Leus angry, and had himself angered him on several occasions, even. It was an experience he wanted to avoid above all else.

When Thoth arrived, panting and sweating at the great hall, a small crowd had already gathered on the uppermost floor directly under the crystal dome. Master Leus stood near a high table set at the far end of the chamber, opposite the heavy doors of the main entrance. He was conversing with another sage whose braided steel-gray hair and severe face made her look as old as him, if not older. Thoth weaved past groups of sages and nervous apprentices and stopped at a respectful distance from his master. He bowed low and waited that way, unflinching.

"I presume you were at the temple, lad?" Master Leus stroked his neatly trimmed gray-and-white beard and raised thick eyebrows. He was tall and sinewy, his figure well-maintained even for his age.

Thoth straightened, his full height not quite reaching Master Leus's chin, but kept his eyes lowered. "Yes, master. The Oracle sent her warm regards."

"I thought you have gotten rid of the child, Leus." The sage's voice was as severe as her looks.

"He may not have any magic in him, but the lad is bright and resourceful. Never in my entire life have I seen another person who can remember any Gesture I show, no matter how simple or complicated, at just one demonstration."

Thoth stood straighter at his master's words.

"Yes, but what use is remembering any Gesture when he cannot cast any spell?"

"Siboea, that is uncalled for."

Thoth cringed even though Master Leus's cold reprimand had not been directed at him. He stole a glance at the female sage. Mistress Siboea sniffed and squared her shoulders, but kept her peace. Thoth had heard of Mistress Siboea before. She was one of the strongest elementalists in known history. She was also the person whose footsteps his friend Isis always wanted to follow.

"Is there anything you wish of me, master?"

"No, but stay close. I want you beside me when the test begins."

Thoth bowed again and backed away. The two high sages resumed their conversation and paid him little heed. Thoth took the opportunity to seek out Isis, who stood by herself outside one of the smaller doors, overlooking the eastern expanse of the great island. In the morning light, the prisms atop the pyramids, famous as the burial grounds of the emperors, glittered as though they were on fire.

"Beautiful, isn't it?" Isis leaned against the marble banister and did not turn to look at Thoth as he approached her.

"What is?"

"Our kingdom. Even the gods are envious of its beauty."

"Do not blaspheme, Isis. Please."

Isis laughed and looked sideways at Thoth. "Forgive me. Sometimes I forget you still keep your faith in the gods."

"Are you nervous about the test?"

"Of course not. The spells required are simple."

Thoth knew it was not true; furiously complicated Gestures were needed to cast the spells set for the test. He also knew how gifted Isis was, and how truly simple the spells were for her. He had even overhead Master Leus mentioning that the test was just a formality for Isis. But he did not tell Isis this, for he did not want her to lose focus.

"I saw Mistress Siboea inside, talking with my master."

Isis turned at this, her eyes alight. "Truly? Then I must do all I can to impress her."

Before Thoth had a chance to reply, a gong was struck from inside the chamber to signify the start of the test. He squeezed Isis's hand before running back inside to stand behind Master Leus, who sat at the center of the high table. Mistress Siboea took her seat beside him, and seven other sages joined them. The nine high sages would preside over the test, and would judge whether an apprentice was fit to join the ranks of the sages.

Seven apprentices would be taking the test, which was held on an annual basis. Two of them had taken the test the year before; one still bore scars throughout the left half of his body from his failure. They were the lucky ones. Many an apprentice had perished taking the test. Thoth looked at Isis, serene and composed, and prayed for her success.

The first apprentice, a young man not much older than Thoth, stood at the very center of the chamber and bowed to the high sages sitting before him. Thoth kept his eyes on the apprentice as he articulated a series of Gestures with increasing complexity. In his eyes, Thoth saw blazing trails of Power with each successful Gesture. Burning red and gold in mid-air, the intensity of the trails increased with the Power of a spell. With a single glance, Thoth committed each Gesture into memory; he knew when a spell was cast less than perfect.

"He has the third and the seventh patterns wrong," Thoth whispered, mainly to himself, when the apprentice failed to cast his tenth spell.

Mistress Siboea turned and raised her eyebrows at Thoth. "How can you tell, child?"

Thoth almost jumped back, but managed to compose himself and lowered his eyes in deference. "Forgive me, Mistress. I did not mean to interrupt your concentration."

"No, you were right. He did have the third and seventh patterns wrong. How can you tell?"

"I can see the Power burning when Gestures are made. They burn themselves into my head, and I can tell when a spell is not cast properly."

Mistress Siboea turned to Master Leus. "You know of this? That is why you keep him?"

Master Leus smiled. He cleared his throat and looked sternly at the sweating apprentice. "Clearly you are not ready. Come back when you are."

Isis came next, and she cast all the spells with speed and precision that sent most of the high sages nodding and smiling. Even Mistress Siboea leaned forward with interest.

"How old are you, child?" Mistress Siboea asked when Isis completed all her spells.

"Seventeen, Mistress."

The other high sages murmured among themselves. Thoth and Isis were the same age, an age considered too young to take the test.

"If you can impress me with an elemental spell, I will take you under my tutelage."

More murmurs, this time throughout the airy chamber. It was well known that Siboea never took any sages under her wing.

Isis bowed low. Thoth could see the excitement in her movements. Isis took a deep breath and raised both hands, each Gesturing a different elemental spell. Her right fingers traced a blaze of fire, and her left ones traced a spell of air. After the first few patterns Thoth knew what spell she was casting.

"Not *that* spell," he hissed, barely audible. "It's too strong."

Mistress Siboea glanced at Thoth but said nothing. She looked at Isis in rapt fascination as the girl executed the complicated Gestures perfectly. When she finished the last pattern, Isis clapped her hands together.

Nothing happened.

Isis bit her lower lip and scrunched her face, but her delicate fingers remained steady. Thoth stole a glance at Mistress Siboea, and saw the disappointment in her face.

"She did everything right," Thoth whispered.

Mistress Siboea leaned back against her stiff-backed chair. "Yes, she did. The girl is not at fault. The spell is indeed strong, and the Power does not respond well to our invocations of late. No matter. When she is more mature, perhaps."

Before Master Leus could say a word, Isis repeated the Gestures with rapid succession. She finished the spell and clapped her hands with a mighty peal. A shockwave blew in a circle, and the image of a stork made of pure fire flew from her hands, flapping toward the tip of the crystal dome. The bird flew into the crystal, and a blinding flare shot out, illuminating all of the land and the islands beyond her borders in midday light for several minutes, before dissipating.

Isis slumped to her knees, panting, but her eyes were alight with triumph.

"What a find, indeed." Mistress Siboea looked at Master Leus and the rest of her colleagues before continuing. "If you so wish it, I will make an elementalist out of you."

"The honor is mine, Mistress." Isis winked at Thoth, and he beamed at her in return.

When the fourth apprentice was in the middle of his test, horns blared from the palace and stopped him mid-Gesture. All the sages present rose to their feet and, without decorum, rushed out of the hall and headed for the palace.

"Thoth, Isis, come with me," Master Leus said as he held Mistress Siboea's hand and guided her out the less crowded back entrance.

The two of them fell into step behind the sages. Though somewhat subdued after hearing the loud horns, Isis could not conceal the spring in her steps.

Thoth smiled at his friend. "I was worried for you. The spell could have backfired."

"That makes two of us, but the risk was worth it, don't you think?"

"An elementalist, Isis. I am excited for you."

"I will miss you, Thoth."

He nodded and kept his focus on following his master.

All the doors to the palace's Audience Hall were wide open, and a large crowd had packed the spacious chamber, from nobles to sages, priests, guild leaders and merchants. All of them made a path for the high sages as they made their way to the heart of the chamber. Thoth and Isis followed closely behind.

The High Emperor Demos leaned against his high-backed throne of gold and orichalc on a dais at the center of the Audience Hall. He was tall amongst his people, and his sharp features were still beautiful even though wrought with consternation. His crown of sacred sea-ram bone gleamed white in stark contrast with his onyx hair. His consort, the Minoan princess Aria, stood beside him in a flowing robe of white silk that clung to her curvaceous figure, with one hand resting on his shoulder.

Before them knelt a general whose plumed orichalc helmet and breastplate were matted with dried blood. Though his tanned face was stern and proud, his shoulders slumped in defeat. He took sharp, ragged breaths, but kept his stoic bearing.

"High Emperor," he began with much difficulty, "we have lost the war with the Greeks."

Pandemonium.

The high emperor raised his right hand, but it took long moments before a hush blanketed the Hall. "Care to elaborate how this is even remotely possible?"

"The Greeks have mastered magic of their own, and they have strong fighters."

"Great-grandfather Prometheus should have foreseen this when he taught those barbarians the secret of fire." High Emperor Demos tapped his throne in a lazy wave of his fingertips. "No matter. Our elementalists have a vastly superior control of magic, and the war elephants are a force to reckon with. How, then, can you come here, bearing this news?" His tone was mild, but his blue eyes bore into the general's, unblinking.

The general started to answer, but collapsed on the polished marble floor face-down. The Oracle was the first to reach his side.

"Demos, you should have sent this man to me first." The Oracle's eyes locked with the high emperor's in a direct challenge, and he had to look away after a few moments. She turned her attention to the man lying with a small pool of blood seeping from under his breastplate and articulated her long fingers in a complex series of healing Gestures.

Thoth kept his attention on her fingers as a trace of feeble blue-white flame formed in front of the Oracle. "Beautiful."

Mistress Siboea tilted her head back toward Thoth. "What is, child?"

"The Power in her Gestures. It's weak, but beautiful. So different from the sages."

Mistress Siboea whipped around and grasped Thoth's shoulders. "You lie. It is not possible for you to be able to see both the sages' as well as the priests' magics! Leus, tell me this isn't true."

The Oracle completed her spell and pressed both palms on the general's head. He convulsed and screamed, but soon his breathing became deep and steady, and before long he was able to sit up again. The Oracle smiled and staggered backward. One of the priests ran forward and held her upright.

The general bowed at the Oracle and turned to face forward. "High Emperor, if it wasn't for the Oracle's magic, I would have thought Poseidon has abandoned us. Earthquakes swallowed our armies, and the magic of the elementalists either stopped working or backfired."

High Emperor Demos shifted his gaze to Master Leus. "Is it true, what he said about magic?"

"It is possible, High Emperor. The Power shows signs of failing."

"The magic of the priests too, Demos." The Oracle held herself upright without support. "The healing I cast just now could have been done by any novice, but it took all I could muster to cast it. I think—"

Before she could continue, the Oracle slumped onto the floor as if boneless. Both the priest and the general reached for her, but an invisible force repelled them. The Oracle floated face-up off the floor, the beads clattering as her braids whipped about in a tempest that affected only her.

"Children of Poseidon," she said, loud enough for the awed audience to hear, but in three voices instead of one: a little girl's, a woman's, and a crone's. "Zeus comes."

The tempest died and she floated gently onto the floor. Just as she landed, a mighty quake shook the palace and cracked the ceiling and pillars. Outside, earth and ocean swallowed a section of the outermost ring-island. The quake was the first of many that shook the mighty kingdom over the next few days.

In the chaos that ensued, Master Leus shouted at Mistress Siboea. "You want to know why I keep Thoth safe beside me? The prophecy is coming to pass."

=[]=

Thoth sat on the uncomfortable high-backed chair and tried his best to ignore the tremors and the black ash that spewed from Mount Olympos at the northern part of the island. Before him stood Master Leus, Mistress Siboea, the Oracle, and twenty high sages and master priests. Isis stood looking worriedly at him from near the entrance of the circular chamber where she had earlier that day passed her test. Thoth was used to being ignored, in the shadows of Master Leus. He found the attention he received now highly disconcerting.

A loud crash came from the east after a strong quake. One of the great pyramids had crumbled to the ground.

"Thoth, stay focused."

He turned to face Master Leus. "Is it true? Has Poseidon forsaken us?"

"It is we who have abandoned Him." The Oracle's voice was gentle, but tinged with sadness. "We have angered other gods. We have angered Zeus with our constant warfare with His beloved Greece. They turn their wrath toward us, and great Poseidon can no longer shelter us from harm."

"Can't we flee to safer grounds?"

This time Master Leus answered. "Most of the ships have perished, swallowed by giant waves. I hope those few that made it out reach their destinations safely."

"Demos and the other emperors are up at the Great Temple, leading others in prayers." The Oracle shook her head. "He is a fool, as all men are. Poseidon can no longer hear them."

Thoth was close to tears. "Surely there is a spell that can protect us."

Master Leus waved his fingers in a four-patterned Gesture. Thoth saw the blazing trail, and recognized the simple spell of lighting a candle, but nothing happened after Master Leus completed the spell. "Our spells no longer work. Not all the time. Even if we could gather all the sages and cast a spell powerful enough to save us from this cataclysm, the spell may backfire and destroy us all much quicker."

"Then what are we doing here?"

"Years before you were born, the Oracle told a prophecy, one that not many took heed, much to our shame. The death of our land has been foreseen, and in the child who can witness all Powers but not use them, hope lives on."

"I don't understand, Master Leus."

"It means," Mistress Siboea interjected, "you are our only hope of keeping this kingdom alive, in your mind."

=[]=

Thoth had never imagined he would be able to remember every single Gesture his elders showed him. One after another, hours on end, they demonstrated different Gestures of varying complexity, from the mundane to the obscure, from common to forbidden, and Thoth drank them all in, feeling each blaze burning into his mind. Through magical Gestures, both sages and priests embedded the accumulated knowledge of philosophy, architecture, military, agriculture and others into his memory. Isis stood beside him, clasping his hand, lending him strength the only way she could.

As the island shook and crumbled around them, the masters fed Thoth with more Gestures in increasing desperation. Over a thousand years' worth of wealth in knowledge had to be compressed within the span of a few days.

At the dusk of the fourth day, with half the city in ruins, Master Leus and the Oracle both articulated the last spell for Thoth to learn.

"Young Thoth," the Oracle said, "When I received the prophecy that foretold the destruction of our civilization, great Poseidon inspired me with a spell only you can cast. I do not know what it is, but you will cast it when the time is right."

"How will I know it?"

"Poseidon will guide you."

Thoth nodded and turned to face Master Leus. "What now, master?"

"Now we send you off to the outside world and hope that the knowledge of our people lives on."

"Where?"

"Anywhere safe."

"Master Leus, let me be his guide." Isis clasped Thoth's hands with strength and determination.

"How do you propose to do that, child?" Mistress Siboea stood beside Master Leus. In the past few days, the severity had left her face, and she looked handsome and matronly.

"I saw you showing him the fire bird spell, Mistress. It is almost similar to the one I casted during the test."

"Do you know what the spell implies?"

"Yes. My life will be forfeit."

Thoth whirled toward Isis. "No, I will not let you do that!"

"I will die one way or another, Thoth. Please, let me have this."

"But you have just passed the test. Being an elementalist has always been your dream."

"A dream that will die with this land. Let me be there for you as you have always been there for me since we were little."

"I—"

"Please."

Thoth reached out and enveloped her in a tight embrace. "I will miss you."

Isis was shaking, but she hugged him back.

Master Leus led Thoth, Isis, Mistress Siboea and the Oracle down a secret tunnel to an enclosed canal where a single-mast boat bobbed with the choppy waves. Mistress Siboea took Isis's hand and led her away.

"It is a shame you were born at the end of our age. Your Power would have surpassed mine. You honor me with your courage, elementalist."

Isis wiped back her tears. She stepped back and followed the high sage's articulations as she Gestured the forbidden spell. Mistress Siboea stopped at the final pattern, but Isis had been instructed how to complete the spell. Yellow flame sparked on her white tunic and spread rapidly throughout her body. She clenched her teeth and kept her peace at first, but soon, as the flames fully enveloped her, she screamed.

Thoth lunged to help her, but Master Leus held him back and locked him in a strong grip. Thoth kept his tear-filled eyes on Isis. He forced himself to stay rooted where he was as she writhed and finally slumped onto the floor, silent.

From her charred remains, a heron made of fire emerged. It flew gracefully and landed on the bow of the small boat. Its flames did not burn, but it gave off a comfortable heat. Its amber eyes glinted with the same intelligence Isis had.

Master Leus enveloped Thoth in a tight embrace. "Quickly now, onto the boat."

Thoth wiped back his tears and nodded at his master. "Master, thank you for raising me after my mother passed away. Thank you for believing in me when others did not."

"I should be the one thanking you. Watching you grow up has been a privilege that I will carry to my grave. Now go, before it's too late."

Thoth buried his tear-streaked face in the folds of his master's tunic one last time before he huddled onto the boat and held on to it as it bobbed to the sides.

"I will call upon the oceanic currents to follow Isis, and Siboea will ask for the winds to speed your way. May Poseidon keep you safe."

"You have never left Poseidon, child," the Oracle murmured. "The Lord of the ocean deep will never leave your side. May the waters be calm, may your journey be safe."

The fire bird let out a shrill cry and took wing. Thoth watched the blazing trails as both the high sages Gestured their spells. At first, nothing happened. After the second try, the boat nudged forward and gradually picked up speed. The boat made its way out of the canal and into a raging tempest. Angry waves slapped its sides, and hailstones pelted at Thoth. But the boat sped eastward despite the storm.

Thoth felt the large tremor as Mount Olympos spewed forth fire and ash. Burning rocks flew from the sky and crashed upon the island. Thoth heard the wails of his dying people, he felt the tears of his God Poseidon, and he wept until there were no tears left to cry.

=[]=

The gentle lapping of waves against his boat roused Thoth from his fitful sleep. The sun had not yet risen, and a thick cover of ash stretched across the heavens. His homeland was dead; Thoth had nothing to return to.

When he finally found the strength to move, Thoth sat up and peered at his surroundings. The fire bird flew around the boat, illuminating the golden hue of the sandy beach. Thoth crawled out of the boat and lay on the cool sand, and listened to the ebb and flow of the waves against the craft and the beach. The death-throes of Atlantis seemed so far away.

The reverberations of hooves on sand told him of approaching company. Three men on horseback, in white headdresses and dusty tunics, waved their curved blades but kept a safe distance from the fire bird that landed beside Thoth. Amongst his people, Thoth had been considered small, but the tallest of these men only reached his shoulders.

"What is this place?"

No reply. He tried again twice, the first using the language of the Greeks, the second using the guttural language of the desert nomads.

"Sa el-Hagar," one of the men replied.

Thoth tried to recall the name his people had used for the place, near the tip of Nile Delta. "Saïs." He knew this would be his home from that day onward. He thought about how he would pass on the knowledge, the memory of his people, when the final spell he learned burned in his mind.

Thoth sank to his knees and Gestured the only spell he knew he could ever cast. The fingers of his right hand articulated the Power of the priests, while his left fingers moved to invoke the Power of the sages. The ground beneath him trembled, and the horses reared back in terror.

Great columns made of sandstone shot up from the desert sands, and walls formed around the columns. Sand sifted away and flew in great tan clouds, and the earth shook and groaned. Before long, a great temple stood proud where there was once only sand and stone. Thoth shuffled into the temple with the fire bird on his shoulder, illuminating the cavernous chambers. He traced the first Gesture he learned onto the inner wall of the largest chamber. The inscription burned itself into sandstone, the first of many he would inscribe on the walls of the temple.

The three men sank to their knees and planted their foreheads on the floor of the temple before Thoth. They uttered the word "gods" over again, but Thoth was too weary to correct them. He also knew he was alone and defenseless, and he could use their reverence to his advantage.

With the first spell safely recorded, Thoth sighed in relief. He turned to face the men. "Nomads of Kemet, I am Thoth, bringer of knowledge, and this is Isis, sacred bird of rebirth. Help us guard this temple, and may the knowledge of my civilization help build yours. Help me guard Saïs. Help the world remember my people . . .

Help the world remember Atlantis."

=[]=

Fadzlishah Johanabas *was born and raised in Kuala Lumpur, Malaysia. When other boys played flattened-coke-can football (soccer), he sat at a secluded corner, lost in the worlds of Krynn, Middle Earth, and Faerun. And when he started exploring worlds of his own, he wrote about them. Being a doctor, pursuing Neurosurgery, has not stopped him from venturing deep into these worlds. Not when he's operating, though. No sir. Fadz can be found tweeting as @Fadz_Johanabas, or at his website* http://www.fadzjohanabas.com.

BARE BONES

Curtis James McConnell

=[]=

I like this next story a lot. It's very sharp and quick and, as Curtis James McConnell likened it when submitting to me, "it's a sort of palate-cleanser for the other stories." Bare Bones *is a humorous little anecdote, which goes to show that good writing can transcend any genre constraints. In a book of dark and ominous discoveries, the author reminds us that revelations can be found anywhere, whether in the ancient Arctic glaciers or the endless shifting deserts or simply an innocuous research office.*

=[]=

I had been with the skull eleven days when Jenkins walked in at five minutes to eight. He had been on vacation. I hoped he enjoyed it. He sure as hell wasn't going to enjoy what I was about to show him.

"Hey, chief, whacha got there?" Jenkins piped. Ignorance is bliss. He poured himself a cup of coffee.

"Two-million-year-old skull," I informed him dully.

Jenkins made a face and a sound like he was bringing up a hairball. "Well I hope it's the guy who made this coffee. If so, justice has been done." He poured it out. I said nothing as he got a fresh pot going. Then he strolled over and looked at the skull.

"Nice skull. Sulfur overdose? Where's the one you called me about?"

"This is it." I wouldn't look at him.

"No, I mean the one Josiah sent us. What's up?"

I stared into the skull's eye sockets. Here it comes, I thought. I tried to keep my tone even. "This is the skull Josiah sent us."

Jenkins still didn't get it. "I thought he sent us one as old as—"

"He did," I said.

"Right. So where is it?"

I took a breath. "This Homo sapien skull, Dr. Jenkins, is, as near as I can determine, two million years old. Give or take ten percent." I waited.

"Pull the other leg," Jenkins said blithely, "it rings."

I continued to wait. He stopped. Something in the tone of my silence got through to him.

"That's impossible," Jenkins said, and the first dark glimmer of what we were in for washed over him in a distasteful bath. He said again, "That's impossible."

"I know," I said dispassionately.

Jenkins came over and looked at the skull. I noticed he didn't pick it up. He dismissed the matter, just as I had eleven days ago. "It's too developed to be that old."

"I know."

Jenkins paused. He looked at the skull. I could almost see him counting the years. Every bit of training from high school geology to his training at this institute denied what was before him. "That's impossible," he said with less conviction.

I was barely audible. "I know."

Jenkins broke his gaze from the skull and looked at me. "Man, oh man. Have you been up all night with this thing?"

"Mostly. Since it arrived, really. Eleven days," I said, rubbing my eyes. I got off the stool and stretched. "I caught little naps. It stared at me with that implacable grin, even in my dreams."

We looked at it. It scornfully defied us with that brain cavity as big as our own, leering at us with those tiny teeth in that impossibly evolved jaw.

The coffee boiled over. I strolled over and turned it off. Jenkins wouldn't need any. He was awake now. I casually wiped up the spill with a paper towel as he looked over the computer printouts of the carbon dating runs I had verified four times. He flipped the sheet away with a loud rattle. He didn't even look at the chemical dating reports. He knew what they said. He bit his lip and thought a moment.

He tried again. "So it's wrong. Some weird soil composition leeched the carbon out at an advanced rate of decay, making this skull seem two million years older than it is. This is probably Jimmy Hoffa's skull."

I showed him Josiah Thibert's letter. As he skimmed it, I told him what was in it, more to hear myself—anyone—speaking. Anything to drown out the scornful laughter echoing down time's misty, dank corridors.

"It was found in a pit with other skulls of the same age, below the flood strata, a pit in a dig with fossils around it all consistent with the era. All the other skulls were as undeveloped as the time frame suggests. Barely Homo erectus. Low ape-like foreheads, large gorilla-like jaws, fangs and diminished brain pans; presumably undeveloped cortices. All except our friend here." The skull grinned, as if with pride.

Jenkins pursed his lips. He started to say something a few times, then went back to the pursed lips. Finally, he got it.

"That's im—what you're saying is, two million years ago, we had a fully developed Homo sapien running around with a bunch of monkeyish Homo erecti."

"That's about the size of it. Unless Josiah is playing a huge prank on us. Not a common practice for a Nobel Laureate who didn't want to hire you because your tie was too loud."

Jenkins paused. "Two million years . . . a brain . . . " It wouldn't catch in his head. "That's impossible."

"You keep saying that," I pointed out.

"I know," he fretted.

I poured a glass of water. I sipped.

"The last time evolution got knocked on its ass this hard was *Piltdown Man*. And that took *how* many years before the hoax was revealed?"

I took another sip, telling myself to let him talk it out, let him get to it on his own.

He walked over to a chart, showing a timeline and evolution down the various branches of the human family tree. "Evolution isn't steady, we know that. Plateaus and spurts. Couple of gaps here and there, a missing link or two."

He looked at the chart, as if willing it to come to life and agree with him.

He turned to me. "But until now, they've all had the courtesy to wait their turn in line. No one skipped to the front of the line two million years early."

I waited. He was almost there. I wasn't gonna do it for him. Not the first leap. Once he took the first one, I'd hit him with the second one, and that would make it all easier. He and I had to be on the same page for me to do it.

"What we have here—if this is really real, we have positive disproof of evolution."

I smacked my lips. "Yup. Either that or we have proof of time travel," I added with casual mischief. I shrugged, but this was just a curve ball for Jenkins.

"I mean—or time travel, yes. Aw, *man*." He confronted the enormity. "Man oh man. Either way, we're in a lot of trouble."

The skull leered smugly.

Jenkins began pacing. "Well thanks a *lot*. Great. Freaking great. So what do we do? If we publish this, we'll be lucky if all they do is laugh at us."

I smiled and pointed at the poster above the coffee pot. It showed a picture of Galileo appearing before a Papal Tribunal. "Every idea goes through three stages to acceptance. First it is ridiculed, then it is violently opposed, then it is accepted as having always been true."

Jenkins just quietly shook his head. His words were quiet, too, at first. "We can't break this. We can't be the ones to break this. We'll become saints, heretics, mad prophets. Josiah—just mailed us the coup of the century." He stopped. I looked up.

He breathed. "I don't want that," he said.

I turned away.

"I didn't sign on for that kind of glory ride. I don't want to be a heretic." He took a breath and continued, "I don't want to be a heretic, I don't want to be a mystic, and I sure as hell don't want to be a saint." He looked at the skull, but addressed me. "Do you hear me?"

With his thumbs on its temples, he asked the skull, "Do *you* hear me?" He broke contact and came over to me. "And why was it just a pit of skulls? That's too weird. This guy and his buddies must've had bodies under those skulls. Where'd they go?"

"Josiah doesn't know anything about this society or its burial rituals. We just discovered it three months ago." He looked at me, demanding more evidence. All he got was, "Africa's a big continent."

"Oh thanks."

I took a conciliatory tone. "There're probably hundreds of unknown proto-cultures within two hundred miles of this dig. If the civil war breaks out again we might even lose what access we have."

Jenkins threw his arms up. "And boy, how convenient for our hoax, the papers'll say. Great."

"I know," I said.

"We have to do something," Jenkins said.

"And what do you suggest?"

"Let's send it somewhere else. We'll have to let others examine it anyway. Let them break it." He looked at the skull.

I spoke what he was thinking anyway. "That's what Josiah did."

Jenkins pursed his lips. "Yeah. Okay. And?"

I pursed my lips. I looked at the incredibly dark and deep sockets of the skull. If it had had eyebrows, they would have been raised.

"And so we'll try not to be tormented too much after today," I said, as I brought the hammer down on it.

The skull seemed to be smiling.

=[]=

Speaking of ancient rituals, **Curtis James McConnell** *is technically BB King's half blood-brother. He has also been to all fifty United States and ventured into Canada and Mexico.*

British Guiana, 1853

Folly Blaine

=[]=

"Touching" is not typically a word selected to describe a work of dark fiction or horror, yet that is how I strangely thought of this piece. Written through correspondence to his wife, we find our protagonist to be cynical and scornful, yet also filled with sweet fondness for his spouse . . . and for other creatures. The author, Folly Blaine, welcomes you to British Guiana, 1853, *in which a paleontologist searches the jungles for "a living relative of Megalosaurus or Iguanodon." As the expression goes though . . . be careful what you wish for as you just might find it.*

=[]=

1 March

My Dearest Ysabel,

The *Whitby* sailed into Georgetown late due to rough weather, yet Mr. Joseph Sutton graciously arranged to meet me at the dock upon arrival. Mr. Sutton, you may recall, is the gentleman who first spotted the mysterious creature in the Stabroek Market and requested the British Museum conduct a formal scientific inquiry. If only the skull hadn't gone missing in transit, or if only there'd been more than those few rough sketches, my superiors would have recognized the implications as I did and honored the request. Imagine, being handed the opportunity to study a living relative of Megalosaurus or Iguanodon in the dark heart of South America. Think of the fame awaiting the man who makes those fossils breathe!

But the crown lies heavy, as they say. I alone grasped the potential. And now the burden falls upon me to tender proof.

Returning to the subject of Mr. Sutton, due to our late arrival he excused himself to attend to other obligations. However, he generously referred me to his man, Azco, to act as interpreter and guide during my stay. As it was a market day, Azco brought me to the stall where the creature had been discovered. Unfortunately we learned the Indians, whether through ignorance or hunger, had consumed all remaining evidence of the beast before it could properly be catalogued. Azco asked where we might procure a replacement and the natives, at first, demurred. I'm afraid I was forced to bribe them with the belt you gave me last Christmas Day.

I consider it a small price to pay for wisdom gained: greed is the same in all cultures of the world.

Darling, do not be angry. I retained the two handkerchiefs you embroidered for luck. I would never part with those.

The Indians reported finding the beast near a wall of stone about three days to the south by boat and a half day's walk from the Essequibo River. Azco believes the men were lying to elicit more trinkets. Regardless, I plan to mount an expedition and charter a boat on the morrow.

I will see these walls for myself.

Ysabel, I thank you once again for obtaining the necessary funds from your father for this voyage. You are a most loving and steadfast wife who understands with perfect clarity that one man's intuition is as great as another man's knowledge. I only hope to repay your father with a discovery worthy of your faith.

2 March, Dawn

Ysabel,

I am bundling my letters to post together. As you may imagine, once we breach the jungle interior, communication will be difficult.

I miss you terribly.

2 March, Evening

Despite Azco's increasingly sour attitude, I have decided he should remain on staff. I find his aboriginal insights useful, his interpreter skills unmatched, and I do not wish to slight Mr. Sutton's generosity. I have relented in one way to his vocal misgivings: Azco insists we need more supplies. Today has been wasted hiring horses to take us to the village where our canoes will launch. An obstruction in the river forces us to walk part of the journey normally traversed by water.

Our party consists of myself, Azco, six Indians, two horses, and numerous containers for holding the specimens I am sure to find. The horses are malnourished creatures. I doubt they'll last two days hard walking.

My excitement grows in leaps and bounds when I think this is the same jungle that fed my insatiable imagination as a child, reading Charles Waterton's *Wanderings in South America*. These hot, green lands are a waking dream.

3 March

Ysa,

The Indians are of a curious stature, small and dark of skin. They move so quietly, I think shadows must flow through their veins instead of blood.

We are committed now, travelling along well-worn paths between Georgetown and the nearest village, whose name I can't pronounce. Even on these constant roads, the jungle threatens to reclaim its own. The men slash the vines and creepers back with practiced strokes. In general, these Indians appear to be peaceful. I have only seen them wield their weapons against the vegetation. Still, I keep my distance.

As I predicted, the horses can barely carry supplies let alone a person. I am forced to walk in their stead, so that they might draw the attention of any predators. I am told predators are a grave concern in this area, however do not fear, dearest Ysabel. These precautions are sure to keep me safe and whole.

With regards to the smallest and most pervasive nuisance in the jungle, the mosquito net I wrap myself in nightly keeps out the worst of the insects. Their buzzing remains an ever present distraction, but I have found a solution.

Ah, Ysa, you will find this amusing, no doubt. The creatures of the jungle squawk and hum so loudly, and I am so starved for respectable music, I've made a game of calling the noise my *symphony of discord*. To pass the lonely hours when other men sleep, I conduct these savage musicians with a swoop of my hands and trill of my fingers, anticipating their next braying crescendo.

Ysabel, it gives me such pleasure to think of you, healthy and warm in our cheerful cottage, attending to your needlework by the fire. You are always in my thoughts.

4 March

No sign of the village yet. Little wonder with the vines (Azco calls them bush-ropes) and creepers blocking our view in all directions. Periodically, one of the Indians shinnies up a tree and confirms our direction, hacking a path for the horses.

I amuse myself with learning more about the flora and fauna of the region. For example, my love, the oulou trees have the sweetest smelling resin, although the wild fig-trees are an endless source of ripe fruit. I am sure this minutia will only add depth to my official report.

In practical matters, there appears to be a hole in my mosquito netting. My arms and legs are covered in welts I am sorely tempted to scratch. Azco has taught me to move my bedding closer to the smoke of the fires to decrease the insect menace, and to rub a concoction of mud and oulou sap on the worst of the bites to deaden the sting.

7 March

It has been several days since I last wrote. I have been battling some kind of sickness and near delirium as we traveled down river. But now that we've reached land again I am sure to be on the mend.

Here is what I remember of the past few days: The village where we boarded the canoes was a sad affair. Every man survived the trip; the horses did not. Since they were already close to death and little use, Azco gave them to the villagers to eat. I fear it was a kindness for both the horses and the villagers.

We landed shortly before nightfall and Azco suggested we camp on the shore of the Essequibo River. I admit relief that we will not set out immediately, for my body is still weak and my senses dulled from fever. Another night's rest should flush out the toxins and set me to rights so that I may properly enjoy this adventure once more.

8 March, Dawn

I suspect the men are talking about me in their odd, choppy tongue. Whenever I meet their eyes, they look away. If I didn't know better I'd say they were frightened, but of what I couldn't say. Azco whipped a man last night for some infraction.

I feigned sleep. I do not like to get involved.

8 March, Late Afternoon

At last, we've arrived! It seems the men from the market gave us an accurate account of the wall's location after all. Ysa, I wish you were here to experience these wonders. It nearly defies description, but I will attempt a record, however flawed. The walls are carved in detailed relief, the human figures rendered so exquisitely, with a skill much advanced for this region. I suspect we will find evidence of European influence once I am able to properly examine the markings.

Imagine the acclaim awaiting an explorer who uncovers such a connection. I may even have the honor of naming the new civilization!

9 March

We are certainly in the right place, Ysa. I caught a glimpse of one of the strange beasts that drew us here, and it was magnificent. I recognized it at once from Mr. Sutton's description.

If I hadn't been looking I am sure to have missed him. His coloring blends in perfectly with the wet greenery prevalent here. He appears to be an oversized lizard, about five feet long. His long tail curls like a snake, but has some maneuverability. I watched him wrap the end around a vine and use it to hoist himself upward, hugging a tree trunk with his thick, yellow talons, and disappear into the canopy. The creature moves very fast on four legs in a kind of graceful waddle. At the center of his forehead appeared to be a large, white spot which, in an illusory way, acted as its own beacon.

Perhaps nature dabbles in trompe l'oeil.

Forgive my crude attempt at humor, Ysa. I know you consider painting a noble and serious art. Although the jungle evokes a levity you may not find appealing I assure you, my dearest, I remain your faithful servant beneath the mirth.

I must catch one of these creatures. Alive, preferably.

10 March, Morning

Two of the Indians disappeared in the night, spooked no doubt by the sniffling sounds around the edges of the camp. Good riddance. Their kind of outdated superstitious prattle was terrible for morale.

I am convinced it was nothing. Perhaps the rustling of wind as it parted the leaves. Or a small rodent scrabbling for worms in the undergrowth. As you well know, Ysabel, I find cowardice disagreeable and yet I must be charitable. The Indians have the form of men, but are children at heart.

10 March, Mid-Day

I led the remaining four Indians and Azco around the wall and discovered it was built in the shape of a semi-circle, butting against a hill. Mid-way round I discovered an opening, concealed by a matted curtain of thorny plants. I instructed the men, through Azco, to clear a space and their efforts allowed me to pass unmolested into a spacious courtyard, measuring roughly three hundred feet across and one hundred fifty feet deep. In the center of the hill, absolutely covered in vines and overhanging tree branches, was a dense patch of vegetation in the shape of a door, about six feet high. My intuition told me we would find something special there.

The men set to work clearing the vines and soon revealed a grotesque relief carved into the door, a caricature of a man's swollen face, eyes bulging and tongue lolling from the mouth. Much of the detail was obscured by grime, but I believe it to be extremely valuable. I will take a rubbing and capture the image before continuing.

It is a marvel, darling, this place. Even the mosquitoes think so, for I have not been plagued since we moved our camp inside the walls.

11 March

The door, I was surprised to find, was unlocked. Although once the vines were moved away from the edges, I quickly saw it was not a door in the traditional sense as it lacked the requisite hinges. It would be more accurate to call it a plug, something to stopper the crude opening at the hill's base.

Time and the elements had taken their toll, and once the vegetation was cleared, bits of stone fairly crumbled away in our fingers. It was a simple matter to pry apart a gap and squeeze through.

Confronted by incessant darkness within, we were momentarily stymied by our need to obtain fresh torches—the wood we'd selected being too damp to catch—however, after finding suitable replacements, we descended.

The torches cast the most delightful shadows on the narrow walls, causing my imagination to run rampant like a child. We descended slowly, the carved steps slick with moss and what appeared to be small piles of excrement. Convenient bush-ropes grew, even here, for us to grip and steady ourselves. As we moved away from the entrance, the rectangle of light behind us grew dim and we became entirely reliant on our torches. As we crept along, the temperature climbed. With each step, the air became denser, more humid. I unbuttoned my shirt three buttons and rolled up my sleeves to the elbow.

With no end to the stairs apparent, the men hesitated and I buoyed their spirits with promises of extra pay. (You see, Ysa? I have learned to speak their language.)

The stairs ended at a square room about one hundred twenty-five feet down—the vines having disappeared about sixty feet down. The men demanded a break before continuing and I granted their request. They crouched on the red dirt floor, fanning themselves and swallowing deeply from their water skins. I myself was perspiring quite profusely and nearly blind from the salty water flooding my vision. Yet what I saw in that room made me forget my discomfort. Every wall was carved into the most amazing panels. The panels appeared to depict progressing events, as if there was a story being told on the walls. I regret to say none of the images were familiar. As I inspected the squiggly lines and contorted limbs by torchlight, the Indians averted their eyes. Perhaps the images hold some mystical significance. I must remember to ask Azco.

Along the far wall, I found an opening about three feet high leading away into darkness. Secured above the opening was an exquisite statue of a young, fertile woman, naked from the waist up, wearing a long black skirt. Her features were blunted by age but she appeared to be decorated in gold inlay, with a third eye carved into her forehead. I imagine the piece will be considered a major discovery by the museum.

I relay this calmly, but Ysa, I can barely stay still. Recalling this experience restarts the pounding of my heart and excites the passion of my brain.

I dropped to my hands and knees and listened at the opening, wondering what other treasures awaited beyond, but only had the impression of vast, unfriendly space.

Then I had the idea to thrust my torch forward. It was still very dark, but I could clearly see the tunnel led into another cavernous room. I could just make out the carved toes of a large ivory-colored statue, proving incontrovertibly that humans once occupied this space, perhaps for ritual purposes. I decided not to advance until we gathered more torches and had obtained sufficient supplies, water being my chief concern due to the sweltering heat.

I noticed Azco's attention was locked onto something in the opposite corner and I approached him quietly. He was fondling several small skulls I had overlooked, skulls that appeared to belong to the mysterious creatures. All showed signs of violent death. Chunks of bone were missing along the back plate, as if a sharp and serrated tool had been used for the death blow. But most interesting were the foreheads. Where a skull typically bulges at the front, I discovered a strange object embedded firmly in the bone. The object glowed dully in the darkness under its own power. The object is the size of my palm, with the general appearance and hardness of a diamond.

I chose one of the better preserved skulls and wrapped it in a handkerchief to investigate in the sun. Azco asked to take one of his own for inspection. I did not see the harm.

Partially obscured by the skull pile I made the most fantastic discovery of our journey thus far: a nest containing four viable eggs, which I assume to be the creature's offspring. I have taken one of the grayish eggs and secured it in my breast pocket, nestling it to my bosom for warmth—warmth I had in spades. I feel the specter of that oppressive heat even now.

With luck I will soon observe the creature's hatching and add to my knowledge of the beast.

I was stopped short by a low keening wail that reverberated through the tunnels and through the low opening in the far wall. The hair on my arms stood on end as I wondered what manner of beast made that sound. To calm the men, Azco suggested it was the wind blowing through cracks in the rock. I have doubts.

Aware of the late hour and uneasy about remaining below ground after nightfall, I instructed the men to return to the surface.

Now I sit in the relative comfort and safety of the courtyard, beside a roaring fire, listening to my symphony of discord, recording my thoughts.

Tomorrow perhaps we will uncover more secrets about this lost civilization. In my wildest dreams, Ysa, these revelations are more than I ever could have hoped.

12 March

Ysa,

I sent two of the men back to the river for water since we have yet to discover a closer source. I learned that although we just came from the river, supplies are already dangerously low. I assumed Azco would oversee the water collection and apparently he thought I was responsible. Hence, we are down to our final drops.

While I await their return, I continue to explore this marvelous courtyard. Abundant evidence suggests this was an outpost for some advanced civilization now lost to the ages, which I am in a unique situation to reveal. Although the jungle has encroached and destroyed several dwellings around the outskirts, I imagine they were sturdy wooden structures in their prime, adept at providing shelter from the frequent jungle rains. In these spaces I have uncovered crudely wrought stone tools and shards of pottery, with faded designs barely visible on the rounded edges. Frequently I have seen similar symbols painted and carved into surfaces that may represent a form of written language. Thus far, my efforts to decipher the complex and interlocking figures have been unsuccessful, however I expect to solve the mystery any day now.

I continue to press the egg securely against my heart. I have not felt so much as a wiggle, but I will not lose hope.

13 March

I have examined the skull in detail. The whitish object embedded in the creature's skull is a new kind of crystal, harder than calcite, about the same toughness as quartz. When I scratched the surface with my fingernail it did not leave a mark.

The egg—

My egg has hatched! I have named the creature Gilberth. More to come.

The men returned with water a short time ago, so I must write quickly. Gilberth is the size of my palm. His skin is scaly, dry, and luminescent-green, with a hard, grey pebble embedded at the center of his forehead. The pebble is the diameter of a child's fingernail. I suspect the pebble transforms into white crystal as the creature ages, in much the same way sand is altered within an oyster to become pearl.

I notice that Azco is of a similar mind. He has pried the gem from his creature's skull and fashioned it into a garish pendant, reminiscent of the impressive Koh-i-Noor diamond we saw at the World's Fair two years ago. Indeed, the two are indistinguishable to the untrained eye.

Ysa, my darling, I have set one of these strange gems aside for you to fashion into something beautiful.

Gilberth's eyes are sealed shut with mucus and when he opens his mouth to mewl, no sound emerges. I do not know what my youngling eats. I will attempt a selection of figs and nuts.

Gilberth has not taken anything but water. Perhaps he relies upon mother's milk. He seems to be in some distress.

I have discovered what Gilberth eats.

I should have suspected, judging by the teeth embedded in the adult creature's skull, but sometimes we are blind to the obvious. As I was handling the skull earlier, I nicked my finger, spilling a few drops of blood in the dirt. The babe must have sensed this, for he jumped from my shoulder to the ground and hungrily lapped up the drops, eyes still sealed. I was able to squeeze a few more drops directly into his mouth, enough to satiate my tiny monster. Then I returned him to my pocket and he slept peacefully at last.

I think it best not to tell the men these creatures are sustained by blood or they may balk at further adventuring. However, I will recommend that every man bring a weapon on our next excursion below ground, and that our torches are dry and well fueled.

It is imperative we uncover the roots of this new civilization. I will not be hindered by superstitious nonsense.

14 March

Dearest Ysabel,

I fear my writing will be illegible. I cannot will my hands to quit trembling. But I owe you a full account.

Fully geared, I took the men into the tunnels at dawn. We quickly passed through the paneled room and entered that vast darkness occupied by the oversized statue. The statue was a larger version of the one I found above the tunnel opening—same full, bare chest, same long skirt with toes peeking under the hem, only this statue had been blinded. Her pupils were hollowed out and the third eye had been replaced with a lump of black coal. The effect was disquieting.

With the benefit of hindsight, I believe the statue was a warning.

The light from our torches soon attracted a flock of inconvenient moths. White wings marred with large black spots gave them the appearance of disembodied eyes. They plunged into our flames without pause, their bodies crackling like bits of burned paper.

But it was not the moths that left me in such an agitated state.

We covered our mouths and noses with cloth and moved farther into the tunnels, eventually leaving the moths behind. The path led down into another large cave, this one with evidence of human occupation. The remnants of abandoned hearths littered the space, the rock ceiling above stained with black smoke. Rotting timbers looked to form a basic bed or chair. All evidence continued to point to a once flourishing and secure settlement. The hearths also helped explain the lack of obvious living quarters above ground.

Those initial moments of discovery propelled me onward. I felt feverish with the promise of academic epiphany.

Wherever possible I kept us moving in a straight line. I regret I had no breadcrumbs; instead I opted to scratch a line of chalk on the walls, which I had brought for that purpose.

We entered a third massive chamber and my God, Ysabel, the colors. You are familiar with the calcium formations that build over time as dripping water dissipates? This room was a treasure trove of natural sculpture. Many looked to be the traditional forms of bare and stacked lumps of gray, but about fifteen had crystallized into blood-red columns hanging from the roof and emerging from the cave floor—I presume the red was due to high iron content in the soil. When our torches met the angular faces of the crystal, the flickering light scattered in an iridescent panoply, splashing squares of red across the rock walls, reminding me of how jeweled colors shine through stained glass windows at church in the afternoon sun. As I examined the walls, I noticed a series of black handprints, all about eye level and sideways, with the fingers directed toward the opposite end of the cave.

The Indians saw the handprints and were afraid. Through Azco, I attempted to boost the Indians' spirits with reminders of extra pay. They babbled a response at Azco, I imagine in an attempt to negotiate, but he stayed firm. When the men still refused to move, Azco removed the whip from his side and struck the closest Indian until the rest complied.

As we gathered to leave the crystal chamber, I caught a glint in the shadows and spotted one of the lizard creatures crouched in the dirt. I indicated the men should wait and I approached it cautiously, intending to capture the creature alive. It watched me all the way, its gem glittering dully in its green forehead, head lowered in challenge.

I patted my pocket gently to assure myself Gilberth was safe. He wiggled sweetly against my hand.

I called for a net and Azco threw me one from his pack. The men refused to come closer. I untangled the lines while the creature watched me warily, a low growl rumbling from his throat. Slowly, I readied the net to toss over the creature. I raised my hands, I held my breath—and the creature leapt at my knees, somehow launching itself off the ground with tremendous force. I stumbled and fell, landing hard on my tailbone.

The beast crouched in front of me, hissing, a red forked tongue flicking the air, and then he lunged. The damn thing must have weighed five stone, and every ounce of me struggled to pry his jaws from my boot. His jaws closed around my foot and his fangs scraped the skin, shredding the leather, tearing the thick sole away with an unsettling rip. When he snapped his powerful jaws around my toes, I felt excruciating pain, and barely saw Azco slip behind the creature. After a short struggle, he slit its throat and dragged the beast off of me. I escaped relatively unharmed all things considered, though Ysa brace yourself. The beast's aim was true.

The creature bit off the littlest toe on my left foot.

I gritted my teeth and checked on Gilberth, who was wiggling fiercely in my pocket but unharmed. Then remembering how he could sense blood, I quickly pulled out one of my two handkerchiefs, soaked it thoroughly in my blood, and shoved it in my pocket to keep the creature occupied. I wrapped the spare handkerchief tightly around my foot. The Indians were too busy watching Azco to notice my odd behavior.

Azco had gutted the beast and popped the gem out of the dying creature's skull to examine in the torchlight. This one was even larger than the stone he wore around his neck.

I was too shaken to go on, so I motioned to the natives to bundle the corpse thinking we could return after I cleaned the wound. But Azco, possessed by some demon, insisted we continue and gather more creatures. When I deferred he brandished his whip but I refused to move, telling him I would surely bleed to death.

He did not whip me then, though I expected it. Instead he ripped the kerchief from my wound, told the Indians to hold my foot steady and, with my blood still spilling on the rough dirt floor, Azco pressed his torch to the ragged flesh where my toe had been.

I screamed.

If there is one smell I had never hoped to know, it is the smell of my own flesh burning.

The pain cannot be described. But it did, in fact, stop the bleeding. I suppose Azco, with his aboriginal logic, considered it a kindness, but I admit to having had enough of jungle medicine.

There were no objections to this mutiny. To the Indians, one master must have been as good as another. Azco forced us on at a moderate pace, and I was barely able to chalk the walls we passed. As we walked I noticed something curious: the pain had lessened in my foot. I could hardly feel the burn any longer, let alone anything beneath my knee. I assumed Azco destroyed some vital nerve in his exuberance.

Azco was on a mission, waving his torch in the corners, checking animal leavings for freshness.

After countless rooms, I was deliriously thirsty and stopped. "Listen here, Azco," I said. "This can't continue."

The damn fool punched me in the nose!

There was nothing to be done. Azco was mad for gems. While I admit they were sufficiently diamond-like to arouse admiration, I failed to see how it excused him from driving us to exhaustion and leaving our corpses to rot in that vast honeycomb of darkness.

I resolved to take the whip from Azco.

No sooner had I made this decision, we entered a chamber twice the size of any other. A furnace-like heat blasted us in the face, drying the sweat from our pores. At the center of the chamber was an enormous boiling spring, milky white and softly glowing. Around the edges of the cave, human remains were piled several feet deep in places, bones on top of bones on top of bones.

We had found their primary nest.

Ysa, forgive me, I must catch my breath.

The charred walls glistened with hot wetness, and the air smelled of sweet decay. I looked down and saw young Gilberth slither from my pocket and climb my chest, his eyes opened at last, bloodshot and wary. He settled at the base of my neck to watch.

An adult creature emerged from the spring and crept toward us, white water trickling off its scaly back. The gem in its forehead burned brightly, illuminating the space around us. Polished river rocks shifted beneath its feet.

The youngling at my shoulder hissed.

A second creature emerged from the depths of the spring, hissing as well, its forked tongue vibrating and retracting smoothly.

I looked from beasts to Azco, who was grinning like a madman, and I backed against a wall, easing a femur from the nearest pile. Azco shouted for the men to ready their weapons.

Then we saw something strange—the memory still gives me chills. Some unknown signal passed over the sound of the bubbling spring and hundreds of creatures emerged from the milky depths at once, the clattering of many claws against the shifting rock bed embedded in my brain. I waved my torch before me thinking the fire would keep them away. Those strange lizard creatures of all sizes, their powerful bow legs gripping through the rock layer to ground below. Their veined bellies scraped the ground and their tails swished.

Azco froze, overwhelmed by the sight of so many gems. I took advantage of his distraction and broke the femur over his head. He stumbled and fell to his knees, dropping his whip and torch, which I retrieved and then backed away. The creatures grew ever closer, their gems glowing like floating orbs in the darkness. Two of the natives behind me ran from the room and I lost sight of them. I can hardly bear to think where they ended up.

The creatures paused to sniff Azco's fallen body and then began to nip experimentally at his trousers.

The remaining two natives and I walked backwards slowly, trying not to attract attention. And then the first creature tore off a chunk of Azco's thigh. Azco screamed and started floundering, which is when the other creatures swarmed his face and legs and hands, until all of his skin was covered by thrashing tails and the loud tearing of flesh. The blood . . . I ran. Dear Ysabel, I ran faster than I have ever run, may God forgive me. It must have been fear that made me forget my wounded foot. I followed the chalk marks out of that accursed place and I plan never to return, although that decision is of little consequence now.

My foot, where the creature bit me, has become dreadfully necrotic. I escaped the underground and, even with my infirmity, have managed to stoke the fire in the courtyard, waiting for the others to find their way out. I fear the wound is not healing. I applied the mud and oulou sap concoction Azco gave me for bites, and it has had no effect. My only hope is to wait for the men to carry me to the river and catch a boat to safety.

My only companion is the innocent youngling who has never left my side. Even in my mad dash from the caves, Gilberth has not abandoned me. I daresay he thinks I'm his mother. His mewling is adorable.

I don't know how long I slept. The moon is overhead and I can barely see to write.

I did not want to alarm you, my love, but the sickness has spread. At first only my toes were numb, but now the paralysis has spread to my waist. I can no longer move my legs.

I lied. I know the men aren't coming. For some time now, I have listened to their screams echo from the cave. Screams and wails and a clattering of many claws. The air is thick with madness and the stink of rotten flesh.

And mosquitoes.

Dearest one, I grow so weary. It is time to fortify my spirit against the dark. It is time to join the symphony of discord.

Gilberth has already eaten the rest of my toes and I fear he hungers still.

I regret nothing, except I am sorry to have ruined your beautiful handkerchiefs.

Your faithful conductor,
—R

=[]=

Folly Blaine lives in Seattle, Washington. Her work has appeared in Every Day Fiction, Flashes in the Dark, and 10Flash Quarterly. You can find her online at Maybe It Was the Moonshine (www.follyblaine.com).

THE NIGHTMARE ORCHESTRA

Chelsea Armstrong

=[]=

In this next tale, Canadian writer, Chelsea Armstrong, takes us to the domain of a unique people we have all visited before. Dark and strange and somewhat melancholy, The Nightmare Orchestra *explores a parent-child relationship where all is not what it seems. Upon acceptance into this anthology, Chelsea told me this was her first publication. My opinion is if she keeps putting out stories as captivating as this, we'll soon be seeing a lot more of her in print!*

=[]=

My friend Jamie is so smart and so nice. And he shares too. He took me to the playground near his house, and we built a sand castle using his shovel and red bucket. We even made a moat and a bridge. We dug windows into our castles, but no one peeked out of them. Tiny sand people were too hard to make. They kept crumbling. That's why our sand windows were empty.

We were turning the bucket upside down, finishing the watchtower, when we heard footsteps behind us, stomping through the grass. My back was to the sound, so, Jamie, he saw it first. His eyes went wide like pancakes, and his mouth dropped open. I could've fit the shovel handle in there.

Slowly, I turned around and saw where the sound was coming from. My dad. I should've known. He found us. He didn't look like his usual self. Not exactly. The skin on his face was missing, and one of his eyes was gone too. A wrinkly hole was where his eye should be. But his smile was the same as always with his top teeth a little bit crooked.

I raised my hand to wave and say, "Hi Dad," just as Jamie started to scream. I turned around and watched my friend run away from the playground. He left his shovel and bucket in the sand. Screaming and flailing his arms, Jamie's body shrank smaller and smaller until I couldn't see him waving anymore. He was gone.

My cheeks were hot. I turned to my dad. His eye and skin had grown back.

"You scared him away again!"

Shaking his head, my dad said, "He'll be fine."

"No, he was really, really scared!"

My dad reached out to touch my shoulder with a serious look on his face. "Skye, you don't need to worry about your friend. He'll be back. He's awake by now. Probably with his mom, Melinda, beside his bed, holding him close, whispering that it was all just a dream."

I pulled away from my dad's hand. "But he still might be screaming and scared. And now he probably hates me. He won't want to be my friend anymore. Maybe he thinks that this is all my fault, but it's not. It's yours. You're the bad guy."

"Skye you aren't supposed to play with the dreamers. I thought I could leave you alone this time."

"Don't touch me."

"I've explained this to you before . . . the way things work. I thought you understood."

"No, I . . . It doesn't make any sense."

"What part of it doesn't make sense?"

"The whole thing! Why do Jamie and all the others wake up when they're already awake? And if they are waking up, why don't we ever do the same? Why do we stay here while they run away, screaming, disappearing? It's just not fair. All my friends hate you, and I hate you too."

My dad sighed. Looking at the ground, he cleared his throat and said, "Skye, I'm sorry. Things weren't always like this. They were a little bit different before." When he raised his chin and looked at me, his eyes were wet. He gave me a small smile. "You probably would've liked our old home better than this one."

I didn't understand. This was the only home that I remembered. "What other home?" I asked.

Reaching down to rub his hand against my head, my dad said, "We used to live in the same place where Jamie lives. We used to wake up like he does every morning or in the middle of the night, but then we moved to this place where Jamie and all the others only visit when they fall asleep."

Dad hadn't told me this before, so I was surprised. I wondered what the other place was like, the place where Jamie runs away to. Just when I was about to ask this question, I felt it.

The call.

It was time to go scare another friend, another man, woman, or grandma. The sand rose from the playground as the wind blew very hard. Then the sand began to move in circles, swirling around us, the monkey bars, and the twirly slide. The wind howled, and I covered my ears to shut out the sound. Then the ground began to shake so hard that I fell to my knees. I felt my dad's hand on the back of my t-shirt, pulling me to my feet.

And he yelled something, but I couldn't hear the words because of the wind and because I was screaming too.

My knees bent, and I fell forward toward the sand again. Except my knees never hit this time. The shaking stopped.

=[]=

We were suddenly in a crawl space behind a set of stairs. Footsteps thudded along the ceiling above us as someone approached the basement door. The footsteps hesitated for a second then someone twisted the knob. As the door creaked open, a small slat of light poured down the stairs, only to be blocked by a shadow. Judging by the silhouette, a tall, thin, elderly woman with curlers piled atop her head would soon descend the stairs. Slowly, cautiously, she lowered one slippered foot onto the first step.

I reached beside me to place my palm on my son's shoulder. He was shaking. As soon as I made contact, Skye wrenched his body away from my hand. I had almost forgotten; I'm a monster, and at the moment he hates me. Leaning to him I whispered, "Skye, pull yourself together. Jamie is fine. The nightmare is over for him."

Skye responded with a sniffle and a whimper. The footsteps above us ceased their descent, and a thin voice called out, "Who's there? Walter, is that you?"

I turned to Skye, holding my finger to my lips. "It's your turn."

"Dad, I don't wanna."

"Dammit, Skye, just do it. This will all be over before you know it."

"But it's not nice."

"You need to scare her before she wakes up."

"But whyyyyyy?"

"Because that's what we're here for. We can't leave until she's had a fright. Now go on."

The woman commenced her walk down the stairs. Skye stayed seated with his head down. He wasn't budging, so I took matters into my own hands. Waiting until the woman's feet reached our eye level, I wrenched Skye's wrist from the side of his body and thrust his tiny hand through a space between the stairs. I then placed my fingertips on top of his own and grasped the woman's ankle with both of our hands.

Skye screamed, "Don't dad!" as she halted her descent. The woman looked down and yelped. As soon as her body lurched forward, her ankle disappeared from our grasp, and the ground began to shake. Wind blew the basement door wide open, smacking it against the wall. Skye began to cry with his head between his knees. Thankfully he didn't look up to see the staircase collapse above us.

=[]=

That poor old woman. I didn't want to grab her ankle. Dad made me, and I didn't like it. She almost fell down the stairs! No matter what Dad says, I can't get used to this stuff. He says I should like it, that it should make me happy, but it doesn't. It makes me sad and angry and confused. Sometimes I feel like throwing up. One time I did throw up when he started bringing me along on his nightmares. He was doing some really bad things this one night. He had an ax and was chasing a man while dragging me behind him through the woods. Eventually, he caught the guy who was screaming and crying. He tied the man to a tree while I sat in a pile of leaves and felt very cold. The guy's glasses were crooked because he had tripped and fallen over a tree root when my dad was chasing him. He was saying, "No, no! Please don't!" and my dad held the ax in front of his face.

My dad said, "Please don't what?"

Then the man said, "Please don't kill me."

My dad stepped closer to him, looked at him real close, and laughed. A mean laugh. Then he held the ax high above his head with both hands and said, "Don't worry about this, Skye. Everything will be okay." I watched him bring the ax down into his own leg, and once it hit, the man with the crooked glasses screamed. I screamed too. There was blood on my dad's pants.

I said, "Dad stop! You need a band-aid. You have an ow-ie!"

But he didn't care. He held the ax up high again and brought it back down into his leg. Onto the same patch of blood. I put my hand in front of my face, so I didn't have to see him hurting himself over and over again. But I knew what was happening anyway because I could hear the ax hitting my dad's bone, and I could hear the guy who was tied to the tree. He screamed louder every time the ax hit.

The screams did stop though. That's when I peeked through my fingers. I shouldn't have done that. I saw the ax, covered in blood, on the ground beside my dad. He was sitting and holding onto the bottom part of his leg that he had cut off. The guy on the tree looked very scared. He was breathing very fast and looking at my dad's leg then he was looking at my dad. Back and forth, back and forth. Then he started whimpering. My dad said, "Shut up," then he chucked his bloody leg at the man. It hit him in the chest and left some blood on his forest-green flannel nightshirt. That's when I threw up into my own lap and cried with my head hanging down.

I looked up when my dad started talking again. He laughed and said, "You should've gone before you went to sleep," pointing at the wet spot on the front of the man's pajama pants.

The man said, "Huh?" He looked down and looked very surprised. Then all of a sudden he wasn't there anymore. It was just me, my dad, the tree, the blood, the leaves and the throw up. My dad turned around to look at me. When he noticed the mess, he said, "Oh Skye," and his face turned from very happy to very sad. He tried to walk toward me, but a bunch of leaves blew up into his face, and the ground started to shake. I was glad for this because I didn't like what he had done in this place, and the shaky ground meant that we would get to leave soon.

=[]=

I'm glad we were able to attend the ball. It's nice to have all of us together in one nightmare once in awhile even if it's just once a week or once a month. Reminds me of old times. These days, everyone is just so busy orchestrating their own nightmares that it has become extremely rare for us to all occupy the same dream.

With Skye at my side, I circled the room with a half-empty champagne flute in hand. We stopped at quite a few tables and chatted with old friends. Mostly, we reminisced, recollecting funny and embarrassing moments of years gone by. Like the time in grade school when Bonnie Dunham brought her tapeworm to show-and-tell and the other classmates, the majorities, didn't cry. They didn't vomit or cringe. They weren't fazed in the slightest. Hell, one of our classmates, a majority named Nancy Corrigan, was downright amused. Our teacher even congratulated Bonnie for bringing the most interesting, educational item to show-and-tell. Poor Bonnie was hoping to gain herself some laughter from the majorities' discomfort. Needless to say, she was quite disappointed that day. Though she'll deny it forever, I remember Bonnie choking back tears when I walked her home from school. But at least now we can look back and find humor in it.

After visiting a few tables and sharing some laughs, it was time to get down to business. We had a job to do. I began to search for the dreamer. He wasn't hard to find. He was alone, a man in his early to mid-twenties, standing next to the band, holding a glass of scotch. Beads of perspiration dotted his smooth forehead. In between furtive glances around the room, he sipped from his glass, swallowed, then cringed. I caught his eye. For a moment he smiled then shifted his gaze elsewhere. Leaning toward the band, he whispered something to the lead singer who nodded his head in agreement then gave a quick cue and a wink to his musical accompaniment.

With a blast from the trumpet, we knew it was time to jive. The dreamer lit right up. He snapped his fingers and swung his shoulders to the beat. We all followed his lead, and his smile grew wider. Two hundred people littered the dance floor in pairs—swinging their arms, clapping their hands, kicking their feet. I held Skye by his hands and swung him from left to right. He squealed with enjoyment, and I laughed, delighted to make him happy for once.

Still bouncing to the band, the dreamer scanned the crowd. His gaze eventually landed on Miss Bonnie Dunham. She was dancing alone, baiting the dreamer. Swishing her skirt from side to side, she returned the dreamer's stare and curved her red-stained lips. It was her time to shine. She shimmied her bare shoulders, leaning in his direction, then beckoning him closer with a bend of her finger. His cheeks colored, and he smiled sheepishly as he made his way to the middle of the dance floor.

Bonnie reached out her arms and awaited his approach while shaking her hips and tapping her foot. Eventually they made contact. We all held our breath in anticipation while Bonnie kept her cool. He grasped her palms under his own, and they began to jive. They were an absolute delight to watch. Their jive was intricate, synchronized, quick paced, and flawless. We all jived around them, glancing from the corners of our eyes, waiting for Bonnie to make her move. She finally satisfied our hunger.

As the dreamer arched Bonnie into a backwards dip, we all heard it— the snap of her spine. Startled, the dreamer dropped her. She hit the crown of her head on the dance floor. The dreamer lurched forwards with his arms outstretched. His mouth was wide open as he yelled an apology to Bonnie who remained in a backwards arch with only her head and feet touching the ground. She smirked at him from upside-down. That's when he noticed the circle of blood pooling around her head.

Eyes wide, he covered his mouth with a trembling hand and yelled, "For Christ sake, she needs an ambulance! Somebody call an ambulance!"

We continued to jive, more feverishly than ever as he stumbled around the dance floor yelling for help. Eventually he got physical. He made contact with a dancing couple. As soon as he touched the sleeve of the jiving man's jacket, the man flung his arms away from his body—still moving to the beat of the music—and dislocated his elbow in the process.

The dreamer screamed.

"I'm sorry . . . I—I I didn't mean—"

The dreamer backed away from the man who was smirking and waving goodbye with his forearm hanging loosely from his elbow joint.

"Oh man," the dreamer muttered as he ran his fingers across his forehead. He turned around and came face to face with another dancing couple. Placing his shaking hands on their shoulders, he leaned toward them with his eyes darting back and forth from one person to the other. With his voice breaking, he managed to say, "You guys gotta help me. There's some people at this ball, they need help. They need a doctor."

The couple just smiled at him. In unison, they tilted their chins upward and craned their necks toward the dreamer. Then they twisted their necks until a sharp crack could be heard echoing from the top of both of their spines. Simultaneously, their chins dropped to their chests, and they continued to jive—smiling, with both of their heads hanging down.

The dreamer ran across the dance floor. Frantic, confused, delirious. He began to babble incoherently and gestured toward the injured dancers. Up until this point, I was able to keep Skye distracted from the events occurring around us. I swung him upside-down and sideways and spun him in a circle until we were both too dizzy to stand. We eventually lost our footing and collapsed to the ground. Our stomachs ached from laughter. Leaning back to lie on the floor, we held our bellies as tears rolled down our faces.

But soon Skye realized that we weren't the only ones laughing. He pushed himself up to a seated position and took a look around. That smile that I had fought so hard to keep stained on his face was washed away in an instant when he saw what was going on. His face twisted into a mask of utter disgust. Tears filled his eyes as he shook his head. My chest grew tight. This was it. He needed to know why he's different.

Moving to him, I slipped my hands around his wrist and gently pulled him to his feet. Defeated, his head hung with his chin tucked into his chest. I guided him toward the nearest dinner table and motioned for him to follow my lead and lower to his knees. Once we were on the ground, I lifted the tablecloth and crawled under the table. Reluctantly, Skye followed.

For a few moments, I held him in my arms and ran my fingers through his hair. He was seven years old but still small enough to embrace in my lap. We rocked back and forth to a symphony of laughter echoing throughout the ballroom.

"Alright Skye. We don't have much time. Ask me anything you'd like. I'll try to tell you everything."

Taking a moment to catch his breath, he eventually whispered, "What was our old home like?"

"Well, it looked a lot like this home, except we could go wherever we wanted—whenever we pleased. We weren't called to different parts of the world every few minutes. We could orchestrate our nightmares for however long or short we wanted."

"So you still made the nightmares in our old home?"

"Yes."

Disappointed, Skye shook his head at me.

"It's what we do, our people. It's what we've always enjoyed doing, scaring others," I continued.

"Not me. I don't like doing that."

I smiled and held his hand. "No Skye, not you. You're different. You're like the majorities. When you see people getting scared or nervous or disgusted, you don't find humor in that."

"Humor?"

"You don't think it's funny."

"No. It makes me sad."

"And that's why you're different."

"Then why am I here? Why aren't I with the other dreamers?"

"Because I didn't want to leave you when I moved."

He thought about that for a second. As soon as our conversation halted, the laughter seemed to echo louder, only occasionally broken by sounds of the dreamer screaming—high pitched shrieks of terror. Skye closed his eyes.

"Why did we move?"

"We agreed to move, all of the adults in this ballroom, because we thought it would be better for the majorities that way. When we all lived together, the majorities eventually became very scared of us. We were hurting them, they said. Mentally, not physically. They didn't like to be scared. They didn't like to watch us torture ourselves. But we liked to see them scared and nervous. That's what made us happy. Do you see? We're opposites, our people and the majorities."

"But I'm like them. Like the majorities. I'm not like you."

"Come on, Skye. We have fun together, don't we?"

"I don't like it here. I want to live with Jamie. I want to wake up."

"I'm sorry, but you can't. We can never leave these nightmares. That's why I wanted to tell you all this, so you'd understand why things are the way they are, and hopefully someday you'll come to accept it."

"I won't. I want out."

"You can't get out. You'll be here forever with me, with us."

Skye's face fell. He quietly asked, "But why?"

"There once was a man, a very smart man, a scientist, who found a way to move us here. He thought it would help society, the majorities, if we only lived in their nightmares. You have to understand; he was only trying to help. He developed a way for us to enter the nightmares, but he . . . ummm, he died before he found a way to bring us back. He never intended to keep us here forever. He just hoped to make things better for the majorities for the time being."

Skye's eyes brightened.

"But what if, what if someone else, another scientist, found a way to bring me back?"

"I'm sorry, but that's not going to happen. At least not any time soon. You see, Skye, I don't think the majorities want us to come back. They don't see a reason to release us from here because they think it's safer for themselves to keep us in their nightmares."

"But I'm different. I'm a majority. I'm not like you."

"They don't know that. They know what I am, and they know that you're my son. So they think that you're just like me, a piece of the nightmare orchestra. Your mom thought the same thing. That's why she let me take you."

As tears trickled down Skye's cheeks, the ballroom began to tremble. Ripples formed in the tablecloth hanging around us. Laughter, shrieks from the dreamer, and the howling wind melded into one deafening roar of sound. The tablecloth swirled outwards, exposing our hiding place. Skye clamped his palms onto his ears and gritted his teeth. Above us, plates clinked against knives and forks. As a champagne flute tumbled to the ground and smashed beside Skye, I yelled, "The dreamer is waking up! Don't worry, everything is going to be okay!" but I'm not sure if he heard me or not.

=[]=

Chelsea Armstrong received her BA in English from the University of Alberta. She currently resides in Edmonton, Alberta in an old house which sits atop of a collapsing foundation. When she's not slowly sinking into the earth, Chelsea works full time, reads any novel she can get her hands on, writes short, twisted stories, and plays Scrabble. She is a large fan of words.

The Funeral Procession

Jay R. Thurston

=[]=

One of the rewards for editing this book is that I was able to read so many brilliant stories that offered explanations and discovery for a multitude of lost lands and peoples. There is no end to ideas of what "could have been" or "may have actually happened." Some stories are entirely imagined in the civilizations that are discussed, while others are mired in historic fact. These latter tend to be the most intriguing to me. You read them and think, "yeah, I know what this legend is all about," only to be thrown for a loop, as the author takes you down a path you did not expect, but realize you were heading toward the entire time. Such is the case with The Funeral Procession, *in which an archaeology team uncovers more than they expected while excavating for the burial ground of the last of a feared tribe.*

=[]=

Along the fringe of the northern Gobi Desert, a lone jeep's dust cloud rose over the rural expanse. Ahead, a single stream of smoke could be seen climbing from a cluster of tents. Rises of excavated earth contrasted against the desert's edge and beyond that, a crescent-shaped lake separated the settlement from distant mountains. The jeep's driver checked the clock on his cell phone; over an hour had passed since he had last seen any other trace of civilization.

The jeep halted beside the only other vehicle at the tents, a pick-up-truck turned makeshift-bus. Around him, faces poked out from freshly dug holes in the earth, no discretion made in trying to catch a glimpse of the light-skinned newcomer.

"Oy, mate," Standing by the truck, a sharp-featured man in safari-styled attire offered a bombastic greeting. "Pleasure to have you on board. Name's Duncan. You're American, I see."

"Yes, how'd you know? I'm Aaron," said the younger man as he got out of the jeep. Duncan met his welcome with a firm grasp and sustained the handshake several seconds after Aaron felt comfortable.

"I don't know of any other Kansas City." Duncan examined the small print of Aaron's cap, above the much larger *Royals* in handwritten embroidery. He smiled, accentuating sun-dried cheeks. "What brings you out this way?"

"I'm doing a thesis on the whereabouts of Genghis Khan. I thought some first-hand time with a research team would help me get started on the project."

"Ah, you go to university. Well you came to the right place then, mate. Spending holiday out here? Or you chucking a sickie?"

Huh? Chucking a what? "Summer break just began, so I'll be able to spend some time before next semester," Aaron explained.

"Good-on-yer-mate."

"Cool accent. You British?"

"Nah, Aussie." He gestured for Aaron to follow. "I'll introduce you around."

"What brings an Aussie to Mongolia, Duncan?"

"Same as you. Intrigue."

Mongolian laborers in the low ground sprung into startled motion with the command from a gaunt man with a goatee. Aaron and Duncan were the only foreigners in sight. Duncan pointed to the leader, scolding a pudgy worker for discarding soil in another's dig space. "See that bloke? He's Qachi, the son of the chief researcher. He's in charge of the labor force."

"Seems a bit strict."

"Bit of an ocker, that one. Got all wobbly on me when I first got here. Racked off after I knocked him one."

Aaron nodded with a blank expression.

Duncan's gesture encompassed the settlement. "There's a lot of expeditions just like this all around Mongolia. Seems everyone's got a different theory about the Khan's hidden tomb. Course, most of it is raw prawn."

"Raw prawn? I'm not following."

"Most of their theories are bullshit. This is the only expedition open to foreign assistance. And the chief researcher allows it because he's closer than any of them other blokes."

"So he wants all the help he can get. But is he really closer to finding the grave of Genghis than the next guy?"

Duncan rolled back the entry to the largest tent. A wrinkled native man hunched over books in Mongol script, grey strands of a long Fu Manchu mustache grazing the pages. To the right, a Caucasian woman with an auburn bun clicked away on a laptop, surrounded by spotlights, cameras, tripods, generators, portable batteries, satellite dish, and other electrical equipment. Neither looked up from their toil.

"You must have found us by our website," Duncan said.

"I did."

"She's our web designer and photographer, Stefania Milanowski. Stef also handles much of the translating."

Aaron asked, "Aussie too?"

Stef's soft lips curled to a halfhearted smirk, but her eyes did not break from the glow of the laptop. "I am Polish."

"You're a photographer?"

"Yes."

Aaron found her accent as attractive as the face speaking it. "I think you're on the wrong side of the camera."

"Easy, mate," Duncan said between laughs. "There's a waiting list for that sheila."

She shot Duncan a cold scowl before returning to work. Duncan rolled his arm toward the elder gentleman shaking his head.

"This is our leader of the operation, chief archaeologist Haguyu. He's dedicated his life to the search for the great Genghis Khan."

"Does he understand English?" Aaron asked in a low tone.

"He understands enough."

Aaron stepped up and offered a handshake. The elder bowed his head and returned to the book.

"Come on, mate, let him be. He's brainstorming, does a lot of brainstorming."

Aaron left the tent on Duncan's queue. At a safe distance, Aaron asked, "So what makes Haguyu think he's closer than anyone else?"

"Fair question. Are you familiar with the tales of Genghis Khan's death?"

"Of course. He got as far as Poland before he was stopped."

Duncan nodded.

"Isn't it a bit ironic that Stef's working here?"

"It was almost eight hundred years ago, mate. The Mongols are over it. Plus she's quite valuable to the group."

"She seems nice."

"Nice to look at is about all." Duncan steered the conversation back on track. "What about *after* Genghis died?"

"His body was returned to Mongolia and placed in an unmarked grave near his place of birth."

"Right, another theory," Duncan said. "Search parties have torn apart the Khentii Mountains based on that rumor. Others say he was taken hundreds of miles away, or that he's under a river bed, or he's covered in permafrost. Raw prawn. What all these stories have in common is what Haguyu stakes his research upon."

"There's a commonality?"

"A handful of slaves and soldiers carried out the transport of the Khan's corpse. Any human or animal that crossed their path was slaughtered. After the slaves dug the grave, they too were slaughtered. The soldiers then killed off one another. The final resting place had to remain a secret at all costs."

"Wow, but, if they all died..."

"The final soldier standing was one of the Khan's most loyal lieutenants, a man named Chagatai. He arrived in Mongolia at a young age from an unknown clan to the west, and earned loyalty from Genghis when he carried out the order to decimate the village he came from. Chagatai massacred his mentors, friends, and even family."

"Wow, brutal."

"He buried the soldiers and slaves of the funeral procession himself. After the burial, rumor was he returned to the nearest settlement and never spoke again for the rest of his days. Others say he wandered hopelessly without guidance from Genghis or presence of his fellow soldiers. Haguyu believes he released his horse to the wild, possibly the Khan's personal horse as well, and sacrificed himself shortly after the burial."

"Why does he think that?"

"Warrior code, mate. Haguyu has researched warrior code for years. It would not be uncommon, almost expected, for Lieutenant Chagatai to have sacrificed himself near the resting place of Genghis, to serve and protect him in the afterlife."

"I see," Aaron frowned. "Imagine the stories Chagatai could have told, serving so close to the villain Genghis."

"Shh. You want to be lynched? Genghis is a war hero to the Mongols."

"He pillaged and murdered most of Asia."

"Genghis was a symbol of power and the potential of the northern barbarians to mobilize and conquer. He brought Mongolia together. Vile as the bloke might have been, these folks revere him. Watch your tongue around here, mate."

"Sorry."

"The Golden Horde always let one live to witness and spread the news they were to be feared."

"Effective advertising," Aaron quivered.

Duncan drew the tour to a halt in front of a smaller tent at the end of the row. "For decades, Haguyu has followed a trail of corpses south by southwest from Karakorum. His examinations have dated each of the findings back to the early thirteenth century."

"Genghis's funeral procession..."

"Exactly right, mate. He's mapped out the pattern and followed the trail for hundreds of kilometers. His mantra has been that if he could find Chagatai, he could find the Khan himself."

"So if he keeps following the trail of bodies, eventually he will find the Lieutenant."

"Look around you, mate." Duncan motioned to the mountains and desert. "If you're travelling southwest, does this not look like a dead end?"

"I suppose."

Duncan disappeared through the nearest tent door. Aaron followed. Inside, a blanket draped over an uneven object in the 'room' center. Duncan tugged at the far side of the sheath, revealing a decayed skull.

Browned patches of flesh and tissue covered the cheeks, chin and ears. The jawbone remained intact.

"Aaron, I'd like you to meet Lieutenant Chagatai."

Aaron's mouth fell to a gape. He removed his baseball cap, wiped sweat from his forehead, and repositioned the cap off center. "What? Where was he? How do we know this is him? Why isn't he in a museum somewhere?"

Duncan returned the blanket gently over the corpse. "Easy, mate. If we get him to a museum, then every pig's arse search team will flock to our side."

"I thought Haguyu wanted all the help he could?"

"Oh he does. But he also wants credit for the find. And the bloke deserves it really. Stef has already sent off a sample and his DNA matches a collection of corpses found near the remains of a village in northeast Kazakhstan."

Aaron looked from the covered body to the Australian, "His family."

"Spot on, mate. Slaughtered by his own blade at the command of the Khan. This body was found at the bottom of the nearby lake."

"In the lake? Why?"

"If Chagatai was the last soldier standing, and had intentions of offing himself, he likely could not have buried himself, now could he?" Duncan flipped back the opposite end of the blanket. The sight of decayed foot bones churned Aaron's stomach. Through the center of the right foot, a clean but narrow penetration resembled the size of a coin slot to a vending machine. Duncan directed his attention to the fracture. "See there? Chagatai did not want his body found, so he swam to the bottom of the lake, drew his sword, and drove it through his foot into the rocks and deadwood."

"His body would not be able to float. A brilliant suicide," Aaron marveled.

"Riding with the Golden Horde for most of his life, Chagatai knew a thing or two about dead bodies. Over time the sword rusted and broke. His buoyancy had been long gone by that time of course. But the corpse remained in good condition for being down there so long."

Aaron scratched his nape, speechless.

"I know it's a lot to take in."

"It's unbelievable."

"Very believable, mate. And quite incredible I'd say." Duncan escorted Aaron from the tent to the edge of the dig site. Laborers worked to the rhythm of a half-dozen spades. Qachi supervised, barking commands more than making use of his own shovel. Duncan continued, "Since Chagatai was discovered, there's been revitalized energy. These men are native volunteers, not slaves as you might think with Qachi over there spittin' the dummy."

Aaron did not anticipate a language barrier from the only other person at camp that spoke English as a first language. "Duncan, what's your role around here?"

"The Archaeological Foundation of Australia offered me a grant to come and assist in the research. To the group, I'm the cook."

Aaron chuckled, "That's assisting research?"

"The team works hard. They got to eat. I was told when I got here to help out as I could. They think Aussie cuisine is exotic."

"Is it?"

"Next to Mongolian cuisine?"

They exchanged a smirk.

Aaron scanned the scene. "There's only manual digging here? Where's the bulldozers?"

"Kidding right? We're hours from what even the *locals* consider civilization."

Aaron reached for his cell phone, tapping and sliding his finger across the screen. *Still works out here. Stef must have some high powered satellite equipment.* Digital blips were drowned out by Qachi, pointing and shouting amongst the laborers.

"Why do the volunteers put up with Qachi?" Aaron asked.

"Haguyu funds the operation, which means free meals for the work staff. Qachi throws his weight around because he's the son of the boss. He hasn't been here long... Haguyu dragged him here for an extra set of hands, because he's close."

"Dragged him here?"

"He's more of a thug than an archaeologist. Doesn't quite have the passion, knowledge, or the delicate hand for this sort of thing. He only works hard so his work can be completed sooner and he can go home."

Aaron switched his attention from Duncan to the smart phone.

"What're you doin', mate?"

"I found a cell phone application on the flight. It records speech from different languages and translates it to English on the screen."

"Pig's arse, that's something."

The pudgiest of the diggers yelled excitedly in Mongolian dialect. Laborers congregated around him.

Duncan observed over Aaron's shoulder. Black text on white backdrop replaced the hourglass cursor, translating the laborer's words. *'Look. Something here.'*

Duncan patted Aaron's shoulder. "Let's go."

Haguyu rushed from the large tent at an impressive speed for someone of his years. Stef accompanied, toting a large camera. Duncan and Aaron joined them on the high ground. Qachi wrestled his way to the front of the laborers, clawing at dirt like a dog intent on burying a bone. An off-white bulb made way to a pair of long, narrow adjoining bones.

Stef spoke in Mongolian, directed at Qachi. She mimed a motion of sliding something onto her hand.

Qachi paid no heed and dug bare-handed, until attaining a two-handed grasp on the long bone.

"It looks like a knee," Aaron said.

Stef repeated the instruction to Qachi. Aaron's phone displayed '*gloves.*'

Qachi secured his footing and pulled back with harsh force.

The foursome observing from the high ground protested in unison. "Qachi!"

A single cracking sound freed Qachi's prize. He fell into the workers, a dislodged upper leg in his hands.

Stef held a hand over her eyes. Haguyu shook his head. Duncan turned to Aaron, "After nearly eight hundred years, the Mongol people still aren't known for gentle demeanors."

Qachi presented the leg bone to his father. No one spoke. All eyes watched as Haguyu stroked his Fu Manchu, perusing the size and condition of the leg. He turned to Stef, spoke in his native tongue, and Stef followed Qachi into the large tent with the disembodied leg. The leader instructed the laborers to orchestrate efforts around the newest discovery. Duncan made for the pit. Haguyu held an arm to halt him.

"Not you. Food."

Duncan bowed and dismissed himself. Haguyu lifted the rim of Aaron's Royals cap with his index finger. "You dig," the elder instructed.

Qachi joined Aaron in the pit. Aaron felt alone amidst the chatter of the Mongol natives. He thought to check his cell phone translator program, but did not want to spark Qachi's curiosity.

First were the hips and other leg, then the upper body of the specimen was exhumed. Stef came and went, snapping photographs with every pass through. Qachi turned sickeningly pleasant in Stef's presence, only to resume sternness with her departure. Aaron expected a recess after the corpse had been unearthed, but Qachi demanded the diggers continue and glared every time Aaron paused to stretch or wipe his forehead. The smell of cooked meat taunted him for what seemed like hours, and he breathed relief when Duncan finally made the announcement to eat.

Dinner consisted of boiled potatoes and an unidentified spiced meat, grilled "on the barbie." *Duncan's culinary skills weren't half bad.* He hoped meal time would provide opportunity to mingle with Stef, but she attained a minimal serving, flashed an uncomfortable smile at Aaron *(Was I staring?)* and returned to her examinations in the large tent. Haguyu indicated the radius he wanted excavated. Duncan stopped to eat only after all had been served. Aaron ate quickly and thought he'd occupy the last of his meal break small talking with Stef. A hand caught his shoulder near the entrance to the large tent, and Qachi guided Aaron back to his shovel.

Aaron dug, slowed by a full stomach. Marinade across Qachi's goatee became a source of amusement for Aaron and the other volunteers. In a matter of minutes, Qachi's spade stopped inches deep with a *clunk*. His brown eyes grew wide and he waved Aaron over.

A second corpse so close by, exactly what everyone had hoped. The mass grave of the funeral procession!

"Think it's the slaves?" Aaron asked as Duncan offered a hand.

"Could be the soldiers too, mate."

"Or both." Stef appeared, speaking from behind a camera.

"The soldiers would not have been buried with the slaves," Aaron protested. "They were a prestigious class."

"Chagatai alone buried them," Duncan said. "He could have put them all together out of convenience."

"An elite soldier would not have been that disrespectful."

"He killed his own family. Don't think the bloke cared much for respect."

Within an hour, the team revealed the top half of another skeleton. A larger bone already identifiable as a horse skull lay even deeper. Haguyu pushed the team onward into dusk, instructed Stef to prop spotlights for as long as the generator would allow, and all hands worked into the night hours.

By eleven, Aaron was ready to collapse. Duncan agreed to share his tent, but when he admitted to sleeping 'in the nick,' Aaron decided to go for a walk. He wandered the handful of dormitory tents until spotting Stef's silhouette across the slant of cloth. *She's still up.*

Aaron adjusted his cell phone before poking his head through the draping entry. "Hello."

"No sleep for you?" Stef kneeled by a battery operated lantern-shaped flashlight. She lowered an old book, unimpressed with the interruption.

"No one warned me Duncan sleeps 'in the nick'."

Stef tilted her head.

"He's naked. It's a bit awkward."

She returned to the book.

"What are you reading?"

"I study about Sword of Khan. Are you excited for discovery today? You come at good time."

Her thick accent and broken sentences were adorable. He had never met anyone from Poland. Stef's smooth, porcelain skin contrasted her dark lashes. *If they're all this beautiful in Poland, I know where my next vacation will be,* he thought.

"Why you stare?" Stef blushed.

Dammit. Again. "Sorry, yes I am very excited. What does your book say about the Sword?"

"Book do not say. Book do not talk."

Aaron felt like Duncan, with nuances of his language missing his target. "Sorry, what does the book read?"

Stef giggled. "I made a joke, silly."

"Oh." He smiled. She returned one.

"People believe Sword have great powers. It can hold a soul. Made from metal of a meteor."

"Do you believe the Sword has special powers?"

"No," she giggled, "It is legend. Only rumor. But Sword could be useful for study. Blood on Sword could tell a lot."

"Good point," Aaron said, "It could potentially have DNA traces of people all across Asia."

"Yes." Stef beamed. *My God, even her teeth are flawless.*

"Do you believe it was made from a meteor?"

"Maybe yes. Maybe no. If yes, could be valuable to chemistry."

"New elements for the periodic chart, I hadn't thought of that." *Maybe the Sword was radioactive. Maybe it strengthened Genghis or poisoned its victims. Maybe it glowed in the dark or shot fireballs...* Aaron's imagination answered far-fetched possibilities, *why not?*

"It would be honor to take first photos of Sword to share with world. A dream for me," she added.

Aaron shook his head in agreement. "Oh definitely. You'd be famous."

She again showed Aaron her teeth. *Perfect teeth.*

"You speak English good."

She rolled her eyes, "Well. I speak well. Not good."

"See what I mean? You speak better than I do, and it's my only language! And you speak Mongolian too!" He retrieved his cell phone and held it at arm's length. "May I?"

"May what?"

A flash of light illuminated Stef. The cell phone mimicked a sound of an instant camera.

A crease formed between her eyes, "Why?"

"Look," Aaron spun the screen to face her. "When I said you should be on the other side of the camera, I meant it."

"Flirt." She reddened with embarrassment.

"Did Duncan teach you that word?"

She burst with a loud chuckle and covered her mouth. "Oops. People sleeping." She examined the photo on his cell phone. "Is good photo."

"Great photo."

She rolled her lower lip inward, "Sorry but I must sleep now. Thank you for talk, Aaron. Masz ładny uśmiech. Good night."

"My pleasure, Stefania. Have a good night." Aaron backed out of the tent to the open night. He admired his latest digital photo for several seconds before changing the screen. The Polish translation read, '*You have a nice smile.*'

=[]=

The unobstructed sunrise from the eastern flats cast an orange light through Aaron's eyelids. He could not bring himself to rest aside a naked man he hardly knew, and chose to sleep on the ground outside of Duncan's tent. *How did Duncan rest so sound with a deceased Mongol warlord in the next tent?* He could not decide if it were discomfort of the bumpy earth, the progress of the excavation, or revelling in the encounter with Stef that had hindered his rest. The Sword of Khan was just as much of a mystery as its bearer. *Could it really have unearthly powers? Was it the Khan that brought about the legend of the Sword, or vice versa?* Duncan released an unconscious groan behind him. *If the Khan and his Sword were found, had Haguyu worked out the details? Stef would want to analyze the Sword. If it really granted power, Qashi would be interested. Who knows how many volunteers had their eyes on it . . . and then there's Duncan.* As straightforward as the Australian seemed, his motives weren't clear.

The soft thump of a sandaled foot startled Aaron. He met the wizened eyes of Haguyu. Empty wooden buckets in each hand, he offered one to Aaron and made for the lake.

Aaron rushed to Haguyu's side. "Good morning."

"Same. I give you my thanks for coming and helping."

"I am honored to be here, Haguyu."

The elder looked Aaron up and down. "Why have you travelled all this way? Why are you interested?"

"Discovering Genghis Khan would earn the attention of the world."

The elder's long silence made him nervous.

"Haguyu, what do you plan to do with the Sword of Khan?"

The old man glanced over his shoulder and sighed, impatience in his expression. "Tourism."

"Tourism?"

"Build a museum. People visit Mongolia from everywhere to see the Sword."

"What about his body? And Chagatai? And the rest of the funeral procession?"

"More displays for museum." He smirked, more patronizing than innocent.

Aaron wanted to ask him if he believed all his help were on board with his vision, to inquire if he was concerned a nearly eight hundred-year-old corpse had only a tent and blanket protecting it from the elements, to ask why his brute of a son ran the volunteers like a tyrant. He knew Haguyu's guard was up; his answers came across as rehearsed default. Aaron doubted his inquiry about the Sword first, and the Khan second, left a good impression with the elder archaeologist.

Haguyu spoke as if delivering lecture. "The soldiers pledged loyalty to the Khan and his Sword in life and beyond. There is an old saying, 'As Sword commands, Golden Horde shall follow'. Both Khan and Sword belong in security of Mongol people."

By the time they returned with full buckets, Qachi had roused the camp into action; his boisterous volume muted only when in close vicinity to Stef's tent.

"I think your son is fond of Stef," Aaron said.

"You are a keen observer. It is best you stay away from Stef, or Qachi may show his unfriendly side."

You call his current personality 'friendly'? Aaron wondered if the old man had translated his words correctly. He set down the bucket and queried Duncan from outside his tent if he could use assistance in the meal preparations *("no slushy today," whatever that means)*, before acquiring a spade and getting to work.

The intact skeleton of a horse had been freed from its grave *(Qachi must not have had a chance to pull it apart)*. Stef undusted the bones with delicate strokes of a painter's brush. She smiled warmly at Aaron. He waved in a subtle motion, to avoid the jealous wrath of Qachi.

Within the hour, the diggers discovered hints of two additional corpses. The pace of the spades livened with excitement. Haguyu issued a work stop, spread the team in a circle around the remains of the funeral procession, and stressed that their focus was the discovery of the Mongol leader rather than his subjects. The elder examined each laborer's progress with a sharp eye. Aaron preferred the concentrated effort over responsibility for his own hole. On either side, Qachi and the pudgiest of the volunteers plowed earth twice as fast.

Aaron's patience thinned as the morning advanced. Not only were the other workers making him look bad, but a groaning stomach nagged him for nourishment. *Will Duncan call meal time already?* Duncan fidgeted, periodically checking a pot on the grill for boiling water. The sun intensified over the fringe of the Gobi. Aaron hurled an excavated baseball-sized rock toward the lake in his best Bret Saberhagen imitation, his favorite all-time Royals pitcher. The pudgy laborer applauded Aaron's form. Qachi glared until labor continued.

Shovels came to a synchronized halt with a clunk of iron meeting buried wood.

All but Duncan clamored to the pudgy worker's hole. Qashi dove to his knees and displaced dirt by the handful in every direction. The corner of a box met sunshine and open air for the first time in ages. Stef disappeared to get a camera. Volunteers squeezed in on either side to dig the rectangular box to freedom. Aaron in the rear struggled to be helpful. Haguyu spoke Mongolian commands to the group.

Aaron's cell phone translator, set back to Mongolian, displayed *'Take caution. Do not break it'.*

The coffin was sturdy, with a featureless exterior. *Could this really be Genghis Khan?* Aaron expected a temple or lavish resting place laden with gold. Then again, his followers went to great lengths to keep the grave a secret. *Much of the known world deemed him a villian. A shrine would have been a target of spite for years after his death.* Lieutenant Chagatai and the funeral procession did their parts in assuring the resting spot was, unlike the Khan, unassuming and peaceful.

Qachi forced grubby fingers around the base. Volunteers shimmied the coffin while he pulled with extreme force. The box jilted. Haguyu echoed his words of caution. Aaron stepped alongside Qachi; each grasped one corner. Shovels wedged into surrounding dirt, used as jacks. A clunk from within came as the team angled the coffin.

Could that have been the Sword?

They slid the coffin to level ground. *It looked more like a produce crate than a leader's tomb,* Aaron thought.

Qachi motioned the volunteers away.

Haguyu watched over Qachi's shoulder.

Aaron gazed in awe over the other shoulder.

Volunteers exchanged incredulous expressions.

Qachi pried the studs along the top of the coffin with his shovel.

"Shouldn't we wait for Stef to take pictures or film this?" Aaron asked no one. No one replied.

With the creak of a stubborn plank, the lid freed. Decay rose with dust. Patches of aged silk and chain mail fell between a rib cage. The backbone was hardly more than powder. The tibia of the right leg displayed a clean break. The legend of Genghis's taking an arrow to the leg was confirmed. The skull rested within a decayed helm, cheekbones stripped of tissue. The arms shifted under the ribcage with the motion of the coffin, releasing what was once held within them. All eyes roamed to the right of the skeleton. The pommel of gold fashioned as a dragon head; atop it, a blade of deep blue not akin to metal worked on earth. The tip of the scimitar arced toward the Khan's cheekbone.

The laborers roared with applause. Haguyu glanced from Aaron's cap to the Sword of Khan. Aaron muttered, "Royal blue."

Qachi reached into the coffin, a threshold unsurpassed for centuries. He ran a finger along the pommel, staring into the empty eye sockets of the Mongol war hero.

"Qachi," his father spoke.

"Don't," Aaron added.

The skull shifted to face Qachi. Aaron and the volunteers leapt back. Qachi stood motionless. He watched for several seconds before releasing an exhale, concluding the skull had detached from the movement. He pointed and cackled; others joined, laughing off their nerves.

Come on, Stef, where are you.

Enjoying the attention, Qachi stood over the skull and mocked a hollow stare. Laughter resurged through the volunteer onlookers. In close proximity to steadfast Haguyu, Aaron remained respectfully humble.

The jawbone moved. An air of sulfurous steam rose from the orifices of the Khan, streaming into the nostrils and mouth of Qachi. He bent forward; his cackling turned to a hacking weeze.

Haguyu approached his choking son. "Qachi—"

Fingers wrapped around the dragonhead pommel.

Haguyu clapped his palm on Qachi's back in steady repitition. The gasping and coughing ceased. The elder aided his son upright and presented a hand for the Sword, a rewarding smirk of fruition across his wrinkled face.

With a vile glare, Qachi spun.

The blade soared without resistance. Greyed lengths of Fu Manchu floated softly downward, before settling on Haguyu's decapitated body. The gushing head rolled into a ditch.

Aaron froze in terror. Two volunteers charged Qachi. The blade struck with murderous grace, as if in the possession of a master swordsman. One laborer fell, a diagonal slash across his torso, the second gushed from a stomach penetration . . .

Aaron shouted toward the camp, "*Stef! Duncan!*"

A piercing pain surged through Aaron's right shoulder. In slow motion, cold, foreign friction slipped along his collarbone as Qachi pulled back the blade. Aaron's fresh blood stained the blue point. He dropped to his knees, then fell face-first to the arid ground, which absorbed the red flow from his body. His cell phone tumbled beside his face.

Qachi leapt at the retreating volunteers, slicing them down one by one.

"Unngh." Agony spiked throughout his neck. The corpse of the pudgy worker toppled onto Aaron's back, pinning him down. The struggle to remain conscious faltered his senses. Tearing flesh, dying wails, and lifeless thuds came through intermittent hearing that Aaron prayed would fail.

A blurred image of Qachi stood amidst the dispatched laborers, admiring the carnage with menacing glee. He wiped the blade clean on a laborer's scalp.

Aaron did not move. His hat rim cast shadow over his eyes. Qachi could easily kill him. *Does he think I'm dead?* The shoulder wound rendered his right arm unresponsive, but pressure on top of him slowed the bleeding. Qachi wiped red droplets from his goatee and surveyed the scene. Both his, and Aaron's, eyes fell upon the large tent.

Oh God, no! Stef get out of there!

Her silhouette along the cloth wall got to its feet, camera ready in hand. The flap of the tent rustled with Qachi's entrance. His shadow advanced on the woman.

Stef! Aaron wheezed, unable to broadcast his voice. He raised his head. Dizziness lowered it.

She spoke scolding words in Mongol.

Qachi is not himself. Blind him and run!

Her body language instructed Qachi to pose with scimitar drawn. She raised a camcorder, giving an approving thumbs-up.

Qachi roared and lunged.

My God! Nooo!

A mortal slice ripped through the air; her silhouette replaced by splatter. Qachi hissed Mongolian words to the fallen woman.

Aaron's cell phone displayed, '*Your people will not stop me again!*'

Duncan emerged from his personal tent. Qachi reappeared, forty feet from where Duncan stood. Duncan raised an arm and cocked a pistol.

"G'day, mate. I'll be taking that off yer hands."

Yes! Shoot him!

Qachi did not advance, withdraw, or relieve the weapon. He raised the Sword, eyeing Duncan's weapon with curiosity. Each held their ground in a glaring showdown.

"Lay it down or I'll shoot."

Qachi grinned.

Fleshless arms grappled Duncan from behind.

"What the hell!" Duncan dropped the gun to pry the hands of Lieutenant Chagatai from his neck. Decayed tendons dangled from the undead's forearms like spaghetti. A jaw sank into Duncan's shoulder. He squirmed, but bony palms clamped on his cheeks denied escape.

"Pig's arse."

The zombie jerked his arms. Duncan collapsed with a broken neck.

'As Sword commands, Golden Horde shall follow.' Aaron bit his lower lip and silenced his breathing. Had Qachi saved him until the end on purpose?

Chagatai hobbled toward Aaron, favoring the foot without a coin-sized slit. Qachi motioned a halt command.

They're not . . . going to kill me?

The zombie Lieutenant joined its master. Both faced the Gobi desert. Aaron craned his head to see what they were looking at.

A dust cloud grew, a black figure approached. A second figure came into clarity.

Galloping horses.

As Aaron identified them, the dust in their wake contorted. Transparent figures, riders, emerged into vision. Three per side became five, then ten, until the entire horizon skewed by hundreds of spirit-riders.

My God . . .

Two dark mares arrived beside Qachi and Chagatai. With fiery eye sockets, their skulls burned from within. Smoke flowed from nostrils while their owners mounted. A thousand hooves in muffled clatter and a chill of undeath surrounded Aaron; the swarm of corporeal horsemen awaited command. Qachi screamed a battle cry, mobilizing the army. He sneered in pure madness one final time at Aaron and spun his steed. The two solid horses led the spirit-riders northward, toward Karakorum.

Gallops diminished to silence. Aaron wrestled free from under the pudgy worker and gauzed his wounded shoulder with cloth ripped from Haguyu's sleeve. He recalled Duncan's words, *'the Golden Horde always let one live to witness and spread the news they were to be feared.'*

Of the Kahn's triumphant return, he had been the one spared to spread this warning.

Aaron glanced from the jeep to his cell phone. He removed his blue cap and pondered the haunting memory of the metal's otherworldy color that had slipped through his shoulderblade. He needed to find shelter right away, to get to a doctor, to *spread the warning.* Reaching for his phone, he read aloud the final translation . . .

'*The Golden Horde rides again.*'

=[]=

Recently accepted into, A Glitch In the Continuum, *anthology by Pill Hill Press,* **Jay R. Thurston** *is honored to present his second published work,* The Funeral Procession. *When not writing, Jay enjoys attending concerts, paintballing, and chess. He has a B.A. in International Relations, and lives in New Hampshire with his wife. Check out his blog site at* www.jaythurston.blogspot.com.

REQUIEM

Jason Andrew

=[]=

Jason Andrew brings a unique perspective to this collection. Humans have long sought to discover life on other planets but, if that day should arrive, what exactly would the implications hold? Would alien life be so different from that of Earth, or would it mirror our own, filled with joy and pain and fear? Could we find commonalities with our galactic neighbors and, if so, what is it that all "intelligent" creatures seek? One suggestion lies forthwith in Requiem, *a quiet passage that is both beautiful and telling.*

=[]=

Tonight, I want to share a story with you. Some of you have lived your entire life with the warm knowledge that we are not alone in the universe. I was but a very young boy when the first message from Tau Ceti was detected.

My father had won tickets to the World Series in Detroit. It was a rare prize. We were from a working poor family and we hadn't spent much time together since the divorce. It wasn't until years later that I realized my father could have sold those tickets for a tidy sum. The White Sox were our home team. It is a rare gift when a father and son love the same baseball team.

Watching the President of the United States throw the first pitch, we knew that was a historic game. We cheered as the Sox led into the seventh inning stretch. The White Sox were going to win the World Series.

The lights then flickered haphazardly. The shrill whistle of the Umpire stopped the game. I remember looking around at the panicked faces of the other fans in the stadium. None of us knew what to expect. What could be so important as to interrupt a baseball game where the White Sox were about to win the World Series? Had there been a terrorist attack? Did someone assassinate the president?

The announcer flipped on the PA system. "Ladies and gentleman. New Comiskey Park would like to apologize for the interruption. This is a day that will long be remembered." I had never heard Ken Harrelson, the Voice of the White Sox, so flustered. "I can't explain the science behind it. I certainly can't explain the religious connotations or the meaning of it all. The Associated Press just reported that two hours ago, the Large Hadron Collider located in Geneva confirmed the receipt of a communication from a solar system known as Tau Ceti, which is located just twelve light years away. We are not alone."

We waited in silence while the Star Spangled Banner played. What did it mean to all of us that we had cosmic neighbors? What did their message mean? The low mutterings of the skeptics were quickly drowned out by the President's speech.

"Citizens of America; Citizens of the World. On this day, we have received a message originating from beyond this world, beyond this solar system. Learned scientists from all around the world have verified the origin of this message, but as of yet, we have not decrypted the meaning of it. Our brothers from Tau Ceti have gifted this day with the knowledge that we are not alone. We ask that you remain patient. This government wishes to assure you that there is no known danger and that all possible precautions are being undertaken."

And then the world, all of humanity, held our breath in anticipation.

The young of today can't fathom what it was like at that time. War stopped. Governments didn't broker peace. Armies and militia simply quit fighting. Lands and people that had soaked in blood for centuries simply went quiet. School was canceled. It wouldn't have mattered as none of us were willing to leave our television sets. We spent our time messaging each other, wondering what it all meant.

My father took me to church the very next Sunday. I had never been inside of a church before. We had to sit in the aisles. The entire neighborhood had come seeking some sort of answer we could all digest. The Pastor smiled and welcomed us all, but he didn't have any answers. Instead, he called us all together to sing.

Amazing grace! How sweet the sound
That saved a wretch like me.
I once was lost, but now am found,
Was blind but now I see.

I realized then that if there was a God, then he lived in the beat of a song. Millions of children that day were inspired to learn the subtle craft of science to meet the challenge of our new neighbors. I followed the beat.

It took the governments three months to finally admit to the world that it seemed beyond our science to decode the message. The possibility contained within the message frustrated us all. The message became a Rorschach test against which the frightened, the hopeful, and the faithful flung their own ideals against. It was a challenge the world willingly accepted.

We tried to learn everything we could about our new neighbors. Our largest telescopes couldn't pierce the debris disk surrounding that star. Through spectral lenses, we caught pictures and shadows of the planets there hidden inside that celestial briar patch. What did our neighbors look like? What sort of world did they live in? Did they laugh? Did they love?

Ten years passed until a married couple from California discovered the solution to understanding the message. It had been delivered through a complex quantum entanglement that pulsed at regular integrals. Standard communication would have taken centuries. The Tauians, as we had come to call them, had managed to link a few quantum particles from their system to ours creating the longest string in the history of man. We simply couldn't figure out how to tie that string to a can so we could communicate.

The Brooks had an argument. Matt decided to blow off steam by playing his oboe in the garage. Jen tried to work on her dissertation while listening to her husband butcher the scales. It occurred to Jen that the human ear and the human brain were programmed via evolution to appreciate music. The pattern from the quantum entanglement mimicked a musical scale that extended beyond the human audio range. It was different than any human scale, but the coincidence seemed uncanny. She made an innocent notation in her personal forum and others noticed a similar pattern.

I was a man of twenty then. I was almost done with school, eager to prove I could make it. I mastered the piano, the guitar, and the cello, but still I feared the cool attention of an audience. It was a good time to be alive. The world had changed.

It might have been the fear of our neighbors that brought out the best of us. I like to think that it was our awakening. We realized that we needed to put aside childish things. The world learned to work together, feed our hungry, and live in enlightened self-interest. Those of you in the audience attending Jerusalem World University might forget the two thousand year struggle of this city. We long had the means to resolve our own problems on this world, but rarely the will.

It took a message to remind us all of the possibilities.

Within the year, scientists had figured out that the notes in the cosmic scale provided them with a mathematical key to build a transceiver. The transmissions were translated by mathematical alchemy into sounds. We had searched the skies for centuries seeking a sign that somewhere else in the universe there was life; that we were not alone. None of us ever expected to hear the song within our lifetimes.

Some of my learned scholars believe that using the word song is an improper anthropomorphism of the Tauians' method of communication. I strongly differ on this point. Music requires a special evolution to appreciate. Our brains are wired by millions of years of evolution to seek out and appreciate connections. It changes the way we think, the way we perceive the cosmos. How eloquent and strange to us would a creature be, that communicates solely through music?

The songs of the Tauians use a twelve-scale pattern that feels to the human mind like a fusion of the Baroque and the Blues scale. Listening to them can bring joy, sorrow, or any emotion in between.

Some of the sounds of the songs are a bit out of our range, but translation software has improved our ability to enjoy them. And through listening, we learned more about the universe. It took a few years to realize that the Tauians use a duodecimal system.

Mathematics is just another way to describe the universe. Once we realized how the Tauians thought, we were able to understand their language of whistles, pitches, and hums and they opened to us a universe of possibilities. We learned about their science, their history, and most important their stories.

We dreamed of their aquatic world of crystal and refracting light. Each of us longed to see their cities carved from the Great Coral Reefs along their equator. They learned to communicate almost telepathically by musical notes alone. They shared everything with each other and realized that their greatest strength was their community.

Our world burned with questions. What did the Tauians think of us? Why did they communicate with us?

It would be years before an answer would come even with the quantum entanglement cosmic line. We waited with as much patience as we could muster and slowly the songs of Tauians became our songs.

I was almost fifty when I wrote my first Tauian Symphony. It had taken a lifetime to understand and master the subtle shifts in tone, the joy of their crescendos, and the sorrow from their andantes. I had locked myself away for the better part of a year ignoring my wife, my grandchildren, and yes, pesky agents wanting their new song.

And then came the answer from the Tauians. A cosmic disaster virtually destroyed the fourth planet in their solar system. It caused a disaster of biblical proportions. By the time we received the message on Earth, the world of the Tauians had been destroyed a century past.

The Tauians reached out to us on their last nights desperately wanting someone to mourn them. They wanted their songs to pass on to another generation and so they launched probes to broadcast their songs.

Some speculate that our neighbors escaped to the stars seeking a new home. Perhaps the children of my grandchildren will find out that answer.

I dream of those dead cities and I think of all that they did for us during their final hours.

And then I remember their courage and that their last wish as a people was to share their songs. I present to you the *Requiem of the Tauians*.

=[]=

Jason Andrew lives in Seattle, Washington with his wife Lisa. He is an associate member of the Science Fiction and Fantasy Writers of America and member of the International Association of Media Tie-In Writers. *By day, he works as a mild-mannered technical writer. By night, he writes stories of the fantastic and occasionally fights crime. As a child, Jason spent his Saturdays watching the* Creature Feature *classics and furiously scribbling down stories; his first short story, written at age six, titled* The Wolfman Eats Perry Mason *was rejected and caused his Grandmother to watch him very closely for a few years. Jason is at:* http://jasonbandrew.com.

Gilgamesh and the Mountain

Bruce L. Priddy

=[]=

One of the earliest known works of literature is The Epic of Gilgamesh, *a series of poems and legends from Mesopotamia, which follows the eponymously named character. Gilgamesh, a tragic hero much like Hercules of Greek lore, travels the land amongst both men and gods. His exploits are great and, so too, are his tales. Bruce L. Priddy brings us his own contribution to the lore of Gilgamesh, written in its traditional verse-narrative. Balancing passionate prose and vivid storytelling,* Gilgamesh and the Mountain *continues the epic of the King of Uruk.*

=[]=

From apocryphal tablets discovered by Hormuzd Rasam in the palace library of Ashurbanipal at Nineveh, 1856. Inscribed in Akkadian and found to be written in the traditional verse-narrative of the Epic of Gilgamesh. Translated by George Smith, 1872; tablets and translation suppressed by the British Museum, same year.

In those strange ages, in those far-off strange ages,
Gilgamesh, king of Uruk,
mourned his friend Enkidu, whom he loved so dear.
Gilgamesh wandered the wild places,
forsaking that he was a man and king.

He had become as an animal, he dressed in their skins,
he slept on the bare ground, nose to tail.
To Sin, the lamp of the gods, he howled his grief.
Like the night-beasts, our king howled.

Ninsun became concerned and bent down.
To Gilgamesh she spoke,
"My son, why have you forsaken your kingship?
My son, why do you live as an animal?"

Gilgamesh wailed,
"My friend, whom I loved so dear,
he is gone! The Netherworld has seized him!
Shall the Doom of Mortals fall on me?

"Shall I become the clay that has become Enkidu,
my friend, whom I loved so dear?
I am afraid of the Doom of Mortals,
of what my friend has shown me.

"A House of Grays, a House of Ashes,
a thirst that can never be sated,
that is what dear Enkidu has shown me.
These dreams and visions have made me afraid.
I wander the wild places, to seek an escape from the Doom of Mortals."

Far east did our king roam.
He walked a land no man had walked,
he saw a mountain no man had seen.

A dream came to Gilgamesh.
The mountain walked,
the mountain stumbled,
the mountain spoke and said to Gilgamesh, "Come."

Gilgamesh walked toward the mountain.
Every night he dreamed.
The first night the mountain spoke in an infant's sigh,
the second night a harlot's gasp,
the third night a jackal's laugh,
the fourth night as men in battle.
On the fifth night the mountain spoke in thunder.

Gilgamesh walked toward the mountain,
and Ninsun became concerned.
She bent down and said to Gilgamesh,
"My son, why do you go to that mountain?
No man was meant to walk it,
No man was meant to see it."

Gilgamesh spoke to Ninsun and said,
"In my dreams, I saw the mountain walk.
In my dreams, I saw the mountain stumble.
In my dreams the mountain spoke to me and said 'come'."

Ninsun spoke to Gilgamesh,
she said, "Turn back.
No man was meant to walk it,
no man was meant to see it."

Gilgamesh said to Ninsun,
"Are those not men I see in the distance?
Are those not men who cavort and dance around bonfires?"

Ninsun said to her son Gilgamesh,
"Those are not men you see,
who cavort and dance around bonfires,
but demons who pretend to be men.
Men do not have the legs of ewes.
Men do not have the horns of rams.
Men do not have the mouths of hyenas.

"They bay when Sin, the Lamp of the Gods, is high,
but do not serve him.
Frog-demons who crawl through the hair on the back of his head
receive their songs.
They will not welcome you in this land.
No man was meant to walk it,
no man was meant to see it.
They will be like wolves on you, they will be like lions,
your flesh they will consume, your remains will go to their masters."

Gilgamesh said to Ninsun,
"In my dreams I saw a mountain walk.
In my dreams I saw a mountain stumble.
In my dreams the mountain spoke to me and said 'come.'
To the mountain I shall walk.
The Doom of Mortals I fear but if it be mine,
I shall face it with ax and knife in hand,
not in bed, not in fever, as the gods cursed Enkidu."

Ninsun pleaded with Gilgamesh,
"Turn back.
The gods cannot follow."

Gilgamesh opened his mouth to speak.
"I weep bitterly for my friend Enkidu,
whom I loved so dear,
but no god helped me.
I fear the Doom of Mortals,

but no god helps me.
So, I shall ask the mountain."

Our king walked toward the mountain.
He saw Ninsun and the gods shudder.
He saw Ninsun and the gods flee.

As he approached the fires of the demons who pretend to be men,
Gilgamesh kept a league's distance.
When the demons who pretend to be men approached him,
Gilgamesh kept a league's distance.

The demons who pretend to be men sniffed the air.
But Gilgamesh had not bathed in water or anointed himself in oils,
so they did not fall upon him.
The demons who pretend to be men looked at him.
But Gilgamesh, dressed in the skins of animals, did not resemble a man,
so they did not fall upon him.
The demons who pretend to be men danced and cavorted.
Gilgamesh danced and cavorted like them,
so they did not fall upon him.
The demons who pretend to be men sang to the frog-demons who crawl in
Sin's hair.
Though it made his throat bleed, Gilgamesh sang with them,
so they did not fall upon him.
Gilgamesh was as the demons who pretend to be men,
until their bonfires were but stars on the horizon.

Gilgamesh came unto the mountain and saw it was not a mountain,
but an alive thing that was not alive.
Not alive but not dead.
Not dead but dreaming.

The face was one thousand plus one thousands of snakes,
each one a hundred rods and half again long,
dancing and cavorting like the demons who pretend to be men.
The eyes were night-oceans, the gulfs above,
but not moon nor stars shown in them.
Gilgamesh saw only the Deep.

The mountain spoke to Gilgamesh,
though it had no mouth to speak.
The words were as a night-insect who sings, "*azif! azif!*"

Birds fell from the skies,

cedars uprooted to crawl away.
Gilgamesh's ears could not understand the words,
but heard them as he would his own thoughts.
"You have come."

Gilgamesh forgot he was a king,
he lost his bowels.
Gilgamesh forgot he was a man,
he wet his legs.

"Are you a demon?" Gilgamesh asked the mountain.
And the mountain laughed.
"Are you a god?" Gilgamesh asked the mountain.
And the mountain laughed.

The mountain spoke to Gilgamesh and said,
"Those who pretend to be gods are but parasites,
lice in the hair, ticks in the skin,
flies that lay eggs in the flesh.

"Usurpers to the throne,
servants who play at being king
while their lords sleep.
That is what those who pretend to be gods are.

"I am they who slumber in beds
the gods turned into graves.
I am they who in sleep
have conquered death.

"I am they who dream
and give the gods torments in their night-beds.
I am they who the gods fear will wake
and bring upon them Doom."

Gilgamesh fell before the mountain and cried out,
"Why did you touch my dreams?
Why did you speak and say 'come',
and bring me to a land no man was meant to walk, no man was meant to
see?"

The mountain spoke to Gilgamesh and said,
"I saw a heart hollowed by sorrow,
as worms burrow through the dirt."

Gilgamesh wept.
"Yes! I weep bitterly for my friend Enkidu,
whom I loved so dear.
He is gone! The Netherworld has seized him!"

The mountain spoke to Gilgamesh and said,
"I saw a mind heavy with fear,
as one burdens a slave."

Gilgamesh wept.
"Yes! I am afraid the Doom of Mortals,
that I shall become the clay that has become Enkidu,
whom I loved so dear.

"You, who are they the gods fear,
can you bring back to me Enkidu, whom I loved so dear?
You, who are they that in sleep have conquered death,
can you teach me to escape the Doom of Mortals?"

The mountain spoke to Gilgamesh and said,
"Release us from our binding,
and you will be as a god.
Release us from our false prison,
You will be as a god.
None shall stand before you,
we will teach you new ways to revel and kill.
Every desire shall be yours to have."

Our king asked of the mountain,
"How did you come to be in this false prison?"

The mountain spoke to Gilgamesh.
"Long ago, before the moon was set in the sky
we who dream were the lords of this earth,
we who dream were the lords of every earth.
Through blood and fire we conquered.

"We who dream were as to the gods as men are to vermin.
Mice and roaches in our palaces,
scavenging in our refuse,
that is what those who pretend to be gods were.

"Then the heavens changed.
The sky broke, the stars went black.
The earth flipped over twice and flipped twice more.

The earth split. Mountains were set ablaze, fell and rose.
The land became the ocean.

"We who dream could not sustain our lives.
In slumber we would conquer death as we conquered earth.
In slumber we would conquer death as we conquered the gulfs between stars.
We who dream would sleep until the sky healed, to awaken and claim our thrones.

"Those who pretend to be gods
huddled and cried in terror of the Cataclysm.
From the ruins of our palaces they crawled,
into a world made anew.

"Famished, starved,
they gathered around the first fool who lit incense.
Those who pretend to be gods
were as flies that cling to rotting meat.

"Those who pretend to be gods
conspired against the true masters of this earth.
They stole our knowledge, they stole our magics,
they sealed our beds, made them into tombs!

"They are liars, they are thieves.
They claim to have created the heavens and the earth.
They are fattened on your worship.
They sealed our beds, made them into tombs!

"We who dream cannot wake,
condemned to watch the world from our graves.
Usurpers to our thrones,
they sealed our beds, made them into tombs!

"Across the land are the locks that keep we who dream in deathless sleep.
Push aside the gravestones and you, Gilgamesh,
you shall be as a god.
None shall stand before you.
We will teach you new ways to revel and kill.
Every desire will be yours to have.

"Release us so that we who dream may tread once more.
Through blood and fire we shall cleanse the earth,
and storm the heavens, to tear down the palaces of the usurpers,

so that you, Gilgamesh,
can take your revenge on those who pretend to be gods."

Gilgamesh stood before the mountain and spoke,
"If you, who are they the gods fear,
can bring back to me Enkidu,
whom I loved so dear,
and if you, who in sleep have conquered death,
can teach me to escape the Doom of Mortals,
I, Gilgamesh, shall call you master,
I, Gilgamesh, shall call you god.

"Tell me, my master,
where I will find the locks that keep you who dream in your graves.
Tell me, my god,
how to undo the seals that turned your beds into tombs."

The mountain spoke to Gilgamesh
and told him where to find the locks.
The mountain spoke to Gilgamesh,
and taught him new ways to revel and kill.

The mountain spoke to Gilgamesh,
and whispered to him the secrets to undo the seals.

Gilgamesh heard the secrets,
and black fled from our king's beard.
Gilgamesh heard the secrets,
and his heart lost a beat with every word.

Gilgamesh heard the secrets,
and our king forgot his vows to the mountain.
Gilgamesh heard the secrets,
and he ran.

Our king never spoke aloud the secrets.
Not to his wives,
when the secrets plagued his dreams and woke him with screams.
Not to the Council of Elders,
when his hands would tremble at the memory.

Gilgamesh ran from the mountain,
the secrets so maddened him.
He ran through the land
of the demons who pretend to be men.

They fell upon Gilgamesh.
Like wolves, like lions, they fell upon him.
Gilgamesh fought as a wild-beast, the secrets so maddened him.
He tore at them with his teeth, he tore at them with his finger-nails,
and Gilgamesh escaped the land no man was meant to walk, no man was
meant to see.

Gilgamesh returned to Uruk, he returned to his sheepfold.
Among them he sought they who worshiped those who dream.
He burned their temples.
He burned the people.

Our king raised an army,
ten thousand men.

His army of ten thousand, Gilgamesh marched
to the land no man was meant to walk,
to the land no man was meant to see.
Gilgamesh slaughtered the demons who pretend to be men.
He extinguished their bonfires.

His army of ten thousand, Gilgamesh marched to the mountain.
And the mountain laughed.

Their swords broke against the mountain,
Their arrows would not bite.
Gilgamesh could not kill that which was not living
but not dead.

The snakes crushed one thousand men, then one thousand more.
The mountain breathed death and two thousand men died.
Two thousand men fell on their knees to give the mountain worship.
Gilgamesh burned them.

The survivors returned with our king to Uruk.
At night no one in the city slept,
the nightmare screams outnumbered the stars.
The temples swelled with those who spoke the tongues of gods.

Gilgamesh raised a new army,
another ten thousand men.
He taught them new ways to revel.
He taught them new ways to kill.

They marched through the land,
Gilgamesh knew the secret places.
Beneath new temples to the gods,
Gilgamesh buried the locks.

His army of ten thousand, Gilgamesh marched,
on other sheepfolds,
to seek they who worshiped those who dream.
One in a city condemned all within the walls.

Gilgamesh tore down these cities.
His army reveled and killed in the new ways he taught them.
The fathers were slaughtered, the mothers burned,
the sons were made slaves, the daughters prostitutes.

Through blood and fire Gilgamesh cleansed the earth.

And the mountain laughed.

=[]=

Bruce L. Priddy is a single father, writer and editor living in Louisville, KY. His works can be found at Flashes in the Dark, Morpheus Tales, the upcoming Bigfoot Terror Tales, and the LovecraftEzine.com, where he also serves as co-editor. He is the creator and editor of the flash-fiction site EschatologyJournal.org. In addition to his fiction writing and editing, he pens a sort-of-monthly column promoting skepticism for the website of the popular Binnall of America podcast. Follow him @MisterPriddy on Twitter or at misterpriddysmarvels.wordpress.com.

BURIED TREASURE

Rob Rosen

=[]=

"Nothing lasts forever," is a truism that affects all civilizations. As generations pass, it really doesn't take long for peoples and monuments, even those considered once-magnificent, to fall and be buried by the sands of time. What wonders of today will be deemed "mysterious" or "archaic" when their relics are rediscovered in the future? Rob Rosen offers one wry possibility. Quick-witted and fun, the author leads us on a fast-paced tale of exploration and revelation. Join him on his trek, as he searches for Buried Treasure.

=[]=

"Ain't no water up there," the patrol guard informed me. "Not for well over five hundred years, anyway. If you want my advice . . . "

Which, of course, I didn't.

"Thanks, but, between you and me, and this here five grand, I'd like to see for myself," I told him, with a polite interruption.

He pocketed the cash and nodded his assent, allowing me to pass with nothing more than an additional, "Just endless desert up there, buddy. Good luck to you, though."

That far up north, the guards were paid little and, naturally, little was what was expected of them. After all, there wasn't much point in guarding a bunch of sand. Still, in terms of public safety, at least the government, what was left of it, was doing something to protect us.

Five hundred years too late, I figured.

Anyway, water, being the most precious of commodities, was worth seeking out. Though, like the proverbial needle, I was sure to find only hay in this here stack; and, of course, a hell of a lot of sand. Still, rumors abounded that water did indeed exist, if you knew where to look for it.

And the map, which I'd stumbled across quite accidentally, was sure to prove helpful in this endeavor.

Those who began the great exodus toward the equatorial regions left tantalizing clues of what once was. In some cases, that something being water. In this case, in particular, a large supply of it, worth untold riches.

But was it worth the risk of traveling into no-man's land? Well, that I was about to find out.

Fortunately, though the map I had in my possession was now five centuries old, it did give longitude and latitude as points of reference. I say fortunately, because there were no longer any road markings. No roads either, for that matter. Just endless dry desert, as the guard had pointed out, and the occasional hawk in search of what meager prey there must have been. There were also mammoth dunes covering Lord only knows what. Or worse yet, things I assumed were buried underneath and didn't have the desire to uncover.

The trek, after all, was depressing enough. We reaped, as the saying goes, what we sewed, and this was living, or not-living, proof of it.

Hours later, my body badly shaken, I arrived at my destination. Judging from the map, this area had always been desert up until an even greater desert encroached, surrounded, and then replaced it. For some reason, water, at some point in the distant past, had been brought to this place; and perhaps, just perhaps, it still remained, hidden below the oddly shaped giant dunes that stood before me.

Hints of what lay beneath poked out high above, though. The tops of towering steel buildings, only skeletons now, shown brightly under the unforgiving midday sun. Oddly shaped structures unlike any I'd ever seen, stripped of their hides, indicated that some sort of giant desert town had once been located in this spot. A city that must've needed a great deal of water to survive. But how could the water still be here? That was the conundrum of the map, which displayed various sized lakes scattered about, one of which, the largest, was situated in the center of the town.

And the makers of the map indicated that it was somehow protected.

The sand, sadly, was my biggest obstacle in getting to it all. But then, as my eyes scanned the lofty, beige horizon, an unexpected grin splashed across my face.

"Then again, maybe not so big an obstacle, after all," I whispered to myself. For there, in just about the location of the lake I sought, part of a still-roofed edifice, just the barest tip of it, actually, could be seen in between squinting eyes such as mine.

"An entrance," I quickly added, already walking up, up, up the giant dune, with a river of sweat now cascading down my face.

The roof, it turned out, was badly damaged, with a gaping, jagged hole at the top. Still, the dune had not worked its way over it yet, allowing my access to the building inside, and then requiring only a minimal drop into a sand-cushioned stairwell.

One story down and I found an open door leading to a long corridor. I flicked on my powerful flashlight and had myself a look around. It was obvious right away where I was.

"A hotel. And, judging from the number of rooms, a large one at that.

But a hotel out in the middle of the desert?" I whispered to myself. It was a strange concept, considering that man had been avoiding these sweltering, merciless places for centuries now. "Maybe even back then they came for the lake," I thought to add.

I returned to the stairwell and proceeded downward, until only the light from my flashlight lit the way through the pitch black darkness. I emerged inside a cavernous room, lined on all sides with brightly colored machines of similar size, all with lifeless monitors that reflected the radiance of my flashlight. The room itself, at one time, had been richly appointed; now it was a dusty, faded memory of what it once had been.

"What is this place?" I asked myself, shivering in the chilly space. Considering how far beneath the dunes I now was, this wasn't at all that surprising. See, the room, it seemed, was more like a desert tomb.

The blue swirling light at the far end of the room, however, was unusual, to the say the least.

I'd seen images like this before, in movies and in pictures. This was the reflection of a pool, flashing a dull blue glow against the farthest walls. My heart quickened as I approached the source.

"Water," I fairly groaned, in shock at the sheer volume of it. The lake, obviously man-made, sat, at one time, outside the building. Except the building's façade had long ago crumbled, making one long contiguous space, covered, it seemed, by other collapsed buildings, creating a protective ceiling over the lake. This explained why the sand had not long ago engulfed it as it had everything else.

The coolness of the air had obviously maintained the lake, and whatever evaporation occurred accumulated on the ceiling above and then dripped back down. In other words, the lake was in a perpetual state of flux, one that had maintained itself for centuries.

At least, this is what I assumed.

Looks, I was soon to discover, could be deceiving, even in such an apparently stagnant place as this.

For the stagnation did not last long.

In the blink of an eye, the water erupted. Like cannon fire, a deafening explosion filled the cavern. And the once-tranquil waters, like a terrifying volcano, shot up from all sides, sending out an ice-cold mist as it slammed into the ceiling above. I jumped back and tripped over ancient debris, landing hard on my rump. The water continued to rise and fall in tremendous sheets, as clear as glass, each time rumbling the enclosure with a noise so loud that I was forced to cover my ears.

Then silence, once again, save for the drip, drip, drip of the water as it trickled down from the roof. And then, out of the nothingness, a voice bellowed.

"Leave now," it said, the words echoing all around me, shaking me to the bone. A figure then appeared. Then two. Then dozens more emerged from the other side of the lake, dressed in garish clothes, tattered and torn, weathered as the building above us. In sharp contrast to their attire, their skin was a ghostly pale, white as the snow I'd only ever seen in pictures.

"Who . . . who are you?" I managed.

The same voice repeated, "Leave. Now."

"But all this water. Do you realize its value?"

The odd group laughed, low and deep, the sound collectively pinging this way and that as it ricocheted off of the walls and the lake.

"Value?" the voice asked. "How do you place a value on a god?"

I paused, realizing what was meant by this statement. Clearly, they worshiped the lake. Before I could answer, however, once again the waters trembled and rocketed to the ceiling, bursting forth in fits and starts, dousing the area once more in its chilly mist.

The figures knelt and bowed their heads. The voice shouted, "See, you have angered the god. You must leave, now."

I stood there and trembled as the lake again returned to its peaceful state. How was I to reason with them? If the lake was man-made, so must be the mechanism that controlled it. But how do you caution a people that what they are worshiping is a false god, and live to tell about it? I stared at the water, in all its brilliant blue glory, nearly salivating as I pondered the wealth that lay within. On a planet long dry, water indeed was a god, but not one such as they thought it to be.

"Yes," I finally shouted. "I see that your god is indeed most powerful. But should you not share it with the world? Shouldn't your god be worshiped by countless men and women, and not just a paltry few?"

They looked up at me from their kneeling positions and, strangely, again began to laugh. Eventually, a man walked toward me.

"You are not the first to find us," he informed. It was then I noticed that his eyes and hair were as colorless as his skin. "You mean to take our god away from us, as the others have tried, for the sake of riches."

I heard no menace in his voice, just a knowing sadness.

"Yes," I acknowledged. "I am sorry, but water is as sacred above the sands as it is below. And therefore valuable."

His frown quivered and turned to a smile, just as the waters again shook and exploded forth, as they had done before, circling round and round the lake in a continuously loud frenzy.

"The god appreciates your honesty," the man said. "And so, we will reward you with what you seek."

And now it was my turn to smile. "How?" I asked. "Are there waters elsewhere?"

For the third time, the group laughed in unison.

"No," the man replied. "You seek riches of a monetary value. Of this, we have as much wealth as there is sand above." He pointed within the building. "The machines you passed," he told me, "contain precious metal. The desert around us abounds in these machines. Riches in unimaginable numbers. For your silence, when you leave here, we will reward you with as much of this as you seek. We simply wish to live in peace, as we have for generations, with our god."

My laugh echoed their own. I came in search of wealth, and this is what I found, only in a surprisingly different form. My map was a treasure map, after all. And so, I looked at the nearly translucent man and then to his people, and I nodded.

"Deal," I agreed.

The man paused. "A strange word," he said, with a tilt of his head. "It has been passed down from our ancestors, but we do not know its meaning."

I shrugged and then watched in awe as his people carted out heavy sacks of silver and gold coins, enough to fill up my buggy with, and then some. Untold riches, just as promised. And then they walked me back through the dilapidated room and up the rusted stairs. Eventually, they covered themselves in hotel sheets, revealing not an inch of tender skin, and joined me on the hot desert sand as they loaded my buggy, bag after glorious bag.

"We have your word then?" the man asked. "You will never return or tell of our god?"

"No," I confirmed as I sat myself behind the steering wheel and looked back up at him one final time. "But one last question."

"Yes?" he said, staring down at me quizzically.

"This god of yours, what do you call him?"

He smiled and bowed his head in reverence. "Bellagio," he replied. "We call him Bellagio."

=[]=

Rob Rosen *is the author of the critically acclaimed novels* Sparkle, Divas Las Vegas, Hot Lava, *and* Southern Fried. *His short stories have appeared in more than 150 anthologies. Please visit him at* www.therobrosen.com.

THE SMALL, BLACK GOD

Caw Miller

=[]=

This next selection caught my attention immediately, not only by its intricate storyline, but also its clever dialogue. Dialogue is one of the most challenging aspects of writing—when done effectively, characters become vivid and "real." When done poorly . . . well, there's simply nothing that ruins a story faster. The Small, Black God *captures the back-and-forth jousting intellects of a young archaeologist and a panel of scientists who have arrived at his dig site, perhaps with motives of their own. Heed this god, but consider still the following: Well done, Mr. Miller, well done.*

Caw also asked to include his own anecdote regarding this tale: "The original version of the story was set on the Black Sea coast of Turkey, but a week before the submission deadline for the anthology, a 7.2 magnitude earthquake struck Turkey and killed hundreds of people. Out of respect for the victims and their families, I moved the location across the Black Sea to Crimea. I hope that Crimea escapes the baleful glare of The Small, Black God.*"*

=[]=

As the ferry chugged closer, billowing black smoke into the sky, Roger hoped that the serpent of the Black Sea would rise up and swallow the ship, taking Frederick Frost and his band of unbelievers with him to the bottom of the sea. The serpent did not appear, though, because the beast was a mirage seen by drunken sailors, so Roger could either run away and never do archaeology again, or face the inquisition of the panel of scientists.

Roger kicked pebbles from the dock into the water as the steamer approached. He had invited his mentor to come see the lost city but somehow his enemy had found out instead. Frost invited himself, no doubt to carry out his two-fold campaign to discredit dear mentor Augustus Le Plongeon and to disprove the existence of the city of Mu, Le Plongeon's progenitor of all historic civilizations.

The steamer ploughed closer and Roger reviewed his arguments and proofs, which coupled with his buoyant nature, convinced him that he had enough evidence to sway the esteemed panel. He would make his own fortune and clear the name of his mentor. Roger waved as the ferry tied up at the dock.

"Welcome to Crimea," he said.

Down the gangway strode imposing Frederick Frost, his signature top hat clamped on his head with a hand against the gusting wind. Tall and broad, Frost looked more like a bare knuckle boxer than the head of the archaeology school at University College Nottingham. He had the reputation of a man who got what he wanted by whatever means necessary.

"You Marsh?" Frost asked, not extending a hand in greeting.

The man's pessimistic expression made Roger wonder if he would ask for identification papers.

"I am." Roger offered his hand, which was ignored.

"Show us to our lodging. The rough seas have been telling on Huxley's delicate innards."

Frost's sneer shocked Roger by its intensity and gave him the impression that he was to blame for the weather. Roger nodded. This man's opinion would be nearly impossible to sway.

"This way, please." Roger turned and led the way up the dock to a waiting carriage. At least here, he knew that he would not disappoint. The carriage was new and would bear them to the Golden Waters, the most famous of the hotels in the resort city of Sudak.

Roger held the door to the coach as the party climbed in. He recognized the oldest member, Thomas Henry Huxley, the noted scientist who so favored Darwin's theory of evolution as to be nicknamed *Darwin's Bulldog*. The last member of the party was young James Churchwood, who smiled sadly through his goatee.

"Is the old Kaiser ever going to let you graduate?" Roger whispered.

Churchwood shrugged. "He feeds me well, at least."

Roger followed Churchwood into the carriage and squeezed into the only space left, between two middle-aged men wearing the worn suits and supercilious expressions of academics.

"Introductions." Frost pointed at the man to Roger's right. "Theodore Willard, archaeologist. He's studied the Maya, like your mentor, and has some questions about Augie's preposterous claims."

Fuming at Frost, Roger nodded to the man. Of course Frost brought with him a well-known critic of Mu. Frost also used a nickname for Le Plongeon since it would trivialize the great man.

"Uriah Gildston, geologist." Frost pointed at the man to Roger's left. "He's looking forward to examining the alleged earthquake that revealed this lost city that you claim."

"Alleged?" Roger barely contained his anger and had to look away for a moment before he could speak. "The earth shook. Buildings collapsed. A landslide blocked the river which cut off the lake. When the water drained out, the city was revealed. It was in the papers as far as London."

"Yes, yes. You found a couple rocks stacked on top of each other and you're claiming it's Mu, your mentor's fictional city that he confused with Atlantis, which was a lie told to Plato. If not for Huxley's desire to take the waters in Sudak, this expedition would not be here."

Roger looked at Huxley, who stared out the window blandly. "I'm grateful for everyone's trouble," Roger said. "You'll find there are more than a couple stacked rocks. The architecture is varied, with Mayan and Egyptian pyramids, bas-reliefs like ancient Assyria, dolmens, and Greek pillars, showing proof of Le Plongeon's theory that all of those cultures had a single origin culture, which he called Mu."

Frost chuckled. "No ziggurats?"

"No. But there is a flat space that is about the right size for one matching the pyramids," Roger replied.

"But what about your mentor's placing of Mu in the Atlantic Ocean?" Willard asked.

Roger felt his cheeks heat in a blush. They had spotted a weak point in the theory. "Yes, well, Le Plongeon might have put the thumbtack in the wrong place on the world map, choosing the most central location, but the hypothesis is still valid."

Frost snorted. "Yes, well. That's the problem with Augie's little story. I daren't legitimatize it with the word *hypothesis*. It's based on ideas, not facts. A resemblance of architecture does not prove a relationship."

"But what about the sun motifs in each culture?" Roger asked.

Frost pointed out the window with a wickedly curved thumb. "The sun is the most dominant feature in every culture, including our own. You're not going to tell me that Mu founded London, too, are you?"

Willard and Gildston chuckled.

Roger squeezed his fists so tightly that he would have drawn blood, but for the thick calluses on his hands from shoveling silt and mud. He clenched his jaw shut to keep from returning insults with Frost, likely what the bully wanted.

"Why don't we keep an open mind about this city until we see it," Huxley said. "Science is best served by observing first, before making decisions."

To Roger's delight Frost frowned, clearly wishing to continue the debate, but respectful of the elder scientist.

The rest of the carriage ride passed in tense silence. At the hotel, the new arrivals went to their rooms and freshened up, then to dinner. Roger presented Frost with the ongoing report he was writing on the excavation. After the meal, while the others sipped brandies, Roger led Gildston out into the city to look at the evidence of the earthquake.

In the morning, Roger was the first one to the carriage. To his surprise Huxley was second.

"I always sleep like a baby when I can hear the ocean," the elder scientist said. "I figure it reminds me of being in the womb."

Willard came next, followed by Gildston who still smiled from the earthquake evidence they had seen last night. "There'll be more today, right?"

Roger assured him there would be much better earthquake evidence. Last came Frost, trailed by Churchwood carrying several satchels. Roger guessed that Frost had waited in his room until he knew he would be the final one to appear.

"Let's get on with it," Frost muttered, acting like it was a tribulation.

Once they settled in the carriage, Roger waited as long as he could before asking his question. "And what did you think of my report?"

"Oh, that." Frost smirked. "I was busy with correspondence last night and never got to it."

Churchwood caught Roger's eye and mimed holding a pen then pointed to himself. Roger knew who had written the letters. Anger at Frost's snub surged in Roger, but then ebbed away. He had expected it, so it just made him feel empty inside. Frost's mind was already made up. If the man would just look at the city, especially Diaspora Hall, he could be enlightened. Roger felt his academic career slipping away like it rested on ice . . . or Frost.

After lunch, eaten in the cramped carriage, they traveled up a narrow road climbing the side of the mountain. Far below, a blue river twisted between rocks. The carriage stopped at the only pull-off.

"We're here? I thought it was at the bottom of a lake?" Frost asked.

"We're going to see some evidence of that alleged earthquake," Roger said, suppressing a chuckle.

Frost frowned.

From their vantage point halfway across the mountain, the party looked down into a steep-walled valley filled with a cloudy lake. A landslide of boulders, whole trees, and talus blocked the valley. The river leaked out of a crack in the side of the mountain on the far side of the valley and disappeared.

"Call me a flannel buzzard if that isn't the most obvious example of an earthquake I've ever seen," Willard said. "You could put that in a textbook."

Gildston sketched furiously on an art pad. "It will be."

Frost snorted.

"When you have a chance, Gildston, I'd like your interpretation of this," Huxley said.

"One moment, sir."

The geologist finished his sketch before launching into a half hour lecture on earthquakes, the shrinking earth, and hydraulics. Roger meant to listen and learn, but Frost's leering and supercilious expression seared through Roger's ability to concentrate. Roger looked at the steep mountains and blue sky, seeking solace in their beauty. It was a pretty place to spend the rest of his life trolling for fish and then cleaning them, the only real job in Sudak likely open to a foreigner like him if this archaeological dig failed.

"Roger . . . ready?" Churchwood said.

Roger realized that everyone stared at him. "Of course. Back into the carriage. Time to go down the mountain now."

"There's no chance of that landslide giving way and flooding the city again, is there?" Willard said, clearly fearful.

"Only if there's another earthquake as strong as the last one," Gildston said. "Unlike lightning, earthquakes do occur in the same place twice, but they're never as strong."

The geologist squeezed the shoulder of the archaeologist and encouraged him to enter the carriage. Roger considered riding on the bench with the driver to escape Frost's brooding presence, but wanted to be near the man to defend himself and Le Plongeon against defamation.

As they neared the city, Roger's spirits rose. It truly was an amazing find that could persuade even a Neanderthal man like Frost.

When the carriage stopped, Roger could not suppress his smile. "Gentlemen, I present to you the lost city of Mu, progenitor to all culture on Earth."

Roger followed the scientists out of the carriage, to find them staring at two huge piles of reeking, oozing silt.

"I think the one on the right is the Egyptian pyramid and the one on the left the Mayan, what do you say Willard?" Frost said.

The scientists laughed, Willard bent over with his hands on his knees.

"No. Why did you stop here?" Roger asked the driver in Ukrainian.

The driver pointed to where the road passed between the piles of silt; it was reduced to a track only wide enough for walking single-file.

"As you can see," Roger gathered the scientist's attentions. "The digging is progressing swiftly. It seems we'll have to walk a bit more than planned. Please follow me."

Roger led the way to a paved courtyard before a massive gate that looked to be a Roman triumphal arch, but instead of praising a victor, half of a rising sun sent out rays across the entablature.

"Queen Moo welcomes all visitors to Mu, is what I've translated the text to read. It appears to be a predecessor to Sanskrit."

The scientists stared, Willard open-mouthed. Even Frost looked more amazed than grumpy. Roger exhaled. His reputation was saved. Mu would make him famous.

"This way, gentlemen." Roger headed for the monument. He tried to keep righteousness out of his tone of voice. "The arch is one of the *least* impressive parts of the city."

Flights of steps, sixty-six feet wide, progressed down into a valley. Hundreds of laborers hauled wheelbarrows of sludge up out the valley to hundreds of piles.

At each landing, Roger paused to point out the interesting finds that slowly emerged from under the thick, muddy silt. He showed the tops of the pyramids, the obelisks, and other buildings, but ignored the columned building in the center of the valley which had already been cleared of debris.

"Is that the Parthenon?" Huxley asked.

All of the scientists stared at Roger. He paused, smiling, enjoying the moment. "It's even better," he finally said. "I call it Diaspora Hall, the origin of every culture on the Earth."

"Preposterous," Frost said.

Roger noted that he spoke with far less vehemence. "Wait until you see inside to decide."

Frost said nothing more.

As Roger led the way across the city, he pointed out the canals where the river water had been channeled and also the many sun and bird motifs and compared them to pre-Christian religions.

The scientists asked numerous questions of Roger as they climbed the five hundred fifty-five steps to the entrance to Diaspora Hall, but he waved them away. "Come inside first."

Even Roger was winded when they reached the top of the steps. Hands on his knees, he pointed to the flowing script encircling the frieze of the building. "I don't know what it says but the script looks like early Arabic."

"I know just the linguist to tackle that," Willard said.

To Roger's delight, Frost was the last one recovered enough to proceed. He still looked flushed and breathed heavily but did not want to delay the exploration.

"Everyone grab a lantern," Roger said. "It's as dark as night inside."

Giddy with elation and relieved at his success, Roger led the way into the voluminous hall. Two rows of huge pillars supported the roof, dividing the hall into three long rows. Plinths stood between the pillars and on each sat the remains of a sculpture. Roger gathered everyone at the first of the thirty plinths.

"Let's play a little game," he said. "Each plinth holds a representation of a god. See the large breasts, here, and there's part of an ample belly. Does anyone know which god this was?"

"Venus, Aphrodite, and many others generally descended from Asarte of Phoenicia," Willard replied, sounding a bit annoyed.

"Right," Roger quickly spoke before the scientists became impatient. "But see that the effigy was smashed and—"

"That likely happened when it was under water," Frost snapped.

"Maybe," Roger said. "But look at how the statue was painted with words of different languages, many of which I haven't translated yet. I believe that when the first worshippers of Asarte took their god out into the world they destroyed the original one here."

The scientists, especially Frost, did not look convinced.

"Who can spot the next one?" Roger asked, pointing at the opposite plinth.

The remains of a bas relief littered the plinth and the ground.

Churchwood pointed to several pieces. "I see the headdresses of Zoroastrianism and a ring. This likely was Ahura Mazda, the uncreated god and lord of light and wisdom."

"Top marks to Churchwood. Shouldn't he have his doctorate by now?" Roger looked at Front who glared and stood with his arms crossed.

"How about the next one?" Roger aimed his lantern on a plinth that contained pieces of tentacles. Even in its reduced state, the statue raised the hair on the back of Roger's neck.

No one could identify the effigy.

"I don't know either," Roger said. "At least half of them I have not been able to identify. I was hoping you gentlemen would assist me there. Let's look at another."

The next plinth held the remains of a statue of an old man with a long beard, wearing a long robe and holding a fan.

"By its hair I'd say Lao Tzu, author of the *Tao Te Ching*," Frost said. "But it could be any old man. Fans like that are as common as student assistants."

Roger winced. It seemed that lobbying for Churchwood would not be tolerated.

After showing several unknown remains of statues, Roger led the group to a winged woman, naked, standing on lions near owls.

It took several moments of looking before Willard smiled. "Kishar. This is Akkadian."

The scientists expressed their surprise. Huxley stood with his chin in a hand, staring at the portion of the torso. "That is a depiction of a penis, drawn here, right?"

Roger agreed.

"I don't believe that's a fertility symbol, however. I'd say it's pornographic in nature. These effigies seem to be defaced." Huxley pointed to black marks around the statue's eyes. "If the diaspora ritual involved destroying the idol before carrying the god to its new culture, then the effigies would not have been vandalized."

Roger did not answer at first. It was a revelation. "There's a great deal unknown. Many a career can be made here."

Roger switched rows and moved deeper in the hall, stopping and showing a statue of Enlil, a Sumerian god of the ghost-land and then Kinich Ahau, the Mayan god of the Sun. "This is where I really see Le Plongeon's work showing up as this is from the Western Hemisphere, a millennium before Columbus."

They moved on and looked at the remains of a turtle statue.

"I know what this hall reminds me of," Huxley said.

Roger turned and stared. He knew this could be a pronouncement that changed his life.

"At my old boarding school we had a trophy room," Huxley said.

Roger wondered if the old man had become demented.

Huxley continued. "We had a small room where we put the trophies we won for sports and academic competitions, but we went a bit further than that. Sometimes we stole the mascot of our opponents, or we created effigies of the teams we defeated, especially hated rivals, and vandalized them and laid them at the foot of the trophies. We made up dirty limericks and sang songs to mock our defeated opponents. We were really quite beastly about it. Eventually our dormitory father got sacked for letting us do it."

Roger stared, stunned into surprise. The brilliant scientist had become a doddering fool.

"Don't you see," Huxley went on. "The inhabitants conquered these people, and then brought back their gods here, where they ridiculed the gods of their defeated foes. This should be called the Hall of Defeated Gods."

There was silence.

"By Jove—is he here somewhere—I think you're right." Frost took off his top hat and bowed to Huxley. Willard and Gildston softly applauded.

Roger derided himself. The hypothesis fit nicely. The only explanation he'd had for the graffiti was that it had happened later, after the city had fallen, but somehow before the flood. But there was still one crack in the idea, although even thinking of it made the hair on his neck stand—the small, black god.

"Excellent reasoning, sir, but there's one idol that you need to see. It's this way." Roger led the party to the farthest corner of the hall. "I'm not sure in what order the statures were placed in the hall so I don't know when this was put here. It may have been first or last. As you can see, this god was not smashed or mocked. I'm thinking it might be the original god of the people of Mu."

Roger illuminated a plinth upon which sat a small statue of a rotund man, naked, holding his toes in his hands, a clever grin pulling up one side of his face. The black color seemed to be flat, yet shined with light at odd angles.

The scientists approached and scrutinized the statue. Most shivered.

Roger looked at the base, being sure to look away from its mischievous eyes. "I've not placed it. Tell me if you recognize it."

"Unsettling," Huxley said.

Churchwood went last, almost as an afterthought. "I think I saw this in Patagonia. Humorous god."

"I don't think it's funny at all. Ghastly, really," Roger whispered.

Churchwood squinted at Roger, looking confused.

The scientists launched into a debate of the small, black god, the purpose of the hall, and the order of the placement of effigies. Roger answered questions and joined a few discussions but he noticed that Frost kept staring at the statue and several times actually picked it up. Frost's satchel, which had been flaccid, now seemed to be rather lumpy. He planned to steal the small, black god.

"I think the black god came last and was the one that brought down the city. They conquered a god that got back at them," Gildston shouted over the men talking with him.

"Uh, interesting," Roger said into the ringing silence that followed. Uncertain of what next to say, he looked at his pocket watch. "Oh my. It's nearly tea. We need to get back. We do not want to ride the carriage over the mountains in the dark."

Roger ushered the scientists out ahead of him. Frost refused to move and actually clapped Roger on the shoulder and pushed him ahead. "Good job, chap. This city is first rate. I might even be able to find you a spot on my staff at the university."

"Oh. Yes. Lovely." Roger scooped up the small, black god and placed it in the pocket of his jacket where it bulged like a canker.

The smile evaporated on Frost's face.

"The exit's this way, sir." Roger led the way. Frost stumped behind him.

The scientists jabbered like school children as they marched out of the city. They peppered Roger with questions, asking for details on his excavation techniques and which textbooks he used for translation. Roger detected a pessimistic tone to their inquiries.

On the carriage ride, Frost was as pleasant as a bull that smelled a cow in heat but could not reach her. The rest of the scientists echoed the attitude and Roger vowed to rent a new coach. The scientists that had been so excited about the city were again doubting it—doubting what they had seen with their own eyes.

The trip back over the mountains echoed Roger's feelings: Depressed at the start of the day, then his emotions soared, then back down again.

By the time they reached the hotel, the scientists had three hypotheses that refuted the claims of Mu. Willard went so far as to call the city a Roman joke built by Nero as a place to perform his theatrical shows.

While the guests washed up and changed their clothes for dinner, Roger cleaned up in the well behind the hotel and brushed the dirt from his only suit. He arrived at the dining room late to avoid the scientists during the aperitif, but Frost and Willard were already inebriated and vicious.

Frost tapped on his wine glass with his large, gold class ring until he had everyone's attention. "I've figured out the whole thing, the city, the gods, all of it."

Roger cringed. This would be a blow.

"This is the Kingdom of Prester John, the Christian city surrounded by Muslims."

The scientists laughed. The few other guests in the dining room chuckled, pretending to get the joke. Roger wanted to run from the room but his feet would not obey his order. He felt like his blood had been replaced with lead. This was worse than his nightmare of being asked to lecture at Cambridge only to find that he stood naked before the assembly. That had been a dream. This was reality.

Willard stood and tapped his ring on his glass. "I thought I had the correct theory, but you've got it, old chap. I was thinking we had found Camelot and the knights of the plinths."

Frost laughed and clapped. "No, I did not make the greatest joke. Le Plongeon did, making up that story about a mother city, which this— guppy—lapped up and spit out like Henry Rider Haggard. Come to Mu, the city that must be obeyed."

Even though this was the only dinner Roger would get—he could not afford another—he folded his napkin, excused himself from the table, and departed. He walked the streets of Sudak for an hour before going to his room, which was barely larger than the cot, on the side of the city closest to the excavation. He slept poorly, plagued by nightmares of failing at every task or career he tried, even one as lowly as being a hauler at his own excavation where he dumped a basket of silt over a huge cliff only to see the small, black god tumble into bottomless depths, smirking the whole way.

The next morning, Roger stayed in bed as long as possible and made sure he was the last to the carriage. He had forgotten to make arrangements for a new one and so expected his luck to be even worse than yesterday. As Roger wedged in between Willard and Gildston, Churchwood covertly pointed to himself and moved his lips. Uncertain of the meaning and wishing to hide from the mocking scientists, Rogers closed his eyes and pretended to sleep.

At the excavation Roger exited the carriage before it came to a complete stop, then hurried between the piles of silt toward the city. Today they would visit the two pyramids and Roger wanted to be by himself as much as possible.

Impatiently, Roger waited at the edge of the excavation of the Egyptian pyramid for the scientists to arrive. Frost came last, sneering and strolling, and staring at Roger's bulging jacket pocket. Roger knew that Frost would not believe anything he said, today.

Churchwood raised his eyebrows at Roger and seemed to be hinting at something, but Roger launched into his lecture on the architecture, which the scientists ignored. Roger did not wait for questions and set off toward the other pyramid, ignoring the calls of the party to slow down.

A hand on his shoulder brought Roger to a halt.

"We need to talk," Churchwood whispered.

"I just want the day to end."

"Unless we talk it's going to end badly for you, and still might."

Roger looked Churchwood in the eye. "It can be worse than this? My reputation is shot."

"Let's pretend to examine that frieze." Churchwood pointed to a small columned temple.

"Keep following this canal to the next pyramid. I'll catch up," Roger shouted to the scientists.

Not looking to see if they had heard, and not caring, Roger accompanied Churchwood a dozen yards off the main path. The mud was thick here and slippery. If he convinced the panel, he would have enough money to buy enough laborers to clean the city properly. He sighed. His dreams were dead.

Near the temple, Churchwood pointed at the script and bird symbol. "I overheard Frost and Willard talking last night. They are very impressed with this city. They don't buy into Mu and the diaspora, but they want to excavate here, so much so that they plan to discredit you and take over."

"What?" The news elated and shocked Roger. All the jokes and mockery were to cover the archaeologists' envy. There really was something here if Roger could just keep it from being stolen. "Damn them."

Needing to strike something to release his frustration, Roger smacked his thighs, hitting the side of the idol in his pocket. He pulled out the small, black god and showed it to Churchwood. "Not so humorous, now?"

Churchwood looked puzzled. "Why do you keep saying humorous with that effigy?"

"That's what you said it was, the humorous god."

"No." Churchwood smiled briefly. "I said the god of hubris. Greek for inflated self-worth. What led to Achilles's death and half the heroes of the Greek tragedies."

"I know what it means," Roger said. "That's a rather different meaning than I—" Roger stared as thoughts collided in his brain. "It arrived here last."

He turned to Churchwood. "Willard was right. I've got to see Frost." Roger hurried through the mud to the cleared road, then jogged.

"Why? What's so important?" Churchwood asked, jogging after him.

"Professor Frost, can I have a word in private?" Roger asked.

Willard checked with Frost, then walked half a dozen steps away. Churchwood joined him.

"What is it?" Frost said, glaring at Roger.

"I want you to have this, sir, for your museum." Roger pulled the idol of the small, black god from his pocket and handed it to Frost.

At first Frost was surprised, speechless, then his sneer returned. He turned to Willard and Churchwood. "You are all witnesses. Roger Marsh attempted to bribe me with this priceless artifact to support his excavation. I declare his dissertation invalid and therefore he is unworthy to continue the excavation here. Someone should take over."

"How about you, Professor Frost?" Willard said. "You're the most experienced archaeologist present."

"I accept." Frost turned his malevolent gaze on Roger. "You are discredited and banned from this site. Get out now or face imprisonment."

"As you wish, sir." Smiling slightly, Roger strolled passed the beaming Willard and the stunned Churchwood.

"What? What are you doing?" Churchwood hissed.

Roger paused, then turned back to Frost. "I don't think I'm trustworthy enough to see myself out. Maybe Churchwood should escort me out of the city?"

"Don't be too long. We have a lot of work to do," Frost said.

"I don't understand," Churchwood said.

"Just come on. Trust me," Roger whispered.

Huxley strode forward and gestured for Roger to halt. "That was very poorly done. I'll support you in fighting that egotistical monster."

"Thank you, sir. But right now I need to get out of the city. I recommend you join me. Where's Gildston?"

"He rushed on ahead."

Striding so quickly that Huxley and Churchwood struggled to keep up, Roger pressed on until he could hail the geologist.

"Professor Gildston, we're heading out of the city to take a closer look at the earthquake line. Maybe you'd like to join us?"

"Certainly more interesting to me than old buildings," Glidston replied

At the next active dig site, Roger realized that he needed to do one more thing. He called over the head laborer. "You've all worked so hard that you should take the rest of the day off, with pay. Tell everyone you meet."

The laborer hurried to his underlings who quickly cast off their baskets and sprinted toward the exit.

"That'll bollix Frost for his trouble," Huxley said, smiling.

"Yes, well, let's keep moving. The effect seems to be quick." Roger marched away.

"Can't you explain this?" Churchwood asked.

"I'm saving my breath for the walk. I won't stop 'til we're out of Mu."

Laborers jogged by, many offering thanks to Roger as his small party exited the city. Outside of the victory arch, they boarded the carriage and caught their breaths. They were partway up the mountain when Gildston asked about the quake line.

"Oh. Sure. I forgot. We'll stop in a moment."

Roger instructed the driver where to go, then sat back in the carriage surrounded by expectant faces.

"Well? What's this all about?" Churchwood asked.

"It stretches the imagination. I'm not sure I'm right, yet, but if I am, I just saved all of our lives." The audience seemed to be suitably impressed, so Roger continued.

"When the committee arrived two days ago they were justly doubtful of my findings. I was justly doubtful of the committee, especially since it was headed by Frost, my mentor's enemy. Things started out poorly, but once you all saw the city you saw how spectacular it was. I knew my reputation was made, but late yesterday afternoon I saw that Frost had been stealing artifacts and his next mark was the idol of the small, black god. To protect the linchpin of Diaspora Hall, or Conquered Gods, I took the idol. That's when my luck turned."

The carriage stopped. Roger led the party to the edge of the road where they could look down on the city in the valley, the closest end of the earthquake line, and the landslide. Gildston headed down the mountainside for a closer look at the scar.

"Shows how much he loves his rocks, that he'd rather look at them than hear the rest of your story," Huxley said.

"Well, I don't think he knows of Frost's treachery," Roger said.

Huxley nodded.

"By the time we were leaving the city yesterday, you all had changed your minds and were mocking me and my theory, and it only got worse after that. Thanks to Churchwood here, who really is a good man if you're looking for a new student assistant, I learned that Frost planned to discredit me and steal Mu from me. But that's where Frost's partner in crime showed me what had happened, along with discovering what Churchwood had said. The small, black god is the patron of hubris, essentially revenge for ego. It was the last effigy to arrive in Mu and the city was destroyed soon after. I took the idol and my luck turned upside down. My ego being rather small, no one had to die to appease the dark god."

"But why did you give it to Frost?" Churchwood asked.

Huxley chuckled. "Frederick has an immense ego, therefore if he possessed the idol it would bring him down, just like it did the city."

A tremendous crack knocked Roger off his feet. The ground trembled, keeping him on his hands and knees.

"Earthquake?" Churchwood shouted.

Roger nodded. Roaring sounds drew his attention to the mountainside below. The crack in the earth widened on the closer mountain and sealed up on the far mountain. The landslide shivered, then water burst from the middle of the debris, soon eroding a channel. The lake surged into the valley, its former bed. The city of Mu drowned in minutes.

Churchwood stared, opening and closing his mouth, but no sounds came out. Huxley looked stunned. Roger sat, trembling so violently that he thought the earthquake continued.

"Frost's ego was even bigger than I thought," Churchwood said.

At least two men had just died, but Roger laughed. His emotions had been so twisted the last several days that he let them out, whatever they were. The great find that would have set his name among the revered of archeology was submerged, again, and out of reach. If it had been buried in rock he could excavate it, but he had no way to remove a lake or walk underwater. He was not sure that he wanted to. The small, black god was best left out of reach of humans and their egos.

A hand reached over the edge of the road.

Gildston hauled himself up, smiling like a fool. "That was stupendous. I finally experienced an earthquake firsthand. It nearly killed me, but now I can write what it really feels like." The geologist looked at the faces near him. "What?"

Churchwood pointed at the new lake. "The city is gone."

"Oh." Gildston shrugged. He turned to Roger. "Sorry."

"I expect Frost and Willard are still in the city," Roger said.

The geologist shrugged. "They were tiresome companions who knew that archaeology is a dangerous profession."

The men stood and watched the water eddy around its old bed, like a dog circling before lying down to sleep.

"What will you do now?" Huxley asked. "Publish your paper, incomplete as it is?"

Roger sighed. "Frost still has my report, which has many of my original sketches. It's at the bottom of the lake now, where I hope it stays. In fact, I would like all of you to promise you won't speak of this city ever again. I want the small, black god to stay where it is."

The men nodded.

"What about the workers?" Gildston asked.

"I'll tell them the truth, which they'll embellish so much it will be like El Dorado and no serious archaeologist will ever look for the city again."

"But this find could have made your career, landed you a professorship?" Churchwood said.

Roger shrugged. "I've decided to switch professions to something a little less dangerous."

"Geologist?" Gildston said.

"I was thinking of joining the army." Roger said.

The men laughed.

"Actually," Roger said. "One of my classmates is digging in Egypt in the Valley of Kings. I'm thinking of joining him."

"Aren't you worried about the 'Curse of the Pharaohs'?" Churchwood asked.

"I've looked into the eyes of the small, black god. What's a dead pharaoh after that?"

=[]=

Caw Miller is a technical writer by trade and is beginning the adventure that is fiction writing. He is enjoying the journey so far, seeing new vistas and even into the depths of hell, and hopes that just over the horizon is a novel or two.

In Eden

Cherstin Holtzman

=[]=

Mortality is finite, but what would occur if man refused his own demise? For that matter, what about a town or an entire era? What if they simply weren't ready to lie down when that black clock strikes midnight? Such an idea seems oddly plausible when one thinks of the cowboy-infused myths of the old "Wild West." After all, who else inspires the phrase, hard livin' and harder dyin'? *Cherstin Holtzman brings us the next story,* In Eden. *Gritty and tough, this town ain't going down without a fight.*

=[]=

"Where life had no value, death, sometimes, had its price."
—Sergio Leone, 1965, *For a Few Dollars More*

The sheriff sat in a corner of the kitchen, clutching the stiffening body of his dead wife, while the sounds of small animals scurrying under the floorboards had him wondering how long it would be until they came gnawing for her. Pockets of dust floated across the wood floor in the fading light, and when he heard shuffling footsteps on his porch, he shifted his wife to the comfort of his left arm, pulling her close, aiming his revolver at the back door. The sheriff had known the West was dying for quite some time. A few days ago, he'd even mentioned it to his friend, Jed Nelson, who now, before the sheriff could pull the trigger, kicked in the door and blew him away.

=[]=

Some said they came from the dust, but that was too literal; the West just refused to die. There was a change, and the land spit them out to wander the streets, and in that moment, the desert was fertile again. The land birthed them, reanimated, and the West itself was resurrected. The town was happy, and the winds died down.

The town was named Eden, and the man walked down the middle of its hardpan street, layers of dust on his boots visible in the light of the moon. He paused once to wipe each boot clean on the back of his pant leg, but reconsidered, afraid of losing his balance or worse. Changes were taking place so rapidly within him that he could hardly keep up, and he was disturbed by the numbness in his limbs, his inability to feel pain.

Up ahead, ragtime music cascaded through an open window, music that was able to lift and float and fly, a moth on fragile, dusty wings. Its crisp treble sound reached infinitely further than the light which drew his attention, as if he were a winged insect. Dirty piano keys banged out a broken tune, and the sound was comfortable among the stars. They were all in there, this resurrected town, and he would deliver this message to his flock if it killed him.

He readjusted his hat, which no longer fit right. The constant rubbing was starting to chafe a break in the skin over his left brow, which he touched in dismay. He spit into the street, a hard pebble reflected in the moonlight, and he watched, offended, as it sat on the surface of the road, the land unwilling or unable to absorb the life he'd offered. As it was, he was tied to this earth, tethered to the land that held him tight in its fist, but as much as the West wanted to have its way with him, the sheriff knew it wasn't too late; he still had a job to do.

From his holster, he withdrew his revolver, the standard Smith and Wesson with which he'd been buried, and from his back pocket, he took a dirty red bandanna. He shook out as much dust as it would release, and he gave the gun a thoughtfully-quick polish, carefully rubbing the honed-ivory handle. He finished by shining his badge before pushing open the swinging doors to enter the packed saloon.

The music played on, its upbeat melody overpowered only by the smell that hung in the air. The West with its desert heat was no place for the bodies in this room, and the collective grin plastered on their faces as they turned to him bore the truth—there was still some knowledge inside each of them. Recognition slowly worked its way to the forefront of every slack-jawed grin, each gaping mouth attempting a unified smile.

He stood in the open doorway and tipped the brim of his hat with one-fingered authority, remembering his duty as sheriff to protect his people from the evil in Eden. The music quieted, slowed, stopped. The breathing of the dead had a faint, audible hum which hung in the stale air just beneath the lifeless odor of decay.

His presence alone commanding their attention, the sheriff rocked back on his heels, scanning the room. He cleared his throat with effort, not having used his voice much in the last few days.

"Listen up, folks."

It was the beginning to every speech he'd ever given this town, hundreds of times over. A long-ago cattle farmer by the name of McCurdy was the first to rise. The sheriff watched him lurch to his feet, watched the way what was left of Ted McCurdy's face contorted into a misshapen grin as he mouthed what could've been "Evenin', sheriff." The only sound that passed from the dead man's lips was a chilling, serpentine hiss.

The sheriff kept his hand on the barrel of his revolver and kept Ted McCurdy in his sight. He'd been the one to pronounce McCurdy and his family deceased just over half a year ago, found dead in their beds from dysentery.

He met their eyes, every one, as they sat at the wooden tables, packing the stools at the crowded bar.

"Townsfolk, listen up."

Blank eyes stared from gaping sockets. Lipless mouths hung open. There was Max Tillman, who'd owned the local grocery, three years in the ground from a rattlesnake bite. The sheriff had been with Max long before, at the death of his wife from a cancer deep in her belly, and she sat now next to her husband wearing fragments of the decayed dress in which she'd been buried.

He spoke to the McCurdys, and he spoke to the Tillmans. He spoke to all of them.

"What we've got here, folks, is some kind of plague." His voice grated, but he continued. "What we need is to fix it."

At this, there was an overall hiss of displeasure. *Easy now*, the sheriff reminded himself. *Tell it to them slowly. Let them take it in.*

"My job, as sheriff, is to make that happen."

The sound of breaking glass drew his attention to a far corner. It was common, the fighting, although what the dead had to argue about, the sheriff couldn't speculate. He drew his revolver and fired a round into the ceiling, raining down splinters of wood, but the townsfolk hardly moved in their seats.

With the acrid smell of gunpowder in the air, ears ringing, he saw for the first time the way the flesh was peeling from his hand. Bone at the outside of his thumb was exposed, same with the knuckle of his trigger finger, tendons holding the framework together, but for how long? He was their sheriff, and he had a job to do, a responsibility to get these people out of this infected town. They were his to save, and he needed to make it quick.

"Friends, we can't live like this anymore. This death, it's not right."

Behind the bar, one of the Lincoln brothers disagreed with a grunt, but the sheriff continued.

"This town, and we in it, is an abomination. I'm here to issue a warning. Tomorrow at dawn, I will burn this town."

His voice sounded different, muddled. Cracked.

"Burn it to the very core. Those of you wanting to escape, leave now and walk to the town limit."

He met their eyes once more, straightened his shoulders the best he could, chest out. "I can't promise you salvation, I can't promise what you'll find, but it's got to be better than this."

He looked to McCurdy, hoping for some sign of comprehension, but could read nothing on his old friend's face. Around the room, the empty stares showed nothing close to intellect. The sheriff stood his ground. He'd never been one for fancy speeches. He waited and watched as, one by one, the light of recognition he thought he'd seen in their eyes flickered out as they slowly resumed their activities: card games in the corner, whiskey at the bar. His speech forgotten, the piano started up again, keys reaching their familiar breakneck speed, and he watched his flock for another minute before he set home to prepare for morning.

The town had other plans.

As he walked down the center of the hardpan street, glass storefronts reflected moonlight from each direction and his left leg began to buckle; a hint of a limp at first, but the more he pushed on, the more focus it took to get his body to cooperate. His frustration grew. Alone, he heard laughter in the wind, coming in off the desert itself, and he was afraid. He paused in the street, looking behind him, still expecting retaliation against the words he'd just spoken to his town, *against* his town, but no one followed.

He looked down at his shirt, still buttoned, and he reached a gnarled finger inside, tracing the empty hole where the bullet had entered just below his ribcage, under a piece of protruding rib. He remembered the pain of his death, his last whispers to his already-dead wife: "Comfort me with thoughts of beyond. Quick—I'm losing grace." Maybe it had never made sense.

He died in her broken arms, but the town brought him back alone.

Halfway back home, he fell. He hit the ground hard with his elbow, landing on his side, dislocating his shoulder as a result of the fall. He felt the split, although he didn't want to believe it, but his arm hung loose in his shirt, still buttoned at the wrist. The West was winning.

The wings of a lone crow cut the air above his face, and the ebony bird landed just out of reach, onyx eyes focused on his own. He rolled onto his back and the wind howled, kicking dust and sand out of its way. He could still hear the piano in the distance, thin bones on ivory, and his thoughts started to stutter as his mind turned to ruin. The town lured him instead with its beauty, leaving him alone in the street on his back under the watchful gaze of a million stars, remembering the copper taste of fear in his original death.

The buildings moaned. The wind picked up, and the sheriff handled his revolver as if it was made of glass, but it was his failing body which gave him concern. One arm missing, he tried with everything in him to cock the revolver with his left hand, but his fingers snapped like twigs under the pressure, broken bones like bits of litter in the street.

From a nearby rooftop, a second crow answered the shrill call of the first. The sheriff lay in the dirt, waiting without giving up, but knowing in what was left of his mind that he'd failed and the town had won.

=[]=

The fire started later that night at the ammunition depot and continued into the day, the white-hot sun adding color to the blinding scorch of the town. McCurdy burned the hardware store next, and the bank after that, orange-red flames licking the sky. He remembered what the sheriff had said and, although he couldn't remember the timeline, he knew he'd done the right thing.

McCurdy watched from a distance, a wide-open grin stretched like plastic over his decaying face, as those who managed to make it over the town line fell to their rightful death as soon as they stepped out of Eden. Others were eventually consumed by fire, and as the town burned, the wind died, too.

McCurdy saw this and was glad, still smiling just before he stepped over the town line, falling in a heap with the masses.

=[]=

Cherstin Holtzman *grew up hating English (to which many a high school English teacher can attest), yet she always loved reading fiction with the stipulation she read on her own terms (which included any dark, speculative fiction she could get her hands on at garage sales, unbeknownst to her mother). After spending three years in the Army, she returned to southwest Florida where she found her love for writing. At 37, she is continuing her education, pursuing a degree in, ironically, English literature. Cherstin has finally settled down enough to earn the title of "wife," and is happily raising two sons and two dogs.*

WE ARE NOT THE FAVORED CHILDREN

Matthew Borgard

=[]=

When I read this next story, I was struck first by its raw sincerity. We Are Not the Favored Children *is provocative and prophetic and just well-written on so many levels. Civilizations may collapse, but so too do gods, replaced by evolving cultures and values. But what falls first, when faith and practicality conflict? Matthew Borgard examines this concept through Mansi'kala, a native maiden, as deities are irreverently replaced in the face of a changing world . . . and who are displeased at their loss of veneration.*

=[]=

"One of those dwellings, high, high in the rocks, is bigger than all the others. Utes never go there. It is a sacred place."
—Acowitz, preceding the discovery of the Ancient Pueblo Cliff Palace, 1885

I found him under the ground, at the bottom of my *kiva*, curled up in a ball. He had carved the words into his own arm, the knife still clutched in his lifeless fingers. Now that Tawa had risen into the morning sky and spread his light across my home, I could make out the message clearly: "We are not their favored children."

This man was Honovi. I did not know him well, only that he had married Sira not long ago, and they had recently produced a child. I had never once seen him here, in this kiva. He may have worshipped in his own—I could not say. But this kiva was mine, and I had never seen him here.

"He must be buried immediately," said Honovi's mother, blotting her tears with a frayed cloth. It was a reasonable thing to ask. He had not disturbed anything, but I could not help but feel uneasy about the message. And why had he bled himself here, of all places, when he could have just as easily returned his water to the earth in his own house?

"Not yet," I replied.

Honovi's mother and sister broke into loud weeping at this. My own family looked at me with questioning eyes, but I did not care. This man had defiled my home, and I wanted to know why.

I had requested that one of the cacique's assistants come to investigate the scene. I did not expect for the cacique himself to appear in my doorway, alone, with none of his usual sycophants. I would have thought Cacique Koa'ki had more important matters to attend to, but I suppose Honovi's message caught his attention as vividly as it did mine.

"I wish to speak to you alone, Kala," he said, using my childhood name. Anyone else, even my family, would have gotten a tongue lashing for speaking to me in such a manner. But he was the Cacique, so I ignored the disrespect.

"Of course, Cacique. If you wish, we may speak in the kiva."

He gave me a slight nod and we descended the ladder into the prayer chamber. The paintings of the *kachina* spirits eyed us as we entered. At the bottom, Koa'ki touched one knee to the ground and brushed his fingers against Honovi's arm. I peered over his shoulder. Even though the dried blood blurred the edges of the symbols, Honovi had carved into his flesh deep enough to retain the meaning.

"It is as you said." Koa'ki placed his hand over Honovi's face and lowered his eyelids.

"Did you think I had lied?"

Koa'ki stood, brushing the dirt from his robes. "No. Of course not. I apologize. You should not have been involved in this. The gods have used Honovi to send me a message."

"To send *you* a message? Then why did Honovi choose *my* kiva, Cacique?"

"Impossible to say." Koa'ki stepped past me to the ladder, placing a hand on one of rungs. "I suggest you put it out of your mind. We have more important worries."

"More important? What is more important than a dead man in my home?"

Koa'ki turned his head halfway around, presenting me with the side of his face. "Kala, you should pack your things. Prepare your family to travel."

"Travel? Travel *where?*"

The cacique ascended the ladder back the to surface, leaving me without an answer, but only for a short time. Later in the day, when Tawa watched us from straight above, Koa'ki addressed the village. We gathered in front of the festival altar, which hadn't seen use in months; there was little to celebrate. I brought my entire family: my older sister, Hwara, her husband, two young children, and one infant, cradled against her breast; my younger sister, Terala, not yet old enough to be wed; and my widowed mother, whose frail utterances of "what's happening?" I answered only with "wait and see."

Koa'ki climbed up the steps and onto the stone plateau, followed by a few solemn assistants in ornate robes. Most of them were old men, accompanied by a few women, just as old. When I was younger, I had asked the cacique—Koa'ki's predecessor—for permission to study with him. I was denied, not because I was a woman, or even because of my age, but because I had not rejected the old gods as they did.

"My people," said Koa'ki, spreading his arms out in front of him. "For many years, we have suffered through famine and disease. War and drought. We have looked to the spirits for an omen, a sign for us to follow. This morning, we were given one."

A murmur rose up from the crowd. I saw Hwara's husband, a short, timid man, whisper something in her ear, which she then relayed to me. "Is this about Honovi?"

I hadn't told any of them about Koa'ki's warning in the kiva; what good would it do? I shook my head and pursed my lips. "I don't know."

Koa'ki's booming voice drowned out mine. "Our friend Honovi took his own life to send us a message. The spirits no longer want us here. We were once blessed, but no longer. We must seek out a new home."

I expected my people to cry out in anguish. I expected them to fight back—violently, perhaps. I was too optimistic. I saw relief wash over the faces of those nearby, disgusting smiles spreading across their faces. My own family, who I hoped would feel betrayed as I did, joined the rest in excited chattering.

Terala tugged on my dress and sidled up behind me. "Where are we going?"

I could not answer her. My throat tightened, and I began to worry that my anger would suffocate me. I worked hard—sewing garments all day, firing pots instead of sleeping at night—to afford a home in the High Palace for my family. It had taken even longer to obtain our own kiva, so that I could pray to the old gods without any disapproving glares. The cacique wanted to take it all from us. I forced myself to breathe.

The people quieted, and Koa'ka continued. "We have no reason to stay here any longer. We have heard of the bounty in the south. Our ancestors have showed us our path. We leave with the dawn, tomorrow."

I spat on the ground. How dare he invoke our ancestors, the ones who built our homes and blessed us with rain and harvest? It was only when we turned from them that they revoked their gifts.

"We must get started," my mother said, limping back toward our home. "Only a single day... not much time..."

"Mother, stop." I placed my hand on her shoulder. "We're not going. We can't. You won't make the journey, you'll die."

My mother's lips parted, revealing the few stubs of remaining teeth left in her mouth. "If we don't leave, I'll die just as surely. There's no food left, and Lowlanders will only leave us be for so long." She patted my cheek, the same as when I was a child. "You must trust the kachina. If it is meant to be, they will protect me. If it is my time, they will take me into the sky with your father."

I glanced at my sisters, who nodded in agreement. Hwara's girl-child clutched her spirit doll to her chest and turned her eyes away. I often voiced my disapproval of the kachina figures, and the children had learned not to flaunt them in front of me. It wasn't as though I disbelieved in the spirits, but to me, the dolls represented a desertion of the old gods. Wasn't there room for both? But now was not the time to reopen those wounds, so I gave the girl a smile, knelt down and kissed the top of her head.

"Hwara," I said, standing. "Take them to our home. Begin gathering our things. I shall be along shortly."

Hwara shifted the infant from her right side to her left and clucked her tongue at me. "What are you planning?"

"I just want to speak with the cacique. Perhaps I can change his mind, or at least get more time."

Hwara snapped her fingers at the two older children and pointed them toward our home. Her husband, Terala, and Mother followed after them.

"Have you considered," said Hwara, "that none of us *want* you to change his mind?"

I did not answer her, so she turned from me and walked away.

Koa'ka was still conversing with some of our people. I hoped that a few of them possessed the same concerns as me, but instead, they seemed only to be praising the cacique's holiness and begging for blessings to keep their families safe. I waited for my turn, as I did not desire to speak to Koa'ka amidst all the adoration. I approached him when he was at last alone. He pretended not to see me, so I spoke first.

"Cacique Koa'ka. May I speak with you?"

He took a deep breath. "We have already spoken, Kala."

I had bitten my tongue long enough. "My name is Mansi'kala, Cacique." It was a name I'd earned in my consecration, and with all the things he wished to take from me, I would not allow him to have this one.

"Of course," he replied. "I apologize. I prefer Kala. It is an elegant name."

"But it is not mine."

Koa'ka snorted and waved his hand at the ground. "What did you want to say to me?"

"You should reconsider your plan. We cannot leave our home."

Koa'ka reached out to touch my arm, so I took a step back. He frowned and rubbed his chapped lips. "Our home is where the spirits watch over us, and they no longer watch over us here. Our people have seen it. Your family has seen it. Your cacique has seen it, Mansi'kala. It is time to move on. The spirits demand it."

"You say the spirits wish this of us, but you refuse to speak to all of them!"

Koa'ka's nostrils flared. "I will never understand why you insist on clinging to the old gods. You are like a wild horse; stubborn, unwilling to accept change when it is demanded of you. This is why you haven't found a husband, I think."

I felt the tips of my nails cutting into the palm of my hand. Were this anyone but the cacique, I would have struck him down with a single fist.

"I have not *found* a husband because I do not *want* a husband. I have a family, Koa'ka. I work hard for them, and for my people." I thrust my hand forward and Koa'ka flinched, but instead of striking him, I flicked one of the leather strips hanging from his ceremonial headband.

"I made this, Cacique, because your wife cannot tan skins or sew. I taught your nephew to use a bow after the rest of your family decided he was no good." Koa'ka began to protest, but I raised my voice and continued. "I have plenty of work to do and people to support without a husband."

The face on Koa'ka's skin tightened and a bulging vein appeared above his left eye. "Do what you want, woman! For all the responsibility you think you have, I have more! It is my duty to ensure our people's survival! If you believe the old gods have a better way, then go to your kiva and speak to them!"

He was goading me. He knew his words would infuriate me.

"The old gods do not visit the High Palace anymore!" I said.

"Precisely," said Koa'ka. "They do not speak to us any longer."

"If you would only send a few men to the Low Temple . . . "

"Out of the question!" Koa'ka raised a finger to my eyes. "The Lowlanders hunt at the Temple now. I will not send what few able men we have left to die on a quest to tell us what we already know. We are not wanted here."

I folded my arms across my chest. "If you will not send them, I will go alone." The Lowlanders did not frighten me. If I was right, the old gods would protect me. If I was not, then I was already lost.

"You wish to abandon your family and your people for this?" Koa'ka mumbled a curse to himself. "If you are so selfish, perhaps you are not as deserving of your name as you think. Perhaps you are a child after all."

I watched Koa'ka leave. I was filled with such blinding rage that I could do nothing except stand in the courtyard and feel Tawa's rays burning my skin. Tawa. The god of light. The god that my people no longer believed in. I watched the sky for hours, hoping for some sort of sign. But Tawa simply fell toward the horizon, as he did every day, lighting the heavens on fire. Dusk drew near, and I had no answer. If there was to be any chance of saving my home, it would be in the Lowlands.

The High Palace was unusually quiet tonight. Normally the children would be taking advantage of the last of the daylight, but a malaise seemed to have possessed the village. My people should have been making the most of their last night here but, instead, they were cowering in their houses. If this is what had become of us, perhaps we no longer deserved our home.

Inside my own house, my family had arranged our possessions in a pile. Put together, they looked so small and meaningless. A few sets of clothing, some utensils, some kachinas, a pair of bows and accompanying arrows. Water. A few sacks of vegetables, nuts and grains. This is what my life was worth.

I thanked my sisters for their help, and Hwara's husband as well, though he only grimaced in response. He had never liked living with me, though he never voiced displeasure with eating my food or sleeping under my shelter.

"Mother's already gone to bed," said Hwara. "And the children as well."

"Good," I replied. "You should sleep too. If Koa'ka wants you to leave at dawn, you should be well rested."

Hwara glanced at her husband, who nodded. It was a common gesture between the two. It meant that Hwara wanted to speak with me alone.

"What about you?" she asked. "You're coming with us."

"I don't know. I will try to come back, but I don't know."

"Come back? Come back from where?" Hwara straightened her back. She liked to flaunt her height when she was angry with me.

"I am going to the Low Temple."

Hwara's eyes widened. "Why would you do such a thing?"

"I must speak with the old gods before I leave. I cannot walk away from our home without knowing the truth."

"The *truth*?" Hwara stood on her toes, towering over me. "The truth is that we don't have enough food to feed our people. What other truth matters?"

I needed to find for myself the meaning of the words Honovi carved into his skin, but I could not tell Hwara that. She accepted things too easily. If the cacique said the sky was brown, then it was brown.

"I don't know. But I have to go." I started to gather what I would need for the night. Nuts to quiet my stomach, a waterskin to quench my thirst, and one of the two bows to fend off any of the Lowlanders I might find.

"No," said Hwara. Her eyes started to water. "I forbid this. Mother forbids it."

"You cannot forbid me to do anything," I said, strapping a bag of arrows over my shoulder.

"I am your elder!"

"In age only, sister." I tied the food and water to my belt, then looked into Hwara's face. Tear streaks cut into the dirt caked onto her skin. "I am sorry, Hwara. But I must do this."

Hwara moved quickly toward me, and I raised my arms for fear that she would strike me. Instead, my sister wrapped her arms around me and squeezed me into her chest. "Please, Kala. Please don't leave us. What would we do without you?"

I stood paralyzed by Hwara's sudden affection. She sobbed into my shoulder, pleading for me not to leave. At last, I circled an arm around my sister and kissed the side of her face.

"If I don't come back, you will do what you've always done. You'll be a better daughter to Mother than I ever was. You'll be a better wife and mother than I could ever be." Though I'd always considered myself more capable than my older sister, I still looked up to her, in a certain way. I had never told her.

"Momma," came a voice from the room behind us. Hwara released me and turned. Behind her, I could see her girl-child, Ankti.

"Child, you should be asleep," Hwara said, turning from me to kneel in front of the girl. "What's wrong?"

"Is Aunt Kala leaving?" The child looked at me with puffy red eyes.

"Just for the night," I told her. "I will be back in the morning."

She sniffled and walked past her mother to hug my leg. "Do you promise?"

"I promise, little one."

Ankti placed a finger in her mouth, and with her other hand, she held her kachina doll up to my face. This one had black skin, elaborate clothing, and a small cloth facsimile of a bow attached to its hand. "Will you take Cha'kwaina?" Ankti asked me. "He'll protect you."

Cha'kwaina was a spirit of exploration, not a protector at all. I felt no kinship to the doll; the grinning face and careless posture reminded me, more than anything, of our cacique. But I felt kinship to my niece, and so I took the doll and tied it to my dress. "Thank you, Ankti. I'm sure he'll keep me safe."

Hwara took her child back to the sleeping den then returned. Her melancholy gave way to a dull, emotionless expression. "When will you leave?"

"Now," I said, checking the knots on my belt one last time.

"Be safe, sister."

"And you." I stepped close to her, forcing her to look into my eyes. "If I do not return in the morning, you must leave without me. Do you understand? You cannot wait for me. You must go with our people."

"But you're coming back," she said simply.

"Yes. But if I don't, you must promise."

"If you insist," said Hwara, crossing her arms. "I promise."

"Thank you." I took my sister's hand in mine, squeezed it, and walked out into the night.

My eyes adjusted quickly to the darkness, and I was thankful to be blessed with a cool breeze. Most of the paths in the Lowlands had been erased years ago, but the faint few that remained were enough to guide my way. I encountered little in the way of wildlife, which was to be expected. It was hard enough to find game even when looking. At one point, I heard a rustling in the grass. Afraid that the Lowlanders had spotted me, I stuck my back to one of the large, wilted spruce trees and peered from over my shoulder. After a few terse minutes, I spotted the culprit: a famished weasel, no doubt hunting for his dinner. I tried to offer him a few of my nuts, but he dashed off as soon as he saw me. Poor creature. The gods had been as cruel to the animals as they had to us.

I continued on, treading for hours through the water-starved grasslands until I reached the village of our ancestors. My grandfather's generation had left it behind when the Lowlanders began their war, and worn bricks that had once been buildings were all the remained. The Lowlanders hadn't taken it for their own, or if they did, it had been a brief occupation, as there was no reason to stay after the creeks dried up and the herds moved on.

The village itself sat in the shadow of a large hill. This, I knew, was my destination. I had only been here a few times, as a girl. My father brought me and my sisters here to show us the place where our ancestors worshipped. It was my father who told me never to forget the old gods.

The entrance to the Low Temple, a cave in the side of the hill, had been sealed with several large boulders to stop the Lowlanders from getting inside the sanctified chamber. As my father told it, the plan didn't work; the Lowlanders simply moved the boulders to their current resting place beside the entrance and looted the few offerings my people left behind.

As I stepped over one of the large rocks, I again heard movement among the nearby grass. At first, I assumed it was the weasel, back to take me up on my offer, but then I heard the voices barking into the wind.

Lowlanders.

As quickly and silently as possible, I ducked into the Temple. I held my breath but kept my eyes open. The voices grew louder, and soon I saw a faint light creep into the cave. A moment longer and I saw them—five Lowlanders with torches and spears, a hunting party by the look of it. I could not say why they would be out at this time, other than to guess that they were as starved as we were. They didn't notice me, and they didn't pay any attention to the Temple. They passed by and soon the light of their torches faded into the distance. I exhaled and rolled onto my back, letting my nerves calm before progressing any further.

The Temple, if it could still be called that, was dusty and overgrown. Near the back, I could make out the faint outline of a small, cylindrical stone pedestal. I put my hands to its surface and found several large cracks running throughout. Any more force and I would have broken it entirely. From one of the pouches on my dress, I took a handful of seeds and placed them on the top of the altar. Then, using the tip of my finger to sort them, I picked the largest of them and placed it between my teeth. I sat, closed my eyes, and waited.

I focused on the image of Honovi. I focused on the message in his arm. I focused on the memory of my father, which had grown fainter and fainter as the years went by. My body tensed and my muscles relaxed as the breath of the gods filled my veins.

I saw Honovi. He sat, legs crossed, in front of me, a serene smile on his face. I reached out to touch his arm. The message was gone, and his skin was as smooth as mine.

"Why?" I asked. "What did you see that frightened you?"

Honovi's smiled widened, but he did not answer me.

"Show me," I said, to the spirits as much as to Honovi. "Help me see the way."

And suddenly, the wind left my lungs. I coughed, grasped my throat, and fell to my knees. My vision blurred. I reached out toward Honovi, but he made no movement to help me. My eyelids fell, and the world went black.

In the darkness, I felt a powerful hatred fill me. I heard otherworldly voices in my head, though I could not make out their words. These were not the kachina spirits that visited us in the High Palace. These were the old gods: frightful, commanding.

"Show me the way," I repeated, gasping to try to regain my breath. "Help us."

There is no path.

I panted and flailed in the darkness.

There is no way.

I held my arms against myself and shivered. A chilled despair overwhelmed me.

You are not our favored children.

My blood ran cold. This is what Honovi had seen. The old gods had visited the High Palace, but they had not brought a message of peace. I was filled with such devastating anguish at that moment that I wanted nothing more than to lay on my back and die. It felt as though all that was good had left the world.

The voice only laughed at me. It taunted me with images of the High Palace in ruins. I saw bodies, hundreds of them, and many more sick and dying. I saw our lands, dried out and desolate.

You are not our favored children.

I cried out for the voice to stop. As my screams grew louder, the visions faded. The voice dissipated, repeating its warning again and again. The old gods had abandoned us, just as we had abandoned them.

When I opened my eyes, the Low Temple had returned just as I had left it. I found myself on the ground, shivering like a frightened animal. I lay there for a long while, reflecting on the message the old gods had sent me. I understood now why Honovi acted as he did. There was no right path for me to take. Nothing I could do to help my people.

As I rolled onto my side, I felt Cha'kwaina, my niece's kachina, roll with me. It landed on the ground next to me, still attached to my dress. I picked it up and stared into the slits that acted as eyes.

"And what about you?" I asked the doll. "What do you have to offer? Do you hate us as well?"

The kachina didn't answer. He simply continued to smile, taking pleasure in my pain. I gripped him hard, tore him from my dress, and tossed him against the rock wall. He hit less forcefully than I'd imagined, landing on the ground with nothing more than a faint stirring of dust.

I turned my head from it and began to hear a strange laughter. I felt my pulse quicken, afraid that the gods had returned to torture me. But this wasn't the same vile laughter from before. Instead, it was the high-pitched, mischievous laughter of a child.

Behind me, I saw Cha'kwaina float up from where I'd discarded him. A peculiar jade glow surrounded the doll, illuminating the cave and forcing me to shield my eyes. I had seen the kachina spirits appear before, in the kiva of the High Palace. But not like this. Never like this.

With his stubby, fingerless arms, Cha'kwaina raised his bow. At once, a green arrow of light appeared against the string. The doll pulled it back and fired it into the wall behind him. The light from the arrow splattered against the rock like spilled dye and began to spread out to all corners of the cave. The light enveloped me, and when my eyes adjusted, I was no longer in the temple. This vision did not fill me with dread, but with confusion. I saw layers of grey bricks piled up to create massive structures that stretched into the sky. I saw the ground layered with black rock. I saw great beasts of shining colored stone moving past me with daunting speed. I saw many people, but they were not like me. They had pale skin and wore strange clothes. Above me, I saw Tawa rising into a shimmering blue sky.

"What is this?" I asked Cha'kwaina.

He only tittered in response. This vision seemed no more useful than the one the old gods had sent me.

I pointed to the pale people walking beside us. "Are these your chosen people? Are these the ones you discarded us for?"

Cha'kwaina raised a single stubbed arm and pointed behind me. I turned, following the doll's gesture, and saw a pair of figures behind me.

My heart pounded. Though they were dressed in the same strange clothes as the pale men, I would have recognized them anywhere: Hwara and Ankti.

No, not quite. The faces were different—a lowered eyebrow, a wider lip—but I still knew them. They were family. They were my people. My legacy.

"Is this real?" I asked the kachina. "The old gods showed me a different path. Which is true?"

And the answer came to me. *Both.* My blood flowed in my sisters. They would survive, even without the favor of the old gods. If they no longer needed us, then we no longer needed them.

"Thank you," I said, tears falling from my eyes. "Thank you for showing me."

Somewhere behind me, I heard more voices crying out. I did not let them distract me. I kept my eyes on the child, watching as she stepped past me and walked, hand-in-hand with her mother, into one of the large buildings. I wanted to follow her, but I found that my feet would not move me forward. The voices grew louder. One last laugh from the kachina, and it fell to the ground, extinguishing the vision around us.

I was back in the Temple now. The Lowlander hunters stood in the mouth of the cave, balancing their spears deftly in their hands. The front one shouted a curse at me. I had nothing to say in reply.

In my head, I saw the spear flying through the air even before it left his hand. I slithered backward and the spearhead missed my thigh by only a hair. I pulled an arrow from the quiver on my back, nocked it into my bow, and fired. I was not the best archer, especially at night, but from this distance I did not need to be. The arrow pierced his neck and he fell to the ground.

I did not have time to savor the kill. Before I could reach for another arrow, two of the other hunters flung their weapons toward me. One missed, clanging uselessly against the wall. The other sailed into my shoulder.

I screamed. A haze fell over my vision, and the pain in my arm prevented it from reaching for my quiver. With my other hand, I retrieved an arrow and fired it. This one entered the leg of one of the hunters, but it seemed like a shallow wound. One of the remaining men stepped forward, appraised me for a moment, and threw his spear. To my surprise, I hardly felt it impale my chest.

As I slumped against the Temple's altar, I felt a jostling on my legs. Cha'kwaina had appeared in my lap. I picked him up and squeezed his soft wool skin against my face. The warmth left my body, and I took comfort in his.

=[]=

Matt Borgard is a software engineer living in Austin with one cat and one wife. He's been writing his whole life, and is still not entirely convinced that the writers of The Nightmare Before Christmas didn't steal the film's plot from his elementary school notebooks. He enjoys reading, writing, and partaking in video games, and does not enjoy that it is becoming increasingly difficult to do all three simultaneously. He has been published in the worlds of academia and journalism, but is a newcomer to fiction.

Rebirth In Dreams

A.J. French

=[]=

An accomplished editor in his own right, A.J. French adds a distinctive contribution to this anthology: Dreams, astral projections, and drugs—a perfect recipe for any mysterious fiction concoction. In fact, when I read this, I thought if Hunter S. Thompson had collaborated with H.P. Lovecraft, this would be their brainchild. The selection, Rebirth in Dreams, *is a journey in which the destination is quite unknown. It is a path of self-exploration, one of transcendental knowledge, and of discovering ancient secrets. And mezcal . . . lots and lots of it.*

=[]=

Dreams have much to tell us about the existential condition of *being.* The native peoples, which some foolishly refer to as savages, know this well. The Aborigines of Australia, the indigenous tribes of the Americas, the shamanistic wizards of the Caribbean Islands—these cultures ascribe transcendental knowledge to their dreams, and rightly so. They even built this knowledge into their grand ancient cities, whose crumbling ruins now remain like esoteric signposts, pointing us toward the origins of the universe.

I became obsessed with the subject during my teenage years. My fascination drew me into the realm of rare books and bizarre records. Away from my fellow human beings, I retreated into a world of symbols, pagan rites, and paths better left untrod. Even after I graduated from college, my appetite remained unsated. This lingering interest in dreams affected my work life, ensuring that I remain a bachelor indefinitely.

Each night was an opportunity for me to conduct some new experiment, which I meticulously recorded in my dream journal, not knowing what to make of the strange visions. Through study I learned of certain individuals who had found a doorway in their dreams, an escape from endless suffering, a portal to their higher selves.

This I wanted.

But where to begin?

I had one idea. Some of these individuals employed substances— narcotics—specific herbs and plants which possessed consciousness-altering capabilities, to achieve their end. Cannabis was among these. Also absinth, opium, and peyote, as well as a vine from Amazonia called Ayahuasca.

According to *The Living Torah* and various other sacred Hebrew texts, the cannabis plant was first found growing on King Solomon's grave, and was therefore reputed to impart godlike wisdom to anyone who ingested it. Peyote, a cactus, apparently took its eater into the spirit world, and the session of the opium eater was akin to that of a waking dream.

I inquired about getting my hands on some of these, and was told of a shop on the edge of town, purportedly run by a local Mexican witch.

I decided to visit her shop on a Tuesday.

It was a shabby tenement half-submerged in shadows, located in the back alley behind two derelict buildings. I arrived just past noon.

Pushing through the front door, I disturbed a set of bells, prompting their chiming. I took myself past dusty shelves, taxidermic animals, mason jars storing herbs and powders, into a chamber alight with glowing candles.

Strange painted effigies, whose origins evaded me, occupied various alters and shrines. The idols had large whitish faces and oversized black eyes. And teeth, too: square, yellow, beaver-like teeth. In some, I noticed a hand-wrapped cigar poking from their mouths. In others, glasses full of foul yellow liquid sat at their feet, collecting mold.

I perused the shelves and display cases, my intellect fully engaged, astounded at the variety of occult relics cached here. Many were accompanied by folded white papers, on which was written the item's price. Even the cost seemed relatively agreeable.

In one corner, I came across an effigy four feet tall, dressed in numerous pairs of pants, shirts, scarves, and a huge hat. This slightly grotesque idol—grotesque because of its severely emaciated body and grinning-bone smile—puffed on a cigar and even had a drink in its hands. More cigar packs and drink glasses cluttered its feat, as if they had been discarded there on purpose. *Like offerings.*

I discovered the witch by the cash register, fussing over a set of bones and stroking a gangly cat.

"Excuse me," I said.

She looked up; her hair, tangled around her shoulders, was black with gray streaks. Pockmarks covered her face and boils festered on her neck. Something was amiss in her eyes—they were too white, almost pulpy. Swatting the cat, she shooed it from the counter and turned to me.

"It's you," she replied.

This was a surprise. "You know me?"

"You came once before. You'll come once again... though never in the same incarnation. What do you seek this time?"

"Sleep—and dream—inducing potions," I said, maintaining my air of authority. "I am interested in escaping my smaller self through dreams."

She placed the set of bones into a burlap sack, shoving them under the counter. "You're in luck, boy. Today I received a shipment of special potions from Mexico. You want to lose yourself into dreams? This drink will get the job done."

Intrigued, I let her lead me to a dark room choked with books and strange devices. It was something like the greenhouses recently made popular. Glass windows lined the ceiling, green vines dangling therefrom. Plants in pots and plants in troughs, some uprooted and strewn across the tables, scattering soil like blood. A constricting smell hung thick in the air, like moist dirt. It reminded me of the cemetery after it rains.

In the center of the room, displayed on a flat piece of stone, was a grotesque idol. A skeletal figure wearing a white robe, carrying a scythe in one hand and a small globe in the other. Its face was like the devil in female form, with the grinning rictus of a weasel.

"How about this?" I asked. "Is it for sale?"

Chuckling, she joined me by the idol. Her close proximity allowed for a closer look. The idol was shriveled in a way that was repulsive, and yet potent. The desire to scratch at some unseen itch accompanied her, for her robes and shawl rustled continuously, as if myriad insects crawled about underneath. I even saw a curious black worm coiling up out of her hair.

"You want nothing to do with that, Señor," she said. "That is Señora de las Sombras—Lady of the Shadows. She is death. Her scythe represents the killing. Her globe, Death's dominion. No, not unless you are looking to kill or be killed do you need that." She glared at me, eyes like ice under a night sky. "Come along. What you seek is over in this direction."

We came to a big wooden crate with a black cat lying on top. Beside the cat, the word *Oaxaca* was stamped in bold black letters on the lid. The condition of the crate implied that it had endured a long journey.

Shooing the cat, the witch pried the lid with a slanted iron bar, revealing a treasure trove of glass bottles filled with amber liquid. The bottles had been packed along with a slew of dried corn husks.

"What is it?" I said.

"Mezcal."

"Hm?"

"Agave brewed from the rugged fields of the Oaxaca Valley. Guaranteed to drive your mind from realty. And look," she held a bottle to the light as she spoke, "a grave-worm with every purchase."

The little drowned invertebrate floated up through the liquid as she shook the bottle; it crested for a moment, swirled, then dropped and resettled on the bottom.

"Grotesque," I said. "What on earth is it? An opiate? Why include the rancid worm?"

She grimaced at my words. "This is the finest, most mystical alcohol the New World has to offer, amigo. And as for the worm, each one was hand-dug from a cemetery in Oaxaca. They're what put the magic into the potion."

"I'm not much for drinking."

"How do you plan to escape your smaller self if you can't indulge a little experimentation? I assure you, a robust glass of this before bed and you'll be whisked to faraway lands."

"Then I'll take a bottle, thank you."

She grinned, displaying a maw of misaligned teeth, and clasped her hands. "Excellent."

=[]=

That night, I sat looking at the gold bottle on the table. A fire crackled behind me. A soft breeze wound through the smokestacks outside the window, producing a monotone howl. My cats, Faust and Fauna, lolled on the shaggy gray hearthrug. I got a glass from the cabinet and poured myself two fingers of mezcal.

"Here's to consciousness alteration," I said, without really knowing what I meant.

The cats peered up from the floor. I swallowed my allotment in a gulp and began to cough and gag. The burn was severe. I rushed to the sink for water. The bloody stuff tasted like a graveyard: earthy and damp. I decanted another glassful, just for good measure, and retired to the blankets of my armchair. I read for a while by firelight, then fell asleep.

The visions came hard and without mercy. My dreams had never been so vivid. I lost all concept of material existence, thoroughly convinced I was in another land.

It started with a group of us climbing a mountain range. We had been nomads for a time, but somehow I knew that we now traveled toward our new home. Families toiled across rocky terrain. We soiled our clothes, as wild trees extended around us.

After cresting one hill, we dropped into a ravine, only to find ourselves climbing another hill. The presence of oak and pine trees seemed to mark our progression through the unyielding landscape. At length, we stopped to make camp.

As the stars came out, I stood by the edge of a cliff, the sprawling campsite at my rear. Little fires glowed between canvas tents. I heard people talking and laughing. Someone was playing a violin. Yet their merriment did not concern me, for my sight had been arrested by a looming presence in the distance. I first thought it to be a great beast lumbering toward us, but with time it became clear that the image was stationary.

I realized it was actually a pair of images; two dark blotches probing the sky. Twin towers erected on the horizon, whose architecture appeared bizarrely alien yet unquestionably human. Silvery columns mounting up and up, faceted with innumerable pane-glass windows, with stars circling around their dreadful apexes.

Were these towers our destination? And was that smoke I saw rising?

I awoke in the armchair, sweating, entangled in blankets, oblivious as to my whereabouts. Slowly, however, the vision uncurled from my mind and I regained composure. The fire had died down and the cats had scooted closer to retain the heat. The room glowed dimly. My mouth still tasted of the mezcal and I was exhausted. Quickly, before suffering a fugue, I recorded the vision in my journal and retired to the bedchamber.

The next day I reread the entry but felt wholly detached from it. It was like something someone else had written. I had no memory of it. Though glad to have achieved the vision, I lamented that I could not remember it.

I supposed the journal entry was evidence enough. Still, the description of the towers sent shivers up my spine.

I repeated the process the following night. This time I took three glasses of mezcal. Was that too much? I had to admit, I was developing an affinity for the stuff. Only a quarter of the bottle remained . . . also that floating, wretched worm. Soon I'd be totally out. I decided it was good the witch possessed so many bottles, for I would have to return and purchase another.

Nestled in my armchair, I awaited sleep while listening to the hypnotic noises of the fire. Faust and Fauna had curled into my lap. Soon my head reclined and my eyelids drooped, and I was transported out to the sea.

I was alone on a thrashing ocean, with a carpet of blue spread out beneath me. Seagulls wheeled overhead, issuing their forlorn cries. Somehow I was perched atop the water like a messiah. A gold sun rode the sky, mitigated by groups of silent, scudding clouds. I saw no land, only row upon row of white, spuming waves.

I began walking across the water. It was strange to feel nothing under my feet. I bestrode fluffy currents of air and evoked God's mightiness, taking great pleasure in each calculated step. If Jesus had done it then I could do it: any man could do it. We were all created in His image and likeness—we were all part God.

I awoke in a state of peace, still sensing the undulant water in my stomach and the cushions of air beneath my feet. I remembered my vision and didn't need to record it. I even translated it: all men (and women) are children of God, possessing the same powers Jesus Christ possessed. We must only wake and realize it.

Pleased, I stretched in the armchair and yawned serenely. Morning poured in through the uncurtained window. The fire was out, and the cats were meowing to be fed. I had slept the entire night.

=[]=

When I returned to the witch's hut, she was not glad to see me.

"What the devil are you doing here?" she snapped. "It's only been two days."

I chuckled. "You know exactly why I'm here."

"You're after more mezcal. How quickly you abandon your temperance." She was stocking a jar of herbs onto a shelf, straining to reach its highest location. The jar slipped and shattered on the floor. A puff of smoke with a demonic image arose briefly. It was a face painted white, skeletal in appearance, with hollow eyes and square teeth, biting on a cigar and sipping a glass of mezcal. The image intensified, waved, then faded from sight.

"Maximón, take it," she muttered.

I stepped forward. "What's that you say?"

Her impatient hand gestures urged me away. "Is nothing. Is not for the likes of you."

"I see. Well, I'll have you know that I gladly indulge intemperance for the sake of altered consciousness."

"Have you finished the bottle? Did you consume the grave-worm?"

Here I faltered. "No . . . not exactly."

"I refuse to give you more until you do. The grave-worm induces the strongest visions. Return when you've experienced those."

At that point she forgot I was in the room and went on with stocking her shelves.

As I headed for the door, turning on imperious heels, I replied, "Yes, I most certainly will. You needn't worry about that," and left the shop.

=[]=

Night found me contemplating the bottle again. I watched the invertebrate grave-worm ascend and descend through the honey-colored liquid. My cats looked on from the hearthrug, heads cocked. At last I drew the curtains, and sat in mounting silence.

To eat a worm? Such a thing was unheard of! No cultivated gentleman would stoop so low.

But I was above cultivation, wasn't I? I was on the brink of revelation, venturing into unknown landscapes possessed of amorphous kernels of true knowledge. I wanted universal wisdom. I wanted power and ascension. I wanted refuge from this dreary mortal coil.

I wanted escape from my smaller self. The part of me that felt lonely some nights, that felt like an outcast, and was bitter for having to live in a world where men had ceased to think.

If to learn the purpose and physiology of the universe meant biting the head off a grave-worm . . . then I was prepared to bite.

I lifted the bottle and depleted it, wincing as the worm bumped its way down my gullet. I started to cough, to become nauseated. I bent forward, resting my hands on my knees, but the feeling passed.

Then I was completely drunk. I fell into the chair, studying the ceiling, imagining the worm in my stomach. Soon the acids would take effect and break it apart, absorb it, filter it through the rest of my body. How long did the process take? I didn't have a chance to wonder: in a minute I was asleep.

But something was different. I hovered above my body, observing the passed-out figure in the armchair. My head was back, my eyes closed, my mouth ajar. I didn't seem to be breathing. My body looked so pathetic without me inside it, merely a . . . husk.

Because I was a specter, I phased through the roof rather easily and shot into the star-strewn sky. A sea of buildings and lights unfolded below me. Streets appeared insignificant and narrow. A gathering of smoke rose from every chimney, and a bulbous moon held up the darkness. In the distance, a string of mountains, dark but visible, cut the horizon in twain.

I could go anywhere; I was free. The world was mine!

The words came too soon, for the next moment I was soaring up at a mind-numbing speed. I tried to scream but nothing came out. The world fell away like a trapdoor—smaller and smaller and smaller, then bigger and bigger and bigger—until colors and topography had blended together. Deep blue ocean crept up at the sides, soon encompassing everything. The earth pulled away from me. I was carried into outer space, and there I saw the whole planet rolling slowly and timelessly in its lonely black void.

It reminded me of my *smaller self.*

When the mad journey ended, I remained suspended in place, the stars twinkling about me. The nuclear sun burned nearby, but I dared not seek it out. Instead, I turned the other way, away from Earth, toward the cosmos, and went insane instantly. The higher spiritual realms were too much for me to comprehend. They filled my brain, wiped it clean, and I forgot my name, my story, my life. I became a part of that Godlike blackness: empty, beautiful, alone.

A fire ignited within—flaming, flaming, flaming. Pain enveloped me and I exploded outward, bursting into ever-widening circles. Pieces of me scattered and were gone, but my core, my soul, remained intact, glinting like a fiery ember. I became aware of others burning around me, for now I was not so alone.

My transformation was complete. I had succeeded in killing my smaller self and was reborn in the fire like a rising Phoenix. I had become the triangle, the triad, the converging balance of the three, the fourth whole.

I am still here, riding my cosmic vessel through oceans of time. Drinking my perpetual glass of mezcal, smoking my cigar, displaying my square wooden teeth.

Perhaps I am a star, you tell me. Go outside tonight and look for my painted white face, my black eyes, and my crooked clown grin. I promise to be blinking ever so brightly . . . just for you.

=[]=

Aaron J. French, also writing/editing as A.J. French, is an affiliate member of the Horror Writers Association. His work has appeared in many publications, including D. Harlan Wilson's The Dream People, *issue #7 of* Black Ink Horror, *the* Potter's Field 4 *anthology from Sam's Dot Publishing,* Something Wicked *magazine, and* The Lovecraft eZine. *He also has stories in the following anthologies:* Zombie Zak's House of Pain Anthology; Ruthless: An Extreme Horror Anthology *with introduction by Bentley Little;* Pellucid Lunacy *edited by Michael Bailey;* M is for Monster *compiled by John Prescott; and* 2013: The Aftermath *by Pill Hill Press. He recently edited* Monk Punk, *an anthology of monk-themed speculative fiction with introduction by D. Harlan Wilson, and* The Shadow of the Unknown, *an anthology of nü-Lovecraftian fiction with stories from Gary A. Braunbeck and Gene O'Neill.*

WHALE OF A TIME

Gitte Christensen

=[]=

Set in a future of prim etiquette and Victorianesque reason, the following story reads a bit like a sensationalist harlequin novel. It is cheeky and smart and may even be considered a "cautionary tale." Heed well our aquatic friends, as the final days of man's dominance on Earth are explored. Gitte Christensen, whose crisp prose is as fun to read as it is thoughtful, captains her characters through an underwater world, finding both peril and romance in a Whale of a Time.

=[]=

Chapter One: Introduction

No one would have believed in the last years of the twenty-second century that keen intelligences were scrutinizing humans on a daily basis as we went about our petty affairs. But newly launched into a golden age of reason, prosperity, and individualism, we had no idea that we would soon find ourselves standing amongst the ruins of our former greatness.

As a prominent player in recent events, I feel obliged to record my memories for the edification of forthcoming generations.

Let me begin with my credentials. I am Dr. Matilde Mayflower Rothbilden-Vandershaft. Due to my infamy, you doubtless recognize both my Real Name and former User Name (Lady Suzanne Claire de Lune). Indeed, you may feel that you already know me intimately, and possibly that is why you are reading this particular record from the Earth Archives, for as the Executive Director of the Earnest Rothbilden-Vandershaft Institute for Understanding Resurrected Cetaceans (ERNIURC), a User Group originally devoted to the Cousteauist Lifestyle, I often, as a child, was featured in my father's documentaries, usually swimming with our whales or cavorting on our exclusive beaches.

You may also have seen adaptations of the Great Conflict with my character portrayed by various beautiful actresses. In renderings such as *Where Whales Sleep* and *Soldiers of Poseidon*, my team and I are depicted as heroes who strove in vain to warn the world of the coming war. Even the comedy *Diving Dimwits* interprets our actions as those of bumbling but well-meaning fools defeated by the bulwarks of human bureaucracy.

Conversely, to this very day, the multiple media presentations distributed by User Groups that were once our rivals mostly misrepresent us as traitors to the human race.

The truth, however, is neither as gallant nor as despicable as either of these versions.

At this point, I feel I must explain that although ERNIURC had indeed been fanatically Cousteauist during my father's time (i.e. very Gallic, all science and minimal clothing), on inheriting the foundation, I realized my dream of becoming a Wellesvernian, and ERNIURC changed with me.

It is important to note this Lifestyle change because it explains much about the events to follow, and the manner in which I present them. That said, I shall begin my tale.

Chapter Two: The Captured Submersible

We were well into our expedition when disaster struck.

For three weeks, we had plied the ocean in our underwater vessel *Nautilus Revisited*, enjoying many Devonshire teas whilst we discussed inter-UG matters such as the strange sexual mores of the recreated Martians as interpreted by the newest faction of Heinleinists.

By the fourth week we were awaiting our scheduled highpoint. Since we had brokered an accord with an aerial chapter of the Wellesvernian Lifestyle called Tripod Raiders, and had negotiated a script which mostly involved much hiding and seeking amidst the waves whilst the Tripod Raiders sought to exterminate us, we were naturally taken aback when our submersible was suddenly seized and dragged downwards on a course contrary to our original agreement.

We were, we surmised at the time, at the mercy of another Lifestyle.

I was most annoyed by the setback. It confirmed my belief that there were simply too many Lifestyles vying for space on a finite planet, and that the World Government was far too enamored with the income generated by UG permits to seriously tackle the issue. Most UGs, I must interject, then as now, did respect each other. The Robinsons were family oriented naturalists and the Tikites provided highly educational adventures, but hooligans like the Buccaneer Coalition and the Viking Raiders were out of control, causing nothing but trouble for more moderate ocean users.

So, the situation was this: our valiant submersible *Nautilus Revisited*, under the capable guidance of Captain Lucan Lightfoot (RN: Stuart Troubadour) and his stalwart first officer, Commander Jeremy Chatham-Smythe (RN: Trevor Brown), struggled to pull free. Communications officer, St. John Fitzgerald (RN: Rajiv Sikh) attempted to make radio contact with the invasive UG to protest our plight. The Right Honorable Catherine Veronica Brontë (RN: Jazee Freecloud), our languages expert, stood at St.

John's side ready to parlay should a tongue other than English be required.

Despite our troubles, all was going well. Faced with such adversity, our only option was to exercise our improvisational skills. St. John, true to his role, placed an arm about Catherine's shoulders, offering comfort as gentlemen do in such trying situations. I was pleased to note that Chief Scientist, Professor Vladimir Boronsky (RN: Bruce Wong) showed great restraint under duress, his intellect visibly peaked by our predicament. The Professor's assistant, Geoffrey (RN: Geoffrey), however, inexperienced at projecting the composure required at all times by our Lifestyle, looked gauchely terrified.

At that point, as befits a lady, I retired to my cabin to record my thoughts and emotions in my diary. Whilst I was seated at my escritoire, Captain Lightfoot rapped upon my cabin door. His report was most unsettling.

Our radar man, it transpired, had just informed Captain Lightfoot that we had been captured by a gigantic creature with tentacles of a prodigious length and suckers large enough to secure our valiant vessel, which he had then insisted must be a kraken. Captain Lightfoot conveyed that the radar man knew about such creatures from his grandfather, also a naval man (Real World not UG), who had run into a similar behemoth after an anti-containment group had liberated specimens from a recognized supplier of Lifestyle monsters and then released them into the wild.

"But those poor, patchwork creatures cannot survive long beyond the comforts of their laboratory tanks," I protested.

"Nonetheless, our evidence supports the hypothesis, Lady Suzanne," said Captain Lightfoot, backing out of my cabin. "We'll know for certain tomorrow."

"Since our radar man is not an accredited megafauna expert, I deem it safest to defer all decisions until then," I said, to which the good Captain concurred and left.

Chapter Three: Kraken

After a night of restless sleeping, and upon completing my ablutions and donning a stunning outfit of blue velvet with yellow trimmings, I discovered that a note had been slipped under my door informing me that breakfast would be served on the bridge.

I found my colleagues, plates in hand, gathered before the large observation window.

"Ah, you're just in time, Lady Suzanne," said Captain Lightfoot. "We're about to discuss our plight."

I secured a portion of marmalade on toast from the buffet which had been set up amongst the consoles, and joined my fellow Wellesvernians. We were no longer in open waters, but travelling through an underwater tunnel lit with multiple rows of running lights. The external illumination allowed us a good view of the beast towing our vessel, and it was, we all agreed, definitely a kraken of the classical type favored by Alfred, Lord Tennyson.

"Told you so," said the radar man.

I threw a disapproving glance at the conversational interloper, who was staring at a luminous screen and toggling a console, but he displayed no shame for having interrupting us, just as he had hitherto shown no gratefulness for his fortuitous position on board our vessel, i.e. the privilege of experiencing our enviable Lifestyle and receiving a substantial remuneration to boot. Once again I regretted that it had proved impossible to procure a paid up Wellesvernian for the position, as being a radar man apparently involved the actual possession of technical skills.

Needless to say, this verification of the kraken caused much excitement. We all wondered how Lord Tennyson had come to know the beast so well, and we speculated whether the great man might have once found himself in a situation similar to ours.

"Forget the damned poetry," shouted the radar man. "Ask some relevant questions. Like who rigged those lights out there? And what power source are they hooked up to?"

A scandalized silence ensued.

Professor Boronsky recovered his composure first and said, "Despite his appalling manners, this radar person is most correct. Who indeed has established an infrastructure capable of functioning so efficiently at such stygian depths?"

"We're obviously dealing with Wellesvernians of the nefarious sort," said Captain Lightfoot. "So this, then, is undoubtedly a secret sea lair."

We all shivered with excitement.

The radar man shook his head. "You're a pack of damned fools," he said, and stomped off.

Captain Lightfoot was furious and directed his ire at me. "As Lifestyle Director, you must do something about that person, Matilde. I cannot immerse myself with his jarring comments," he said.

"The rest of you concur?" I asked.

Everyone nodded. So, with as much decorum as I could muster, I ran after the radar man, my skirts skimming the sides of the narrow corridors and requiring much angling and hoisting at each hatchway. When I caught up with him, I confronted the radar man about his frequent contractual breaches. He simply smiled, stepped up, took me into his arms and, ignoring my ladylike struggles, kissed me.

After three minutes of unrestrained ardor, he released me, whereupon I seized his hands and led him to my cabin. Alas, my Lifestyle prevents me from revealing too much of what happened next. It is enough for me to say that even though my radar man might not be a gentleman in the conventional sense of the word, Henry's skill as a lover combines the best aspects of a tradesman's physical power with the judiciously applied regulation of a naval officer.

And so, like entangled krakens, Henry and I pulled each other down into an abyss of passion.

Chapter Four: Embassy Island

When Henry and I finally emerged from my cabin, I accompanied my radar man into the bowels of our submersible.

Squeezing my skirts between the banks of brass-encased computers that all emitted picturesque jets of steam, I leaned over a console, cupped my chin in hands, and watched Henry moved amidst the machinery. With practiced ease, he stripped each crewbot of its blue and white striped sailor's jersey, flipped open its chest panel, and fiddled with its innards.

"They're basic models, not designed for original solutions," grumbled Henry.

"We're purists. I was loath to even include clockwork servants on this expedition, but someone has to wash the dishes," I said.

"Sounds like a job for Geoffrey," said Henry.

I sighed. "He is foolish and ineffective, I know, but his father is a World Governor. We were eager to be underway, and Geoffrey Senior granted ERNIURC a Rapid Departure Lifestyle License on the condition that Geoffrey Junior joined our expedition."

"Power corrupts," said Henry in that practical way I would soon come to know so well. He slapped the nearest automaton. "I've done what I can with these."

Since it was well past noon, we rejoined our compatriots on the bridge for afternoon tea, and discovered that countless dolphins were probing the exterior of our captured vessel. According to Catherine, they were searching for a way to breach our submersible, and she reported that they were arguing about 'calling in the bulwark busters'.

Henry and I pondered that phrase as we sipped our Earl Grey. Our fears that it had a decidedly ominous ring were soon confirmed when *Nautilus Revisited* began to thrash about. Maritime equipment and the paraphernalia of high tea flew about the bridge. A sandwich platter hit Geoffrey on the head and he instantly crumpled to the floor. There was a resounding boom and more shaking, then finally a blessed stillness.

"They've lifted us from the water," whispered Henry.

Through the observation window, I saw a stretch of silver sand broken by an eruption of mauve vegetation, beyond which purple palm trees swayed to the rhythms of an underworld breeze. I knew it was a subterranean scene because of the rocky vault I spied between the palm fronds.

Suddenly, the purple bushes parted and a group of tentacle-waving monsters stepped into view. I joined Catherine in a perfunctory scream before leaping to my feet.

"Where are you going?" cried Henry.

There was no time to explain. I hurried to my cabin and gathered a few necessities: my science journal, a sketching pad, a set of pencils, a box of paints, my needlework, my personal diary, and a fountain pen. I secreted these items into a pouch, hoisted my bustle, and hid the bundle within its folds.

I met Henry on my way back to the bridge, and he demanded an explanation for my odd behavior. He was, and remains to this day, impressed by my cool-headed foresight. I, on the other hand, even though I felt him fondle my bustle, was yet to appreciate his equally prescient precautions.

Back on the bridge, a strange sight awaited us.

Three outlandish creatures stood pointing bulbous objects which, since everyone but Geoffrey had their hands above their heads, I surmised must be weapons. Scientifically driven to categorize, I instantly labeled the artillery 'conch-guns', and, even though they were obviously amphibious, I thought of our captors as 'fishmen'. To my trained eye they were clearly hybrid beings created by technical intervention, for I could not imagine the natural environment that would encourage the evolution of such a muddled assembly of scales and fins, limbs and webbing, tails and hands, and oddly placed tentacles.

"Come," said the tallest of the fishmen.

"Oh, you speak our language," said Catherine, visibly disappointed.

"Of course. What cultured creature does not?" said the tall fishman. He twitched his conch-gun. "Please, climb the ladder."

Captain Lightfoot bore the still unconscious Geoffrey from the submersible. St. John and Henry helped us ladies haul our wieldy attire up the ladder and through the hatch, and then to negotiate the climb downwards to the glittering beach. I noted the curve of the silver sand, measured the sapphire water stretching in three directions, and peered at the stony vault far, far overhead. With the artist in me satisfied, the scientific side of my character began her investigations.

"This is an underworld sea?" I asked.

"It is the Lower Kingdom, an ocean that circumvents the entire globe," confirmed the head fishman, whom I shall henceforth call Tallfish. "And this is Embassy Island, which was built millions of years ago to foster relations between The Lower Kingdom and Atlantis."

"Not for meetings with humans!" retorted the next tallest, whom I instantly baptized Snapper.

"This island is for parlaying with all land-walking species, humans included, or guests from another planet with special requirements," corrected Tallfish.

"Were the Atlanteans native to this planet, or extra-terrestrial visitors?"

I queried, noting how my UG companions seemed cowed by events. I was particularly disappointed by the Professor's silence, for I had anticipated his support in matters scientific, but I knew in my heart that I could rely upon Henry, who, I saw, was even then studying our surroundings with a military man's methodical eye.

"All dead anyway," said the third fishman, whom I had already dubbed Shorty.

"Hopefully humans soon too, and riddance," said Snapper, laughing in an unpleasant manner.

Henry flinched. His hands balled into fists. I reached out and gently stroked his arm. When Henry glanced at me, I shook my head. He nodded. I resumed my research.

"Are you taking us to the leaders of the Lower Kingdom?" I asked.

"Yes," said Tallfish. "You will meet with the Cetacean Council."

His words surprised me. There were only fourteen resurrected whales in the world, and I then knew each one of them personally. They were uncomplicated creatures, somewhat bland and bovine of character, and had not, I knew for certain, ever formed any kind of political alliance. This left me with only one logical conclusion.

"You are, I take it, referring to unlicensed whales?" I said.

Snapper lunged at me, but Henry stepped in and blocked the attack. The belligerent fishman then whipped a tentacle at Henry, but my radar man was too burly a specimen to be felled by such a paltry blow. Henry grinned defiantly, even making encouraging gestures with his hands to signify that he was eager to do battle, and Snapper was about to oblige when Tallfish ordered the fishman to desist.

"They must show more respect for the Great Ones," insisted Snapper.

"Is that how should we address them?" I asked, "As the Great Ones?"

"For you, it is Powerful Lords Who Will Feed Us to Sharks," said Snapper, and he and Shorty chortled at the trifling joke.

"Great Ones will suffice," said Tallfish. "We have arrived."

The colorful jungle gave way to a clearing, and our team of adventurers stepped into a dramatic vista that reminded me of an Incan city I had once visited as part of a Lifestyle exchange program. There, in the centre of a tract paved with tiles of gleaming gold studded with fist-sized pearls, rose a gigantic ziggurat made of a nacreous substance that subtly shifted colors like a shell that is held up to the light and tipped this way and that.

"Welcome to the Plenipotentiary Embassy of the Lower Kingdom," said Tallfish.

Monsters gathered to watch us pass. We endured the angry gazes and garbled insults of many bizarre beasts which, like the fishmen, seemed to have been concocted in a laboratory, until finally, our tiny band of weary humans passed through the many columned portico of the mother-of-pearl ziggurat.

Chapter Five: The Crystal Shaft

The Plenipotentiary Embassy was so richly appointed with all manner of treasures from the oceans of the world, and the proportions were so vast, that the overwhelming effect was such that we felt like ants traversing an Oriental sultan's palace.

Tallfish guided us into an enormous, circular room, the wall of which was decorated with images of underwater creatures cavorting through detailed seascapes.

"This is most interesting," said the Professor, peering at the artwork. "The style is Minoan, though the inclusion of this fleet of merchant vessels, the so-called Ships of Tharsis, suggests a Phoenician influence."

"I'm glad to hear you finally speak, Professor," I said. "I'd begun to think we might have to review your membership."

The Professor had the good grace to look ashamed. "My apologies, dear lady."

The fishmen herded us into the center of the round chamber. Once we were in position, the floor jolted and began to descend. Catherine and I clutched our respective gentlemen. Captain Lightfoot carefully put down the still- unconscious Geoffrey. A colossal tube rose around us and soared overhead, an awe-inspiring sight that robbed us of our collective breath, and just when it seemed it was our fate to be swallowed by darkness, the floor began to glow. The illuminated slab at our feet dropped at what seemed a steady pace, but when I measured the shrinking disc of brightness at the top of the conduit, I calculated that we were moving at an astounding speed. The hydraulics required for the swift transfer of so much floor space suggested the possession of a technology far more advanced than what I would have typically ascribed to whales.

The descent halted. At that moment, Geoffrey awoke whimpering, saw the fishmen, and screamed. Captain Lightfoot helped the youth to his feet and held a steadying hand on his shoulder. In fearful silence, our team watched the obsidian wall around us change. A soft glow from beyond steadily suffused it and then intensified, the dark stone growing lighter and clearer, until finally the once substantial barrier became so lucent as to be technically a cylindrical window.

The scene beyond exerted as much pressure upon our psyches as no doubt the surrounding water exerted upon the transparent tube which was our only protection from the ocean's crushing embrace. The shock of what we saw pushed our little band closer together as we instinctively sought the companionship of our own kind.

For there, arranged in countless tiers around the tube, floated hundreds of whales, each and every one of them focused upon our tiny shapes, their combined intelligence a palpable force bearing down upon us. Despite my fear, I automatically began to catalogue all manner of extinct and extant cetacean types until the sheer number and diversity overwhelmed me.

"I wonder if they speak English," whispered Catherine.

"Welcome, despoilers of the Upper Kingdom," boomed a voice.

"Drats," said our superfluous translator.

Chapter Six: The Cetacean Council

The conference began.

Anticipating accusations about humankind's myriad of failings, I was surprised when the proceedings commenced in an unexpectedly personal manner.

"Which of you is Dr. Rothbilden-Vandershaft of ERNIURC?" boomed a voice.

I looked around, not knowing which of the leviathans to address.

Tallfish cleared the matter up for me. "The Great Ones speak in a collective voice."

"I'm Dr. Matilde Mayflower Rothbilden-Vandershaft," I said.

"Does this belong to you?"

Again I was confused, and again Tallfish helped me, this time by pointing at a large globe whizzing through the water accompanied by a school of shimmering fish. The silver mass tumbled and twirled between the whales, the thing in their midst heading straight for us. At the last moment, the fish veered off, abandoning the mysterious object.

"It's going to crash into us!" shouted Commander Chatham-Smythe.

Henry turned to Tallfish. "Can this shaft withstand such a collision?"

The fishman merely indicated that we should watch. Helpless to resort to any alternative action, Henry and I joined hands as the torpedo hurtled toward us.

"Ah, see there," said the Professor, pointing outwards, "That disturbance in the waters is caused by some kind of an energy field."

The globe slowed and gently bumped against the shaft. Then, to our amazement, the object pushed against the glass and eased through that seemingly impenetrable barrier. The wall closed behind the entrance point without a single drop of water entering the shaft, the orb fell to the floor and rolled. It stopped but half a meter away from me.

"Is this your property, Dr. Rothbilden-Vandershaft?" asked the collective voice.

I wondered why he asked since the letters ERNIURC were prominently stamped upon the surface. "Yes. It's a probe, one of seven AI prototypes launched nine years ago by my late father to explore the depths of our planet."

"We have five more like it," said the Cetacean Council. "Each of them discovered a secret gateway to the Lower Kingdom and was seized by guardians."

"Which explains their mysterious vanishing," I responded.

"We initially possessed all seven of your probes, but one of them escaped two months ago," said the Cetacean Council.

I frowned. "It hasn't returned to our institute."

"We know. After years of captivity, the probe is most likely paranoid. However, bound as it is by its programming, it must eventually present itself to ERNIURC."

"Which explains our abduction," interposed Henry. "This was no random seizure. We're hostages to be exchanged for the escaped AI and its cargo of information."

"Our agents in the Upper Kingdom have already initiated a dialogue with your institute," agreed the Cetacean Council.

"And did they also organize ERNIURC's Rapid Departure License by manipulating Geoffrey's father?" said Henry.

"It was a simple matter for our undercover operatives to arrange," said the collective behemoths with a hint of communal smugness.

"Just for the record, your whaleships have no intention of releasing us, do you?" said Henry.

"What are you saying?" demanded Commander Chatham-Smythe.

"He is obviously saying that since these creatures do not want humans to know about the Lower Kingdom, we can hardly expect them to return us to the surface with our own accounts of their secret underworld," said Professor Boronsky.

"I want to go home!" wailed Geoffrey.

Censorious blasts hit the crystal shaft. "You cannot! And heed this warning—if you escape from our hidden realm, we'll take the offensive, and the Lower Kingdom will erupt with a power that your simian minds cannot comprehend. The future of humankind depends on your compliancy," said the Cetacean Council. "Now take them away!"

The clear glass darkened, the great tube hardened once more into a rock chasm, the floor carried us upwards, and then the fishmen marched us out of the pearly ziggurat and off to prison.

Chapter Seven: Want of Freedom

Our incarceration was devoid of any drama or pain.

We were kept in a compound, separated from the population of Embassy Island so as to not infect them with our progressive ideologies, and made very comfortable in sumptuous apartments. We lacked for nothing but our freedom. We were allowed out once a day for a stroll, but always under strict supervision. Henry and I walked about hand in hand, the very picture of a contented couple, while the others likewise affected a meek satisfaction with their lot.

For a week, I busied myself with writing accounts of our dealings with the Cetacean Council, sketching the outlay of Embassy Island, embroidering a handkerchief with a representation of the pearly ziggurat, and painting a series of miniature portraits depicting the varied denizens of the Lower Kingdom.

Secretly, however, I readied myself for escape, for as we had walked away from the crystal shaft after that initial meeting with the whales, Henry had put an arm about my waist as if to comfort me, but his true purpose had been to discretely rummage around in my bustle. He had pulled forth an unidentified object and quickly stowed it in his pocket. So I was not surprised when on our eighth night of captivity, I awoke to find a hand placed firmly over my mouth and Henry looking down upon me. Behind him loomed the figures of Captain Lightfoot, Commander Chatham-Smythe, St. John, and the Professor.

"Get dressed quickly. We have disposed of the guards," whispered Henry.

I flung back my blanket to reveal myself as fully dressed. Henry smiled at me, offered a hand, and then gave me a quick kiss on the cheek once I was upright. Out in the corridor, Catherine and Geoffrey stood watch, each equipped with conch-guns. The gentlemen, I noticed then, were likewise armed.

"How did all this come about?" I asked.

"I called in the infantry," said Henry, handing me a weapon of my own. He held up some sort of device, no doubt the object he had stashed in my bustle. When I frowned, Henry pointed at the door opposite mine, which was the guards' room. A moment later, the door slid open and six familiar figures in striped jerseys emerged.

"Enemy secured, sir," reported one of the crewbots from *Nautilus Revisited*.

A revelation came to me. "The changes you made to their programming the morning we . . . "

"Indeed," said Henry. "Technological complexity has its advantages."

We headed along the corridor at a brisk pace, our newly liberated spirits buoyant and our hearts bright with hope, but just as we reached the main entrance, the door was suddenly flung open to reveal the shape of Snapper and nine other fishmen, each of them pointing a conch-gun.

"We're armed," warned Catherine, waving her weapon.

"And we have crewbots," added Geoffrey in a firm and very manly manner.

"Stand off," said Snapper gleefully. "A good excuse to kill you."

"Wrong again, Craaaya," said a more cultivated voice from the darkness behind Snapper. The remark was immediately followed by shots.

Seizing the advantage offered by our unseen ally, we too fired our conch-guns, and the ten fishmen blocking our way soon fell down dead as they were caught in the ensuing crossfire. When it was over, Tallfish emerged from the shadows. He held up all his arms and tentacles in the universal gesture of surrender.

"I knew that we could not contain you for long, so I've kept watch here every night in anticipation of your departure. As did Craaaya, it seems," said Tallfish, glancing at Snapper's corpse.

"But why would you betray your own kind?" I asked.

"I wish to accompany you back to the Upper Kingdom," said Tallfish.

"Why?" said Henry. "Is the Lower Kingdom not a pelagic paradise?"

"Anything but, sir," said Tallfish. "The Cetacean Council rules without public consensus. I long with an artist's soul for the freedom of the upper reaches."

"I don't trust him," hissed Commander Chatham-Smythe.

"Without me, you cannot maneuver your vessel past the guardians of the secret entrances," insisted Tallfish.

"Let's kill him right now!" snarled Captain Lightfoot, raising his conch-gun.

Henry and I both stepped in front of Tallfish. We smiled at each other. More than anything that had hitherto happened, this confirmed our compatibility. One by one, after Henry and I made moving speeches about honor and indebtedness, our comrades came to their senses and lowered their conch-guns.

And so with Tallfish's help, we fled the Lower Kingdom, glad to leave a place that was so inimical to humans.

Chapter Eight: The Great Conflict

We all know how the story progressed after that, for we live with the outcome of it every day.

True to their word, soon after our escape, the Cetacean Council declared war upon humanity. Whale scientists in hidden sub-Arctic bases commenced a program of accelerated evolution. They prodded dormant ancestral features back into duty and spliced genes from other life forms to create an army of invincible land-walking soldiers with which to conquer the Upper Kingdom. A month later, these gigantic monsters strode across the landscape incinerating buildings and crushing humans underfoot.

Our civilization proved to be but a fragile edifice when challenged by the superior firepower of those cetacean behemoths.

Humankind didn't know what hit it. Or rather they did know, because we, the former crew of the *Nautilus Revisited*, had forewarned the World Government and the media of the imminent invasion, using my diaries, notebooks, embroidery, and watercolors as evidence. Humanity, however, had chosen to ignore the peril.

Too late, the Real World came to understand that it should not have so hastily dismissed our claims as a collective Lifestyle delusion. Too late, a delegation of World Governors visited our band of adventurers in the secluded asylum to which we had been unfairly consigned and pressed us for counsel. Too late, our armed forces realized they should not have dissected Tallfish, the one creature who might have provided them with valuable strategic information.

Given that we, the former crew of *Nautilus Revisited*, had suffered weeks of embarrassment at the hands of unsympathetic physicians, you can well imagine that we felt a great satisfaction when those World Governors and generals suddenly turned to ash before our eyes, their demise caused by a passing battalion of whale behemoths which destroyed half of the asylum around us as we endured yet another cross-examination.

How we all cheered at that convenient event. Henry scooped me up in his arms and swung me about amidst the rubble. And so we were free and no one cared to recapture us, for human civilization had been reduced to anarchy and ruins.

On the first anniversary of what they called Subjugation Day, the Cetacean Council published a twelve point restructuring plan. Point four announced that humans had been deemed incompatible with the long-term aspirations of a whale-centric world.

Point five, as we all know, ordered humankind to build a space fleet and vacate the planet.

Chapter Nine: Epilogue

The tragedy of this tale, of course, is the part played by humankind's epic ignorance.

For it was eventually revealed that "our" whales, the creatures which for millions of years had once plied the waters of the Upper Kingdom, had in fact been the political rebels and the freethinking artists of the whale world who, like Tallfish, had fled from the despotic rule of the Cetacean Council. Had we not slaughtered them, these outcasts might have warned us of the danger hidden beneath the mantle of our world, something ERNIURC's fourteen resurrected whales could never have done, cut off as they were from classical cetacean history, culture, and traditions.

But I will now end this tome on a brighter note. For though it is true that we humans are now a dispossessed species, and that we endlessly sail upon vast starry seas in search of a new world to call home, it is a grand adventure that we're living. I, for one, with my stalwart radar man at my side, watching for any cosmic krakens that might lurk out here amongst the nebulae, am happy to have swapped my skirts for a spacesuit, and I recommend that morose souls weighted down by what we have lost let themselves be guided by the best aspects of the Wellesvernian credo.

So be not afraid of the future. Instead, let us all go bravely forth into this most exciting and most original of Lifestyles, and carry the flame of human civilization to another galaxy.

=[]=

Gitte Christensen was born and raised in Australia, but also lived in Denmark for 12 years before returning to study journalism at the Royal Melbourne Institute of Technology. Her speculative fiction has appeared in Aurealis, Andromeda Spaceways Inflight Magazine, Moonlight Tuber, *and other publications, as well as the anthologies* The Tangled Bank: Love, Wonder and Evolution *and* The Year's Best Australian Fantasy and Horror 2010. *To escape keyboards, she regularly grabs a tent and a horse and goes trailing riding through distant mountains.*

SINS OF OUR FATHERS

Wendra Chambers

=[]=

So many of the stories in this anthology discuss aspects of eras long ago lost, be it relics of land uncovered by exploring hands or tales passed down through fireside lore. But in this next selection, Sins of our Fathers, *it is a youth's own past that is discovered. Finding a centuries-old diary, he learns that his own life is not what he thought it was. Rich and provocative, Wendra Chambers has crafted a story which is multi-layered and leisurely peels away to unravel each underlying mystery. Whether seventeenth century Ireland or twenty-first century Massachusetts, human nature has not much changed.*

=[]=

The first clue came on my ninth birthday. Though I was his only son, it was the first time Dr. Phillips, as my father insisted on being called, had given his blessing to a party. One of the servants had solemnly given each of my young guests a unique little poem to start us on a scavenger hunt. Because of what happened, I remember everything leading up to it, including the first poem:

> *Over the wall*
> *And into the trees*
> *You'll find flowers*
> *The color of bees*

An adventure over the wall! In my eagerness, I overlooked the low wall surrounding our elaborate garden with blooming black-and-gold pansies. Instead, I excitedly ran beyond the centuries-old iron gate that stretched across our long drive. It was usually locked, but not that day; it stood open to welcome all of my guests, a rainbow of balloons waving across the top. Outside the gate, a forest ran on the right side of our property where the servants lived. For as long as I could remember, I had been forbidden to play in the forest, but that day I was convinced that the poem had given me permission.

I slowed my pace abruptly in the forest as its darkness closed in on me.

I felt uneasy and shortly realized why—I did not hear any birds. Twigs crunched under my feet, disturbing the strangely silent forest as I cautiously edged my way around, looking for flowers. As I neared a copse of trees, my right foot struck something hard and I pitched forward onto my hands and knees. I twisted around to see what had tripped me and saw a long piece of stone. When I scrambled closer, I realized part of it was buried.

As I pawed at the dirt and leaves, it became clear that I was unearthing some sort of headstone. I had never been to a graveyard, not even to my mother's grave, but I'd seen headstones in the scary movies I loved to watch back then. Perhaps because the sun didn't penetrate strongly there, the soil gave away easily and in no time I was brushing off the front of the slab to reveal the etching on the front. I squinted at the one word that emerged from beneath my dirty fingers:

~ *William* ~

The chill started at the base of my neck and traveled swiftly to my fingers and toes. At the same moment I heard Sarah, my favorite servant, calling my name. I don't remember running, but all at once I was in Sarah's arms, my face buried in her apron. I could hear the laughter of the children around me as they found their various treasures, but I didn't let go of Sarah for what seemed a long time. I never told her or anyone else what I found in the forest.

It was my name on that headstone.

=[]=

The next clue came two years later, when I was eleven, on Christmas Day. I saw the small, plain white box nested in the Christmas tree with a "W" scrawled on the top. Dr. Phillips was adjusting the tie he'd received from a colleague and didn't notice me opening it. A necklace lay curled at the bottom, a brass oval held by a well-worn leather strap. I noticed a tiny clasp and opened the necklace.

Dr. Phillips looked up when I gasped. He narrowed his eyes when he saw what I held. Even sitting in his old velvet high-backed chair, he looked imposing as he drew himself up and peered at the object from afar.

"Where . . . " he intoned, reminding me of a sorrowful bell, "did you get that?"

I distinctly remember feeling fearful and wanting to hide the necklace. I swallowed hard and pointed to the tree branches. "It was there, it was just sitting there. It had my initial on it." I then stood up taller and tried to return his wintry gaze. "Did Sarah want me to have this?"

His eyes flicked away. "It would seem so," he replied.

I licked my lips nervously. "Do you know who is with her in this picture?"

His eyes still focused on something else as he said, "That would be her husband."

Sarah had died only days before. Our most trusted servant, I had been there when Dr. Phillips tended to her in the final hours. He personally treated her and all the servants for their ailments, which seemed numerous in retrospect. It seemed as though he was always giving them injections for something. I suspected at the time that no one left because they were so grateful for his kindness. How many people had their own personal physician, a renowned medical geneticist at that? As sick as she was, yet another servant ravaged by cancer, Sarah's eyes had lit up when she saw my father. Before her last breath she had whispered, "Thank you."

Sarah had been there when my mother could not; she died in childbirth when I was quite young, Dr. Phillips said. Sarah had been endlessly kind, always telling me stories about "her people, the Irish" and "that damned Cromwell" to distract me from my loneliness. She was also very protective— "Never come to my quarters, William, nor any of the servants' houses." Because so many of the servants were often ill, she feared contagion. But she was also sad in a way that made me avoid her as I grew older and had friends my own age.

I remember wanting to ask Dr. Phillips who he thought had put the necklace there and how they knew Sarah wanted it for me, but he was already standing with his back to me in front of the large French doors, gazing out at the forest. When he clasped his hands behind him, I knew he would not tolerate any questions.

=[]=

The final clue changed my life. It was summer and I was home from boarding school, age seventeen. It was my junior year, and I was well on my way to applying to pre-med programs. As a result of the intensity of my classes, summers usually passed in a haze of novels, swimming, trips to town to see friends, and as many movies as I could squeeze in.

That summer it rained incessantly, making me feel lazy about venturing out. I'd been back from school only a few weeks and was bored with my usual routine. Dr. Phillips was in England, so in the absence of his gloomy, watchful eye, I wandered aimlessly from room to room, even trying doors that I knew would be locked. Most of my childhood had been segregated to such a small area; only then, wandering for what seemed like hours, did I fully appreciate how much of the house remained a mystery to me.

I knew Dr. Phillips had a "museum" somewhere. I'd heard the servants whispering about it since I was a boy. I had never found it myself, but with so much time to spare and having looked into a great number of rooms, I discovered it on the fifth floor. When the handle gave under my hand, for a moment I could not bring myself to enter. I had never entered a room in the house without permission. I then laughed at my own childishness and shoved open the heavy oak door.

The room stood apart from the rest of the austere house, decorated in a garish manner by the Doctor's standards: Deep burgundy walls, plush green window seats framed by brocade curtains, gold-framed mirrors in various places, and delicate lights illuminating hundreds of objects under glass throughout the long room, easily the size of a dining hall.

As I began peering at the various objects, I realized the theme—medicine. Every artifact had a date and as I walked around the room in a clockwise fashion, the dates grew more modern. Pictures of what I assumed were families dotted the walls starting in the nineteenth century showing the fashions of that age, though I noticed some of the people in the picture wore clothes I could only describe as "proper" and others in the picture wore clothes that leaned more toward "practical." Everyone in the pictures seemed to be holding children of various ages—lots of children.

The oldest artifacts were from the seventeenth century and intrigued me the most: Rusty-looking saws and knives among the scalpels and clamps. Books on herbs and even "astrologie" lay carefully on silk under dimly-lit glass. One leather-bound book in particular riveted me. The spine was very cracked, but the embossed silhouette of a once-colorful lion on the cover seemed like buried treasure to me. I lightly touched the sides of the glass casing to look more closely at the book and my hand brushed a latch. I swallowed and peered to see if a heavy padlock rested on the latch but found it completely free.

I think I honestly looked around before I touched the latch again. I could imagine that such an act might inspire Dr. Phillips to try out his riding whip on me despite my age. But with each passing moment, my curiosity grew to the point of not caring about the consequences. I took a deep breath and crossed the room to close the door to this museum before returning to gently lift the latch. Out from under the glass, I realized the book cover was tightly laminated to protect it from the oil of human hands; I felt a little better knowing my fingers couldn't damage it. Feeling the closed pages, I could tell they had been laminated too.

I'm not sure what I expected beneath the exotic cover, but it was better than I'd hoped: it was a diary. It started in 1650. 1650! This *was* buried treasure, and looking at the various pages, it looked like it had not only been buried but also burned and beaten. Some pages were crumpled, smudged, or singed, and several had deep brown stains in various places. I wondered how long this had been here and if the Doctor had kept it from me because he'd known I couldn't resist it.

But the Doctor wasn't here now. I gave into my urge completely, stretching my legs out in a window seat, determined to read as much as I could before I was discovered.

=[]=

When the natural light from the window waned to the point that I was squinting to read, I realized how much time had passed. My stomach groaned with hunger, though I was sure I could not handle any meat tonight. The diary had been written by a seventeenth century battlefield surgeon and even though there were spellings that were strange to me, "cutting" was the same and the only anesthetic his patients ever received was their own loss of consciousness. The surgeon discussed the use of herbs for treatment and, since he was called upon to treat not just war wounds but diseases the men would catch, he alluded to creating "decumbiture" charts, something that sounded like an astrological diagnosis of the patient.

But, what really shocked me the most were not the details of the surgeon's methods. It was the fact that he started his diary while on Cromwell's campaign in Ireland.

=[]=

A hastily-eaten peanut butter and jelly sandwich later, I could feel Sarah's sad eyes over my shoulder as I plunged back into the surgeon's world, a standing lamp providing me light far into the night in the window seat. I shivered when the surgeon walked through snowdrifts to reach people in need and winced as he cut into each patient, more often to remove something than to save it. And Sarah was right—Cromwell and his supporters were ruthless to the Irish. I admit, though, that I wasn't prepared for the siege at Limerick in 1651, with the surgeon supporting General Ireton's army. Beginning in July of 1651, the surgeon's entries, always on Sundays, became less frequent.

Sunday 16 July 1651

My conscience compels me to wryte, to somehow try to understand how this can be happening. A fierey temper always holds the General, but I saw it mostly in battle. Now I know it's through and through.

You made this famine and it will kill us both, O'Neill told our General. And I fear it will come to pass as I watch the men grow weaker each day, the lack of fighting eating at them as much as their hunger. My herb that tempered their desire for food is almost gone.

By day's end, we saw forty people standing outside the town walls. They could not go around us. The men escorted them into the fort and I wondered of the General's wayes.

When the slow smile spread across the General's face, I divined his intent. And as a surgeon, a healer, I would have no part of it. But the barber, he obliged. Nothing but a blindfold and an axe, and the savage completed his work in a matter of hours. Old and young, women and men. Forty humans, and despite being Irish, human they still were.

What struk us all as strange was their lack of cryes. Not once. Their bravery was impressed upon us.

But the hunger pressed harder. No one looked at each other at our late-nyght dinner tho I noted the General had himself many servings.

Never have I known a man so cruel. To this victualling he hath reduced us. May the Lord protect us from ourselves.

I looked up from the diary, feeling the sandwich flip in my stomach. I'd read about the Donner Party and that was shocking enough, but this . . . this seemed like a war tactic. Had General Ireton deliberately cut off both of their supplies to destroy the enemy *this* way? Or was this merely a way to survive a situation he'd unwittingly created? My sense of revulsion was so strong I wasn't sure I cared. And the surgeon . . . ! He'd been part of this; he survived on those people too!

But I couldn't stop reading now and things only got worse for the Irish from there. And then, something completely unexpected happened.

Sunday 27 August 1651

My heart cannot help but wonder if O'Neill is ever seized by the knowledge of what is happening to his people, the endless supply of people he forces outside of his city each week. I confess, having little to do after tending to the men's ailments or wounds, I have at this point examined many of them before the barber finished his "work" and noted after a month's time they all bear something in common—no one looks a day over five and twenty and they all have a crescent-shaped mark on the back of their neck.

Among thos pushed outside the town walls one early morn was one with child. God's eyes seemed to bore into the men that day and even the barber could not do it. She was instead sent to the dungeon. It had not been twelve hours before we heard her howling birth cryes. Nerves seized the men and many crossed themselves for this first time in the campaign. Her tongue pleaded with strange Irish words, but we all recognized the suffering. Fortunately, no wounds needed tending so I went to her. My training offered me the experience of assisting in birth so I could try to lift her suffering.

In the grip of Venus, I gave her an herb I usually saved for amputations, as her spirit seemed so strained and her face bloodless. My hand she squeezed until the bones seemed to crack and water poured from every surface of her body. When the child suddenly came forth in a rush, her hand went limp and I went immediately to see to the welfare of the child. I could not help but smile when I noticed it was a boy. Scraping the insides of his nose he issued a mighty crye, a good sign. Severing the cord, I took off my coat and wrapped him up and put him beside the mother, but she did not stir. Her breathing was shallow and soon the afterbirth followed. But with the afterbirth also came blood, more blood than is usual. It soaked my clothes and poured over the stones and made the straw crimson. Never had I seen such a syght. No attempt to staunch the blood succeeded. I held her hand until her chest moved no more. Light no longer entered the fort and the baby wailed against its dead mother.

I am terrified. I cannot let them kill a baby, not a boy, especially. Yet no women are with us to tend to it.

May Gold help this child.

Sunday 17 September 1651

God must care for this child because He hath made me do wonderous things on his behalf. The morning after the death of the mother, I let it be known that I was going to look for a new supply of herbs amongst the locals in Irish Town in the garb of one of our deceased, lest my English clothes reveal my loyalties. We knew all fighting men were barricaded in Limerick so the risk was not overly great. Plus, I bore no arms so unless I spoke, the locals would have no cause to fear me. None of the men said anything but I suspect they kept my trip from the General—they noted the babe lying openly in my medical bag. Upon reaching a village, I acted mute but pointed frantically to the baby who was now too weak to crye. Everyone looked at me suspiciously but eventually I found myself at the door of a woman with a young babe of her own. She looked frightened of me at first, but when she saw the state of the baby, she said not a word, but took it into her arms and went into the house. I followed, but she held up a hand and pushed a chair into a corner with her back to me and the baby crooked in one arm. I averted my eyes and then heard the sounds of suckling. This sound did not stop for some time and then was at last followed with, to my relief, a fresh bellow of cryes from the lad. She tidyed herself and then turned around and silently returned the squalling baby to my medical bag. I reached underneath the babe until I felt a certain-shaped bottle that I knew would be of use to a new mother. I pointed to it, mimicked drinking its contents, and then smiled to show the health it would bestow upon her. She gently led me from her house, but it was the first of many visits that would save the child's life.

Sunday 29 October 1651

Last week was the first time that no townspeople were forced outside the walls. We all suspect this is a sign that O'Neill's will is breaking. Tho this meant hunger for us, it was worth knowing that the siege might be ending. It also lifted the General's spirits to the point of risking some men to batter a section of the town wall.

To our surprise, by week's end, one of O'Neill's men turned against him and his troops demanded a negotiation with the General. When we entered the town at last, we all fell silent. We knew thousands had lived here at the start, but now less than a hundred remained. A few of the bodies I passed *lay face down and I could not help but notice the crescent-shape mark on the back of their necks. This great culling was not only due to O'Neill forcing his citizens to leave but also the Plague.*

My only thought was getting home to my wife and, God willing, presenting her with the miracle God had never blessed us with: a son. Dizziness briefly seized me at the thought of a babe surviving the journey, but he hath survived a famine—surely he would survive the journey to his new home. And with the knowledge that home was before me, I touched the boy's crescent-shaped mark that night and vowed to be a good father, to atone for what we had all done here.

And then the most shocking thing of all—the diary ended there. I stared at the binding for a few seconds and then suddenly recalled where I was. The grandfather clock at the far end of the room read three a.m. I nearly dropped the diary before I realized I had nothing to fear—Dr. Phillips wouldn't be back until tomorrow.

I stared hard at the diary as if I could will the pages to fill themselves with the surgeon's life after the campaign. Had the child survived the trip? Was he a good father, as he'd promised? Maybe, I thought, maybe I could get a clue to what happened if I read the diary again, more closely. Maybe . . .

And that's the last thing I remember thinking before I felt a hand on my shoulder.

=[]=

"I'll take that, if you don't mind," Dr. Phillips said, removing the diary from my lap. I wiped the drool from my mouth and swiveled my head painfully, having fallen asleep propped up in the window seat. Fear completely wiped my mind and I stared as the Doctor placed the diary back into its case and settled into the other side of the window seat. Crossing his legs at the knee as he always did, my throat tightened. He'd never sat this close to me.

He looked down thoughtfully at his knee before speaking. "I suppose you have some questions for me," he began and then looked at me with cool expectation.

I stared at my hands. Was I not going to get punished? Was this a trick question?

I hadn't spoken in so long that my voice sounded like a croaky whisper. "Is that surgeon . . . are we . . . related?"

The Doctor looked up at the ceiling and seemed to ponder the question. Then he got up and walked across the room to an ornate mirror and turned on the small light above it. He left briefly and returned with something in his hand. He stood in front of the mirror and gestured for me to come to him.

Fearing the punishment was coming at last, my leaden feet dragged as I made the long journey to the mirror. The doctor put his hands on my shoulders and guided me close to the mirror, then pivoted me so my back was to it. He then put a small mirror into my hand, positioning it in front of me but slightly to the left of my face. I looked at him, bewildered. He pointed to the small mirror so I looked into it.

In my shaking hand was the blurry reflection of a small, crescent-shape birthmark on the back of my neck.

I somehow ended up back in the window seat. I spoke the first thought I had. "The baby . . . lived."

Doctor Phillips nodded.

"And married one of the surgeon's relatives?"

Doctor Phillips shook his head. "No, but it would be wrong of me to say the child and his descendants were not a part of this family."

The room began to tilt and I heard myself say, "But I have the mark . . . how . . . "

Never one to miss an opportunity to teach me something, the Doctor turned it back on me. "Well, let's be logical. Yes, you have the mark. But no, the child never intermarried with the surgeon's family. The surgeon is related to *my* family. Then what do you conclude?"

I heard myself say, "I would conclude that I am not related to you."

The Doctor replied, "And you would be correct."

My voice continued, "And that's why you've always been Dr. Phillips, not . . . not . . . " I couldn't bring myself to say *Dad.*

I actually heard the pride in his voice this time. "Nicely done, William."

He leaned forward and, seeing the deep lines in his face for the first time, I mused on the fact that I didn't know his age.

"Now," he said, with an eagerness I'd never heard before, "let's solve the rest together, shall we? If I am not your father, then my wife . . . "

"Was not . . . my . . . mother," my voice said.

"Good, William!" the Doctor pronounced. "Then your real mother . . .?"

It's strange how the brain works under stress. I don't remember saying anything or even thinking anything, but then I heard my father exclaim, "Excellent, William, excellent!" He was looking excitedly at my hands so I looked down too. My right hand was covering a place on my chest. Sarah's necklace lay hidden beneath my undershirt, every day.

My face must have shown confusion because he chuckled. He actually chuckled.

"My dear boy," he said, "Despite what you may think, I too was once a sentimental boy who loved his mother."

I stared mutely at him, unable to form the question. As usual, he kept one step ahead of me.

"Oh, I'm not a monster, William," he continued. "Sarah asked me never to tell you. It was her personal request. She was able to be close to you yet felt so grateful that you could be a doctor's son, that I would be willing to do that for her. And, it was critical that I have a son. It's part of . . . it's part of *The Tradition.*"

I was trying not to listen anymore. Instead, I brought out the necklace and looked at the face of my real mother and father. But then I suddenly had a burning question.

"My . . . real father . . . when did he . . . "

"He was 21 when he died of natural causes. You were named after him."

The name on the headstone flashed in my mind. "Natural . . . ?"

"Yes, William," and this time the Doctor actually moved closer to me. He reached out and for the first time ever, his hand shook. He placed it on my knee. I stared at his hand, never remembering a single touch from this man I had thought was my father.

"Completely . . . natural . . . causes," Doctor Phillips's voice lowered in a conspiratorial tone. "You, William, will be the first outside of the circle of families to know . . . The Tradition."

I had no idea what he was talking about except that I'd never seen him express any emotion until now. "Why," I asked in a dead voice.

"Because you are the only child I have and you have turned out . . . perfectly," he finished. "William, because you want to be a doctor and because you are my only son, I know you can be trusted with The Tradition. I know that you will understand."

He paused, then continued solemnly, "What I'm about to tell you has not passed outside the circle of families since the seventeenth century. While unplanned, The Tradition evolved into a moral code for the families, one continued solely for the good of humanity, really, for the perpetuation of our very race."

He cleared his throat. "Quite simply, William, *your* family line has, against all odds, managed just barely to survive despite the genocide of your clan by General Ireton. The Plague, the ongoing war, and sadly, the ah, unfortunate consummation of your people, almost annihilated your clan, William. Except for the baby the surgeon saved. But more importantly, this . . . " he touched the back of his neck, "your birthmark . . . is the persistent indicator of a genetic defect that guarantees your death before you reach the age of thirty."

My head suddenly snapped up. "What?"

The old Doctor Phillips returned swiftly. I had interrupted him and his jaw clenched. But then he composed himself. "William, you are . . . you will be fine. I promise you. Now let me continue and you will understand."

He began again. "Among the families who are related to the surgeon by blood or law, *we*, my family, are the direct descendants. As you know, every male in my family has been a doctor and always had more than one son . . . until me, that is. The surgeon was no exception; he ended up having several sons after adopting the Irish baby. Birthright is everything in England and therefore the land, the house, and all responsibility would always go to the blood-related sons. Not wanting to be cruel, however, your family was always kept on the land as caretakers and treated . . . "

"Like servants," I finished.

The Doctor stared at me until the room felt frosty. "Like . . . *family,*" he finished at last.

He stared at his knees once more and then cast his eyes to the ceiling. "Perhaps . . . perhaps I'm mistaken. You've learned a lot of startling information for a teenage boy. Perhaps that is enough for now." He stood up, brushed at his pants, and started to leave the room.

"Wait!" I cried, startled at the loudness of my own voice.

He stopped but did not turn around.

I persisted, "Am I going to die?"

He turned around and said seriously, "Not for a very long time, once I take care of things. When you're ready to know The Tradition, you'll understand."

=[]=

The rest of the summer passed quickly, perhaps because I was determined to spend as little time at home as possible. I did everything to forget what I'd learned from Dr. Phillips. The fact that Dr. Phillips was not my father felt like trying on a new pair of shoes that felt stiff and awkward. The fact that Sarah had been my mother and I'd never known my real father felt like my heart was slowly eating itself.

Dr. Phillips set off for England a week before I planned to return to school. Once he left, my restraint against everything he'd told me slowly gave way. The night after he left, thoughts of Sarah, my father, and my genetic curse all overwhelmed me as I tried unsuccessfully to sleep. At some point I gripped the sides of my bed as I realized something: Would any of the servants tell me about my father?

I leapt out of bed and started pacing my room. I had barely interacted with any of them my entire life . . . it was only Sarah that I knew at all. I had never entered one of their houses because Sarah always warned me not to. Now my emotions overwhelmed her warnings.

Not quite sure what I was doing, I got dressed and crept outside. As my eyes adjusted to the dark I made my way toward the forest because I knew the servants' houses were right behind the first tree line. When I heard the forest floor crunch under the weight of my foot, though, I stopped. It was after eleven at night . . . why did I think anyone would be awake? And even if they were, why would they talk to me?

I'm not sure how long I stood there, but the next thing I recall is a strange sound piercing my thoughts. I tensed, thinking it was an animal, but when I cupped my hand around my ear, I realized it was a woman. Crying.

I half-wished it had been an animal. I'd never seen any woman cry before and just hearing it made me want to run back to the house. When

I heard her whimper, "Please God, no!" however, I worried that she might be in trouble and headed quickly toward the source, a dark house no more than twenty feet from me.

A light came on inside just as I was approaching a window. I hesitated, but then peered discretely inside. A man stood over a woman who sat weeping in a rocking chair in front of a cold fire. They both had their backs to me.

"Colleen," he was saying, "I promise you'll be okay, it can't be the same thing Sarah had. That's not possible."

She withdrew tissues from a robe pocket and dabbed at her nose and eyes and looked up at him, her lips quivering. "I think we are a cursed lot!"

The man put his lips to her ear and I couldn't hear what he said.

She blew her nose and then continued. "If it weren't for Dr. Phillips, I don't know what would become of us. So many of us suffer so, from God knows what. He's tireless in trying to help us, but even with yesterday's injection, I fear that I may soon follow Sarah. I have," her voice broke, "all the same signs." And she broke down crying again.

The man drew up a chair beside her and took her hands. William heard him say, "Not contagious."

"I know, I know you can't catch cancer," Colleen said, "but why am I getting all the same signs? I'm so tired I can barely keep up with my duties! But Dr. Phillips, bless him, said not to worry, he would never dream of putting me out, no matter what. And he tends to me and all of us like we were his own. God bless him!" She pressed the tissues to her eyes briefly. "I don't understand what plagues us. I fear it is a curse because I have no other explanation. Who among us has lived to see thirty? Only Sarah's child might break the curse . . . thank the Good Lord we have kept him away from us. It has probably saved him."

I slowly withdrew from the window. I didn't comprehend what I was hearing, but I became increasingly uncomfortable in my *Peeping Tom* role. I crept silently back to the house.

=[]=

My eavesdropping left me more confused and heartsick. I slept a few hours that night and then tried to actually visit this "Colleen" in the morning, but no one answered to my knock. I glanced at the other houses, all equally quiet.

On my way back to the house, I kept thinking about what she said—all of them were cursed? How was that possible? They weren't all related, they couldn't all have the genetic curse Dr. Phillips had described. Wasn't it bad enough that my people were cursed—how is it that others who came into contact with them were also afflicted with something?

Back at the house, sleep-deprived and restless, I wandered aimlessly from room to room. I didn't know what I was looking for until I stood before the room that had changed everything.

This time I walked past the seventeenth century displays and moved to the eighteenth century. It looked like more diaries, possibly, and again surgical tools, medicine vials. I moved onto the nineteenth century and the books under the glass changed—they looked like old record-keeping books, though nothing on their covers indicated that, only their size and shape. I stared at one and without looking reached around for the latch on the case, only to find myself fumbling with a large lock. I frowned and moved to the next glass case and found the same thing. And the next, and the next.

At the end of this long hall I was in the twenty-first century. Tools and vials were no longer on display, only more record-keeping books, also locked, and pictures. The last picture on the wall I recognized because there among the servants was Sarah, young, smiling, an infant in her arms. My chest ached as I looked at the robust young man with his arm proudly around her. I instantly saw myself in the dark hair with the awkward cowlick and pale blue eyes. Then I turned my gaze to the stern-looking Dr. Phillips standing to the side in the photograph.

It was at that moment that I decided to ransack his study.

He had never shown me where it was, but since he went there every single night, of course, I secretly followed him one time. I wanted to see what was in the record books and surely he kept the keys to them in there.

I'd never been inside his study and was surprised to find it almost as plush as the museum. An enormous desk dominated the large room with leather couches on either side, a closet, and even a fireplace facing the desk.

I pulled on every desk drawer, but of course they were locked. I felt under the desk and under the chair to see if he had a secret compartment that would release when I pressed the right place. The closet held a few suits, but nothing else. I even pushed the couches around the room, but nothing was under them, and I punched every single cushion—nothing was in any of them.

I fumed in the middle of the room. As always, he was one step ahead of me.

I found myself staring into the fireplace. The fireplace surprised me. I had never smelled even a hint of smoke from the room. Why would he never use the fireplace? And how could it work without a chimney?

I looked hard at the logs. They looked real. When I touched them, to my surprise they did not feel like wood. I started to get excited, but then realized it was not unusual to own a fake fireplace.

Not satisfied, I tried to lift the logs up but they wouldn't budge. They felt connected to the iron grating they were piled in. Was that normal? I held the sides of the top log and instead tried to push it away from me. I felt the top log give and retract in a mechanical way. I jerked my hands back, worrying that I had broken it, but then realized it was some sort of container. I peered into the bottom log.

For a moment it looked empty; I could see only darkness. But to be sure, I reached my hand in to feel the bottom. I felt a bumpy exterior and grasped the edge of something flat. My hand emerged with a record book. My heart started to race and I reached in again. This time I came up with a smaller book. I flipped the pages and instantly recognized the Doctor's handwriting. I reached in once more but there was nothing else.

I stared at the two books, suddenly five years old again, afraid of Dr. Phillips, afraid of what might happen if he knew what I'd done.

Then I flipped open the record book. I was right. It was records. But what kind?

I glanced at several pages. All of the servants' names were in here, as well as some names that I didn't recognize. I swallowed hard when I saw 'William Sr.' with an asterisk beside it and then 'William Jr.' with another asterisk. Everyone except for me was preceded with a combination of letters and numbers and then a list of dates with checks underneath them, followed by what I took to be codes—a plus sign, a minus sign, two plus signs, etc. For example, William Sr.'s entry said "DoM, EG1" followed by his name and then a series of dates that looked months apart. The last symbol was a minus sign. Sarah's entry ended in a plus and minus sign. I looked at Colleen's entries. The day the Doctor left for England there with a check mark.

Since he was their doctor, I would expect Dr. Phillips to keep medical records, but these were not normal medical records. He was recording something, but in code. If he gave Colleen a shot, why wouldn't he want to keep clear records of what he gave her and why? Or for that matter, for any of the servants?

I turned to the other book. It was filled with the Doctor's cursive. I opened it to one of the last entries. It was this year, 2020, and the date of our "talk."

I realize the risk I am contemplating, but I cannot let The Tradition die. It is far too important, especially considering the discovery I made. William is not ready, but he must be soon. I cannot risk his life by waiting for him to mature psychologically. I am also aware of my own mortality as I will turn eighty-five this year. He has to know soon in order for him to accept the therapy and live beyond the span of his predecessors. My discovery, which should allow him to live a normal life, is the first step in fulfilling The Tradition. William's life is key to this fulfillment.

And that was it. I turned to an earlier date. The Doctor's writing was shaky.

It is only forty-eight years later after family #83's discovery that I have been able to correct the defective gene in the DoM cells using gene therapy techniques. Now that I've discovered the right therapy from building on my English colleagues' work on pluripotent stem cells, at least I can enable Sarah's DoM son to live. Regrettably not, as we had hoped, forever. As long as any of us, however, and long enough to keep The Tradition alive for his son in turn.

I suddenly remembered an expression from when I was little, when I would shudder unexpectedly due to a sudden draft or chill. Sarah would say, "Someone step on your grave?" and ruffle my hair.

Someone had just stepped on my grave. I turned back several more pages to a date I knew well—the date Sarah died.

I can hardly believe that I have succeeded. To be clear, I have not succeeded in the original intent of The Tradition, but it is a success nonetheless. The latest trial outcome—Sarah's death—replicates the previous trial outcome, supporting my hypothesis that preventing normal telomere shortening might be associated with longevity, but also appears to be associated with producing various cancers as well. I therefore intend to make an adjustment in the therapy which will be administered to a new subject, Colleen, a non-DoM who shows remarkably good health.

My hands shook as I flipped to much earlier pages.

While I appreciate the dedication of trying to extend the lives of the Descendants of the Mark, I believe it has been a mistake to have only one experimental group. I made the following argument at our latest private conference in London: Continuously focusing on the DoM as the sole experimental group has resulted, at times, to even further limiting their lifespan, thus reducing the available experimental subjects that are most critical to our success. Because of the indirect manner in which the gene appears to function (based on our many years of observation and experimentation), it is highly likely that the ability to create the same defect in a normal subject would indicate that this therapy would suppress the expression of the faulty gene in the abnormal (DoM) subjects. I am officially introducing the latest therapy into the normal servants because if my hypothesis is correct, when I have perfected it, a normal subject will not reach the age of thirty.

I found myself unable to take a breath as I turned to the very first page of the diary. This was the longest entry by far and took place forty-five years ago.

. . . and it is with a heavy heart that I accept the burden of The Tradition from my father. He will carry it until he cannot any longer, but with this

knowledge, I am just as responsible as he is. I feel both horrified and enthralled by what I've been told, which I am required to document here in order to pass onto one of my own sons. Only the Nazi studies parallel these findings though I shudder to make the comparison—these are hardly subjects, but well-loved members of my adopted family and that of others across England, America, and Europe.

It is stunning that we have the evidence of "patient zero" in the good doctor's seventeenth century diary, but of course I would have assumed, given the nature of the genetic disorder, that the Descendants of the Mark would never have survived more than a couple of generations, at best. The discovery in the eighteenth century that the survival of the DoM was not only due to the quiet permissiveness of the English family to allow the DoM and their families to practice traditional Catholicism (which involved shunning birth control) but even more startling, the persistence of the faulty gene in "normal" descendants. It turns out many were passive carriers and their children, in turn, often bore the Mark and consequently, the faulty gene. Of course, once the Descendants became systematically tracked and studied, their religiosity was actively encouraged to perpetuate the Descendants.

The words began to waver and blur and my fingers turned white as I gripped the book.

. . . but it was family #83 that really made the most significant progress of the twentieth century. Using hair and skin cells from the DoM, the doctor of #83 used the adenovirus vector to locate the single nucleotide polymorphism among the FOXO genes, as anticipated. An unparalleled discovery to date—identifying the faulty gene—but it is my hope to make an equally startling discovery.

It is against everything in my training to not offer informed consent. But when I was told of the intent . . . how could I refuse? How could I single-handedly destroy years of data, throw out years, no, centuries of work toward this admirable answer? I was advised to repeat The Tradition's mantra whenever I felt my resolve weakening, coined by the first Doctor who formally documented his study of the DoM: "The Key to Death is also the Key to Life." In short, discovering why the DoM die so young could, ultimately, lead to the discovery of eternal life.

Eternal. Life.

When I finally looked at my watch, it was morning. I was not even halfway through the diary, but I couldn't read anymore.

The diary felt as cold and hard as the gravestone I'd found as a boy. I felt controlled by terror and dizzy with everything I'd learned. My mind ran in circles, a caged rabbit, frantic to find a way out. I selfishly wished that I'd never entered the museum, never come home that summer. I felt a panicked urge to hide in a very dark place.

My real mother had died . . . so I could live? He, they, ALL of these "families" had experimented on my family *and now others* for centuries. And for what, to carry on this *Tradition*? How many had died, how many had suffered for a theory about the key to eternity? Unwitting subjects believed they were being treated for their illnesses, but in reality their kind English "fathers" were killing them.

Feeling numb, I got to my feet and left everything askew in his study, not bothering to close the door behind me.

I clutched the railing as I made my way downstairs. Was the intent of these families and Dr. Phillips to ultimately help humanity? Did they all really think they were doing this for the good of the human race?

All these thoughts were endlessly spinning in my head when the Doctor returned close to noon that day. I was sitting in the breakfast nook when I heard him come through the front door. A relentless workaholic, I could tell by the number of stairs he took that he was heading for his study.

It wasn't long before he returned downstairs, his feet thudding faster than normal on the stairs. He headed straight for me, intuitively guessing I'd be in the breakfast nook.

To my surprise he grabbed my chin like he'd done when I was under the age of ten, forcing me to look at him. His skin felt dry and papery.

"How dare you, *how dare you*," he growled. "This is *my Tradition* to pass onto you properly, when you are ready, not something for you to grab like a petulant child whenever you like, whenever *you* think you can handle such knowledge! I had deemed you immature and you knew this, you knew exactly what I thought. You have completely violated my trust and more importantly lost my respect. God help me that you are my only son."

As he said, "son", the fire seemed to go out in him a little. He dropped my chin and both arms hung limp at his sides. He turned away and entered the old cold storage room off the kitchen, which, like several other rooms in the house, no one was allowed to enter but him. He returned shortly bearing a metal tray and plastic gloves. He sat the tray down carefully on the table in front of me.

"If you are so eager to grow up, then you shall accompany me today for a treatment. I expect to see you appropriately groomed and waiting for me at this table in fifteen minutes." With that he turned sharply and headed for the stairs.

My eyes flicked to the metal tray. A full syringe gleamed in the kitchen light.

In one crystalline moment, I realized that I didn't care about the intent of all those English doctors. All that mattered was what they did.

And with that certainty, I realized I knew just what to do.

Tears filled my eyes and I pulled out Sarah's necklace, gripping it fiercely. "I'm sorry," I whispered.

If I was the key to preserving The Tradition, then I was the key to ending it.

In the end, at last, I would be one step ahead of the Doctor.

=[]=

The Weston Town Crier
December 28, 2020

Famous Geneticist Dies at 85, Son to Carry on Legacy

By Stephen Walsh

John Bennett Phillips, 85, died on Sunday, December 27, 2020 at the Massachusetts General Hospital, following a courageous battle with cancer. Trained at the University of Oxford, Dr. Phillips was highly respected in his international professional community for his innovative theories on genetics and longevity.

Though Dr. Phillips was a reclusive member of his community with his grand house tucked away from town thoroughfare, prominent members of the medical community in Boston were well-familiar with his work.

"We attended several private conferences together in London," said Dr. Maye at Boston Medical Center. "He was a great risk-taker and put his work above all else. It's hard not to admire that." When asked to expound on his risk-taking and why the conferences were private, Dr. Maye smiled and said I was more than welcome to read Dr. Phillips's publications.

His doctor at Massachusetts General refused to be interviewed.

Dr. Phillips is survived by his only child, William Bennett Phillips. At age seventeen, William is well on his way to following in his late-father's footsteps, already applying to various pre-medical programs.

"I am going to pursue genetics as well. I've never been more certain about anything in my life," William said, his skin pale and his eyes stained with dark shadows, clearly bereft. "As for your question about my inheritance, I plan to give most of it to the . . . caretakers of the estate here. Them," he said, gesturing to the various servants who scurried about the grounds and house, cleaning furiously. I asked about their hurried state of cleaning and William explained that he was putting the house on the market as soon as possible. He would share the profits of that eventual sale with the "caretakers" as well.

When I inquired about the responsibility of all these dealings and the subject of power of attorney considering his age, he said his father's will clearly indicated that everything went to him and that meant his father's lawyers worked for him now. But what about his extreme generosity toward the "caretakers"? William appeared to hesitate before responding. "They've been extremely loyal," he finally said. "More loyal than they know."

William accepted no further questions from me.

Most of the caretakers avoided me, but I did note one woman weeping bitterly in a quiet corner of the ornate garden. A man, another caretaker I believe, stopped me from going to her.

"Don't," he said. "She's been through enough."

"What has she been through?" I asked.

He seemed lost in thought when he responded, "She thinks it's our fault." And with that he abruptly left to console her and I, Loyal Readers, was unfortunately escorted from the grounds.

Just before I had to submit this story, however, I received an unexpected boon—a large package from William. The package contained a thick manuscript, which William's cover letter indicated to be a copy of his father's diary. He said he thought I might find it of interest and that I was free to write about it. The letter was co-signed by one of his late-father's lawyers.

William's intent remains a secret, however—he has not returned any of my calls.

I have received permission from my Editor, pending the nature of the content, to write a short series based on the diary. Keep your eyes on this column, Loyal Readers. Many of us are very curious to learn more about the secluded Doctor Phillips. And, no doubt, the Doctor will have something to teach us as well. Perhaps his diary will enlighten us to the mysterious epitaph on his headstone, which I stumbled upon in a strangely remote area of the house grounds:

Beware of Grand Hubris
In the Guise of Goodwill
Guard the Rights of the Living
For Good or for Ill

=[]=

Wendra Chambers *is a psychologist by day and artist by night. She has published op-eds, short stories, and scientific articles, and hoards mostly unfinished screenplays. Most of all she hopes to outline a book in the coming year. When she's not begging her husband to please read her stories just one more time, she is lavishing adoration on her rescue dogs. She hopes very much that one day the world might operate according to her very nocturnal circadian rhythm but is not holding her breath.*

THE TALISMAN OF HATRA

Andrew S. Williams

=[]=

An authentic tragedy may be defined as, "A character of high estate who experiences a reversal of fortune, and who is involved in a conflict which ends in catastrophe." With these elements in mind, Andrew S. Williams invokes a brilliant sense of classicism with his story, The Talisman of Hatra. *Haunting and epic, the author explores a profound struggle within his character, Princess an-Nadira, who is torn between the loyalties to her family and the loyalties to her people. As with all tragedies, however, there is never a "right" choice . . . all decisions lead assuredly to bitter despair.*

=[]=

I try to stride unnoticed through the palace forge, but such a task is impossible for a High Priestess. No matter how little noise I make, my presence draws eyes. But only a few apprentices and slaves are still awake this late, cleaning up after the smiths and keeping the fires lit. They notice me, then hurriedly turn away, and for once I am grateful for their fear.

The fires are so bright, they are difficult to look at. The blades forged here have drawn the blood of Romans, of Lakhmids, of Persians, all for the glory of the City of Hatra.

The gems of my robe dance with orange radiance, and the silver talisman around my neck shines brightest of all, the face etched into its surface glimmering with light and heat. From her emerald eyes, I can feel my Goddess watching me, judging me across five hundred years.

I glance at the others in the room; they're still pretending I'm not here. Good. I slip the talisman from around my neck, and kiss the figure at its center. "Forgive me, Atar'atha. I do this to save your people."

For half a millennia, the talisman's magic has protected the city walls, giving us a safe haven from which to reach out and build a kingdom: the Kingdom of Araba, which at its height stretched across the whole of Mesopotamia. From Petra to Palmyra, the Kingdom of Araba—with Hatra at its heart—held sway.

But now the kingdom is swept away, and the armies of the Sassanid Empire swarm unchecked across our lands. The same walls that sheltered us now threaten to become a prison, a place to wither and starve as the world goes on around us.

My brother is dead, and I am bound to inherit a useless throne. There is only one way for Hatra to live in this new world.

I kiss the goddess on the cheek and hurl the talisman into the fire.

=[]=

Have you ever seen the walls of Hatra from the East, when the dawn sets the red walls aflame, and the gem on the temple dome sparkles as though we were witnessing the birth of a second Sun? I have never laid eyes on Rome, or Alexandria, but surely there is no greater sight than Hatra and her mighty walls towering over the desert.

When I was young, my father would take my brother and I outside the city just to see it, to be awed in the same way countless merchants and peasants and would-be-conquerors have been over the past centuries. He would tell us stories of how those walls had withstood Syrian armies, Lakhmid raiders, even the fearsome Roman legions. I fell in love with the stories and the city at their heart—my city.

I joined the ranks of the priestesses on my tenth birthday. And of all the gods and goddesses of Hatra, I dedicated myself to Atar'atha: goddess of love, and beauty, and war. She was Ishtar to the Babylonians; Astarte to the Syrians; Aphrodite to the Greeks. But she has been with Hatra from its birth, and it was her talisman that held the city walls secure.

Atar'atha rewarded my passion: as I blossomed into womanhood, I began to feel her power flowing through me. My prayers were no longer merely words: I could spread sickness among opposing armies, or bring needed rain to our fields. I was no longer merely a priestess; I was a sorceress.

Some even said I was Atar'atha come to life, with bronze skin and long raven hair that grew down to my waist. Suitors came from across the world to seek my hand in marriage, and my father, bless him, turned them all down. I was bride to my goddess and my city; how could I take a husband?

By the age of sixteen, I was the High Priestess of all Hatra. And my father did something unprecedented: so loved was I by the people, and so blessed by my goddess, that he placed the Talisman of Hatra in my care.

My brother was away, leading the armies of the north, or I'm sure he would have protested—he was the heir, and the talisman was his by rights. But for me, the weight of Atar'atha's icon around my neck felt like the most natural thing in the world. The Kingdom of Araba may have belonged to my father and my brother, but in every way that mattered, the City of Hatra belonged to me.

=[]=

Now I watch through the flames, eyes squinted, as the talisman turns red and molten. The necklace chain has turned to rivulets of gold, and tears stain my eyes, whether from the light of the fire or the hurt of my own betrayal, I do not know.

I leave the forges and walk alone through deserted streets. The great inns, once famed for their roaring fires and hospitality, are shuttered and closed; we have seen no traders for months. When I was young, I could stand on the palace wall and look out across the streets at night, and the city seemed every bit as alive as during the day—even more so on summer nights, when the heat made the air almost unbearable. In those months, as Shamash led the Sun over the Western horizon and Sin's disc lit the night, people would emerge onto the streets. And as the city came alive, the songs of bards mixed with the shouts of merchants into a beautiful cacophony that filled the night.

Can this truly be the same city as that Hatra of old? The temples look no less grand; as I walk, I pass shrines to a dozen different gods from a dozen different countries, all of them residents of Hatra, now.

Or, at least they were. Now the temples look as deserted as the rest of the city. There are no priests outside offering blessings, or asking for alms. There is only darkness, and nothing but silence echoes from between the massive stone pillars. Perhaps even the gods have fled.

Beyond the walls, the sky is lit with a faint orange glow from a thousand campfires: Shapur is coming with his armies. Only one thing can save us now . . . invasion.

=[]=

The first time I heard the name of Shapur was in a letter from my brother. He wrote in his usual arrogant manner about an upstart faction—the Sassanids—fighting for control of the Persian Empire. The Parthians, long the rulers of Persia, were struggling, and my brother committed our armies to defend them. We had relied on the Parthians for many years, joining forces to keep both Araba and Persia free from Roman invaders.

Besides, Parthian gods resided in Hatra, and it would not do to anger them.

But the Sassanids were unstoppable. And Shapur, son of their king Ardashir, was their commander. He was a brilliant tactician, a ferocious fighter, and he inspired a loyalty in his men that verged on fanaticism. The Sassanids won their Empire, and then they came for us.

The armies of all Araba, united under my brother, met them in a terrible battle at Shahrazoor. Aided by my prayers, we killed Ardashir and drove their forces from our lands. But in the process, our army was devastated. And two weeks later, my brother's body returned to the city, resting in a palanquin and wrapped in a burial shroud. It was said that he had been stabbed by Shapur himself, driven to rage by Ardashir's death.

My father, with the death of his only son, was consumed not with rage but with grief. He stopped holding open court, and as the pleas of the people went unanswered, rumors began to spread through the city that the king was sick, or dead, or that the Sassanids were already marching on us. Shapur was their king now, and no one held any illusions that he was gone for good.

Shapur did return, swiftly and violently. He rebuilt his armies with astonishing and disturbing speed, and his men fought with a zeal we could not match. He plucked away the cities of Araba one by one, leaving Hatra stranded and alone, its invincible walls protecting us from the Sassanid storm.

Amidst the despair, I heard one bit of news that gave me hope. Despite the fact that Hatra was cut off, I still held a fearsome reputation as the beautiful and powerful Sorceress of Atar'atha. And from the few travelers who still arrived, I heard an interesting rumor indeed: of the suitors who were still enamored of me, one of them was Shapur himself! He was mustering an army, determined to stake his claim, to conquer the unconquerable and take me as his bride.

Being bride to a Persian did not fill me with joy. Still, as Queen of the Sassanids, my city would be safe and prosperous. I could protect Hatra, and lay favor on it from afar, in a way that even Atar'atha could not.

When I told my father of my thoughts, the rage that illuminated his face was like nothing I had ever seen. "Shapur has already taken my son from me. I will not let him take my daughter!"

"Please, Father," I said. "Hatra has been cut off from our trade routes; the grain stores are running low. If I am Queen to Shapur, then Hatra can rise to prominence again as part of the Sassanid Empire! If I only—"

But my father's enraged bellow cut me off. "I will not hear of such a thing! Hatra has stood independent for five hundred years. It has withstood the onslaughts of Roman Emperors, of Lakhmid Kings, and it will damn well withstand a Persian whelp!"

"Our walls may stand," I said, "but our people will starve! Shapur is smart, and cunning, not like the Romans, who were too full of themselves to pay attention to the gods. He rotates his men out of the front lines to keep them fresh; he does not let his supply lines languish; he even ensures that his army camps are kept clean and free of rot. Sickness does not take hold there, and he has priests of his own to counter my prayers. He will come, and he will wait, and until we give him what he wants, nothing will dissuade him."

My father grit his teeth. "This madness that you counsel—I will not hear it!" He stood up, but clenched his back almost immediately, wincing in pain. He glared at me as he sat back down. "You wear the Talisman of Hatra around your neck, Daughter. Never forget. You are bound to the city now, and its fate is tied to your own."

I bowed my head. "I will always be loyal to you, Father. I am the High Priestess of Hatra, and I will always fight for its people."

My father nodded. "Then go to the temple and pray for our victory."

=[]=

But there are no more prayers to be offered. I stand on the steps of Atar'atha's temple, dressed in my finest robes, with flowers laced through my hair, when Shapur's army storms the gates. Without the talisman's magic holding the walls secure, the gates breach easily, and his men pour inside.

Shapur is a fair conqueror. He gathers all the people in the square, but it soon becomes clear that there will be no massacre, no collection of slaves. He is not a demon like the Lakhmids, or a brute like the Romans. He cares for his people, even those he has just conquered.

He lays claim to the Palace, and sits on my father's throne. My heart aches to see a foreigner sitting there, but I push those feelings aside; it does not matter who sits on the throne of Hatra, as long as the city prospers.

When he calls me before him, I am struck by how young he is; I knew he was not old, but he looks even younger than me. His eyes are green and piercing, and when he looks at me, I return his gaze.

I am defiant, confident, and I smile when he turns away first. I have seen that reaction in countless men. He is intimidated. Good.

Then my breath catches in my throat; two soldiers are dragging my father to Shapur's feet. They drop him to the ground, and he lies prostrate, but Shapur barks an order and the soldiers help him up.

"We found him in his bedroom, my Lord," says one of the men. "He was preparing to commit suicide with a dagger."

Shapur rises and walks down the dais to my father, until he is standing only a few paces away. The 'whelp' looks strong and kingly in comparison. It is clearer than ever now: my father is the past. The man who would be my husband is the future.

"Suicide?" Shapur says. "I would have expected better from the King of Hatra. Should you have not been standing on the walls, the legendary Talisman of Hatra in your hand, rallying your troops to defend your city?" Scorn lines his face. "And you call yourself a king."

My father's head is bowed. "My daughter wields the Blessing of Atar'atha; the Talisman is hers. But it has failed to protect our city." His voice fades to a whisper. "The power of the Goddess is broken."

Shapur turns to me, and for the first time, speaks. "Princess an-Nadira. The rumors of your beauty pale in comparison to the reality." He offers his hand, and when he presses his lips to my fingers, there is genuine warmth in his kiss. "If the City of Hatra will accept me as its Master and rightful Lord, there is no further need for strife or bloodshed. Your father and your family will be well-treated. And you will return with me to Persia and reign by my side as Queen." He smiled. "What say you?"

I bow before him. "You do me a great honor, Shapur of the Sassanids. I would be honored to be your Queen."

Then my father rises and spits at Shapur's feet. Strength has returned to his eyes, and he pulls himself loose from his guards.

Shapur raises his hand. "Your spirit does you credit, Sanatruq, but you have been beaten in battle. Hatra rightly belongs to the Sassanids now and to me as their King."

"Hatra can only be defeated," my father grimaces, "by treachery and lies! As long as the Talisman of Hatra is worn by one of the royal bloodline, the gates will stay intact!"

"And yet here we are," Shapur smiles. "My forces have been victorious, and Hatra lies defeated." He turns to me. "Show your father that my victory was honorable. Show him the Talisman."

I grit my teeth, but I do not regret my decision. "The talisman is no more. It lies melted in the fires of the palace forge."

It is hard to say who looks more shocked, my father or Shapur. I glare at my father, whose shock turns to disbelief. "I counseled you to yield to Shapur," I tell him, "but you did not listen. You would rather have our city starve behind a siege, or wither from a years-long blockade, as people died behind its sacred walls. Hatra may be conquered, but it will survive!"

My father opens his mouth, but no words come out. I can almost see the last of his sanity giving out under the hurt of my betrayal, and I turn away.

Then Shapur speaks. "Your father gave you the Talisman, did he not?"

I look to him, hoping to find refuge in his warmth, but there is only disappointment in his eyes. "Yes," I say.

"You were the keeper of the Talisman, and yet you destroyed it. You betrayed your father, your family, even your goddess."

Not Shapur, too! "I did it to save Hatra. The Power of the Talisman would have suffocated us until we died!"

Shapur shakes his head, and gestures to the guards. "I must think on this. Take them both away."

They throw us in the dungeon. My father has gone silent; he lies on the cot, staring at the ceiling. I huddle in the corner, facing the wall, and pray to Atar'atha, but I can feel that her power has left me. My words are just words now, and nothing I can say will bring my goddess back.

I am trapped now, with the man I have betrayed, surrounded by the walls of the city that is no longer mine. All night, my wailing echoes through the tiny dungeon, but the pain in my ears and throat is only the tiniest shadow of what lies in my heart.

=[]=

I have no strength left, and my dreams and hopes are crumbling around me. Word of my deed has spread, and people line the street, pelting me with rotten food. A rock hits me, and I stagger to my knees, only to be yanked to my feet by a guard.

Shapur has set up a pavilion in the main city square, and his army is assembled. I limp through a narrow corridor between the soldiers, to the foot of his throne. I stand straight and look him in the eyes, determined not to show him weakness. I cried everything away last night. My father was right—this man is nothing more than a whelp.

Unlike yesterday, Shapur does not turn away under my gaze. And when he speaks, his voice booms across the square. "Soldiers and warriors of Persia, long have I fought by your side as your leader and your king. And through it all, I have always done right by you, have I not?"

The soldiers shout, and I wince at the raucous cheering, the swords banging on shields, the sound of spears, and feet thumping against the ground. The cheering goes on so long, I think it will never stop, until Shapur raises his hands. "I carry no jewels in my crown, or fancy robe, or retinue of servants. I may be your king, but I am also your fellow soldier."

The cheering is even louder this time, and I close my eyes to brace myself against the onslaught. When it finally dies down, Shapur's voice sounds again. "And do you know why? It is because I value not gold or jewels or spoils of war, but loyalty, pride, and Persia!"

The cheering sounds again, and I have no doubt that these men would happily die for their king. How can even a Sorceress fight such power?

"Through loyalty and honor we gain our strength. I came to Hatra to find a Queen worthy of that honor, a Queen whose devotion was so strong that she had been entrusted with the very power of the gods. And when I got here, what did I find? A Queen who had betrayed her father, betrayed her Goddess, betrayed her people!"

"No," I whisper. "No, I love my people."

But Shapur does not hear. "How could I ever accept such a treacherous woman as queen?" He shakes his head. "To do so would be to betray the very principles that make us strong!"

Then he makes a quick gesture, and I am roughly seized from both sides. My hands and feet are bound, and my robes are stripped from me. I am pushed roughly to the ground, and through the pain, I feel wetness on the dirt . . . blood. I look up at Shapur, and for a moment, I see pity in his eyes. Then the rope attached to my arm jerks, and I roll on the ground, and terror fills me. The other end of the robe is being tied around the neck of a horse. The horse has no reins or saddle, and it bucks against the ropes that hold it. It's clearly untamed; a wild horse, captured from one of the herds that roam the desert oases.

"Let an-Nadira be dragged through the streets and the deserts, to die as she deserves. Hatra will be razed to the ground, and its ruins left to be claimed by the sands. It is tainted by treachery now, and if I add it to my

Empire, that treachery will taint us in turn. Honor must be preserved. Only by doing so will Persia thrive!"

Using every bit of strength I still possess, I struggle to my knees, and tears splash down my cheeks for Hatra's fate.

In the depths of my disgrace and despair, I suddenly feel a tiny whisper in my mind, a whisper that grows, until it turns to a surging of power, like it used to during my most intimate prayers. Atar'atha is within me!

"You think you are so mighty, King of the Sassanids, but your reign will be short and brutal." My voice is quiet, but I can tell there is power in my words. "Destroy Hatra if you wish, but your own great cities will fare no different. You think you value loyalty, but in killing this woman you betray the person who would give you power; who would make you the mightiest Emperor east of Rome! Instead you will fall, and your name forgotten to history."

I take a deep breath and shout, "So sayeth an-Nadira, the Princess and High Priestess of Hatra, the Sorceress of Atar'atha!"

Shapur looks stunned for a moment, then he raises his hand, and I can hear behind me as the horse's ropes are let go. It bolts for the gates, and when the rope pulls me off my feet, Atar'atha's presence leaves me, and the world turns to screaming agony.

=[]=

Andrew S. Williams *is a speculative fiction writer living in Seattle. His work has appeared in* Every Day Fiction *and* Jersey Devil Press. *You can find his thoughts on writing, life, and more modern civilization at* http://www.offthewrittenpath.com.

SUMERIA TO THE STARS

Jonathan Vos Post

=[]=

It's hard to find someone else who has as many and as varied accomplishments as Jonathan Vos Post (see bio). In the course of one month, when I requested status of a rewrite, he politely informed me that it was, "in progress," while during that time he had also written two more complete novels, submitted a dissertation for yet another PhD, and was running multiple businesses, all while teaching at colleges and conferences. How he had time to write this in the first place, is beyond me. The following story, Sumeria to the Stars, *was originally written as a novella and integrated excerpts of the latest research papers in quantum physics and algebraic theories and other subjects I cringed at in school. Now condensed, it still maintains its original triple plot which explores the discovery and subsequent research of ancient clay tablets, suggesting man's past is not quite what we think it is. Oh, and there's still a bit of that quantum physics and algebraic theories stuff, too.*

=[]=

1. Cuneiform Clay Tablets as Computer Memory

Before today's nanotech molecular memories, or the previous generation's Blue-ray discs; before the earlier DVDs and CD-ROMs, floppy discs, videotapes, audio 8-track cassettes, mimeographs, typewriter paper, parchment, or even papyrus, was the first widely used recording medium: the enduring clay tablet of cuneiforms, made by the hundreds of thousands in the Old Babylonian period. What we are staggered to now realize is that these discs suggest around 1700 B.C. in Mesopotamia, the secret of a starship civilization was buried.

Leading historians and cosmologists squealed like stuck pigs.

"Impossible!" swore one historian. "Sumerians barely had their base 60 sexigesimal number system by then. How could anyone in Larsa, one hundred twenty years before the city was captured in 1762 B.C., possibly have had calculus or that crazy string theory stuff?"

"Ludicrous, and certainly a hoax!" insisted a cosmologist. "How could mud-daubed primitives in the Fertile Crescent, thirty-seven and a half centuries ago, have known about Clebsch-Gordan coefficients in nuclear physics, let alone mass ratios of leptons and baryons?"

Duncan J. Melville of St. Lawrence University pointed at the first photograph on the wall-sized projection screen with his laser pointer.

"YBC 7289 is a small clay disc containing the rough sketch of a square and its diagonals. Across one of the diagonals is scrawled 1, 24, 51, 10—a sexagesimal number that corresponds to the decimal number 1.4142129, an approximation of the square root of two. Below is the answer to the problem of calculating the diagonal of a square whose sides are 0.5 units. This bears on the issue of whether the Babylonians had discovered Pythagoras's theorem some 1,300 years before Pythagoras did."

Dr. Dugan Dwamish, sitting next to me, whispered in sushi-stinking breath: "They knew a hell of a lot more than the Pythagorean theorem."

Melville went to the next slide. "No tablet bears the well-known algebraic equation, that the squares of the two smaller sides of a right-angled triangle equal the square of the hypotenuse. But Plimpton 322 contains columns of numbers that seem to have been used in calculating Pythagorean triples, sets of numbers that correspond to the sides and hypotenuse of a right triangle, like three, four, and five."

Melville then showed and explained a photograph of the University of Pennsylvania's excavations at Nippur in 1899. The photo looked like a cross between a *Raiders of the Lost Ark* set, an M.C. Escher etching, and a Piranesi print of uncanny towers beside a pit with descending staircases. Nippur was the principal center of scribal training in the Old Babylonian period. The tablets excavated there provided the basis for research through about 2015 A.D. on mathematical education and curriculum, and now the new, almost unbelievable finds.

"Institute for the Study of the Ancient World," said Melville to the packed audience of scientists, educators, and reporters, "assures us that, since the second half of the nineteenth century, thousands of cuneiform tablets from the Old Babylonian period have been found at various sites in ancient Mesopotamia."

The map showed a mix of familiar and exotic names. The Tigris and Euphrates rivers, with Mari to the northwest, Babylon and Sippar, Uruk, and Ur farther southeast. There was Larsa, where the strangest tablets had been found, down from Nippur and Kish.

Melville put up a photo of a thin-faced man with hair cut short on the sides, wireframe eyeglasses, and pursed lips. "The considerable mathematical knowledge of the Babylonians was uncovered by the Austrian mathematician, Otto E. Neugebauer," he said, "who died in 1990. Scholars since then have turned to the task of understanding how the knowledge was used."

"What about the Calabi-Yau data?" whispered Dr. Dwamish.

"Ssshhh," I said. "He's getting to it."

Melville pointed to Neugebauer's hand drawing, of two sides of YBC

4713. "In the 1920's, he became aware that hundreds of Babylonian mathematical tablets lay unstudied in European and American museums."

"YBC?" said Dugan.

"Yale Babylonian Collection," I whispered back. "Keep up."

"YBC 4713 is a tablet showing a series of abstract problems," continued Melville, sweating, perhaps not only from the spotlight. "While some mathematical techniques learned in scribal schools were intended for use in scribes' later careers, many would never have been applied in practical situations."

He jumped to the next slide, with a much simpler tablet. "This is a school tablet with an incomplete calculation. The early training of scribes consisted of copying lists of units of measure and arithmetic tables. Later, they practiced calculations and simple problem solving."

"Simple? He calls Calabi-Yau manifold simple?" Dugan asked.

"Ssssshhh."

"Sumerian math was a sexagesimal system, meaning it was based on the number 60. Why the Sumerians picked 60 as the base of their numbering system is not known. The idea developed from an earlier, more complex system known from 3200 B.C. in which the positions in a number alternated between 6 and 10 as bases."

"That's nuts."

Melville showed a slide of a tablet, bearing rows and columns of squares, with complicated combinations of wedges. "A 59 x 59 multiplication table is too large to memorize, so tablets were needed to provide essential look-up tables. Cuneiform numbers are simple to write because each is a combination of only two symbols, those for 1 and for 10."

"Look-up tables. Now he's talking like a computer guy," said Dugan with a smile.

"This tablet shows a list of practical problems, worked out step-by-step, to calculate width of a canal, given its other dimensions. These calculations," he pointed with the laser, "are the cost of digging the canal, under different assumptions about a worker's daily wage."

This made perfect sense to me. We have vestiges of sexagesimal. "1:23:45" on a digital hologram computer display means 1 (times 60-squared) seconds + 23 times 60 seconds + 45 seconds. 60 seconds in a minute, 60 minutes in an hour.

"The students doing these homework problems spoke Akkadian, a Semitic language unrelated to Sumerian. The Sumerian in their problem sets was in a language already extinct during their time. But both languages were written in cuneiform, meaning wedge-shaped, because of the marks made by punching a reed into softened wet clay."

So the notation was a unifying force, like the alphabets that swept the modern world, or the 0 and 1 in the molecular memory of a computer.

"Here," the soundtrack music swelled, "is YBC 8886. These tables are what scientists today call *Clebsch-Gordan coefficients*. These are mathematical symbols used to integrate products of three spherical harmonics. Clebsch-Gordan coefficients commonly arise in applications involving the addition of angular momentum in *quantum mechanics*."

"Quantum mechanics!" whispered Dugan, loudly enough that someone in the row in front of us turned around and shushed him.

"If products of more than three spherical harmonics are desired," said Melville, "use a generalization known as Wigner 6j-symbols or Wigner 9j-symbols. These," he pointed with the sparkling dot of the laser, "are undoubtedly Wigner 6j-symbols or Wigner 9j-symbols, although in base 60 numbers. Gentlemen, the ancient Babylonians either knew quantum mechanics, or were in communication with someone who did."

The audience jumped to their feet and bombarded Melville with questions. He held up his hands. "Please wait until I've shown all the slides. Then I'll take questions, one at a time."

Melville continued, pointing at the projection screen as the slides shuffled through. "Here is the most recent dig at Larsa. This next slide is of the principal investigator supervising the *in situ* hologrammetry. Next is YBC 8886. Tables in this slide are look-up tables of the most sophisticated math we've ever seen in any archeological artifact."

Melville squinted at his glowing NotePad, as if still not familiar with the terminology. "Calabi-Yau spaces are important in string theory. One model posits the geometry of the universe to consist of a ten-dimensional space of the form M x V, where M is a four-dimensional manifold of space-time and V is a six-dimensional compact Calabi-Yau space. Although the main application of Calabi-Yau spaces is in theoretical physics, they're also interesting from a purely mathematical standpoint.

"Also called Calabi-Yau manifolds, they have interesting properties. One is that the symmetries in the numbers forming the Hodge diamond are a compact Calabi-Yau manifold. It is surprising that these symmetries, called *mirror symmetry*, can be realized by another Calabi-Yau manifold, the so-called mirror of the original Calabi-Yau manifold. The two manifolds together form a mirror pair, through the *Supercompactification Triality Theorem of 2023*. Although the definition can be generalized to any dimension, they are usually considered to have three complex dimensions. Since their complex structure may vary, it is convenient to think of them as having six real dimensions and a fixed smooth structure. The ancient tables are very similar to these."

He advanced to a page of last year's Nobel Prize acceptance speeches from Stephen Hawking, Roger Penrose, and Jacob Bekenstein.

"The authors of these tables knew results in *black holes, string theory, M-theory,* and *multiverse cosmology* 3,750 years ago that our greatest minds just rediscovered last year."

The room exploded in hub-bub. Melville couldn't get them to settle down. I left as several beefy security guys came into the auditorium. Good time to hit the men's room.

And then I needed a stiff drink.

2. Nippur and Nanotechnology

"I mentioned today's *Nanotech Molecular Memories*," said the Director of the ultra-secret Interstellar Intelligence Directorate to the President of the United States, "which use no science beyond what was known in the late twentieth century. But how could anyone in what's now Iraq know mid-twentieth century nuclear physics and early twenty-first century black holes, string theory, M-theory, and multiverse cosmology?"

The President responded, "My science adviser told me black holes are an eighteenth century idea. He briefed me that the concept of a body so massive that even light could not escape, was first put forward by English geologist, John Michell."

"That's true, ma'am," said the IID Director, glancing at his NotePad, "And in 1796, French mathematician and astronomer Pierre-Simon Laplace promoted the same idea in his book, *Exposition du système du Monde*. His work was pivotal to the development of mathematical astronomy and statistics. However such *dark stars* were largely ignored in the nineteenth century, since it was not understood how a massless wave such as light could be influenced by gravity."

"Hair-splitting," said the President. She sipped coffee from an oversize mug designed by Teddy Roosevelt. "What does that tell us about the clay tablets dug up in Nipple, or whatever the damned place was."

"The first batch were from Larsa, south of Nippur. The point is, if they were about John Michell's idea, we could chalk that up to ingenuity, but it still would be qualitative reasoning. Problem is, it wasn't eighteenth century stuff, which would be amazing, but not such a top priority national security matter. Not even early twentieth century stuff."

"How so?"

"It was in 1915," he continued, "that Albert Einstein developed his *Theory of General Relativity*, having earlier shown that gravity does influence light's motion. A few months later, Karl Schwarzschild, a German Physicist, gave the solution for the gravitational field of a point mass and a spherical mass. Schwarzschild accomplished this triumph using *tensor calculus*, while serving in the German army during World War I. Unfortunately, he died the following year from disease contracted while at the Russian front, so his work was not completed. We see no tensor calculus as such in the Nippur tablets, but there *are* tables of results that we don't know how else could be computed."

"Schwarzschild," said the President, "as in the *Schwarzschild radius*?"

"Exactly. This solution had a peculiar behavior at what is now called the Schwarzschild radius, where it became singular, meaning that some of the terms in Einstein's equations became infinite."

"Physicists, unlike mathematicians," she said, "seem to hate infinity."

"That's right. It hurts them when their theories blow up. Monsignor Georges Henri Joseph Édouard Lemaître proposed what became known as the *Big Bang Theory of the Origin of the Universe*, which he called his *Hypothesis of the Primeval Atom*."

"I don't like to hear the words *atom* and *bang*, except from my Secretary of Energy, or the Joint Chiefs," said the President.

"I quite understand, Madam President, but this is potentially a greater threat than nukes. In 1931, Subrahmanyan Chandrasekhar calculated, using general relativity, that a non-rotating body of electron-degenerate matter above 1.44 solar masses would collapse."

"I'm not familiar with this Chandrasekhar."

"Subrahmanyan Chandrasekhar was an Indian-born American astrophysicist who, with William A. Fowler, won the 1983 Nobel Prize in Physics for key discoveries on late evolutionary stages of massive stars. Chandrasekhar was the nephew of Sir Chandrasekhara Venkata Raman, who won the Nobel Prize for Physics in 1930."

"I've heard that Nobel prizes run in families like seats in Congress," she said.

"Yes. Chandrasekhar served on University of Chicago faculty from 1937 until his death in 1995. Arguments were opposed by many contemporaries such as Lev Landau, who argued that some yet unknown mechanism would stop the collapse."

"Landau, the one from the former USSR?"

"Yes, ma'am. Lev Landau was a prominent Soviet physicist who made fundamental contributions to many areas of theoretical physics. But I digress."

"I'm not going anywhere," she said. "I have a meet-and-greet with some Girl Scouts in a half hour."

"Okay, I'll move it along. In 1932, Landau proposed that every star has a condensed core consisting of *one gigantic nucleus* that does not behave in accord with *the ordinary laws of quantum mechanics*. Later he suggested all stars have a neutron core that generates energy as nuclei and electrons condense onto it. He received the 1962 Nobel Prize in Physics for developing a mathematical theory of superfluidity that accounts for the properties of liquid helium II at a temperature below -270.98° Celsius."

She raised an eyebrow.

He tapped his NotePad. "In 1939, Robert Oppenheimer predicted neutron stars above three solar masses collapse into black holes as per Chandrasekhar, and that no law of physics could stop some stars from collapsing to black holes."

"Oppenheimer? He ran the physics side of the Manhattan Project? Security risk?"

"Yes ma'am. Oppenheimer interpreted singularity at the boundary of the Schwarzschild radius as indicating this was the boundary of a bubble in which time stopped."

"And this whole tablet deal makes us think long and hard about time?"

"Precisely. Oppenheimer's theory is a valid point of view for external observers, but not for infalling observers. Because of this, collapsed stars were called *frozen stars*. An outside observer would see the surface of the star frozen in time at the instant where its collapse takes it inside the Schwarzschild radius. Light from the surface of the frozen star becomes red-shifted very fast, which is what quickly causes the *blackness* of the black holes."

"Better dead than red," she said.

He gave a forced laugh. "Many physicists could not accept the idea of time standing still at the Schwarzschild radius, and there was little interest in the subject for over twenty years. But then modern math kicked in. It was 1958 when David Finkelstein identified the Schwarzschild surface as an event horizon, a *perfect unidirectional membrane in which causal influences can cross in only one direction*. Rather than contradicting Oppenheimer's results, this extended them to include the point of view of infalling observers. Finkelstein's solution extended the Schwarzschild solution for the future of observers falling into the black hole."

"More names than I need to know," she said, putting her hand over tired eyes.

"Just trying to be complete. These results came at the beginning of the golden age of general relativity, with weird things like black holes becoming mainstream subjects of research. This process was helped by the discovery of pulsars in 1967, which were, within a few years, shown to be rapidly rotating neutron stars. Until that time, neutron stars, like black holes, were regarded as just theoretical curiosities. However, the discovery of pulsars showed their physical relevance and spurred a further interest in all types of compact objects that might be formed by gravitational collapse. Oh, and D. C. Robinson emerged with the *No-Hair Theorem.*.."

"Einstein had long hair," she said. "Maybe this was a step backwards."

Again a polite chuckle. "That math states a stationary black hole solution is completely described by the three parameters of the Kerr–Newman metric; mass, angular momentum, and electric charge. So some of the tables on the Nippur tablets are at least late twentieth century intelligence, which bothers us considerably.

"But it gets worse. The black hole stuff, and the *anthropic principle* which made multiverse theory at least semi-respectable, leads to the Calabi-Yau stuff which, in the form we see on the tables, were at least early twenty-first century. That lets us grasp how anachronistic the tablets are. But I'm here this morning, madam President, more so because of something else.

"Our scanning ion microscopes show us unimpeachable evidence of traces of nanomaterials stuck to the surface of some tablets."

"Nanotechnology? But then the Sumerians weren't just doing theory."

"Exactly. They, or someone they knew, built things that worked. Our microscopy shows broken-down remnants of *nanobots* and *nanocomputers*! They had very dangerous stuff and we can't understand how."

"Mud bricks are not a national security nightmare," she said. "But nanoweapons or time travel are."

A West Wing staffer poked his head into the oval office. "The Girl Scouts are ready," he said.

The President sighed, then snapped her face to a telegenic smile. "Okay. Thank you, sir. Next?"

3. Cheating on a Final Exam

"This is Van Damm, your Uncle Sam on the hologram," his voice announced as the theme song by *Viola & the Terrorists* swelled, and the exploding red, white, and blue icosahedron logo flew apart into spinning faceted fragments. "Tonight's interview is with that dashing Indiana Jones of the maddening mud tablets, Dr. Dugan Dwamish."

"Actually *clay* tablets, Van. I'm happy to be here," said Dr. Dwamish.

"Sure you are. Mud tablets and clay bricks, clay tablets and mud bricks, whatever. Twenty *million* viewers want to know—*time travel*, or *secrets of the ancients*, or *contact with extraterrestrials*?"

"First, Van, let me say I'm not on the payroll of St. Lawrence University, where Duncan J. Melville is doing a bang-up job of explaining what his team has excavated. I'm just a humble millionaire software consultant, and so I can say what the tenured professors are afraid to say."

"No conflict of interest like those pointy-headed college boys, afraid to bite the hand that feeds them, right. So—contact with extraterrestrials?"

"That would explain a lot. Civilizations in other star systems might be thousands of years ahead of us, and master both starship technology and whatever will make the local humans think they're gods. Remember the founding myth of the city of Babylon?"

"You betcha! Roll those holograms."

Images flashed on the projection screen and Dr. Dwamish pointed at the first one.

"That's Oannes right there, the name given by the Babylonian writer, Berossus in the third century B.C., to a mythical being who taught mankind wisdom. Berossus describes Oannes as having the body of a fish, but underneath the figure of a man. He is described as dwelling in the Persian Gulf, and rising out of the waters in the daytime wearing a helmet filled with water. See? Looks like a space helmet, doesn't it? The half-fish was said to have enlightened mankind with instruction in writing, the mathematical arts, and the various sciences such as metallurgy."

"Not biblical Onan, who spilled his seed."

"Um, no. The name, *Oannes,* was once thought to be derived from that of the ancient Babylonian god, Ea, but it is now known that the name is the Greek form of the Babylonian, Uanna, or Uan, a name used for Adapa in texts from the Library of Ashurbanipal. The Assyrian texts attempt to connect the word to the Akkadian for a craftsman, ummanu, but this is a merely a pun."

"If you say so, Dr. Dwamish. I'm lucky if I can make a play on words in English that doesn't offend someone. So spill. Your words, I mean, not your seed. So this fishy guy in the helmet. He looks to you like an ancient astronaut?"

"I'm hardly the first to say so. Iosif Shklovsky and Carl Sagan cited tales of Oannes as deserving closer scrutiny as a possible instance of paleocontact due to its consistency and detail."

"Paleocontact?"

"Yes, Van. According to certain authors, intelligent extraterrestrial beings called *ancient astronauts*, or ancient aliens, have visited Earth, and this contact is connected with the origins or development of human cultures, technologies, and religions. Deities from most, if not all, religions are actually extraterrestrials, technologies taken as evidence of divine status. These proposals were popularized in the latter half of the twentieth century, by Erich von Däniken, Zecharia Sitchin, Robert K. G. Temple, and David Icke."

"Okay, ancient astronauts are often used as a plot device in science fiction. Remember the big tablet and the ape men in *2001: A Space Odyssey?* But the idea that ancient astronauts actually existed is not taken seriously by most academics, is it, Dr. Dwamish?"

"The notion has received little or no credulous attention in peer reviewed studies. You said it yourself. Professors are afraid to speculate in ways that might get them fired or could cut off their grant money. In this case, let's use *Occam's Razor.* Is it more likely that primitive people in the Middle East thirty-seven centuries ago mastered nuclear physics and black hole Calabi-Yau Manifold Mathematics, or that someone who already knew those things came to Earth and told them?"

"I've never been shaved by Occam. So you tell me, and the ghost of Carl Sagan, and our twenty *million* viewers."

"Suppose you hand in your final exam to the teacher. You have the right answer, written down plain as day. However, the teacher gives you an 'F'. You ask the teacher, *why'd you give me that 'F'—I got the right answer*? The teacher responds, *I told you to show your work, but you didn't show me any calculation, and I didn't let anyone use their computers in the classroom.* What are we to think?"

"I think the teacher is an A-hole. Not being allowed to use a computer?"

"I mean about not showing your work."

"Well, Doc, you could be a lucky guesser—"

"But nobody thinks the Babylonians could be lucky enough to guess the right Clebsch-Gordan coefficients in nuclear physics, or the mass ratios of leptons and baryons."

"Baryons in Babylon, baby! Or, Doc, you could be so smart that you did it all in your head."

"But if I was that smart, Van, I'd be the teacher, not the student."

"Maybe you cheated. Maybe you copied the answer from someone who hit the books more than you."

"Exactly, Van. Maybe the Babylonians cheated on their final exam. Maybe they cribbed the answers from a vastly superior civilization of underwater beings who lived a thousand years each, but were more comfortable undersea in the Persian Gulf, and had to wear helmets full of water when they walked upon the land and taught the Babylonians."

"And then they climbed in their flying saucers and zoomed away?"

"Your guess is as good as mine."

"Not really. If your guess was as good as mine, you'd be the holo-host, and I'd be the badly made-up college boy. We'll be right back after these words from my sponsors, about many fine products and superior services. This is Van Damm, your grand slam with an oral exam in the traffic jam."

The imploding red, white, and blue icosahedron logo reconstructed from spinning faceted fragments and morphed into a globe of Earth, while the last chords from *Viola & the Terrorists* echoed like the trumps of doom.

4. Time, Time is on My Side

"The media doesn't know about nanodevice fragments found on tablets such as YBC 8888," said the Director of Interstellar Intelligence Directorate to the audience of committee chairmen and researchers. "That buys us time. What else have we deduced? I need to brief the President. She was quite clear that nanoweapons and time travel are both threats. So which is it? Time travel, or secrets of the ancients, or contact with extraterrestrials, or what? And if this is a national security threat, *who* should be doing *what* about it?"

The Chairman of the Ancient Astronauts Committee replied "We're skeptical about the *Chariot of the Gods* notion. But, on the other hand, we must keep an open mind." Then he quoted Shklovski and Sagan:

"Stories like the Oannes legend, and representations especially of the earliest civilizations on Earth, deserve much more critical studies than have been performed heretofore, with the possibility of direct contact with an extraterrestrial civilization as one of many possible alternative explanations."

"Weaknesses in that approach?" asked the IID Director.

"Proponents of ancient astronaut theories maintain humans are either descendants or creations of beings who landed on Earth thousands of years ago. Much of human knowledge, religion, and culture came from extraterrestrial visitors in ancient times, as ancient astronauts acted as a *mother culture*. Or civilization may have evolved on Earth twice, so visitation of ancient astronauts was the return of descendants of ancient humans whose population was separated from earthbound humans. Although these ideas are generally discounted by academic and skeptical communities.

"In his 1979 book, *Broca's Brain*, Sagan said he and Shklovski might have inspired the wave of 1970's ancient astronaut books, disproving von Däniken and other uncritical writers. Sagan reiterated extraterrestrial visits to Earth were possible but unproven, and improbable," the chairman said.

"Strengths of the approach?"

"Proponents argue that the evidence for ancient astronauts comes from supposed gaps in historical and archaeological records, but that's the same fallacy as the *God of the Gaps* argument by creationists. We can do much with mere artwork and legends."

"What kind of legends?"

"Such as *vimanas*, mythological flying machines found in the Hindu epics and in the Book of Ezekiel in the Old Testament. A vimana was a flying object seen as a fiery whirlwind which, when descended to the ground, gave the appearance of being made of metal. It was a wheel within a wheel containing four occupants, *living creatures*, whose likeness was that of man. Wherever the wheels went, the creatures went, and when the living creatures were lifted up, the wheels were lifted up. In chapter four of *Chariots of the Gods?* entitled, *Was God an Astronaut?*, von Däniken refers to Ezekiel seeing a spaceship, just as Morris Jessup also said in 1956. The *Book of Enoch* tells of similar flying objects and beings called *the Watchers* who mutinied from 'heaven' and descended to Earth, and Enoch is taken to various corners of the Earth in the object and even to heaven. But there no maps on the tablets of, say, Antarctica, or other indication of such travels."

"Assessment?"

"These, and others such as in Genesis 6:1-4: *Nephilim were on the earth in those days, and also afterward, when the sons of God came in to the daughters of men, and they bore children to them*. In the King James Version they are identified as *giants* and are loosely interpreted as depicting extraterrestrial contact or technologies. Characteristics of the Ark of the Covenant and the Urim and Thummim are identified as high technology, from alien origins. Absent or incomplete explanations of historical or archaeological data point to existence of ancient astronauts. We differ. *Absence of evidence is not evidence of absence.* The evidence of the crackpots include archaeological artifacts they argue are anachronistic or beyond the technical capabilities of the historical cultures. Sometimes referred to as OOP or *out-of-place* artifacts. We have the most solid OOP ever."

"Nonanachronistic but anomalous constructs?"

"For example, the ancient Nazca Lines comprise hundreds of enormous ground drawings etched into the high desert landscape of Peru. But they could have been made with appropriate technology. Joe Nickell of the University of Kentucky showed that pretty conclusively. Likewise to all the absurd claims of aliens assisting in the construction of ancient monuments and megalithic ruins such as the Giza pyramids of Egypt, Machu Picchu in Peru, Baalbek in Lebanon, or the Moai of Easter Island. Mainstream archeologists have shown how they could have moved large megaliths of at least forty tons. No mysteries there."

"Bottom line?" said the IID Director.

"None of the tables show data of the solar system, the Milky Way Galaxy, or the locations of pulsars, or anything. On one hand, they knew too much about the underlying physics of a cosmos with black holes. On the other hand, where's the evidence of extraterrestrial contact?"

"Genomics Team?" asked the IID Director.

"Biological disciplines maintain there's no evidence to support ancient astronauts or paleocontact," said the Chairman of the Genomics/Epigenomics Committee. "Francis Crick, co-discoverer of the double helix structure of DNA, strongly believed in what he called *directed panspermia*, that Earth was intentionally 'seeded' with life, probably in the form of blue-green algae, by intelligent extraterrestrial species, to ensure life's continuity. This could have been done on other planets of this class, using unmanned shuttles. We don't care about biogenesis, the origin of life billions of years ago. There are no inexplicable DNA in cells, functionally, nor in the noise of *junk DNA*, let alone anything showing that we interbred with extraterrestrials, notwithstanding movies like *Mars Needs Women*."

"Setting aside Nanoanalysis for last, what do we have? Secrets of the ancients? Nope. Paleocontact with extraterrestrials? Weak. That leaves time travel. Srinivasa?"

The Chairman of the Time Travel Committee, Srinivasa, stood up and continued the conversation. "Sir, Professor Paul J. Nahin, in *Time Machines: Time Travel in Physics, Metaphysics, and Science Fiction*, led us to interview Kip Thorne, author of *Black Holes and Time Warps*. Let me flick quickly through this PowerPoint."

"Slide 1: Nahin's presentation of the various arrows of time are illustrated as follows:

1a: The perceptual arrow of time or of time as perceived by the human observer;

1b: The cosmic expansion arrow of time believed conventionally to be *the* arrow of time from which all others are derived, although we received a more nuanced discussion by Professor Sean Carroll at Caltech, in *From Eternity to Here*;

1c: The gravitational arrow of time, which is more interesting, as that's where black holes come into the picture, and the Nippur tablets show too much understanding of black holes;

1d: And the quantum arrow of time including K particles which, unlike any other matter in nature, actually show a time asymmetry. For this reason Oxford's Roger Penrose suggested that K particles or *kaons* might be responsible for *the* arrow of time.

2: Methods that have been proposed for evading the implications of these arrows of time:

2a: Einsteinian relativity allows for limited time travel where local observers, through greater acceleration toward light speeds, experience time more slowly than their nonaccelerated peers, irrelevant to our inquiry;

2 b: Kurt Godel's solutions of Einstein's equations allowing for time travel in a rotating universe, unlike our universe which is not spinning like a dervish, and which is also much bigger than his;

2c: Kip Thorne's black hole wormhole solutions of time travel. Such time travel could only work at subatomic levels;

2d: J Richard Gott's black hole solutions which both allow time travel when the universe's mass is compressed to subatomic levels *and* allow the universe to create itself. However, our charter is no more able to explain the origin of the cosmos than the biology team is able to explain the origin of life;

2e: J Richard Gott's supposed cosmic strings for time travel assume the existence of as yet undiscovered cosmic strings;

2f: Ronald Mallett's gravitational laser solutions that suggest sufficient amounts of laser light create a gravitational force which can be capitalized to stir time and create a local field variance for the sending of signals through time. From this, we've gotten no positive results in the lab;

3: The various arrows of time are the academic side of mere wish fulfillment fantasy; eternal human yearning to revisit the past and remedy its wrongs or re-enjoy its joys, a task that may occur anyway owing to:

4: So-called time travel paradoxes that plague philosophical discussions of time, meaning, there is *zero evidence*.

"This casts a dim light on the potential of time travel. All we really know about what lays beyond the event horizon of a black hole or, in the *10 the minus 43rd power of the first second of the universe and with it multiple universes and quantum gravity and time travel,* is: we have a lot to learn. Not in time for your next White House briefing."

"Bottom line?"

"Physics and mathematics do not quite exclude time travel, but neither do they give us any workable engineering designs for time machines. We know whomever or whatever gathered the data for the nuclear physics and M-theory data on the tablets may have had fundamental science beyond our ability to interpret. We cannot exclude that there are scraps of such super-human science on the tablets, and our quantum supercomputer network has been crunching away cryptographically in search for incomprehensible needles in clay tablet-haystacks."

"So we don't know diddlysquat?"

"No sir, except for the Nanoanalysis."
"We'll break for breakfast and get back at 0900."

5. Molecules of Mari

That morning in a hardened deep underground conference room, the Director of Interstellar Intelligence Directorate asked Dr. Daisy Weal to speak.

"Dirt," said Dr. Weal. "The first point I want to make is how complicated the molecular database is in soil, which we had to establish as a baseline to figure out the anomalies of the dig."

"Talk *dirty* to me," whispered an IID researcher to another, who glared for a moment and then returned his attention to Dr. Weal.

"This is the way that Craig Tyler at Los Alamos puts it:

'There is an invisible world all around us. Air molecules mix and mingle. Radio waves course silently by. And in the soil under our feet, countless trillions of microscopic organisms perform important ecosystem services. They break down plant matter, protect crops from disease, and filter the groundwater. Yet less than one percent of them have been studied in a laboratory. Most of their activities—and most of the organisms themselves—remain unnamed and unexplored by science.'

"Such is the secret life of dirt," continued Dr. Weal, "and our ignorance of this is no small omission. But Los Alamos scientist, Cheryl Kuske, is changing all that with a sweeping approach to genetic study called *metagenomics*."

People around the table nodded, even if they weren't entirely clear on this.

"Traditional microbiology lab work entails studying the genetic information from a single organism grown in a culture. Metagenomics, on the other hand, works directly with the complex mixture of DNA found in samples taken from the natural environment—as in our soil sample from around the YBC 8888 dig, where the first fragments of ancient nanomachinery were found. While a genome is the complete set of genetic information for a particular organism such as the human genome, a metagenome is the complete set of genetic information for an entire community of organisms, and metagenomics describes the gathering and processing of this rich swath of biological information.

"A soil metagenome is a diverse and complicated thing. On average, one gram of soil contains a billion microorganisms, typically spanning thousands up to millions of different species, representing all three major biological domains of life.

"Kuske says the following: 'Although these organisms are microscopic, they collectively impact human activities and the Earth's processes at regional and global scales. Most of their roles are beneficial.' Indeed, the lure of such beneficial, collective impacts is part of what makes soil metagenomics so promising. Emerging technologies derived from microbes hold potential for human health, industry, biofuel, greenhouse gas absorption, and even the cleanup of large-scale environmental contamination. Scouring every gene of every microbe by traditional methods might seem inadequate. Kuske asserts, 'We have all these pressing environmental issues, and we don't have time to do this step-by-step. We have to jump.'"

"We did need to jump," said the IID Director. "So what did you find as the signal, once you analyzed and subtracted out all the metagenomic noise?

"Well," said Dr. Weal, "my second point is that the metagenomics completely confirmed the age of the soil from which the tablet was removed. It's exactly right for that time and place when compared to other samples, and it's aged exactly the right number of years.

"Third, we could then carbon date the nanomachinery fragments. And that was the first big surprise. They were not 3,750 years old, not even close."

The Time Machine Committee perked up.

"How old were they," said the chairman of that committee.

"Approximately 117,000 years old."

"What?" several people at the table cried out at once. "That's impossible, human civilization only goes back 5,000 to 10,000 years."

"I wouldn't be telling you this if my team hadn't checked and rechecked, and had it independently confirmed. The last glacial period was the most recent glacial period within the current ice age occurring during the last years, from about 110,000 years ago to about 10,000 years ago, of the Pleistocene," Dr. Weal said.

"Nanotechnology before the ice age? How can that be?"

"That glacial period is sometimes colloquially referred to as the *last ice age*," said Dr. Weal, "though this use is incorrect because an ice age is a longer period of cold temperature in which ice sheets cover large parts of the Earth, such as Antarctica. Glacials refer to colder phases within an ice age that separate interglacials. The end of the last glacial period is not the end of the last ice age. The end of the last glacial period was about 12,500 years ago, while the end of the last ice age may not yet have come. Little evidence points to a stop of the glacial-interglacial cycle of the last million years."

People were tapping and finger-wiggling on their NotePads, although anything written there would need to be cleared as properly encrypted before removal from the room.

"The last glacial period is the best-known part of the current ice age and has been intensively studied in North America, northern Eurasia, the Himalayas, and other formerly glaciated regions around the world. The glaciations that occurred during this glacial period covered many areas, mainly on the Northern Hemisphere."

"Glaciers never got as far south as Babylon," said one IID researcher.

"True, not for millions of years, but the glacial in question could have easily disrupted settled agriculture all over the inhabited world," replied Dr. Weal.

"What settled agriculture? That only began approximately 10,000 years ago."

"Our current civilizations, such as Mesopotamia, the Indus valley in what's now Pakistan and western India, Mesoamerica, southeast Asia, and China may only be 10,000 years. But there is evidence that many plants and animals were undergoing domestication before the ice age. We just had a long break. We lost all direct record and oral history."

"You're saying there was prehistoric civilization, with quasi-modern mathematics, and nanotechnology, a dozen times older than any consensus history?" asked another IID researcher.

"Exactly what I'm saying," said Dr. Weal.

"We can return to that at another meeting," said the Director. "Prehistory as such is not yet in our mandate, except so far as it explains the Nippur tablets. So what about the ancient nanotech fragments?"

"Sir, the long-term goal is to repair what the decay of a hundred millennia has broken. Imagine what we could learn if we had operational ancient nanodevices." said Dr. Weal.

"What would that take?"

"If you had a handful of gears and ratchets that came from an exploded clock, could you reconstruct the clock? The beta-test of such reverse engineering is the Antikythera mechanism, the ancient mechanical computer designed to calculate astronomical positions and the dates of the Olympics. It is now thought to have been built about 150–100 B.C. The degree of mechanical sophistication is comparable to late medieval Swiss watchmaking."

"Yes," said the Director. "We know all about that. Technological artifacts of similar complexity and workmanship did not reappear until the fourteenth century, when mechanical astronomical clocks appeared in Europe. But we need to focus on the nano."

"Exactly, sir. Instead of mechanical clocks or macroscopic computational components, we have bits and pieces of designed molecules. Instead of something to analog computer astronomical positions and Olympics, we have something digital and quantum to do, who knows what? These nanofragments are fifty times older than the Antikythera mechanism. There are many more parts. We don't know if all the parts came from one nanodevice, or two, or a hundred. So what to do?

"Fortunately, the NSA and IID and Los Alamos supercomputers are, in principal, able to put together a jigsaw puzzle with a billion pieces, even if we can't see the picture on the box they came in. But the combinations are staggering. Just to look at the different ways that 'n'-identically sized spheres can be packed together in minimal rigidity, so that there are three contacts per particle and at least 3 x n-to-the 6th power total contacts, they could barely get up to ten spheres in the computer technology of 2010 A.D. Minimal rigidity is necessary, but not sufficient, for a structure to be rigid. Due to the large number of packings that must be evaluated, this analytical method is implemented computationally, and near n = 10 we reach the method's computational limitations. There are exactly 750,352 minimally rigid 10 x 10 adjacency matrices of sphere packings in 3-dimensional space, for example. And the nanofragments are not even identical spheres, either," said Dr. Weal.

"Bottom line?" said the Director.

"Bottom line, sir, we started with three categories of hypothetical explanation for the tablets. *Time travel*, or *secrets of the ancients*, or *contact with extraterrestrials*. We haven't completely slammed the door shut on time travel, or on contact with extraterrestrials. But the one I would have said was least likely, *secrets of the ancients*, fits the evidence best out of everything my team can see."

"Or maybe some combination?" said the Director. "If people were so advanced before the ice age, how can we exclude that they had paleocontact with extraterrestrials?"

"That's above my pay grade."

"Okay. Break for lunch and subcommittee data fusion. Report back at 1300 hours. Before we go home, I'll have a briefing hacked together for the President."

6. Heironymus Georg Zeuthen

"Now we'll hear from the Math Semantics Committee. What do we know about what we *don't know*?"

"Sir, that's the right question," said that committee's chairman. "How to find math beyond what we already know, in the symbols of the tablets? Let me start with someone fairly obscure who died in 1920, but whose writings gave us some tips. Hieronymus Georg Zeuthen was born and began his education in Grimstrup, Denmark. The first research topic on which Zeuthen undertook was *enumerative geometry*."

"The history of mathematics?" asked Dr. Daisy Weal.

"Yes," said the committee chairman, "that would seem to have some clues. Hass said the following about Zeuthen's style:

'Zeuthen saw things intuitively. He constantly strove to attain an overall conception that would embrace the details of the subject under investigation and afford a way of seizing their significance.'"

"Such as?" the Director asked.

"Zeuthen was an expert on the history of medieval mathematics and produced important studies of Greek mathematics. He wrote numerous papers and books on the history of mathematics, some classics. Unlike many historians of science, Zeuthen explained the ancient texts like a colleague of the ancient mathematicians. In a major work in 1885, he looked in detail at the work of Apollonius on conic sections and showed that Apollonius used oblique coordinates. Zeuthen further argued Pythagoras himself discovered that 2 was irrational when computing the diagonal of a square. The passage from Plato's *Theaetetus* where it states that Theodorus proved the irrationality of 3, 5, 7, 11, 13, and 17 was also carefully studied by Zeuthen. He suggested that the end of Theodorus's proof somehow involved the continued fractions for 17 and 19, a conjecture which is very much in line with modern ideas about Greek mathematics. Zeuthen's largest historical work was published in 1896 on work of Descartes, Viète, Barrow, Newton, and Leibniz, developing algebra, analytic geometry, and analysis."

"Bottom line?"

"When doing the history of mathematics, he wanted to uncover ideas and motives of ancient masters. These ideas were usually formulated in an unfamiliar language, but the ideas themselves had not changed over time, so a modern mathematician can appreciate the work of a colleague two thousand years earlier. Zeuthen said that one cannot evaluate or understand mathematics of an earlier period on the basis of the mathematics of today. He thought it indispensable to be acquainted with the techniques and symbolism of former times to contrast those tools and what they could be used for with what they *had* actually been used for."

"Is that how we recognized Clebsch-Gordan coefficients and tables of Calabi-Yau manifolds?"

"Basically. We looked for ideas around the border between what we know from the *Supercompactification Triality Theorem* of 2023, and what we know that we don't know. Like making a map of the frontiers of ignorance, to get some sense of the shape of what we don't know."

"What did they know about physics, beyond Clebsch-Gordan and Calabi-Yau stuff?"

"They saw more deeply than us about how quantum mechanics and relativity connect. These are two of the three big scientific theories of the twentieth century, but the dirty little secret of physics is that they have yet to be reconciled. They seem inherently incompatible. That's why string theory and quantum loop gravity were developed, yet they still fail to solve the deepest mysteries.

"So, what does all this mean for physics?" continued the math chairman. "The spin factors have an intriguing relation to special relativity, since its cone of positive elements can be revealed to be none other than that of a *future light cone.*"

The Time Travel Committee leaned forward in their chairs at the mention of 'future light cone.'

"A future light cone is the path of a flash of light emanating from a single event and travelling in all directions of space-time. Furthermore, we can utilize a field of abstract algebra, *Jordan algebra*, which is infinite and has some interesting coincidences to the spin factors."

"And what do we think in IID about coincidences?" asked the Director.

"Show me an alleged coincidence," said Dr. Weal," and I'll show you someone with something to gain, and a reason to cover it up."

"Okay. This is not a mere coincidence, but part of the frontiers of ignorance. This is the tip of a huge and still not fully fathomed iceberg," said the math chairman.

"How does that mystery connect with the physics that these guys knew 3,750 years ago? Or 110,000 years ago?" asked the Director.

"Exceptional Jordan algebra remains mysterious," said the math chairman. "For example, when it was first found that quarks come in three colors, Okubo and others hoped that 3 x 3 self-adjoint octonionic matrices might serve as observables for these exotic degrees of freedom."

"Didn't Zelmanov have something to say about that?" said the IID Director.

"Yes. In 1983, Zelmanov generalized the Jordan–von Neumann–Wigner classification to the infinite-dimensional case. There are two *27-dimensional exceptional Jordan algebras*. There's the one described above, and its sister, which is defined the same way, but with the so-called split octonions taking the place of the octonions."

"27-dimensional?"

"Yes, way beyond the 10 or 11 dimensions of string theory and M-theory. Further, Jordan algebra is built upon split octonions and then makes an appearance in string theory. Thus that leads us to the concept of a Hilbert space, which extends the methods of algebra and calculus from a standard two or three-dimensional plane into spaces with any infinite number of dimensions.

"My goal for next session is to tell you how the result of Jordan, von Neumann, and Wigner reappears as a classification of certain cones: cones that can be used to describe nonnegative observables, but also quantum *mixed states*. And here is where we'll meet state-observable duality."

"Bottom line?"

"If the deep ancients 110,000 years ago understood physics applications of the two 27-dimensional exceptional Jordan algebras, they might have been able to build a . . . ahem, a warp drive. A spaceship that can go completely outside on Einsteinian space-time and appear somewhere else, absurdly far away, in the universe. They may have reached a technological singularity before the ice age, and some of them might even have left Earth far behind."

7. We Missed the Singularity by 110,000 Years

"We missed the singularity by 110,000 years?"

"Yes, Mister Director."

"Then why is there not more evidence?"

The Chairman of the Math Semantics Committee nodded and said, "In higher latitudes, glaciers scraped away archeological traces of whatever cities there may have been. Along sea coasts, settlements were drowned and eroded when the ocean levels rose. Steel rusts and bricks wear. Most of the clay tablets were only preserved because they were in buildings that burned, and so the wet clay was fired, and became very hard and enduring. There must be more evidence, but in places and forms we have not yet found."

"Are we abusing the terminology in saying that they reached the singularity?"

"Not in the sense of black holes, of course, but in the sense of Stanisław Marcin Ulam, a mathematician, whose work in Los Alamos was mainly concentrated in the theory of relativity as well as quantum theory. His broad scientific interest was not limited to mathematics and physics; it included also technology, computer science, and biology. He is now famous for his research in nuclear physics and also for other non-mathematical achievements; in particular, he developed original methods of propulsion of vessels moving above the Earth's atmosphere.

"As to the singularity, we take *Vergil Ulam* in Greg Bear's *Blood Music,* to be a double reference to the Roman poet Virgil and to Stanisław M. Ulam who, as we said, was a mathematician who participated in the Manhattan Project and originated the Teller-Ulam design of thermonuclear weapons. He also invented nuclear pulse propulsion and developed a number of mathematical tools in number theory, set theory, ergodic theory, and algebraic topology. Because Ulam was among the first to refer to the technological singularity—and possibly the originator of the metaphor itself—in May 1958, while referring to a conversation with John von Neumann:

'One conversation centered on the ever accelerating progress of technology and changes in the mode of human life, which gives the appearance of approaching some essential singularity in the history of the race beyond which human affairs, as we know them, could not continue.'

"Stanisław Ulam, while working at the Los Alamos National Laboratory in the 1940's, studied the growth of crystals, using a simple lattice network as his model. At the same time, John von Neumann, Ulam's colleague, was working on the problem of self-replicating systems. Von Neumann's initial design was founded upon the notion of one robot building another robot. This design is known as the *kinematic model.* As he developed this design, von Neumann came to realize the great difficulty of building a self-replicating robot, and of the great cost in providing the robot with a *sea of parts* from which to build its replicant. Ulam suggested that von Neumann develop his design around a mathematical abstraction, such as the one Ulam used to study crystal growth. Thus was born the first system of cellular automata."

"Okay, singularity it was. How advanced were they, 117,00 years ago?"

"They had nuclear physics, or at least advanced theory. *Quantum field theory,* or *quantum chromodynamics,* or whatever else gave them the lepton and baryon data. If that was from first principles, they need not have built gigantic accelerators such as the Tevatron or Large Hadron Collider or the Higgs-Hunter in the Australian nullarbor. String theory or M-theory or something beyond that which we have not rediscovered."

"Are you sure we're looking in the right places?"

"We've used the supercomputers to re-scan archived data on the surface of the moon, Mars and its moons, and asteroids and comet nuclei we'd mapped before. There are some anomalies, but no firm evidence that they expanded out into the solar system. But then again, since they had nanotechnology, we'd hardly see nanodevices from orbit."

"Assessment of national security threat?"

"We recommend you tell the President there is no need for heightened alert of time machines popping up in the Rose Garden. And if there was, what good would our countermeasures be? Second, there is also no heightened alert for extraterrestrial invaders, though this in no way undermines IID's long-standing charter. We'll keep watching the skies, tapping every byte from the deep space network, the great orbital observatories, the neutrino detectors with their Cerenkov radiation photarrays, and isotope decay sensors in the liquid oxygen tanks below the Farside Lunar Observatory. We're still working the protocols for archaeonanotechnology reconstruction. Obviously when and *if* we rebuild a working nanobot from before the ice age, we'd better be as close to one hundred percent sure as we can, that it won't self-reproduce and escape and, you know, *gray goo* the world."

"Thank you all for the long hours you've put in, great research, and clear executive summaries. Get some sleep, A-team. Let's reconvene at 0900 hours. Sweet dreams of nanotechnology!"

8. Gilgamesh's Galaxy

The moment arrived full circle. Since the earliest announcement of the Nippur tablets, I had been a part of every discussion and committee forum, merely listening, taking copious notes. Now it was my turn to present to the Director and assembled chairmen. My conclusions were beyond incredible.

"Please explain to this IID group why Niels Bohr matters, since his model of the atom as a little solar system with electrons whizzing around the nucleus like planets orbiting the sun, is *wrong.* We non-physicists have a hard time understanding why Bohr is considered such an influential scientist. And, of course, how does this bear on the matter of the tablets?" the IID Director asked.

I stood and faced the packed audience. "Sir, physics observations must be expressed in unambiguous language with suitable application of the terminology of classical physics."

"How did they deal with this 117,000 years ago? And what does it mean for us now?"

"They seem to have invented or discovered *topos theory*, way beyond *category theory*," I said.

"What's a topos?"

"A universe of discourse, to which a mathematician or observer may wish to confine himself. Even the internal language and associated logic can alternatively be studied externally with classical meta-logic. Various entities at play in our application of topos theory to quantum physics are illustrated in figure one."

I put up the first slide. On the projection screen appeared an image of a rounded rectangle labeled *Ambient Topos*. Inside that, a fancy-font letter 'A' with a label *C*-Algebra*. Near that was an icon of an open human eye and the label *Mathematician using Meta-Logic*. Inside the rounded rectangle was a smaller rounded rectangle containing an underlined-font letter '$\underline{A}$' labeled *Inner C*-Algebra*. Near that was another icon of an open human eye, and the label *Internal Observer*.

Everyone squinted at the slide. It looked profound, but I could tell its meaning was unclear to them.

"This illustrates that our quantum logic is meant to be the logic of an *internal* observer, with all the restrictions it brings with it. Whereas the quantum *logic* of Birkhoff and von Neumann, to the extent it is a logic at all, rather pertains to a fictitious entity like *Laplace's demon*, to whose intellect *nothing would be uncertain and the future, just like the past, would be present before its eyes*."

"This may be clear to you, but I don't see anyone nodding their heads in agreement," said the Director.

"Not many people have expertise in *quantum physics, category theory,* and *operator algebras*," I said. "That's what one needs to follow the state of the art as of, say 2007 in Communications in Mathematical Physics, let alone what the ancients did with it 117,000 years ago. Let me try to explain, more precisely.

"The goal is to relate algebraic quantum mechanics to topos theory, so as to construct new foundations for quantum logic and quantum spaces, motivated by Niels Bohr's idea that the empirical content of quantum physics is accessible only through classical physics."

"Sorry, you lost me again. Are you suggesting that the Proto-Sumerians went into a quantum phase space like some kind of Hilbert space?"

"No. I'm saying they had some deep understanding of infinite dimensional Hilbert space that gave them a handle on how to reconcile *quantum mechanics, general relativity,* and *string theory*. If we even begin to understand what the equations imply, and it's going to take new departments at a hundred universities to even scratch the surface, they could have skipped the solar system completely. They could have wormholed to anywhere in the galaxy they wanted to go. Or *beyond*."

"They could travel faster than light by going off the brane?"

"That's what the tablets hint at, although we're not sure. If we read the cuneiforms correctly, they figured out how the supersymmetric actions of closed multiple M2 branes with flux for the BL and the ABJM theories have been extended to the construction of the case of open M2-branes with flux, and derive the boundary conditions. This allows them to derive the modified Basu-Harvey equation in the presence of flux. As an example, when they considered what we call the Lorentzian BL model, they get a new feature of the fuzzy funnel solution describing a D2-D4 intersection that is obtained as a result of the flux."

"Fuzzy funnel?"

"Yes. Informally, our team calls it a *chronosynclastic infundibulum* after the science fiction novel *The Sirens of Titan,* by Kurt Vonnegut. It's kind of a wormhole through time and space."

The Time Travel Committee leaned forward again.

"I want a full briefing before close of business today. Tell me again how this connects with Niels Bohr? At least I get the little solar system atom thing."

"In a short yet immensely influential 1948 essay titled, *On the Notions of Causality and Complementarity,* Niels Bohr articulated a principle that has served the quantum physics community well for more than sixty years:

'Well-defined experimental evidence, though not analyzed in terms of classical physics, must be expressed in terms of ordinary language making use of common logic.'

"Thus for more than eighty years we have been able to read the quantum literature without any risk of feeling cheated, confident that toward the end of most articles, a concrete reduction to *experimental evidence in terms of ordinary language making use of common logic* will be presented.

"It seems to this committee, as we contemplate the wisdom of the tablets, that the world would benefit substantially if a similar principle was explicitly formulated and widely adopted, regarding in particular the discussion of oracle-dependent theorems. Here the point is that oracular models of computation differ as substantially from physical computation, as quantum state-spaces differ from classical state-spaces."

"That's where Hilbert Space comes in?" asked the IID Director.

"Yes," I replied. "What is conspicuously missing from many quantum information theory articles, even articles that explicitly link theorems to experiments, is a Bohr-style discussion of the analysis of experimental evidence that expresses its conclusions wholly *in terms of ordinary language making use of common logic.* That is, without any reference to Hilbert spaces or computational oracles."

"Are we equipped to do the experiments?"

"Not yet. Decades of quantum physics articles have conditioned many people to expect a conclusion to the Bohr-reduction in the first article that can link theoretical models to concrete experiments. Perhaps this has been a globally beneficial practice that the community would do well to embrace in coming decades."

"Does this connect with that *Pratt Principle* thing?" said the Director.

I nodded. "Yes. Vaughan Pratt is a pioneer of computer science and asked the following:

One. Is the space that quantum mechanics currently models as Hilbert space really flat?

Two. If not, would that compromise quantum computing in any way? Is there some curvature, positive or negative, at which the current best error correction methods fail?"

"Bottom line?"

"The point here is that the IID accommodates many Holy Grails. It very commonly happens that in seeking one Grail, researchers find a very different one!" I said.

"Gentlemen, ladies, I think we should break until the end-of-day breakout sessions. It is my considered opinion that the national security threat is actually the greatest opportunity in human history. Our species had our singularity, and we don't even remember it, or we scattered out fragments of its memory into myths and legends. The ice age wiped out almost all physical evidence. We have been incredibly lucky to unearth these tablets. And we have worked incredibly hard to figure out what they mean," the IID Director said.

I replied, "We've got to search for more Sumerian tablets, reconstruct the ancient nanotechnology, and figure out if this was mere theory, or whether they really built a fuzzy funnel *chronosynclastic infundibulum*.

"And if they did, where did they go, these interstellar pioneers of 117,000 years ago?

"If they did, then they have achieved the kind of immortality that King Gilgamesh sought in his epic story.

"If they did, then we can do it, too. The human race may be on the brink of going from Sumeria to the stars. Of exploding out into Gilgamesh's Galaxy!"

=[]=

Jonathan Vos Post has been a Professor of Mathematics at Woodbury University *in Burbank, California. His first degree in Mathematics was from* Caltech *in 1973. He has been also a Professor of Astronomy at* Cypress College *in Orange County, California; Professor of Computer Science at* California State University, Los Angeles; *and Professor of English Composition at* Pasadena City College. *He is a widely published author of Science Fiction, Science, Poetry, Math, Drama, and other fields. In his so-called spare time, he won elections for local political offices and produced operas, as Secretary of* Euterpe Opera Theatre.

Co-Webmaster, Vice President, and Chief Information Officer of Magic Dragon Multimedia
4,200+ publications, presentations, broadcasts
co-author with Ray Bradbury
co-author with Richard Feynman, Nobel Laureate physicist
co-editor with David Brin and Arthur C. Clarke
co-broadcaster with Isaac Asimov
quoted by name in Robert Heinlein's Expanded Universe
Winner of 1987 Rhysling Award *for Best Science Fiction Poem of Year*
Published in Nebula Awards Anthology *#23, 1989*
Semifinalist for 1996 Nebula Award

THE TALL GRASS

Joe R. Lansdale

=[]=

Joe R. Lansdale . . . what else can I add that has not already been said of one of the most accomplished names in modern writing? Master, legend, inspiration; his list of honors is a long one. Personally, I've been a Lansdale fan since 1992 when, as a high school sophomore, I first read Love Doll: A Fable *in the* Borderlands 2 *anthology. That's two decades since, of enjoying Lansdale fiction. To bring it full circle now, by including him in my own collection, is beyond thrilling. His contribution to the* Dark Tales *anthology is actually a bit of a departure from his characteristic rough-and-tumble characters and outrageous adventures. The following tale is a quiet one, written in the fashion of traditional ghost stories. The people found in this tale are not ones you'd ever wish to encounter.*

=[]=

I can't really explain this properly, but I'll tell it to you, and you can make the best of it. It starts with a train. People don't travel as readily by train these days as they once did, but in my youthful days they did, and I have to admit those days were some time ago, considering my current, doddering age. It's hard to believe so much time has turned, and I have turned with it, as worn out and rusty as those old coal-powered trains.

I am soon to fall of the edge of the cliff into the great darkness, but there was a time when I was young and the world was light. Back then, there was something that happened to me on a rail line that showed me something I didn't know was there, and since that time, I've never seen the world in exactly the same way.

What I can tell you is this. I was traveling across country by night in a very nice rail car. I had not just a seat on a train, but a compartment to myself. A quite comfortable compartment, I might add. I was early into my business career then, having just started with a firm that I ended up working at for twenty-five years. To simplify, I had completed a cross country business trip and was on my way home. I wasn't married then, but one of the reasons I was eager to make it back to my home town was a young woman named Ellen. We were quite close, and her company meant everything to me. It was our plan to marry.

I won't bore you with details, but that particular plan didn't work out. And though I still think of that with some disappointment, for she was very beautiful, it has absolutely nothing to do with my story.

Thing is, the train was crossing the western country, in a barren stretch without towns, beneath a wide open night sky with a high moon and a few crawling clouds. Back then, those kinds of places were far more common than lights and streets and motor cars are now. I had made the same ride several times on business, yet I always still enjoyed looking out the window, even at night. This night, however, for whatever reason, I was up very late, unable to sleep. I had chosen not to eat dinner, and now that it was well passed, I was a bit hungry, but there was nothing to be had.

The lamps inside the train had been extinguished, and out the window there was a moonlit sea of rocks and sand and in the distance beyond, shadowy blue-black mountains.

The train came to an odd stretch that I had somehow missed before on my journeys, as I was probably sleeping at the time. It was a great expanse of prairie grass, and it shifted in the moonlight like waves of gold-green sea water pulled by the tide-making forces of the moon.

I was watching all of this, trying to figure it, determining how odd it looked and how often I had to have passed it and had never seen it. Oh, I had seen lots of tall grass, but nothing like this. The grass was not only head high, or higher, it was thick and it had what I can only describe as an unusual look about it, as if I was seeing it with eyes that belonged to someone else. I know how peculiar that sounds, but it's the only way I know how to explain it.

Then the train jerked, as if some great hand had grabbed it. It screeched on the rails and there was a cacophony of sounds before the engine came to a hard stop.

I had no idea what had occurred. I opened the compartment door, though at first the door seemed locked and only gave way with considerable effort. I stepped out into the hallway. No one was there.

Edging along the hallway, I came to the smoking car, but there was no one there either. It seemed the other passengers were in a tight sleep and unaware of our stopping. I walked through the car, sniffing at the remains of tobacco smoke, and opened a door that went out on a connecting platform that was positioned between the smoking car and another passenger car. I looked in the passenger car through the little window at the door. There was no one there. This didn't entirely surprise me, as the train had taken on a very small load of passengers, and many of them, like me, had purchased personal cabins.

I looked out at the countryside and saw there were lights in the distance, beyond the grass, or to be more exact, positioned out in it. It shocked me, because we were in the middle of absolutely nowhere, and the fact that there was a town nearby was a total surprise to me.

I walked to the edge of the platform. There was a folded and hinged metal stair there, and with the toe of my shoe I kicked it, causing it to flip out and extend to the ground.

I climbed down the steps and looked along the rail. There was no one at first, and then there was a light swinging its way toward me, and finally a shadowy shape behind the light. In a moment I saw that it was a rail man, dressed in cap and coat and company trousers.

"You best stay on board, sir," he said.

I could see him clearly now. He was an average looking man, small in size with an odd walk about him; the sort people who practically live on trains acquire, as do sailors on ships at sea.

"I was just curious," I said. "What's happened?"

"A brief stop," he said. "I suggest you go back inside."

"Is no one else awake?" I said.

"You seem to be it, sir," he said. "I find those that go to sleep before twelve stay that way when this happens."

I thought that a curious answer. I said, "Does it happen often?"

"No. Not really."

"What's wrong? Are there repairs going on?"

"We're building up another head of steam," he said.

"Then surely I have time to step out here and have a smoke in the open air," I said.

"I suppose that's true, sir," he said. "But I wouldn't wander far. Once we're ready to go, we'll go. I'll call for you to get on board, but only a few times, and then we'll go, no matter what. We won't tarry, not here. Not between midnight and two."

And then he went on by me swinging the light.

I was intrigued by what he had said, about not tarrying. I looked out at the waving grass and the lights, which I now realized were not that far away. I took out my makings and rolled a cigarette and put a match to it and puffed.

I can't really explain what possessed me. The oddness of the moment, I suppose. But I decided it would be interesting to walk out in the tall grass, just to measure its height, and to maybe get a closer look at those lights. I strolled out a ways, and within moments I was deep in the grass. As I walked, the earth sloped downwards and the grass whispered in the wind. When I stopped walking, the grass was over my head, and behind me where the ground was higher, the grass stood tall against the moonlight, like rows of spear heads held high by an army of warriors.

I stood there in the midst of the grass and smoked and listened for activity back at the train, but neither heard the lantern man or the sound of the train getting ready to leave. I relaxed a bit, enjoying the cool, night wind and the way it moved through the prairie. I decided to stroll about while I smoked, parting the grass as I went. I could see the lights still, but they always seemed to be farther away than I thought, and my moving in their direction didn't seem to bring me closer; they receded like the horizon.

When I finished my cigarette, I dropped it and put my heel to it, grinding it into the ground, and turned to go back to the train.

I was a bit startled to discover I couldn't find the path I had taken. Surely, the grass had been bent or pushed aside by my passing, but there was no sign of it. It had quickly sprung back into shape. I couldn't find the rise I had come down. The position of the moon was impossible to locate, even though there was plenty of moonlight; the moon had gone away and left its light there.

Gradually, I became concerned. I had somehow gotten turned about, and the train would soon be leaving, and I had been warned that no one would wait for me. I thought perhaps it was best if I ceased thrashing about through the grass, and just stopped, lest I become more confused. I concluded that I couldn't have gone too far from the railway, and that I should be able to hear the train man should he call out for *All Aboard.*

So, there I was, standing in tall grass like a fool. Lost from the train and listening intently for the man to call out. I kept glancing about to try and see if I could find a path back the way I came. As I said before, it stood to reason that I had tromped down some grass, and that I couldn't be that far away. It was also, as I said, a very well-lit night, plenty of moonlight. It rested like swipes of cream cheese on the tall grass, so it was inconceivable to me that I had gotten lost in such a short time walking such a short distance. I also considered those lights as bearings, but they had moved, fluttering about like will-o-the-wisps, so using them as markers was impossible.

I was lost, and I began to entertain the disturbing thought that I might miss the train and be left where I was. It would be bad enough to miss the train, but here, out in the emptiness of nowhere, if I wasn't missed, or no one came back this way for a time, I might actually starve, or be devoured by wild animals, or die of exposure.

That's when I heard someone coming through the grass. They weren't right on top of me, but they were close, and of course, my first thought was it was the man from the train come to look for me. I started to call out, but hesitated.

I can't entirely explain the hesitation, but there was a part of me that felt reluctant, and so instead of calling out, I waited. The noise grew louder.

I cautiously parted the grass with my fingers, and looked in the direction of the sound, and coming through the grass were a number of men, all of them peculiarly bald, the moonlight reflecting off their heads like mirrors. The grass whipped open as they came and closed back behind them. For a brief moment I felt relieved, as they must be other passengers or train employees sent to look for me, and would direct me to back to the train. It would be an embarrassing moment, but in the end, all would be well.

And then I realized something. I hadn't been actually absorbing what I was seeing. They were human-shaped alright, but . . . they had no faces.

There was a head, and there were spots where the usual items should be, nose, eyes, mouth, but those spots were indentions. The moonlight gathered on those shiny, white faces, and reflected back out. They were the lights in the grass and they were why the lights moved, because the faceless men moved. There were other lights beyond them, way out, and I drew the conclusion that there were many of those human-shaped things, out in the grass, close and far away, moving toward me, and moving away, thick as aphids. They had a jerky movement about them, as if they were squirming on a griddle. They pushed through the grass and fanned out wide, and some of them had sticks, and they began to beat the grass before them. I might add that as they did, the grass, like a living thing, whipped away from their strikes and opened wide and closed up behind them. They were coming ever nearer to where I was. I could see they were of all different shapes and sizes and attire. Some of them wore very old clothes, and there were others who were dressed in rags, and even a couple who were completely devoid of clothes, and sexless, smooth all over, as if anything that distinguished their sex or their humanity had been ironed out. Still, I could tell now, by the general shape of the bodies, that some of them may have been women, and certainly some of the smaller ones were children. I even saw moving among them a shiny white body in the shape of a dog.

In the same way I had felt it unwise to call out to them, I now felt it unwise to wait where I was. I knew they knew I was in the grass, and that they were looking for me.

I broke and ran. I was spotted, because behind me, from those faces without mouths, there somehow rose up a cry. A kind of squeal, like something being slowly ground down beneath a boot heel.

I heard them as they rushed through the grass after me. I could hear their feet thundering against the ground. It was as if a small heard of buffalo were in pursuit. I charged through the grass blindly. Once I glanced back over my shoulder and saw their numbers were larger than I first thought. Their shapes broke out of the grass, left and right and close and wide. The grass was full of them, and their faces glowed as if inside their thin flesh were lit lanterns.

Finally there was a place where the grass was missing and there was only earth. It was a relief from the cloying grass, but it was a relief that passed swiftly, for now I was fully exposed. Moving rapidly toward me from the front were more of those moon-lit things. I turned, and saw behind me the others were very near. They began to run all out toward me, they were also closing in from my right.

There was but one way for me to go, to the left, and wide, back into the grass. I did just that. I ran as hard as I could run. The grass sloped up slightly, and I fought to climb the hill; the hill that I had lost such a short time ago. It had reappeared, or rather I had stumbled up on it.

My feet kept slipping as I climbed up it. I glanced down, and there in that weird light I could see that my boots were sliding in what looked to be rotting piles of fat-glazed bones; the earth was slick with them.

I could hear the things closing behind me, making that sound that a face without a mouth should be unable to make; that horrid screech. It was deafening.

I was almost at the peak of the hill. I could see the grass swaying up there. I could hear it whispering in the wind between the screeches of those pursuing me, and just as I made the top of the hill and poked my head through the grass and saw the train, I was grabbed.

Here is a peculiar thing that from time to time I remember, and shiver when I do, but those hands that had hold of my legs were cold as arctic air. I could feel them through my clothes, they were so cold. I tried to kick loose, but wasn't having any luck. I had fallen when they grabbed me, and I was clutching at the grass at the top of the hill. It was pulling through my hands and fingers, and the edges were sharp; they cut into me like razors. I could feel the warm blood running through my fingers, but still I hung to that grass.

Glancing back, I saw that I was seized by several of the things, and the dog-like shape had clamped its jaws on the heel of my boot. I saw too that the things were not entirely without features after all; or at least now they had acquired one all-encompassing feature. A split appeared in their faces, where a mouth should be, but it was impossibly wide and festooned with more teeth than a shark, long and sharp, many of them crooked as poorly driven nails, stained in spots the color of very old cheese. Their breath rose up like methane from a privy and burned my eyes. There was no doubt in my mind that they meant to bite me; and I somehow knew that if I was bitten, I would not be chewed and eaten, but that the bite would make me like them. That my bones would come free of me along with my features and everything that made me human, and I knew too that those things were originally from train stops, and from frontier scouting parties, adventurers, and surveyors, and all manner of folks who, at one time, had been crossing these desolate lands and found themselves here, a place not only unknown to the map, but unknown to human understanding. All of this came to me and instantly filled me with dread. It was as if their very touch had revealed it to me.

I kicked wildly, wrenching my boot heel from the dog-shape's toothy grasp. I struggled. I heard teeth snap on empty air as I kicked loose. And then there was warmth and a glow over my head. I looked up to see the train man with a great flaming torch, and he was waving it about, sticking it into the teeth-packed faces of those poor lost souls.

They screeched and they bellowed, they hissed and they moaned. But the fire did the trick. They let go of me and receded back into the waves of grass, and the grass folded back around them, like the ocean swallowing sailors. I saw last the dog-shape dive into the grass like a porpoise, and then it and them were gone, and so were the lights, and the moonlight lost it's slick glaze and it was just a light. The torch flickered over my head, and I could feel its heat.

The next thing I knew the train man was pulling me to the top of the hill, and I collapsed and trembled like a mass of gelatin spilled on a floor.

"They don't like it up here, sir," the train man said, pushing the blazing end of his torch against the ground, rubbing it in the dirt, snuffing it out. The smell of pitch tingled my nostrils. "No, they don't like it at all."

"What are they?" I said.

"I think you know, sir. I do. Somewhere deep inside me, I know. There aren't any words for it, but I know, and you know. They touched me once, but thank goodness I was only near the grass, not in it. Not like you were, sir."

He led me back to the train. He said, "I should have been more emphatic, but you looked like a reasonable chap to me. Not someone to wander off."

"I wish I had been reasonable."

"It's like looking to the other side, isn't it, sir?" he said. "Or rather, it is a look to one of many sides, I suspect. Little lost worlds inside our own. The train breaks down here often. There have been others who have left the train. I suspect you met some of them tonight. You saw what they have become, or so I think. I can't explain all the others. Wanderers, I suspect. It's always here the train stops, or breaks down. Usually it just sort of loses steam. It can have plenty and still lose it, and we have to build it all up again. Always this time of night. Rarely a problem, really. Another thing, I lock all the doors at night to keep folks in, should they come awake. I lock the general passenger cars on both ends. Most don't wake up anyway, not this time of night, not after midnight, not if they've gone to sleep before that time, and are good solid in. Midnight between two a.m., that's when it always happens, the train losing steam here near the crawling grass. I guess those of us awake at that time can see some things that others can't. In this spot anyway. That's what I suppose. It's like a door opens out there during that time. They got their spot, their limitations, but you don't want to be out there, no sir. You're quite lucky."

"Thank you," I said.

"Guess I missed your lock, sir. Or it works poorly. I apologize for that. Had I done right, you wouldn't have been able to get out. If someone should stay awake and find the room locked, we pretend it's a stuck doorway. Talk to them through the door, and tell them we can't get it fixed until morning. A few people have been quite put out by that. The ones who were awake when we stopped here. But it's best that way. I'm sure you'll agree, sir."

"I do," I said. "Thank you again. I can't say it enough."

"Oh, no problem. You had almost made it out of the grass, and you were near the top of the hill, so it was easy for me help you. I always keep a torch nearby that can easily be lit. They don't like fire, and they don't come up close to the train. They don't get out of the grass, as far as I can determine. But I will tell you true, had I heard your scream too far beyond the hill, well, I wouldn't have come after you. And they would have had you."

"I screamed?"

"Loudly."

I got on the train and walked back to my compartment, still trembling. I checked my door and saw that my lock had been thrown from the outside, but it was faulty, and all it took was a little shaking to have it come free of the door frame. That's how I had got out my room.

The train man brought me a nip of whisky, and I told him about the lock, and drank the whisky. "I'll have the lock fixed right away, sir. Best not to mention all this," he said. "No one will believe it, and it could cause problems with the cross country line. People have to get places, you know."

I nodded.

"Goodnight, sir. Pleasant dreams."

This was such an odd invocation to all that had happened, I almost laughed.

He went away, closing up my compartment, and I looked out the window. All there was to see was the grass, waving in the wind, tipped with moonlight.

The train started to move, and pretty soon we were on our way. And that was the end of the matter, and this is the first time I have mentioned it since it happened so long ago. But, I assure you. It happened just the way I told you, crossing the Western void, in the year of 1901.

=[]=

Joe R. Lansdale is the author of thirty novels and over two hundred short pieces of fiction and non-fiction. He has written for animation, film, comics, and newspapers. He is the founder of the Martial Arts System, Shen Chuan, Martial Science and has been inducted into both the U.S. Martial Arts Hall of Fame and the International Martial Arts Hall of Fame. He has produced films, and his novella, BUBBA HOTEP was made into a cult film starring Bruce Campbell and Ossie Davis, and his short story, Incident On And Off A Mountain Road, was filmed for Showtime, both directed by Don Coscarelli. He is writer in residence at Stephen F. Austin State University. He is also the editor or co-editor of over a dozen anthologies.

THE ISLAND TROVAR

JC Hemphill

=[]=

We now arrive at the final tale of this anthology. I selected JC Hemphill as the closer, as his is another tale that really captures the spirit of this collection. It seemed quite fitting to end with a final excursion of intrepid explorers travelling to mysterious territory. What is it, after all, that draws us inexplicably to lands that "none have returned from?" Wealth? Adventure? Prestige? Of course, what explorers often discover is not quite what they sought. Dark and inviting, The Island Trovar *is no exception . . .*

=[]=

The mast of our ship pierced the low lying clouds that had shrouded our vision for an hour or more, and the sea opened before us like an indigo field waving in the wind. A general whoop went around the ship at the sight of our destination.

The Island Trovar.

It was as beautiful and mysterious and chilling as the rumors had said. More so, even. A black crag protruded from the sea like the jagged remains of a seaman's half-rotted tooth, giving way to sloping land that graded into the ocean where the mountain grew to leviathan proportions. Beneath the tropical waters, where even light dared not delve, Trovar hid its molten-beating heart.

The leeward side of the island was rough with black cliffs and sprays of white foam as waves crashed upon the rocks with deadly force. The windward side was a stark contrast of lush jungle edging a serene bay. The idea was inexplicable, but I could sense a dark presence hiding in those thick tangles of wilderness. Something with eyes. Beady, ignorant, ravenous eyes—

"You put any stock in the natives' lore?" Herb Flenderson said from beside me.

I heard him speak, but not the words. The island had me. The watchful jungles and threatening peaks reminded me of the penny dreadful tales that fascinated me as a child. In those, all manner of objects seemed to exude evil in the same way a man sweats. And at the time, no better means of description came to mind—Trovar *sweated* evil.

"Come now, Felix, I know you too well. It's no good feigning deafness this late in our friendship." Herb, a leather-skinned fellow with an amiable grin, glanced around the ship as if he mistrusted the men around him. "If you ignore me, I'll only have the English and natives to talk to." He spit over the railing. "How dismal life would be."

"Indeed," I said, breaking the island's hold over me. "I'd pity those poor souls who'd have to suffer through your tiresome accounts of misguided debauchery."

"Ah, the infamous Kingway wit. How sharp it is." Herb pulled a cigar from his shirt pocket and held it between ivory teeth without lighting it. "The ladies tell me they dare not disrobe around you for fear of being cut by that wit."

"Liar," I proclaimed, smiling. "You know, such postulation would require you actually *speak* to a woman. And as every man on this ship knows, your bladder would never allow such bravery."

We chuckled and feigned disinterest in the island.

Through the village on Gilbert Island where our voyage originated, we'd heard legends of a dead island. It was said that it hid from those who knew not where to look. And those who knew where to look, never returned to tell. The stories caught the attention of Paul Schmeck, a man known for specializing in the imports and exports of hard-to-find items. He had investigated the legend as best he could, but differing rumors made any real knowledge vague. Some said the human body melted the instant anyone set foot on its sands. Others claimed that plants came to life at night and dragged men into the earth, kicking and screaming, where they were digested over millennia. I, myself, heard a drunken native telling of an evil so consuming it drove men mad by the mere sight of it.

Schmeck became enthralled by the idea of finding the island. He came to Herb and I and asked for our assistance. We had worked for him in the past, and he valued our rare brand of discretion. The conversation was lengthy, but in the end, he enticed us with promises of posterity. He reasoned that since the island appeared on no map and no records existed, we could name every mountain peak, river, beach, and stream. Our names would piggyback eternity with the likes of Cook or Columbus.

And for a sea-tramp like me, who's never owned his own horse or commanded a ship or saved a cent of what I earned, the prospect of fame came on like a hunger. Real or not, I seized the opportunity.

Now, with the island standing testament, I believed every one of those stories. Notwithstanding their uncanny nature, every grotesque detail became fact in my mind.

Schmeck lumbered toward us. His limp caused him to stumble as the ship keeled with the course change. He struggled to keep his hefty torso from dragging him to the deck and composed himself before continuing. "Sirs," he said, gripping the rail with both hands.

Herb smiled. "Quite the sea legs you've got."

"Yes, well, I couldn't appear any queerer than the two of you at the moment. I've only seen such grim expressions on battered women. Haven't we found what we came for? Haven't we accomplished something of merit? Herb, break out the bottle I know you smuggled aboard, for Christ's sake, and let us celebrate."

Herb patted his back pocket where he kept his flask. "No bottle. Just a personal serving today."

"A shame. We'll need more sauce than that to ease our thirst tonight. From the looks of the westerly skies, I'd say we'll be spending the night on that rock."

"Impossible," I said. "We were to make landfall, survey the area, christen a few streams and bays, and depart. You mentioned nothing about spending a length of time on Trovar."

"Come, now," Schmeck said with irritating pleasantness and an unwavering grin. "We need to map the island, gather samples, take notes—"

"Take notes? Map the island? That will take weeks, if not months."

"Don't be childish, Felix. The gap for exploration is closing. Almost every reach of our planet has been trampled by man's heel, and here we face one of the final specks of unexplored land remaining. Think of Lewis and Clark. Or Hudson. Think of the legacy."

I began to protest, but he raised a palm. "Now that we found the island, I fully intend to reimburse you for your troubles. How would three hundred pounds each sound?" Instead of waiting for a reply, he pivoted awkwardly, and yelled for the captain to prepare a landing.

"This isn't done," I said over the commotion.

Schmeck gave a dismissive wave.

A storm conquered the sky, and men scurried beneath it across the deck like frenzied ants, checking sails and riggings. Herb and I turned back to the sea—back to Trovar. We were closer. Close enough to smell the humidity and hate wafting from the jungle. Close enough to feel a pressure building in our chests.

The idea of being watched and waited for crept back into my thoughts. The island wanted us. It *needed* us. And we went willingly.

=[]=

Resh and his son watched from the tallest tree as a small ship broke free from the cloud-barrier that surrounded and masked Trovar. The clouds floated on the water and never moved or shifted and lay so thick that most any traveler with sense invariably avoided them. Those who didn't fell prey to Trovar's children.

His eyes narrowed as the ship grew near, approaching the village side of the island. He counted at least a score of men on board. He motioned to runners who waited on the jungle floor, and they sprinted off to spread his orders. Within minutes, every flame on the island was extinguished and every one of Trovar's children was in place.

Resh shut his eyes and spoke aloud to his son in a language that was harsh, laborious and older than the trees or the sky or the waters.

"It will not be long. Soon, the moon-skins will arrive to steal what is ours. Moon-skins always more dangerous than the time before. Always more of Trovar's children die. But Resh grows more dangerous, too. Resh learns from mistakes. Watch. Learn. Trovar not happy when His children die, so we must be stronger and smarter. Trovar demands it." His eyes snapped open, and he ran a red tongue over cracked lips. "Tonight, we offer Trovar a bone-sacrifice. Tomorrow, Trovar will smile on us."

Resh locked with his son's obedient eyes and hefted a scepter made of bone that represented Trovar's power. "One day, Trovar will choose you to replace me. On that day, you must be ready to ensure wayward souls don't spoil this land."

Resh's son nodded with the cold dispassion of a warrior.

They remained in the tree until the vessel stopped in Trovar's sacred bay, and the men aboard split into smaller ships.

"The rain comes. Good. Better for hunting."

=[]=

We dropped anchor in an emerald cove lined with black beaches. My stomach churned as our raft splashed down, and something hidden within urged me to dive in the water and swim away; swim fast and far, never looking back, never slowing down. But something else, something wiser, told me that there wasn't enough distance in the world to save me from Trovar. The island had seen me, and no matter where I went, it would *always* see me.

I looked to Herb, but his face was masked by his silver flask. When he was done, a ruddy face appeared. "What say you?" he asked.

"My appreciation for Schmeck is fading."

"Ah, toss that old fool," he burst. The liquor had set in. "We simply keep our heads down for the time being, then we can take some time in Australia or those Hawaiian Islands the government mules are always naying about. With three-hundred pounds we could even find us some top-shelf women and not those washbasins we get back on Gilbert, either. So toss Schmeck. Toss him right to the sharks."

"I still don't like it. A man should have a choice in what he does."

"I don't know about you," he said as he began to row. "But I *choose* to bury my face in the bosom of a Hawaiian woman."

The wind gusted in strong bursts as we approached the shore. We unloaded our provisions and set about searching for a place to make camp. A few feet into the jungle, we discovered a clearing. The sands from the beach extended there, creating a soft, ebony floor. Schmeck declared the spot perfect and gave the order to settle in. The crew was split into two groups. The first to pitch tents, build fires, and prepare meals, while the second explored the surrounding area for sources of water and any landmarks of note. Herb and I ignored Schmeck's orders and focused our attention on security. From what, we did not know.

Due to the bizarre stories of the island, Schmeck had brought a rifle for each man—oiled and clean—a pair of dueling revolvers, and enough ammunition to put a hole in every leaf on the island. Herb discovered a crate containing a long bore rifle with a dark wood finish. He inspected the sights, the muzzle, and grunted his approval.

"Any experience with guns?" he asked.

"A bit. Somewhere between Pennsylvania and California I worked for a corn husker who paid a half-cent for every crow I shot. But the deal ended when he said my poor aim cost more in bullets than it was worth."

"I guess I'll take this slender lady, then. A gun like this deserves a keen eye."

"No argument there. I'll do fine with a repeater."

I scanned the jungle. We were losing light, and soon the green walls would become enigmas in the dark. Death's cold breath filled my body. Herb opened the mahogany box containing the revolvers and handed me one.

"In case the rumors prove true," he said while shoving the second gun into the back of his pants.

=[]=

The night came on fast and thick. A gift from Trovar.

Four children, each covered in black mud, crept into the canopy where Resh waited. The tallest child, a girl with fine bones hewn into her hair and no real trace of adolescence other than her size, reported that the moon-skins were in the clearing. Yes, the same clearing as always. Resh smiled. The moon-skins were predictable. There were twenty-three men. They were scared, but they also had weapons. Yes, the kind that fire smoke and metal.

Resh pondered the report. He had watched the bigger ship ever since the smaller ones separated from it. In that time, he hadn't seen any movement on board. But the moon-skins never leave the big ship unattended, so he assumed they were hiding. He'd have to send his best swimmers to handle them.

A stone-faced man approached. His skin was also covered in black mud. All that separated him from the night were the whites of his eyes and the sharpened length of bone he carried. "Resh," he said and kneeled.

"Are Trovar's children ready?" Resh replied in a voice that scratched the air.

"Yes."

"Good. Strike when sky weeps. Trovar only requires four. Kill the rest."

The man stood, turned, and exited, quickly melding into the shadows. Resh bent by a stream and scooped mud into a large mound. He then dumped black sand from a pouch onto the mud, kneaded until the mixture became a thick paste, and applied it to his skin.

He clicked his tongue, and a woman approached with her eyes to the ground, holding his communing ornaments. She helped him dress, and when she was done, Resh proceeded to the altar. He had much to prepare for Trovar's offering.

=[]=

Our camp consisted of three fires, eleven tents, twenty-three souls, and forty-six watchful eyes. On the surface, our mood was light and jovial. The sailors told stories of past employment and discussed which captains were fair and which trading companies paid the best. They were Dutch and English and American and islander, and although they laughed together, not one left their rifle more than a few feet away.

I sat with Herb near the biggest fire, and we talked of our lives. A man born from Poseidon's own lineage, rough and humble, Herb lived a nomadic life, skipping from one South Seas rock to another. As he spoke of the world, one got the sense that beneath his carefree mannerisms hid a man who understood the world around him on an intimate level. And as he discussed the varied peoples of his travels, his voice became smooth and wise, coaxing my fears away.

Schmeck waddled over and sat across from us. The storm had wiped the smirk off his face, revealing a rawness one rarely saw in the stubborn man.

"Good evening," he said, humbled. "Before we get off to bickery, let me express my gratitude for your general acceptance of the situation. I made assumptions concerning your involvement, and I deserve nothing less than to have the two of you tie me to the anchor. I apologize."

I studied him for a long while and knew him for the shrewd negotiator that he was. His apology was a ruse. If making money required a heart of gold, Schmeck would cast his in twenty-four karats. But the second that heart lost its utility, you'd find him smelting it for profit. "That's not a bad idea," I finally said.

"What?"

"Tying you to the anchor."

We chuckled, and the air lightened.

"So when are we doing this note taking?" I asked.

"Don't forget the sample gathering and map making," Herb added.

"First light. I hope you gents have some proper names in mind, because I expect to fill the map with our legacies. Think of all the times you've carved your initials in decking. How many ships brandish the name Felix in some secret location? We, my fine friends, are doing just that, but on a much grander scale. Also, keep an eye for local flora and fauna. Imagine if we returned with a black tiger or a slower burning tobacco."

Herb perked. "Folks state-side would shell out a week's pay for a look at a black tiger."

"My thoughts exactly, Mr. Flenderson."

"You know," Herb said, "I think I might remember bringing a bottle along after all."

"Really?" Schmeck asked.

"Perhaps. Let me—"

A scream in the distance cut him off, followed by three quick rifle shots. The camp collectively froze, then roared to life. Men grabbed rifles, taking sight at the tree line. Others shouted orders. Two more shots rang out, followed by a gangly man running into the camp. Flecks of blood covered half his face.

We ran to him.

"Drew, who's shooting?" Schmeck yelled.

The man—Drew—appeared bewildered. His lips moved without words.

"Drew. Say something, man."

Drew broke from his daze. "I saw 'em," he said in a cracking voice. "Four of 'em."

"Who?"

"Sk-Skeletons." Drew whispered the word as if he were cursing in church. "Me and Faulk w-was out patrolling when we came across 'em. They stood in the distance watching us. Their bones cleaved the dark, clear as day, but they didn't move. We figured they were made up that way, you know, just old sets of bones that someone stood up instead of burying. But when we got closer, the four of 'em took a step toward us like they was attached at the hip. I know it sounds crazy, but . . . but I swear it. The sight hit us something awful. The four skeletons never made another move. They just stared without eyes. I fired, but they didn't even flinch. And why would they? They got nothing to shoot. Nothing. And . . . and then I heard Faulk screaming. I looked over, and this black figure was on him, ripping him to shreds right there next to me. Oh, God, the blood." He looked around the camp, and we saw the truth in his face. "It was like his own shadow had come to life and started killing him."

Panic rippled through the collected men.

"Let us return to the ship," one man said, and soon everyone was in agreement. Everyone except Schmeck.

"No. The thought of bones walking about is preposterous. And demon shadows? Where's your marrow? I refuse to cow to such fantasy."

Just then, the laden clouds decided to release their burden, and fat, warm drops of rain fell. The fires singed and drowned. Commotion broke out and shouts erupted behind us. Small black demons, maybe ten, maybe fifty in total, slithered from the dark in all directions. They moved like blurs.

Shots rang out, followed by shouts for assistance. Then shouts of terror. Then pain. Agonizing pain.

My mind clouded with indecision. I couldn't process the chaos. I watched as two sailors fired into the thicket. A child-sized demon ran up behind them and struck the backs of their knees. Thin lines of blood sprayed, and both men crumpled backwards. With a fluid motion the demon was at their throats. The two men kicked and convulsed in the mud next to each other, and the demon quickly moved on.

Drew's high-pitched screams caught my attention. Ivory skeletons stood among the trees, watching. Drew raised his rifle and fired twice before the gun clicked dry. He dropped the useless weapon and fled toward the beach. Schmeck followed, his limp pronounced by fear, but stopped when faced with more of the ghastly skeletons cutting off his retreat.

I found the courage to act when Herb's rifle exploded with a plume of white smoke. One of the skeletons dropped away. In reaction, the encircling line began to move. They cinched in closer, holding a perfect band around the clearing as demons darted among us. We were routed. Men were dead or dying and those who weren't were in wild disarray.

Schmeck bellowed inanely for everyone to rally around him, but those who stood, wouldn't for long. Already the desperate cries outweighed the gunfire.

Herb fired again, hitting a skeleton next to the first one he had shot, and aimed at the next. He was creating a gap. I tried to help, but my shots went wide. I didn't know where to aim. At the bone? The head? The heart? Did they have hearts? For that matter, would they even stay down if hit?

When it came time to reload, Herb grabbed my shirt, and yanked. We made for the gap. As we punched through undergrowth, Schmeck's voice rose behind us like a terrible wind.

I had no concept of direction as we ran, but I sensed we had set ourselves inland. We tore through all manner of brambles until we came upon a mass of broad-leaved vines and hid. My chest burned. We could no longer smell the sea or hear the brutalized screams.

Struggling to control my breath, I listened for followers, and heard only the soothing patter of rain on plant. Everything was happening too rapidly. I couldn't move or think. I needed to reload, but couldn't find the will to do so. Herb spoke, but I couldn't understand the words. They were foreign and odd. He pointed toward the camp, toward the slaughter. I looked, comprehending on a primal level that he needed me to aim my weapon in that direction. I wanted to tell him that I couldn't, but he was already firing.

My name penetrated Herb's incoherent words. " . . . Felix . . . "

Dozens of dark souls scurried forth, spread across the entirety of my vision. They leapt over deadfalls and passed through wilderness with ease. Herb cursed when his gun jammed. He howled, raised the rifle over his head, and greeted the onslaught. As they descended on him with white clubs and red rage, I noticed the black on several of the demons melting in the rain. Beneath was *flesh*. The inhuman was human.

My mind made connections it was previously incapable of making. I yanked the dueling pistol from the back of my trousers and pulled the trigger. Red splashed as one body spun with contact. I kneeled for better accuracy, emboldened, and fired again. A black demon spewed blood from its chest, but the swarm came on. I had time for two more shots before I was forced to swing the pistol like a hammer. I connected, but the impact slowed my next swing and then they were on me, clawing, punching, biting. I saw a cold dispassion in their young faces and not the savageness I had expected. They were calm in their brutality. And then I saw no more.

=[]=

"Trovar happy," Resh declared to the congregated tribe. He stood on the stone altar, gazing over them with pride. A few of Trovar's children were lost, but only half as many as the last time. Resh attributed this to Trovar's gift of rain. And now that the tribe had gathered and the offerings were ready, Resh would ensure Trovar gave them many more gifts in the time to come. "The moon-skins are defeated. Now we offer Trovar their bones."

His son had perished in the battle, but Resh did not mourn his young one. Trovar had a plan and would provide. The death had purpose, as did all things on the island.

=[]=

I awoke to fire crackling and a sinister, well-practiced murmuring that reminded me of chanting monks.

I moved to my knees, but a powerful force pushed me back to the ground. A sharp pain spiked my arm as I fell sideways, and I realized that my hands were bound behind me. I twisted to face my oppressor. A skeleton towered there, silent. Eyes glimmered from within the sockets of the skull, and I remembered seeing flesh on the demons. Human flesh. I saw these monstrosities with new eyes. What I saw wasn't a skeleton at all, but a costume. The bones lacked depth. The ribs curved inward as they should, but didn't circle around to a spine. Nor did the skull completely enclose. My eyes focused on the dark areas between the white frame, and I noticed dark mud concealing the man beneath.

The man dressed as a skeleton was but one of many that circled a large pit dug from the side of the black mountain. Across from me was a polished stone altar. The demon-children kneeled before it with their heads bowed in obedient order, mimicking glazed statues in the orange firelight.

The evil chanting came from atop the altar where a man dressed in an ornate version of a human skeleton stood. He wore a full skull, split at the sides and widened, like a helmet. A spine, polished white, curved with his back from which a fan of longer bones, possibly human femurs, protruded in parody of a long deceased peacock.

The bone-man raised his hands over his head, and I noticed Drew's slender figure lying on a slab beneath him. The chant quickened, becoming more of a yell than a prayer. Anxiety overwhelmed me as the bone-man swept his hands back and forth. Drew lay still for a moment, but his body suddenly arched, fighting against the restraints binding his arms and legs. He writhed and flexed, but through some power not his own. As the chanting grew in intensity, so did Drew's struggle. Soon he was screaming.

The bone-man continued to wave his hands. A crack sounded through the gruesome words. Then a whole succession of cracks like a forest worth of trees snapping in half all at once. Drew wailed with purgatorial agony, and I could see his skin shift with inner-movement, his flesh bending in grotesque bubbles as his own skeleton tried to force its way free from his body. More cracking sounds. More screams. Ribs expanded within his chest. An elbow exploded, revealing the rounded ends of his joint, toes separated from their feet, collar bones buckled and folded upward, the scream tapered into a gurgle.

The bone-man started jerking his arms in an upward motion as if ushering Drew's bones forth. Drew continued to arch away from the altar, mutilated, lifeless. With a sickening tear, his rib cage began to surface through his skin. The other elbow exploded, followed by both knees, and red pulp rained in a cloudy mist.

I shut my eyes, squeezed them tight, and prayed they never opened again.

But I couldn't shut my ears. I listened as his body was shredded. Tissue and bone conspired to form a squishing, *ripping*—

I heaved.

When my eyes fluttered open, the bone-man stood holding a red skull in one hand and a polished scepter that radiated religious significance in the other. Various bloodied bones were being shared among the children, and before the bone-man lay the red gore that remained of Drew, and behind his skeletal mask, an imagined sneer.

The bone-man stepped down from the altar. His stride was long. Each step brought him unbearably closer. Someone whimpered, and I became aware of a quaking presence. I craned my neck. Herb and Schmeck lay in similar positions. Schmeck's face shone with tears. Herb gave a slight nod.

As the bone-man approached, all others watched. He stopped within arm's length, raised his scepter, and pointed. My heart shriveled. The end of his scepter had a crude etching of a man's face, bearded and primitive. I saw this because the image was pointed directly at me.

The bone-man didn't need to speak. Powerful hands grabbed my arms and yanked me to my feet. My legs tried to fold, but failed under my captors' hold. The bonds on my hands were cut. I tried to thrash free, but a blow to the back of my head extinguished any fight.

"No," Herb bellowed. "You sons of bitches, leave him be."

Hundreds of tribesman looked on with blank detachment.

Orange streaks from the firelight trailed across my vision. I tried to focus, but the ground pulled away as I was lifted off my feet.

"You sons of bitches, I said *no.*"

I was dropped. I crumbled to the ground in a daze. Running feet pounded the ground. Surprised exclamations. A skeleton crashed beside me, bones clattering.

I lifted my head to see what had happened. Herb was pinned to the ground a few feet from the bone-man. He had tried to fight them; tried to save me. The bone-man pointed his scepter at Herb and spoke a single line. Impossibly, Herb's forearm twisted clockwise until it met resistance. Then a snap. Herb wailed and tried to cover his broken and still twisting arm.

I looked around, the streaks of firelight a permanent part of my vision now. Schmeck was wrapped into a fetal ball. The children, those emotionless shadows, gathered around. I watched as the bone-man magically broke Herb's other arm, and a feral instinct ignited in me.

I stood with an effort. The men around me were too enthralled in the torture to notice. Some of the skeletons with a wider view must have seen, but they were too far to react. I staggered, then lunged forward in a desperate grab for the bone-man. I had no plan, I only understood the need to stop him.

One hand found the fan of bones at his back and the other found his outreached scepter. I pulled on both, separating the two. I continued to pull him backward and, in a blind fury, I brought the scepter down on his face in pulverizing swings. His mask shattered, driving shards of bone into his eyes. I loosed the beast within. All my fear, disgust, and hate powered my strikes, each landing with more viciousness than the last. I couldn't, wouldn't stop. When he toppled to the ground, I followed by straddling his chest.

I raised the scepter over my head, hot blood streaking my face, and prepared for a final strike. I froze. The children stood inches from me in a tight pack. They didn't move. Nor did the skeletons behind them and, for once, there was emotion in their faces. Awe.

Schmeck fled as best he could. No one tried to stop him. He stumbled over a black mound of dirt and vanished.

The indifference sent a cold chill through my body. Why weren't they reacting? Why weren't they swarming?

And for a moment the world seemed to freeze and only I could move. A powerful presence consumed me, burning at first, but then soothing as its influence spread throughout. I could suddenly sense all life around me. It was as if I was looking at a map of the island with every single organism marked with a red dot. I had knowledge of every bird, beetle, and man that made contact with Trovar. More than that, I held a connection with all life, both present and ancient. In my mind's eye, I could see through the tribesman's eyes. But they weren't tribesmen. They were Trovar's children; my brothers and sisters. I looked into Resh's life and knew his history. He had been the tribe's longest lasting Voice of Trovar.

But now it was my time. Trovar had chosen me. I held the scepter—a remnant of Trovar's physical body long destroyed—and with it, Trovar's power.

I looked at the scepter in my hand, and reality came crashing back. Herb moaned on the ground, the fire cracked, the clouds let out a weak rumble of a storm that had moved on, and a primeval voice whispered in my ear.

Three of Trovar's children helped Herb to his feet. He looked at me with worry and wonder. The tribe watched, waiting for direction.

"We take care of you," I said in harsh words that were older than the trees or the sky or the waters. "Felix promise."

The worry stayed with Herb, but he would understand with time. If Trovar let him heal, then he would be allowed to assimilate with the tribe—become one of Trovar's children.

I climbed the steps to the altar, stood erect in front of my people, and spoke. "One still lives. The fat one. Bring him. His thick bones will please Trovar."

A flood of Trovar's children lurched into the jungle in search of Schmeck.

He won't escape, for I am the Voice of Trovar. I am Felix. And I have been chosen to ensure wayward souls don't spoil this land.

=[]=

JC Hemphill was born yesterday, so if you found his writing infantile, then you're spot-on. But you gotta admit, he's pretty damn good for a toddler. His work has appeared in The Washington Pastime, Pulp Modern, SNM Horror Magazine, *and* Spinetinglers, *with upcoming work in* Buzzy Mag *and* Cover of Darkness. *Follow his scribblings on* Facebook *or at* www.JCHemphill.com.

ABOUT THE EDITOR

=[]=

Eric J. Guignard is an award-winning author and editor living in southern California.

He writes fiction short stories in the genres of horror, speculative, and young adult. He also writes research and knowledge-base articles in genealogy, woodworking, and ecology. Eric has been published in numerous print and online media, recently including publications in: *A Very Short Story* competition (first place), *Coscom Entertainment, Dark Moon Books, SNM Horror Magazine, Another Realm, Indie Gypsy,* and many others.

When not writing, Eric designs and builds custom furniture.

Eric holds degrees in Communications and Environmental Science, as well as a Master's Degree in Public Administration (*California State University Northridge*).

Most importantly, he is married to his high school sweetheart, Jeannette, and father to an adventuresome toddler son, Julian James.

Please visit Eric at: www.ericjguignard.com
or at his blog: www.ericjguignard.blogspot.com

CPSIA information can be obtained at www.ICGtesting.com
Printed in the USA
LVOW100842140513

333702LV00002B/229/P